Heaven

··

Violet Scomber

Copyright © 2023 by Violet Scomber

All rights reserved.

No portion of this book may be reproduced in any form without written permission from the publisher or author, except as permitted by U.S. copyright law.

Contents

Prologue	1
1. 1. Home	5
2. 2. Fresh Start	20
3. 3. First Meetings	34
4. 4. Fear	46
5. 5. Help	58
6. 6. Threat	71
7. 7. Debt	80
8. 8. Revelations	92
9. 9. Problems & Promises	104
10. 10. Safe	118
11. 11. Grief	137
12. 12. Panic	151

13.	13. Dinner	163
14.	14. Coward	189
15.	15. Fight	204
16.	16. Senseless	213
17.	17. Protection	230
18.	18. Storms Eye	249
19.	19. Hope	262
20.	20. Date	274
21.	21. Fangs & Fur	288
22.	22. Normal	302
23.	23. Visit	314
24.	24. Preparations	325
25.	25. Gathering	339
26.	26. Truths	350
27.	27. Turning Point	361
28.	28. Ready	370

Prologue

Lightning flashed outside her window and Norah sighed as she poured herself another cup of tea.

This weather was ridiculous. A storm with no rain seemed silly to her. Could you even call it a storm when there wasn't any rain? There wasn't enough lightning to classify as a lightning storm and the thunder was far off so she didn't know what to call it. Lightning flashed and looking out her kitchen window, she saw her neighbour in his backyard having a smoke. She knew his wife hated him smoking and he always snuck out in the middle of the night to have one. He looked over, saw her observing him and gave her a salute. Saluting back, she watched him take a final drag and go back inside, their porch light flicking off.

Grabbing her tea, she walked back into the living room and sat on the couch in front of her laptop. Wrapping her rug around her, she settled back in, determined to get past this block. A blank document shone from the laptop screen and she took a sip of tea, inspiration lacking.

For the past two hours she'd been stuck on her latest chapter. The protagonist needed to discover a big secret her boyfriend had been keeping from her but she was having trouble revealing it in the best way. So far, every attempt had lacked the impact the revelation was meant to have. Her protagonist needed to feel the impact in the core of her being, but Norah couldn't find that emotion. It was something she had no experience in. Her last boyfriend had been three years ago and he'd been the clingy type. In the end, she had to let him go. It was hard to like someone who spent their time breathing down her neck while she was trying to write. She'd told him how much it annoyed her but he didn't listen. If he wasn't going to listen, then she didn't want him around.

The clock on the mantle chimed two in the morning and she bit her lip. Part of the reason she was having trouble was because her brain was scattered. Her brother Adam had said he was doing a job tonight, something that never made her feel good. He'd been hanging out with a bad group of men for the last few months and these 'jobs' always took place in the middle of the night.

She knew he was doing something illegal but she couldn't bring herself to talk to him about it. Whenever she had tried to broach sensitive topics in the past, he would clam up and disappear for months, returning when he needed something from her, usually money. She didn't like to lend him money all the time but he was the only family she had left and she didn't want to push him out of her life, but at the same time she didn't want him becoming a criminal. In the end, the only way to keep him in her life was to remain quiet and never question what he did.

Her patience was beginning to wear thin lately, mainly because of Daniel, Adam's new best friend. He was always hanging around the house, looking for Adam when he wasn't around and he didn't know how to take a hint that he wasn't welcome. His random visits had been occurring more frequently over the last two weeks and she had decided to tell Adam she didn't want him hanging around anymore. Adam was usually protective of her and the last time one of his sleazy friends had tried something on her, he had gone nuts and beat his face in. Again, not something she was comfortable with but at that point in time, it had been preferred to him touching her and groping her. She didn't get a sleazy vibe off Daniel, but it was creepy enough for her alarm bells to ring whenever he was around. He was the wrong kind of dangerous and she didn't want him anywhere near her.

Bang bang!

Norah jumped, spilling tea down her top and cursed, fanning the material so she didn't burn her skin. The only person who would come to her house at this time of night was Adam. Still, just to be safe she grabbed her baseball bat she kept near the front door. Holding it behind her back, she called out. "Who is it?"

"Norah, open up its Adam!"

She was alarmed at the panicked tone in his voice and dropping the bat she opened the door, eyes widening at the sight.

Adam stood in the entryway, shoulders slumped. His eyes looked bloodshot and a flash of lightning cracked across the sky, lighting up his hands, stained with blood. The red liquid was splattered across his shirt and face. His left cheek was smeared and she guessed he'd wiped at his face. His brown hair was plastered to his face from a mixture of rain and sweat, a single strand hung over his left eye but he wasn't bothered by it. His eyes looked at her with a mixture of desperation and fear, his hands held out in front of him as if he didn't know what to do with them.

"Adam," she whispered, taking a small step back. Her eyes were drawn to his hands, the blood causing a ball of fear and nausea to form in the pit of her stomach. "What did you do?"

"Norah, you have to help me," his voice broke. "I really fucked up this time."

1. Home

"I really think you're groovy, let's go out to a movie..."

Norah hummed along to The Turtle's classic, fingers tapping away on the steering wheel as she drove through the night. The Blue Briar forest loomed on both sides of the road, the large trees melting into the dark and she drove below the speed limit, afraid an animal would jump out in front of her. Earlier she had passed a dead wolf on the side of the road which had put her stomach in more knots than it already was. There was something about seeing animals on the side of the road that upset her. If it had occurred naturally, it wouldn't bother her but because it was humans who had ended those poor creature's lives, it made her feel guilty in a way she knew she shouldn't, but couldn't help.

The other reason her stomach was in knots boiled down to one person; Daniel. The last two weeks of her life had been a nightmare. After Adam had appeared on her doorstep, explaining what he had done, Norah knew things were only going to get worse.

She had been right in thinking his job with Daniel had been illegal. Apparently, they had planned on stealing some diamonds from a businessman who was passing through town that night to attend a fundraiser. Unfortunately, for Adam and Daniel, the businessman decided to return home early due to an upset stomach and had caught them in the act. The man had stopped Adam from escaping and Daniel, being the great 'friend' that he was, escaped and left Adam to fend for himself.

During their scuffle, the man had tripped and they both fell through the coffee table, smashing the glass top and the man cracked his head open on the foot of the table. In a panic, Adam had tried to stop the bleeding before realising the man was dead.

After explaining to Norah, she could see he didn't know what to do, but she did. A situation like that, Norah couldn't let it slide by. She loved her brother, despite his flaws, but she couldn't keep this a secret for him. A life had been taken and Adam needed to turn himself in before things got out of hand. It took Norah seven hours of tears and shouting to convince him to do the right thing. She had half expected Adam to run the moment she turned her back but he hadn't.

For two weeks she had put her life on hold to help Adam sort everything out. The case had gone through quickly as Adam had confessed and the only thing he left out was Daniel and the location of the missing diamonds. Norah thought Daniel would have skipped town with them by now and she didn't care if they both never resurfaced.

Sadly, on the fifth day after Adam had been jailed, a knock had sounded at her door and there was Daniel, smiling his 'innocent' smile which shot a bolt of fear through her being. Despite her assurance that she didn't want his help or 'sympathy', he continued to plague her. The first few visits had been standard Daniel, hovering too close, offering his version of pity at Adam's situation when it wasn't wanted. Every time she saw his face, she wanted to threaten call the police if he didn't leave her alone, but was too afraid of how Daniel might react, and she also didn't feel the police would believe her since no mention of Daniel had been made in the initial report.

Rain started to splatter across her windshield and she turned the wipers on as her brain went over what had happened three days ago.

Juggling with three bags of groceries, she managed to unlock the front door without dropping anything. Her fridge had been empty for three days but with Adam and an annoying subplot that wouldn't sort itself out, she'd been too busy to care, simply surviving on what was left in her pantry; cashews and museli bars. Walking down the hall to the kitchen, she was thinking of how to make her pasta when she stepped through the kitchen door and bit back a scream, dropping her bags and the ingredients rolled across the floor.

Daniel leaned against the kitchen island, her large cutting knife in his hand as he tested the tip's sharpness.

"W-what are you doing in my house?" She demanded, trying to cover the fear she felt coursing through her veins. She stood still, afraid to run in case he gave chase. The house phone was in the hallway but she knew she wouldn't reach it before he reached her.

Daniel sighed, glancing at the knife before lowering his arm. "Norah, Norah, I've tried to be patient but I'm afraid I've run out. Now, let's do this the easy way and no one will get hurt; tell me where Adam hid the diamonds."

Heart pounding against her ribcage, she was momentarily confused. "But I thought you already had them?"

This wasn't what Daniel had wanted to hear; he moved fast, grabbing her by the shoulder, he slammed her against the wall, pressing the blade's edge against her throat. Norah's mouth went dry and she froze, terrified.

"Tell me where the fucking diamonds are, or I spill your pretty blood all over this kitchen." He snarled.

"I honestly don't know," she croaked, the knife moved against her skin as she spoke and her hands trembled, wanting to reach up and shove him away. Norah wasn't weak, she kept fit, but Daniel was larger and stronger; she wouldn't stand a chance against him. "Adam told me you had them, I've never even seen them!"

Daniel's eyebrows furrowed and he glanced down in thought. "Clever bastard," he muttered. Looking back up, he steadied his hand and pressed her shoulder harder into the wall. "All right, change of plan; you ask your brother where the diamonds are and I'll be back tomorrow to collect. Call the police and I'll sneak into your room and slice this knife across your throat, ear to ear. You try to get me arrested and I have plenty of other friends who will come and do the job for me."

The knife moved as he spoke and her legs threatened to collapse. "If the diamonds aren't in my possession by tomorrow night, you'll be dead anyway." Stepping back, he placed the knife back on the island. "See you tomorrow, Norah."

She waited until she heard the front door slammed shut before her legs folded, sliding to the floor and she burst into tears.

Her situation hadn't gotten any better when she rang Adam straight away and he had denied knowing where they were. The fact that he obviously knew something about them but wouldn't tell her set her on edge. Surely her life was more important than some stupid diamonds he was probably never going to see again?

In the end, too afraid to call the police, she rang Alice, her best friend and only person she trusted with something like this. Alice was the only person who had ever seen her writing so far and was the one who convinced her to try and do it professionally.

Alice's first reaction was to call the police but after hearing Norah's panic, she looked at their other options. Her best option was to leave town until they could deal with Daniel. Coming around, she sat with Norah and explained her idea. "Ray's father has a beach house in this place called Bellvale. The family won't use it since he had an affair there for five years. It mostly gets rented out to holiday goers and it's free at the moment."

"So you're suggesting I just run? What if he follows me?" She asked incredulously.

Alice squeezed her hand. "He won't follow you, Ray and I will act as your cover story. I don't want you to run, but this Daniel is a creep and without those diamonds, he's going to keep hounding you until he gets them or you get hurt. At this point, apart from the police, running is your best option. You've still got your inheritance money from your dad so you won't have financial trouble. Just head out there for a month or so, lay low and Ray and I will keep a look out for Daniel. If I see him hovering around and I'm sure he doesn't know where you are, then I'll get the police involved and get him put on stalking charges or something."

"But he's coming tomorrow, I won't have time to organise everything –"

"No time for organising, sweetie only time for action. Leave everything to me. Now," she said seriously, "how fast can you pack?"

In one night, Norah and Alice had packed up her life, putting only what she needed in her car. Alice took whatever had value to keep it safe should Daniel break in again. As the sun had risen, Norah had hugged Alice farewell and directions to her safe house in hand, she got on the road. For three days she had driven nonstop, sleeping in her car when she got too tired, her kitchen knife resting on the seat beside her. It had now become her weapon and after waking from nightmares of Daniel finding her, she often touched it for reassurance.

Tired, hungry and drowning in fear, Norah was finally near Bellvale and a night of sleep in a proper bed. At this point, she didn't even care if it was an adulterer's bed. As long as it was comfortable, she would be happy. The rain pounded heavier and she turned the stereo up, her iPod had switched to The Kinks and singing softly under her breath, she paused as she passed a young woman walking on the side of the road.

Turning a bend, the girl disappeared in her rear view mirror and Norah started putting her foot on the brake. She didn't want to stop, the adulterer bed was calling to her but she wouldn't be able to sleep anyway if she didn't turn around. Checking the road, she did a u-turn and headed back. Reaching over, she grabbed the knife and tucked it under her seat. Performing another turn, she pulled up beside the girl.

Leaning over, she wound the window down and the girl stopped walking, standing away from the vehicle. "Uh, hi. Can I give you a lift somewhere?" She called out the window.

"Where are you heading?" The girl asked warily.

"Bellvale."

The girl paused and Norah offered her a friendly smile. "If you don't feel safe, I understand. I can give you an umbrella instead?"

As she was reaching into the backseat to try and find it, the door opened and the young girl hopped in. "It's okay, I'll accept the ride. You don't scream 'highway murderer' to me."

Already half in the backseat, Norah grabbed a towel from under a pile of books and passed it to her. "No, I prefer back roads with less traffic when I do my murdering."

Rubbing the water from her hair, the girl grinned. "Thank God we didn't meet on the back roads then. I'm Olivia Montoya."

"Norah Jacobs."

"Thank you for stopping, Norah, most people don't stop for strangers around here."

Norah pulled onto the road and cranked the heater up to high. "I guess I'm not most people. What were you doing walking out here at this time of night?"

"This time of night? It's only eight," Olivia grinned, wiping her face. "Well, I was out here with Rylan, my brother's friend. He had to pick up something from the mill and I went along for company. So anyway, we're at the mill and he gets a call from this girl he's been seeing and poof! Just like that, he up and leaves while I'm out answering to nature's call. Stupid jerk."

"So he isn't your boyfriend then?"

"Ew, god no. He's attractive, I guess but he's like a big brother to me. Just the thought makes me want to gag."

"Sorry," Norah smiled, eyes on the road. "Change of subject then. Where can I drop you off?"

"The café in town, I've got a spare change of clothes there so I'll slip in. Its quiz night, which I hate, but my brother's there so he can give me a ride home." Olivia placed the damp towel on her legs and started rubbing her legs. Norah moved the vents so they were all aiming at her and Olivia grinned. "I'm not that cold, but thanks. So, are you just passing through?"

"No, actually I'm moving here for a month or so. I'm staying at a beach house my friend's family owns."

"Oh, you must mean the Jones' house. It's the only vacant house on the beach."

"That's the one. I have to get the keys from a man named..." she searched blindly for the piece of paper in the console.

"Jack Richards?" Olivia offered. "He usually keeps the keys for them."

"That's the name. I might have to wait until tomorrow though, it is a bit late to be bothering him –"

"Oh no, Jack will still be awake. We'll stop there on the way into town and pick up the keys."

Norah glanced at Olivia. They'd known each other for maybe twenty minutes and Olivia was acting as if they'd known each other longer. "Are you sure?"

Olivia waved her hand, the other adjusting the heater. "Of course! It won't take long and I'm sure you must be tired of driving. How long have you been on the road?"

"A few days."

"Wow, that's insane! What brings you to Bellvale?"

"Ah, I'm a writer and I wanted to get away from my life for a while." Norah tried to twist the truth as little as possible. She wasn't the best liar and she did plan on writing while she was here.

"That's cool, Wendy will get a kick out of a writer staying here." Olivia pointed ahead, as the town came into sight. "Go straight through the roundabout and take the second left. Written anything I've heard of?"

The forest thinned out and houses started appearing. They passed a small sign which read, Bellvale. Population est. 600. At the roundabout, she followed Olivia's directions and went straight though.

"I haven't written anything yet," she answered her. "My first story is still in the development stages. I'm hoping I'll be inspired while I'm here."

The area became more suburban and taking the second left, Olivia told her to stop in front of the third house on the left. Lights shone through the curtains and Olivia stopped her from unbuckling her seatbelt. "Hang on."

Jumping out, she ran up to the front door. A few seconds later the door opened and Olivia started talking to a man in his fifties. His bald head shone in the door light and thin legs looked out of place with his beer belly.

As they spoke, Norah glanced about. In the dark, there wasn't much to see, but his garden seemed nice. It was well kept and his garbage was out on the sidewalk for collection the next day. The recycling box glittered in her car lights and looking closer, she saw it was overflowing with glass bottles.

Looking back up to the house, she saw both heads turn in her direction and she waved awkwardly. The man went back inside and Olivia headed back to the car, two thumbs up. Sliding back in, she grabbed the towel again. "Jack's just getting the keys."

"I could've done that," Norah protested.

"Nah, no point both of us getting wet and Jack's a bit of a grump once he's started drinking."

"Oh, when does he usually start?"

"As soon as he opens his eyes, every morning." Olivia wasn't joking and Norah laughed breathlessly.

Knock knock.

Norah jumped, head hitting the roof of the car and flushed. Rolling down her window, Jack Richards leant over her car, one arm resting on the roof. The smell of whiskey mingled with the rain and she resisted the urge to shrink away.

"You Norah?" His voice sounded like it was buried in gravel and she nodded.

"Yes, nice to meet –"

"Ray rang," he interrupted. "Said you were coming. Place ain't much, hasn't been used in a few months and Ray's wiring some money tomorrow so you can buy some furniture. Come by and get it. I ain't your landlord, you break anything, you fix it yourself. Electricity and water are in my name and I'll send you the bills. Any questions?"

"Ah, how do I get there from here?"

"It's all right, Jack," Olivia called from behind her. "I'll show her the way."

"Much obliged." He passed the keys to Norah, water dripping down her arm. "See you tomorrow, don't make it as late as this though."

"Thank you, Jack."

Offering nothing more than a grunt, he ambled back to the house and slammed the door. Olivia put her seat belt back on and moved her hair away from her face. "Head back to the roundabout and turn left."

Norah did as she was told and turned the car around. "Is there a certain time I should come back tomorrow?"

"Probably best to leave it until the afternoon."

"Is he always like that?"

"Yep," Olivia laughed. "He's the best functioning drunk I've ever met. Liver of steel, I recon. He can be a bit blunt but learn to look past it and you'll be fine."

They turned at the roundabout and the street gradually declined and levelled out, the centre of the town looming ahead. "I wonder what happened to make him drink like that." Norah wondered out loud.

Olivia hesitated. "Did the owner's tell you about the affair?"

"Yes, Alice mentioned it."

"Well, the woman that guy was screwing around with was Jack's now ex-wife."

Norah's eyes widened, slowing down to the new speed limit. "How does that work, him keeping the keys for their family?"

"I don't know, Jack doesn't speak about it and his ex-wife left town not long after it ended. I know Jack gets along with the guy's son, Ray. Maybe they bonded over their mutual disgust or something. Who knows? If you're that keen to know you'll have to ask Jack."

Norah snorted at the thought. "I think some things are better left a mystery."

"Exactly," Olivia grinned. "The café is a few blocks ahead. This is the main street too. Most shops are located here which is convenient. It's only a small town but we have everything we need."

At night, Bellvale didn't seem like much to her. The street lights were dim, casting a soft orange glow across the road. Olivia pointed out a few shops but Norah couldn't tell them apart in the orange light. Looking into the distance, she could see the waves of the ocean and thought that it must look pretty during the day.

A group of cars lined the next block and Olivia sat taller. "Pull over here, this is my stop."

Putting her blinker on, she pulled up behind a motor cycle. The silver metal and maroon body shone in her car lights and Norah had to admit it was a good looking ride. She'd never been one of those girls who melted for a biker boy but then again, she'd never seen a bike like the one in front of her.

"Thanks, Norah. You really saved my butt tonight." Rubbing her hair a final time, she passed the towel back to Norah. She motioned to the café as she opened the car door. "This is the Twilight café. I work here most mornings, stop by sometime if you want to catch up."

Norah smiled. "If you're selling caffeine you can definitely count me as a regular."

"Sweet! Good luck unpacking and welcome to Bellvale."

Climbing out of the car, she raced around to the shop, pushing the front door open. Through the rain, she saw Olivia hit a tall brown haired man across the back of the head before the door shut.

Shifting back into gear, she pulled back onto the road, idling down the street as she tried to follow Olivia's directions. Reaching the wharf, she followed the curve of the road and the town lights faded as she reached the outskirts of the town.

After driving through the dark for a few more minutes, she saw the old mailbox Olivia had described and slammed on the brakes as she was about to pass it. Everything in the back seat shifted and she winced as a loose book hit her shoulder.

Clenching the steering wheel, exhaustion seeped through her bones and she leaned back, staring at the car roof.

"Almost there," she mumbled. "Keep it together for a few more minutes."

Turning off the main road, the tires crunched on the gravel and she peered into the night. Tall grass grew everywhere and she tried to keep track of the small road. Turning up a small rise, a house came into view and she slowed down. Cream weather boards were the first thing she saw as she came to a stop. The sound of the ocean was close and she could see the waves a few yards away. Turning the car off, she stared at the house for a moment before opening her door.

Reaching under her seat, she grabbed the knife for protection. A part of her felt ridiculous carrying it around but there was also a scared, slightly crazy part of her that thought Daniel might have found her and was waiting in the long grass. It didn't matter how rational her brain normally was, that small part overrode any attempts to believe otherwise.

The smell of the ocean was salty sweet and she inhaled deeply, trying to calm her nerves. The rain had slowed and she walked up the two steps onto the porch.

"This would be less scary if it wasn't dark," she grumbled to herself. Unlocking the door, she found a switch and flicking it down, the house was bathed in light. The empty room eased her fear just enough for rational thought to take back control and she lowered her knife, secretly glad no one had been around to watch her act like a fool.

It was a small house, the dining area, lounge room and kitchen all melded into one large room. A stale smell hung in the air and she covered her nose. A small table with four chairs were the only furniture visible and now she understood why Ray was sending money for more. Past the small kitchen, she could see another door in the shadows. There were no paintings or photographs on the walls, no colour other than the faded brown wood wall and dark brown counter tops.

This was it; her new home. Olivia's welcome echoed in her ears and a lump formed in her throat.

"Welcome home," she whispered.

2. Fresh Start

Sunlight pierced her eyelids and Norah rolled over, opening her eyes.

She'd forgotten to the close the curtains the night before and she squinted, seeing the cliffs in the distance. She'd been exhausted as she lay down last night, she'd drifted off before she could worry about unpacking the car. It was the best sleep she'd had since the Daniel incident. She couldn't decide if it was due to exhaustion or the adulterer bed being so comfortable, but she wasn't about to complain.

Rolling out of bed, she walked over to the window, stretching the kinks from her neck and looked outside. The large cliffs were the first thing she saw; intimidating, they reached their peak at the ocean line and then slowly descended back down towards the road. The forest covered the top and it was at least a five storey drop to the beach. Long grass grew in the area between the house and the cliffs, the different shades of green creating a pretty collage.

Looking further left, the grass stopped and gave way to golden white sand. It was filled with contrasting black rocks which seemed to accumulate closer to the cliffs wall. The sound of gentle waves was calming and a small smile began to form as for a brief moment, her worries faded away.

Opening the window, the salty air wafted in and she walked into the kitchen, opening the window above the sink which had the same view as her bedroom. Upon further exploration last night, she had discovered that the bedroom sat opposite the bathroom which was tiled from the floor and halfway up the walls which were a faded white. A large old tub stood near the far wall, a shower head protruding from the wall. The wall opposite the tub was a large glass block window, the natural light ridding any need of overhead lighting during the day. Norah was desperate to have a shower but the tub needed a little maintenance before she dared step foot in it. Much of the house was in need of cleaning and so she decided to put the shower off until the house was more tolerable to live in.

The laundry was in a small room just outside the back door and she was grateful she wouldn't have to buy a washer and dryer. A large cupboard lined the wall near the backdoor and it had a few changes of linen which smelt mouldy. Everything would be getting washed today. At least she'd brought some linen of her own so she would have a clean towel for her shower later.

Walking out to her car, she started the long process of dragging everything inside. It took an hour to pile her belongings on the small kitchen table and by the time she was finished, her body was covered in a fine sheen of sweat. Grabbing a suitcase, she took it to the bedroom and changed into some clean clothes. She felt better, after wearing the same clothes for three days. If she was going to mingle with the locals, she didn't want their first impression to be that she smelt disgusting.

Spraying half a can of deodorant over herself to mask the lingering smell of sweat, she tied her brown hair in a knot at the base of her neck and finding a notepad in the kitchen, took stock of what she needed to purchase. At the top of the list was cleaning supplies and she added some food, only writing down the essentials. She'd worry about filling her pantry once she was settled in. Once the list was finished, she grabbed the home phone to ring Alice. She'd shut down her mobile account, afraid Daniel would be able to track it, so now this phone would be her only life line to the world.

Finding Alice's number from her emergency contact list, she dialled the number. She knew Alice wasn't fond of her being without a mobile, but Norah wouldn't be deterred. On the fourth ring, the call went through.

"Ray Jones speaking."

Norah smiled at his mannerism. "Hello Ray Jones, speaking this is Norah Jacobs speaking."

"Norah!" He sounded relieved. "Alice will be annoyed she missed your call. She's just gone to the library. Did you have a safe trip?"

She played with the phone cord. "Yeah, there were no problems."

"I take it you found the place okay then?"

"I had some local help." She thought of Olivia. "I don't think I would have found Jack otherwise."

"Ah, Jack." She could hear the smile in his voice. "I'm sending some money through today for furniture. There used to be more, but Jack has a tendency to go down there when the place is empty and burn pieces when he's on a bender."

"Ah, that's not comforting to hear..."

Ray laughed. "Don't worry, he doesn't come down when people are staying."

"How can you be okay with him just burning furniture?"

He sighed. "When it comes to that place, Jack and I are on the same page. We don't like it but we keep it because it's a good investment. Furniture is easily replaced and if it makes Jack feel better, then I say let him. Just a word of advice; don't lash out on anything expensive. Once you're gone, it will probably get burnt."

"Duly noted." Norah still couldn't believe he was okay with Jack burning furniture but then she'd never gone through what they had been through, so she couldn't judge.

"If there are any problems, don't hesitate to call and don't worry about that bastard, Daniel. We'll keep an eye out for him."

She felt tears beginning to form. She loved Ray and Alice. "Thanks, Ray."

"No problem. Sorry Norah, I'd love to chat more but I've got an appointment to head to –"

"Not a problem. You get going and send Alice my love."

"Will do. Talk soon."

"Bye."

Placing the receiver back in the cradle, she grabbed her list and headed out the door. At the mention of Daniel, she just wanted to crawl back into bed and wallow but her neurotic need for a clean house, and more importantly, a shower made her get in her car and head into town.

Reaching the road, she saw that the entryway was difficult to see even in the daylight. She was surprised she'd caught a glimpse of it last night, the edge of the road was covered in long grass and the gate was so small, if you didn't know it was there it would be easily missed.

As she neared the wharf, in the daylight the town appeared quite charming. The wharf went far out into the water, many older gentlemen lined the walkway, their fishing rods dipped in the water as they waited in silent contemplation for a nibble.

A restaurant sat at the end of the main street, large glass windows providing a beautiful view of the ocean. Many people were already sitting at the outdoor tables, the rain from last evening a forgotten memory as the sun promised a good day. Turning onto the main street, people walked along the streets, some leading dogs and up ahead, she saw a sign for the Twilight Café.

It was a blue wooden board with white cursive writing and a star over the 'i' where the dot should have been. Pulling into an empty car park, she headed for the blue door, caffeine a high priority on her list. Without it, she would be brain dead by lunch time, and zombie Norah was no fun to be around. A bell chimed as the door opened and she saw Olivia look up from behind the register, her face splitting into a grin.

"Norah! How are you?" She called out through the doorway behind the counter. "Hey Gail, this is the new girl I was telling you about."

A woman with bright red hair peered around the corner and shot her a smile. "Heard a lot about you, Norah. First coffee is on the house."

Not one to say no to free coffee, Norah accepted.

"So, what's your poison?" Olivia asked. Today her ash brown hair was braided down her back, blue eyes full of energy and she wore a black short sleeve shirt and shorts.

"A latte, in the largest cup you have."

"Are you sitting in?"

"Sure, why not." Eyes travelling over the glass cabinet of pastries, she selected a spinach filled croissant to nibble on. Taking a seat near the window, she took a better look around the café.

The walls were a cream white with baby blue moulding. Big open windows let enough natural light in and artwork hung around the shop, many depicting images from the town. Looking up, the ceiling was covered in fairy lights and she hoped she would get to see them at night, it would look beautiful. The chairs were made of big heavy white painted wood and the cushions a deep blue. They were comfortable to sit in and Norah had a feeling she had found her new writing place.

Near the counter, she saw a sign she had missed. It read, A warning: all those who quote or reference the Twilight series as a joke will be forced to pay the sparkle tax. A jar was placed below the sign, filled with dollar notes and she grinned.

Pulling out her list, she added some food to the grocery section as she waited. Coffee and chocolate topped the list as she'd learned that both were important to her writing process. Without them, nothing got done.

"Here we go," Olivia placed her coffee and pastry down with a smile.

The smell of caffeine rose from the cup and her body began to relax from the comforting scent. "Thanks, Olivia. Did you get home okay last night?"

Olivia waved her hand. "Yeah, it was fine. Rylan was here, apparently he called it off with his girl, that's why he took off. She was a real clingy type and had been avoiding him for a few days because she knew he wanted to end it. She must have missed him though and called him. He had an opening and he took it, hoping that by doing it in a public place would mean she wouldn't go bat shit crazy, which she still did by the way. It was hilarious."

Norah took a sip of coffee. "Damn that's good. Still, he shouldn't have ditched you."

"True, don't worry, he got what was coming to him."

A customer walked in and Olivia smiled before going to take their order. Eating slowly, Norah doodled notes for her story on the edge of her list until the food and coffee was gone and she had run out of room.

Next time don't forget the notebook, she reminded herself. Olivia was making a coffee and she walked over. "Can you tell me where the supermarket is?"

She looked up from the coffee machine. "Sure, just walk up the block and you'll see a pathway of trees. If you follow that to the end, the grocery store is right there. It's only a three minute walk."

"Thanks Olivia." She grabbed her bag and Olivia called out.

"Will you be back tomorrow?"

"Of course, I get the call for caffeine every day, and I must heed the call."

Olivia laughed. "You're so weird. Must be why I like you."

"The weird do tend to flock together. See you tomorrow."

"Bye, Norah, see you then!"

Norah stepped out and paused when she saw a man looking at her car. "Can I help you?"

Turning around, the man grinned and Norah was surprised that he was actually kind of cute even if his clothes were dirty and old. "I know most of the cars in this town and I was just wondering who this one belonged to."

"Don't a lot of tourists go through here though?"

The man took a step towards her, running a hand through his dirty blond hair. He had a five o'clock shadow, a grease stain smudged his chin and she guessed how he knew the local cars. "They do, but most tourists walk around Bellvale and park by the wharf to avoid getting parking fines. Only locals bother parking up along here because they know the police around here are pretty lenient when it comes to parking."

"I'll keep that in mind…"

He held out his hand. "Brad Smith. And you are?"

"Norah Jacobs. I'm letting the Jones' beach house for a month or so." She shook his hand and noticed his brown eyes giving her the once over.

"If your car needs to be looked at, I'm more than happy to take a look under the hood. I'm the local mechanic, my place is just up the road."

If Norah didn't know any better, she would have thought he was flirting. "Thanks, Brad I'll keep that in mind. At the moment it's fine, it still does all the important stuff; start, stop, brake, honk at people who annoy me."

An eyebrow raised. "Do people still say honk?"

He hadn't let go of her hand. "I assume they do, if not I'm going to bring it back. Now, I've got some shopping to do so can I have my hand back please?"

Momentarily confused, he looked down and laughed, withdrawing his hand. "Sorry about that. I'll see you around, Norah."

"If my car stops honking, I'll let you know." She felt his eyes on her as she headed up the street. He seemed cute, in a puppy dog kind of way. Norah had dated a guy like him before and it didn't work out. They were all about pleasing you, which was nice at first, but it didn't allow her to connect with them on a deeper level because they never opened up about themselves and were too scared to have an arguemnt. She wanted someone who, strangely enough, argued with her but was willing to stay by her side and work it out at the end of the day.

Some people thought she was weird, wanting someone she could fight with, but she felt it was important to fight for love, in all aspects of the term. A love that was filled with nothing but sunshine and happiness just seemed boring.

She reached the trees Olivia had mentioned and a motorbike came rumbling down the street. It drove slowly, Norah recognised it as the same bike from the night before and she glanced at the rider.

Broad shouldered, wearing black jeans and short sleeved grey shirt, the wind pressed the fabric against his body and she couldn't stop herself from looking. His arms had two black circle tattoos around his biceps and she thought it was a strange tattoo set to have. He wore a black helmet, the visor down and she felt a stab of disappointment. She was curious to know who owned it.

The rider's head turned as he passed and Norah didn't know how, but she knew he was looking right at her. Flushing, she turned away and hurried down the small path. She had probably looked like an idiot, ogling at him. The sound of the bike faded and she made her way between trees, trying to forget she probably looked like she had just climbed out of bed, which she had.

The path was lined with apple trees, the red fruit beginning to ripen and she hoped they did something with them. It seemed like such a waste to let them fall on the ground and grow rotten. She loved to cook from time to time and if possible, she could use them to bake pies. The small lane ended and opened up to a small parking lot and the grocery store was at the other end. The only visible sign that it was a grocery store was a faded sign above the door, the 'g' and 'c' faded from age.

The doors slid open as she entered and she grabbed a basket, pulling out her list. Walking slowly around the store, her basket grew heavier with each aisle she went through and she regretted not grabbing a trolley. She always grabbed a basket and spent the last half of her shopping dragging the basket around on the floor because it was too heavy to carry.

Standing in the household cleaning section, she was trying to decide which window cleaner to get when the hairs on the back of her neck stood on end and her spine stiffened. Glancing to her left, she saw a man leaning against the far wall, eyes fixated on her. He looked too large to be inside the store. He was of average height, but the bulk of his body consisted of muscle. Black scraggly hair hung in his brown eyes and he wore tight dark clothes.

As she met his gaze, a leer etched across his face and kicking off from the wall, he walked away. Filled with unease, she threw a random bottle of window cleaner into her basket and grabbing everything else in a rush, she dashed to the check out. As the teenage girl put everything in bags, Norah kept glancing around the store for the large man. He seemed to have disappeared but the damage was done. One day and already she was seeing creepy guys.

Grabbing her bags, she hurried back to her car. Walking down the lane, she felt as though she was being watched but there was no one around. Reaching her car, she fumbled with the keys and threw everything inside, once she managed to unlock the door. Sliding in, she locked the doors behind her and closed her eyes, taking deep breaths.

"I'm just imagining it," she whispered. "Why would a creepy dark version of Thor be following me?"

Turning on the engine, she decided to go and get the money off Jack now. One trip into town and she was already losing it. It was time to harness that crazy and put it into cleaning the house.

She found Jack's place without needing directions and the garden looked slightly unkempt now. The night had hidden most of the weeds but it was still pretty to look at. Climbing out, she shut her car door and walked up the small path to the front door, hand hesitating as she raised it to knock. Olivia had said to wait until the afternoon…

The door opened and she stumbled back. "What are you hovering out here for?" Jack growled. He was still wearing the same clothes as yesterday, the smell of whiskey stronger and his eyes were bloodshot. "You're early."

"I'm sorry, I just thought…" she trailed off, not wanting to tell him about her freak out at the grocery store.

Jack's eyes narrowed as he studied her. "You all right? Look like you've seen a ghost."

"No, I'm fine," she said faintly. "I can come back tomorrow for the money if you want?"

"Nah, don't want you bothering me again. Wait here a minute." Leaning on the frame for support, he turned around and disappeared down the dark hallway into a side room. He returned a few moments later, an envelope in hand. "Went and got the money this morning. There's an address there too, for second hand traders. They'll give you a good deal, tell them I sent you.

"Okay." The envelope felt thick and she wondered how much Ray had sent.

"Anything else?" Jack glanced over his shoulder and she shook her head.

"No, thank you."

"Bye then."

Shutting the door in her face, Norah tried to take Olivia's advice and brush it aside. Since she had cold items in the car, she wasted no time heading back to the house, following the main street and the trip back was a bit faster now that she had her bearings.

The waves crashed gently against the shore as she pulled back up at the house and took everything inside, putting it all away in the empty cupboards. Leaving the cleaning supplies out, she found her laptop in the messy pile of belongings and turned it on. If she was going to clean, music might help to make the time go by.

Scrolling through the music library, she finally settled on The Ramones and got started as 'Sheena is a Punk Rocker', blared through the small speakers. The afternoon passed quickly as she opened up the house, dusting, scrubbing and wiping the house from top to bottom. She stripped the bed and washed the linen, and the curtains too which smelt old and stale. Every wooden surface was polished and soon the house began to smell fresh. Cleaning had always calmed her whenever she grew stressed. Those ugly feelings were scrubbed away and her stress over Daniel and the man from the grocery store faded with the dirt in the house.

The sun was beginning to set as she finished wiping down the bathtub which was now a gleaming white. She spent the next hour unpacking her belongings and putting everything away. Once she had put the last of her linen away, she walked out to the kitchen to close the front door and stopped at the sight. Stepping down the steps and onto the sand, she walked down to the water and stared. An orange glow was cast over the sky, tinged with pink dotted clouds, fading into the horizon. The waves sparkled in the setting light and the wind had quietened, blowing her hair softly against her face and she brushed the brown strands aside. Her body ached from cleaning but she felt peaceful.

Maybe it won't be so bad here, she thought. A fresh start could be just what I need.

The sound of a wolf howling floated on the wind and she looked up at the cliffs. She thought she saw a tail disappear into the trees but she was probably seeing things. They hadn't mentioned any wolves in the area. She would have to ask Olivia tomorrow when she got her coffee. She would worry about the furniture tomorrow too. Right now, she was content to simply watch the waves, enjoying a peace she hadn't felt in some time.

3. First Meetings

The drive into town the next day was faster now that she had her bearings. It only took her a few minutes and she thought about walking from now on to keep fit. She needed the car today for furniture but after that it would be better to cut down on costs.

She didn't have to worry about money since her father had passed, he had left her and Adam a considerable sum each. Adam had blown through his in a few months, but not Norah. She put it all away, collecting interest and adding to it when she worked for Ray over the summers. Alice had always made him employ her to be what he affectionately called, a 'paper bitch', and Norah realised, as she pulled up in front of the café, that this would be her first summer in four years that she hadn't worked at Ray's company. A pang twisted in her chest and she walked into the shop, thinking it was a weird thing to be sad about.

Olivia came over from the far window, empty china in her right hand and she surprised Norah with a quick one armed hug. "Hey, how are you settling in?"

"All right, I spent yesterday cleaning so at least the house is looking better. Now I just need some furniture."

Olivia went behind the counter and putting the cups down, she started preparing Norah's coffee, remembering what she had ordered the day before. "How much did Jack burn this time?"

Norah raised an eyebrow. "Does everyone just turn a blind eye to his pyro habits?"

"Pretty much. He's actually a decent guy, he's been good to my brother, Luke over the years, when he isn't completely tanked. Also it's fun to watch sometimes, he really knows how to start a fire."

"Weird," Norah muttered, before raising her voice. "Can you make the coffee to go? I want to go and check out this second hand place."

"Sure, it's just up the road by the way. Across the street from Brad's mechanics. You know, Brad," she teased, "the guy who was flirting with you yesterday?"

Olivia handed her a cardboard cup and she wrapped her fingers around its warmth. "You were watching?"

"Hells yeah, not much else to do around here, except gossip and snoop into other people's business."

Norah didn't like the sound of that. She'd prefer they knew as little about her problems as possible.

"He was all over you," Olivia continued. She looked Norah up and down. "He doesn't seem like your type."

She laughed. "You've known me less than two days, Olivia, for all you know my type is scrawny, balding, middle aged men."

Olivia held up her hand. "Okay, first of all – gross. Second of all, you are just like me; you like them well defined, with a rock hard –"

"Don't finish that sentence, Olivia!" Gail called out. "Or I'll be telling your brother."

Norah guessed her brother was the over protective type as Olivia rolled her eyes. "I was going to say, personality!"

"Sure," Gail muttered and Olivia grinned. The door opened and more customers walked in.

Saying goodbye, Norah got back in her car, taking a long swig of coffee before she started the engine and headed up another block, pulling up in the small lot beside the second hand furniture shop. Having everything so close together was quite convenient. Grabbing the cup and her bag, she headed inside.

A short stocky man stood near the front counter, clip board in hand and looked up as she approached. "How are you doing ma'am? What can I help you with today?"

She glanced around at the array of oddly organised furniture. The smell of dust and moth balls was strong and she wondered if he ever opened the windows. "Hi, I'm just looking for some new furniture, a couch and maybe a coffee table?"

Realisation dawned and the man broke into a smile. "Ah, you must be the little lady renting Jack's place down on the beach. So, he destroyed the couch this time, huh?"

"I guess so." She decided to just go along with it. If everyone didn't care what he did to the furniture, then she would have to learn to go along with it too.

He touched her arm briefly. "My names, Frank. Feel free to look around and let me know what catches your eye. I'll give you a good deal, just make sure you pick the wooden pieces so it's easier for Jack later on!"

Frank laughed at his own joke and Norah laughed awkwardly under her breath as she turned away. Savouring her coffee, she made her way down the disorganised aisles trying to find a decent looking couch and coffee table. The sound of a motorcycle drifted through her ears as she tested out a brown leather couch. It still had a good seat and seemed to be in good condition for a two seater. The leather had faded on one of the cushions but she would probably put a blanket over the seat so it was more comfortable. It was too big for her car, but maybe Frank could deliver it for her.

Memorising its location, she kept going behind some old shelves and at the end, sighted a few coffee tables. She was about to walk over when Frank's voice called out – "Rylan, how are you?"

Norah's ears perked up at the name and she snuck a glance between the shelves over at the front counter. A man stood talking to Frank, he appeared to be in his late twenties, a five o'clock shadow adorning his jawline and he smiled at Frank, giving her a glimpse of the dimple in his right cheek. Light brown hair was swept from his face and he looked like he had just come from work, his white shirt was covered in dust and had stains where he had obviously rubbed his hands. The same marks were only slightly visible on his black jeans.

He didn't seem to mind, and Norah couldn't help but notice that his clothes accentuated the fact that he was in good shape. Examining his average frame, she noticed he did have a rock hard – personality, she corrected her thought. Dammit but Olivia had been right.

So, that's the guy who left Olivia on the edge of the road, she thought. She wanted to go over and chastise him but since he didn't know who she was, it would probably be awkward. He started to turn her way and she quickly went back behind the shelves, pretending to examine the tables beside her, heart pounding in fear of being caught perving. His soft voice didn't reach her ears and she waited for them to finish talking before coming out of hiding.

When she walked out, Rylan was gone and she went over to Frank. He looked up as she approached. "Have you found anything?"

"Yeah." She showed him the coffee table and couch she had picked out. The coffee table was a simple dark wood and it was just long enough to maybe fit in her car.

She asked him about delivery and he said that was fine. "I can bring out the couch this afternoon, if you're home? I would bring the table too but I won't have any room in the tray for it."

"That's fine, it should fit in my car." Frank helped her carry out the long coffee table. It was heavier than it looked and she wondered how she was going to get it into her house. Frank waited as she folded the back seats down and helped her lift it inside. They had it halfway in when the phone rang inside.

"Oh shoot, I bet that's my insurance, give me a second." Dropping the end, he raced inside and Norah's legs buckled under the weight. She tried to push it in but it seemed to be caught on the seat further in. She tried to lift - cursing Frank for ditching her - when two hands appeared beside hers, lifting the table with ease and sliding it in. The scent of saw dust and pine and drifted over her and her back brushed against someone's chest.

She spun around to say thank you and paused; her mystery helper had been Rylan, who was already walking away. She stared at his back for a moment, confused that he hadn't stuck around for her to say thank you.

"Thanks, Rylan," she said it softly and turned as Frank came running back out.

"Sorry about that, oh look, you got it in yourself."

"I had some help."

"Good, good, lucky we are such a friendly town. I better get back in there, I put them on hold. I'll see you this afternoon then."

Shutting her trunk, she paid Frank for the furniture and headed back down the main street. Her thoughts drifted back to Rylan. It was strange he had taken the time to help her, but didn't hang around to wait for the praise. Most men were like puppies that way; they craved women's gratitude – or at least the ones she knew did.

Maybe these Bellvale men were different.

As she passed the next block down, a white brick building caught her eye and she came to a stop, mentally kicking herself for not noticing the book shop sooner. Her book radar must have been on the fritz, normally the book shop was the first place she located in a new town. Unable to go home without taking a look first, she got out of her car and headed inside.

The brick work inside matched the outside but retained its natural red colour, faded from age. The walls were covered in shelves and the owner had made use of the small space, cramming every available surface with books. New books faded into old books as she went down the small aisle towards the voices at the end. Two women stood near the counter in a heated argument. They appeared to be in their late twenties, one woman had dark olive skin that made her green eyes stand out. Her black hair was tied back in a messy bun and as Norah approached, she heard what she was saying –

"Karl Urban is one of the sexiest men alive. To say that he isn't is just preposterous. Have you even seen Star Trek?"

"I have," the woman with strawberry blonde hair replied. "And I think he holds a certain charisma, but I wouldn't go so far as to say he is sexy. He's not in my top ten anyway."

The black haired woman scoffed in indignation and saw Norah observing them. She motioned her to come over with her perfectly manicured hand. "We need a third party to settle this; is Karl Urban sexy, sweetie?"

Norah saw a metal pole behind the counter, leading up to the next floor and tried to refocus on the conversation at hand. "I think you both have solid points from what I've heard, but I have to agree with – I'm sorry I don't know your names."

"I'm Wendy," the dark haired woman said. "And this person with no taste in men is Madison."

Madison smiled and waved. "Hi."

"Okay so –" She looked at Madison. "First of all, who's your number one?"

"Jensen Ackles."

Norah nodded in approval. "Then you do have taste. Damn good taste at that, but I think I still have to side with Wendy. Karl Urban is definitely sexy in my opinion."

"Ha!" Wendy raced around the counter and tackled Norah in a bone crushing hug. "I like you."

"You like everyone who agrees with you, Wen," Madison said wryly.

Wendy stuck out her tongue and gave Norah's shoulders a small shake. "Sorry about that. Was there any book in particular you were looking for before we dragged you into our discussion?"

"I'm just browsing, actually. I'm new to town so I'll probably be floating through here on most days of the week –"

"Oh, you must be Norah!" Wendy hugged her again. "Olivia raved about you the other night. I do hope you let me see your writing sometime. I'm a pretty decent critique."

"Maybe one day." Norah, stepped away, unused to so many hugs in one day. "Would you recommend any books about the area? I've been busy the last month so I haven't been in a book shop for a while."

Wendy went to a shelf at the front of the store and pulled out a thick book. "If you're going to be staying in Bellvale, then you need to get on the wolf train."

"Wolves?"

Wendy handed her the book. It was about wolves and their history and surrounding mythology. "It's more of a research book, but it's one of our best sellers."

"Why is that?"

"Because of the wolves in the forest," Madison interrupted. "Also, because Wendy spreads false rumours about werewolves."

"I would never!" Wendy declared, while Madison mouthed, 'she does' behind her back.

"Are the wolves sighted often?" Norah thought of the tail she had seen on the cliffs the night before.

"They tend to keep to the centre of the forest," Wendy explained. "It's rare that anyone sees them near the town."

"That's good," Norah breathed a sigh of relief.

Wendy nodded, tucking a stray hair behind her ear. "I'm pretty sure whatever pack it is, is up further north at this time of year, so don't stress."

"Good. Now onto my next important question; why do you have - what I can only assume to be - a stripper pole behind your front counter?"

Wendy grinned. "No, girl, it's a fireman pole. This building used to be part of the old fire station. It ironically burned down fifteen years ago and they decided to relocate rather than rebuild here." She spun on the pole for effect. "This is one of the surviving structures from the old station."

"Well that makes more sense than a stripper pole." She weighed the book in her hand, an idea forming. "If I buy your book, can I slide down it?"

Madison laughed as Wendy leaned over the counter. "Blackmail, I love it! You do drive a hard bargain, Norah but you've got yourself a deal. Come on."

Norah followed her up the old steel stairs behind the counter, they creaked under her weight and she stepped tentatively. The second floor was obviously Wendy's private room. Books were strewn across every flat surface and a laptop was open on the coffee table, a picture of Karl Urban on the screen, the instigator of the sexy argument.

The pole came through the floor and Wendy held out her hand. "Go for it."

"So glad I wore jeans today." Feeling more excited than an adult should, she grabbed the pole and pressed her knees into the sides. The air howled as gravity took hold and Wendy disappeared. She reached the bottom level quickly and her feet hit the ground.

"Have fun?" Madison smiled.

Norah nodded, eyes shining. "That was awesome!"

"Look out below!" Norah stepped aside and Wendy came sliding down after her.

"It's fantastic, right?" Wendy nudged her. "It would be better with a sexy shirtless fire man sliding down it though."

Madison shook her head, a soft smile gentling her features as Norah paid for the book.

"I expect regular visits from you, Norah." Wendy handed her, her change.

"Definitely." Norah gave her a wave. "Thanks for the book."

Madison was leaving at the same time and Norah offered her a lift. "Oh, no thank you. I'm just heading down to the beach, it's not that far and I could use the exercise. See you next time."

"Bye Madison." She headed for home, thinking that Madison didn't need the exercise at all. She was a petite girl, it looked like a small puff of wind could blow her over, or snap her in half. She seemed like a sweet person though. Her fingers brushed the hardback of the book, intrigued to learn more about these Bellvale wolves when she got home.

*   *   *   *   *

Frank's car honked as he drove off and Norah waved before heading back inside. She had waited until he turned up that afternoon before trying to get the table out. Her living area now looked homier with the two new additions.

She had spent her time writing as she waited for Frank and was pleased with her progress for the day. Her story was set in two different time periods and followed an old police report about a gypsy girl who supposedly murdered her troupe in the early nineteen hundreds. The people in the present time were descendants of the gypsy, and were following the case by reading an old journal the gypsy had written during her incarceration which reveals the truth of what happened. At the same time, they are discovering who they are, they are dealing with their own problems.

The modern people were a hassle for Norah to write. Their chemistry and the problems they were facing were difficult to write. It was strange, that it was easier to write of characters in a time past. Norah put it down to things being simpler back then, but if she didn't get on top of it, the modern part of the story was going to get unbalanced by the past.

Needing a break after writing and moving furniture, she grabbed the wolf book and went outside, sitting on the edge of her deck. Flipping through it, it seemed to be filled with facts but Norah liked that. Research books were like a drug to her. She loved learning about different creatures and their history. The first half of the book covered the facts of the wolf and second half was the mythology. Choosing the facts first, the sound of the ocean faded into the distance as she became immersed in the book. She was reading about their eating habits, when her skin raised. Feeling as though she was being watched, she looked around and saw a lone wolf on the cliffs above, watching her. Shaking her head, she looked away.

"It's just looking down, it's not looking at me, idiot," she muttered to herself. She watched from the corner of her eye as it stared for a few more moments before melting back into the forest.

I'm just being paranoid, she thought and started reading again.

4. Fear

It took a week for Norah to finally settle into the beach house and way of life. She spent a lot of time at home, writing her story and reading novels Wendy kept recommending her. It had only been a week and her reading list was as high as the kitchen table. Every morning, she got up and jogged into town for a coffee before she started her day.

Olivia was beginning to know her routine and her latte was now waiting for her when she walked through the door. The weekend had been busy, the tourists came in droves and Norah avoided the town at that time. She wasn't a big fan of crowds, they often left her feeling frustrated and a little claustrophobic.

One thing that hadn't settled was her irrational fear of Daniel showing up. She kept a small bag in the back of her closet, filled with money and clothes in case she needed to run again. Something she hoped wouldn't happen.

The weekend was over and Norah put on her sneakers to go for a run. Standing up from the bed, she tucked the kitchen knife in the top drawer of her bedside table. She found she slept better knowing it was close by and if she woke in the night, it was the first thing she checked, the cold of the blade easing her fears.

Locking the front door, she started running down the long drive way, her legs still stiff from sleep. The first day she had started running again, her legs had seized up, unused to the sandy terrain. She was a bit out of shape, but she was slowly getting back into her routine. All the coffee and chocolate had taken its toll, but she wasn't going to stop consuming them. Not a chance in hell.

She reached the main road and stuck close the edge. It was a ten minute run into town so she would pass through and go up the cliffs on the other side for a real workout before heading back into town for her coffee. Her breathing grew heavier as she passed through the town, waving to some of the locals who were beginning to recognise her. She didn't know their names but they always sent her a smile so she would return the favour.

The path to the cliffs came into view and she started to mentally brace herself. It was a fair hike and she still had to stop halfway for a breather every day. Today, she wanted to make it with no breathers. It was going to kill her but she was determined. The path grew steep quickly and she focused on her breathing, keeping her eyes down. Looking ahead and seeing the way to go was always a motivation killer.

Her legs started screaming in protest and she pushed harder, secretly loving the feeling which told her she was doing a real workout. Twenty minutes later, the ground levelled out and she laughed in relief. For the last three minutes she had been groaning in pain but she refused to give up. Looking around, she glanced over the top of the cliffs and at the ocean grinning in triumph. She'd done it.

Heart pounding, she stretched out her legs, waiting for her breathing to even out a little more before starting the walk back down. She wanted to stay and savour the moment, but her stomach was demanding food. The sound of the ocean was muted by the cliffs and blended with the sound of the wind blowing through the green and straw coloured long grass. It was a simple but pretty path and at this time of morning, there was no one around and Norah felt peaceful, as though she were the only person around for miles and her troubles were long forgotten. Apart from writing, it was becoming her favourite time of the day. The grass on the cliffs was still wet with morning dew and she breathed in the fresh smell.

By the time she had reached the main street, her breathing had slowed and her heartbeat had returned to normal. The bells tinkled as she stepped into the café and Olivia was waiting with her coffee and croissant. "Wow, you're early today."

"Didn't stop today," she grabbed the bottle of water from the fridge and took a swig before grabbing her breakfast and sitting in her favourite place by the window.

"That's pretty impressive, Norah. You're making me feel lazy." She grabbed at the non-existent fat on her stomach. "I am getting fat."

Norah rolled her eyes. "Shut up, Olivia. You're skinny and you know it."

She grinned. "Thanks, Norah. You have such a way with words."

The front door opened as she took a bite of her croissant, mouth-watering at the sweet taste and Wendy walked in with her brother Charlie. He had the same skin tone as his older sister and his hair was shaved close the scalp leaving nothing but a faint shadow. He was taller than Wendy, his sister only came up to his shoulder and his job at the saw mill seemed to keep him in good shape. His height alone was enough to leave Norah feeling a little intimidated but his overall build sent out an aura of danger. She had met him during the week and discovered he was actually a sweet guy who was over protective and slightly scared of his big sister.

From the look of annoyance on Wendy's face, she guessed it wasn't a good morning for them. Wendy saw Norah and made a beeline for her table. Norah braced herself for the incoming argument. "Hey, Norah, what's happening?"

"Just having breakfast –"

"You can't just ignore me, Wendy!" Charlie dragged a chair over and sat at their table.

Wendy glared at him and gave Norah a sweet smile. "How's your story coming along?"

"Good –"

A fist slammed on the table and Norah jumped.

"Hey!" Gail walked over and slapped Charlie across the back of his head as some tourists tried to pretend they weren't looking. "You break my table and I'll break your legs, Charlie Jackson. Get your shit together!"

"Sorry, Gail," he muttered. She gave his head a small shove and went back behind the counter. Wendy was smirking.

There was a small bubble of tension around them and Norah eyed them. "What's going on between you guys?"

"Nothing –" Wendy started.

"Our cousin dropped by last night," Charlie spoke over her. "Was demanding that bastard's share of the profits from the bookshop! The nerve of that bi –"

"Charlie!" Gail called and he winced involuntarily.

"I take it you don't get along with your cousin?" Norah asked.

"Not since Dante ran off with her." He growled.

"Dante?" She glanced at Wendy. "As in the name of your store?"

She nodded, lips pursed. "Used to be my boyfriend. We were together for nearly six years and I came home one day to find him in bed with Mara, our cousin. Everything in the bookshop was in my name, though it was ironically called Dante's Emporium, so I kicked him to the curb, quite literally."

"You didn't change the name though?"

Charlie opened his mouth to speak and Wendy raised her fist, shooting him a warning glare to shut it. He closed his mouth and shrunk back in the chair. Wendy sighed. "I didn't change the name as a reminder to myself. It's a memento of the mistakes I've made and a reminder not to make them again. Now, can we drop the subject before I start to get really pissed?"

Norah nodded, taking a sip of her coffee. "Done."

"Dammit, Wen –"

"What subject are we dropping?" Madison walked up behind Charlie and he shot out of his chair.

"Hi, Madison. Take a seat." She shot him a smile as she took the offered seat and Norah swore the poor boy's knees melted.

She bit back a smile. "We were talking about Dante."

"Oh, not that awful man." Madison frowned. "How did he come up?"

"He came up because Charlie doesn't know how to keep his big fat mouth shut." Wendy snapped.

"Oh Charlie, you know not to upset your sister like that." She said gently.

He mumbled something incoherent under his breath and stalked out of the café. Madison turned to Wendy. "Did I say something wrong again?"

Wendy shook her head, murmuring something about, 'unable to keep it in his pants' and Norah guessed Wendy knew of her brother's obvious crush. Madison however seemed completely oblivious.

Norah finished her breakfast, listening quietly to Wendy and Madison discuss the latest episode of Witches of East End. Norah hadn't gotten into the show, but then, she rarely watched T.V these days. Saying goodbye once she'd finished her coffee, she walked out, waving to Olivia and ran right into Brad.

"Hey, Norah." He sent her a smile and braced herself for the same question – "what are you doing for dinner tonight?"

"Not much, I plan on writing so I'll probably be having left overs." Every time she ran into Brad, he never hesitated to try and ask her out. At first it was cute and rather flattering, but now that it had been just over a week, it was beginning to wear a little thin. He obviously thought he had the charm to win her over, and it might have worked with any other girl – but Norah wasn't going to change her mind.

"All right," he said, disappointed. "Maybe another time."

Norah just smiled and nodded before turning to walk back home. As she walked down past the wharf, she thought about the latest scene she was working on. Her modern characters were heading to a party to let off some steam and she wasn't sure how to write the atmosphere of the party. Her last party had been back in high school when she was seventeen, which was seven years ago now. The only reason she had gone to parties had been because of Adam. He had wanted her to get out and meet new people, rather than staying home with her nose buried in a book. She had never enjoyed herself; the girls were too preppy or slutty and the boys were wasted before the party had even started.

Adam had never gotten completely trashed when she went with him. He said he liked to keep a partly clear head so he could keep an eye on her. Any guy who had tried to hit on her was kicked to the curb, even the owner of said house in one instance. Her eyes stung; she missed that Adam.

A motorcycle roared past as she turned down her driveway. Adam had never been perfect, he held countless flaws but at the end of the day, he had always come through and protected his little sister.

"Just not this time," she whispered to the wind. Her house came into view and she refocused on the story, pushing the memories to the back of her mind.

Heading inside, she saw the answering machine's red light flashing and clicked the button to hear the missed call.

Hi, Norah, I haven't heard from you in a week! A week! Even Ray has heard from you. I don't like this radio silence. I've got tomorrow off work so you better call me or I'm going to come down there and drown you in the ocean for not letting me know you're alright! Love you!

The message ended and Norah smiled. Alice had a flair for the dramatic sometimes. She would call her in the morning. Alice knew Norah hated talking on the phone, it was never something she had been comfortable doing but Norah did used to make the effort to call Alice every couple of days. Being in Bellvale though, it seemed easier to forget everything and get lost in her writing. Speaking of which – she grabbed her laptop and settled on the couch to try and hammer this scene out.

*   *   *   *   *

This was such a bad idea.

Standing beside her car, her keys were raised to unlock it as she debated her decision for the ninth time. The party scene had been written, it had taken most of the afternoon but she had got it done. It was the next scene's turn to torment her. Her character had left the party and she was walking through a thicket of trees back to her car in the dark. She was meant to be afraid of the shadows, the noises and the dark, but Norah couldn't write it.

Sure, she had her fears, Daniel being numero uno, but she had never been in a forest at night before. Looking at pictures did nothing to help, she was better at describing these sort of scenes if she had experienced them in some way herself; and what better chance did she have, on a clear night with a full moon and a forest just above her...

She thought of the wolves and shook her head. Madison and Wendy had said they were far off. That lone wolf must have been a stray or something and the odds of running into it were crazy low. Jumping up and down a couple of times to try and shake off the fear, she finally unlocked her door and slid in, placing her notebook, torch and knife on the seat beside her.

"I am so going to regret this," she muttered, turning the key in the ignition.

She pulled out onto the main road, turning left away from Bellvale and the butterflies in her stomach started beating ferociously. Fingers tapping on the steering wheel, she stared into the darkness and followed the signs to the walking trail. She had read about it during the week and it would do for this.

Turning left again into a small parking lot, she pulled up beside a familiar maroon motorcycle. There was no one around and she hesitated; what if he was a crazy axe murderer just waiting for someone like her to come along?

Idiot, a voice in her mind whispered. Where would he put the axe on the bike?

Grabbing the torch and knife, she slowly stepped out. She left the notebook, she would fill it in when she was back in the safety of her car. Her torch flickered into life as she took small steps into the dark forest. The cool air burned her lungs and a howl of wind tore through the trees, making her jump.

"Suck it up," she whispered to herself. Taking larger steps, she kept walking as she counted to one hundred. When she reached one hundred, she would stop and turn back. Because of the full moon, the shadows were larger and each sway of a tree branch made her want to shriek. The old trunks creaked in the wind, the leaves rustling overhead blending with the pounding of her heart in her ears.

Ninety eight, ninety nine, one hundred.

Coming to a standstill, she took a shaky breath and did a slow circle. The trees appeared to be surrounding her from each side and she swallowed a scream when a bird flew overhead. Apart from the wind, the forest was quiet. That silence was enough to keep a chill in her bones. Her hands shook as she held the torch out in one hand, the knife raised in the other.

"Okay," she whispered after standing still for what she hoped was at least a minute. "I think I've got enough data."

A snarling sounded from the darkness at that moment and she dropped the torch, the light dying as the sound drew away, accompanied by another. She scrambled on the forest floor, her fingers shaking as she desperately tried to find the torch. The growling continued, though it was getting more distant but her panic continued to grow. She finally brushed against the cool cylinder and grabbed it, flicking it back on when a new sound made her freeze.

The wolves were growling again but she could have sworn she heard a man shout this time. She thought of the motorcycle and shut her eyes in dread. She wanted nothing more than to run back to her car, but if he was in trouble...

Groaning, she stood and started heading towards the noise. Stupid stupid stupid, she chanted in her head. Why didn't she have a cell phone so she could call for help? More importantly, why did she feel the need to go and help when she didn't even know the person?

Rounding a large pine tree about a yard into the forest, she flashed her torch and let out a small gasp. A large grey wolf stood over the prone figure of what appeared to be a completely naked man. The wolf turned to look at her and not thinking, she stepped into the clearing, brandishing the knife.

"Get back!" She snapped. The wold snarled, teeth bared and she raised her knife. "Get lost, you stupid wolf!"

For a moment, it looked as though the wolf was looking at the knife, assessing it in the dark. Its teeth snapped in her direction before it turned and ran into the forest. Adrenaline pumping, she raced over to the prone figure. "Are you okay?"

She rolled him onto his back and gasped. Three large slashes ran across his chest and his left eye was bloodied. His skin seemed pale in the light from her torch but the light could be misleading. She tried to keep her eyes above deck, so to speak and she took a closer look at his eye. Her eyes widened as she recognised the face –

"Rylan?"

5. Help

What on earth was Rylan doing naked in the middle of the forest?

Norah touched his arm, surprised at how warm he still was. "Rylan, can you hear me? My name is Norah, I'm not going to hurt you. I'm going to help you, okay?"

He moaned and she took that as consent to help him. She had to get him to a hospital, in the dark she couldn't determine the full extent of his injuries but she knew it was bad. She didn't have a phone to call for help and he obviously didn't have one either. Her next plan would have to be carrying him back to her car but that was still going to be a problem. "All right, Rylan, I'm going to help you, but you need to help me as well."

She pulled him up to a sitting position and frowned. The guy was heavy. "Okay buddy, I need you to stand up. Come on," she groaned as she tried to pull him to his feet.

He hissed, struggling to stand as he tried to help her and she winced, knowing she must have been hurting him. But she couldn't leave him in the forest while she went to get help. What if the wolf came back? She shifted, trying to put most of his weight on her back as he finally got to his feet and her own legs threatened to buckle. His head and arms hung over her shoulders but his feet were still dragging on the ground. The metallic scent of blood, combined with dirt filled her senses and she breathed through her mouth.

"Okay," she gritted her teeth. "You better stay awake or we're both screwed."

She walked slowly through the forest, her torch tucked tightly under one arm. With each step, her legs wanted to collapse but she kept a steady pace, knowing if she stopped she wouldn't be able to start again. Rylan's laboured breathing sounded in her ears and her back started to feel damp from the blood coming from his chest. It took her nearly ten minutes to find the path again and with each step, his weight grew heavier.

"Come on, Rylan, help me even a little bit here."

"Sorry," he murmured lightly and she felt a stab of guilt.

"Just focus on staying awake, please." It felt like forever before she saw the outline of her car. Relief swept through her and she struggled over to the passenger door. She cursed as the torch dropped and she fumbled with the key in the dark before finding the keyhole. In an awkward manoeuvre, she somehow managed to get him sitting in the passenger seat, shoving her notebook onto the floor in the process.

Picking up the torch, she rushed around the other side and froze, turning to look at his bike. A small pile of clothes were on the ground, on the other side, his keys and wallet buried in them. She hadn't looked on the other side of the bike earlier so she hadn't seen them. She picked up the small bundle and put them in the backseat of her car before climbing in. Quickly starting the car, she turned to look at him in the dark, secretly glad so she couldn't focus on the fact that he was very naked. "Where is the hospital around here?"

"No hospital," he breathed, eyes closed.

"You need a hospital," she demanded, "and I don't know where it is –"

She jumped as his hand grabbed her arm and his eyes flew open, staring at her in pain. "No hospitals, please, Norah."

His eyes closed again and she wanted to ask why, but the need to attend to his wounds took priority.

"Stubborn man," she cursed, banging the steering wheel as she shifted into reverse. Spinning around, she headed back for home. She didn't know where Olivia lived and had never bothered to ask for her phone number. She thought of checking the address on his license, but she still wasn't familiar with the streets here and he needed attention now.

She tried to drive carefully, every bump made him hiss in pain and she bit her lip in worry. She wished he'd just tell her where the damn hospital was. She couldn't believe that it was him she had seen every time she saw that motorcycle. She wondered if he would be annoyed that his motorcycle had been left out near the forest. Someone could steal it. At least she had thought to grab the keys, and unless it was possible to hotwire a motorcycle, she felt it would be safe for the night.

She turned down her driveway and her next problem arose; how was she going to get him in the house?

Coming to a stop, she rushed out of the car and unlocked the front door before going back for Rylan. His skin was pale and she kept her eyes on his face as the car light came on. "Rylan, we're getting out of the car now, I need you to help me again."

He seemed to understand and was able to twist his body so she could pull him out. He fell into her and she stumbled back. "Whoa, stand up, Rylan."

With one arm draped around her shoulders, he was able to take slow steps into the house. They reached the couch and she placed him on it as gently as possible. His legs hung over the edge and she grabbed a blanket to place over his lower half. Her mind was in overdrive as she tried to think of what to do first.

"I'm going to call an ambulance –"

"No," he breathed. "I'll be fine but no ambulance and no hospitals."

"I'm not qualified to do this, Rylan. I'm calling an ambulance."

"Then I'm leaving." He tried to sit up on the couch, face scrunched in pain as he grabbed at his chest. Norah watched him for a second before shrieking in annoyance. Grabbing his shoulders, she gently pushed him back down.

"Fine, but if you get an infection and die, don't blame me." She looked at his wounds, wondering what she should do. "Clean," she murmured, staring the blood all over his chest. "Clean the wounds."

Grabbing a large mixing bowl from the kitchen, she filled it with hot water and grabbed some towels and her first aid kit from the bathroom. It only had gauze and bandages but she would use whatever she could at this point. Bringing everything over to the coffee table, she placed it down in a rush. His chest was sticky from the blood and she bit down her nausea. Even after helping Adam clean up, the sight of so much blood made her feel ill.

"Okay, Rylan," she said hesitantly. "I'm going to clean the wounds now."

Wetting a face washer, she started wiping the blood away. The bleeding appeared to have slowed and she did her best to clean the wounds without pressing too hard. His face was twisted in pain but he didn't make a noise. "Nearly done," she tried to assure him.

The puckered flesh looked bad and she knew he probably needed stitches, but there was no way she was doing that. Her mind was going through how people cleaned wounds in the movies since it was her only reference point for this sort of thing. "Sterilize with alcohol."

Getting up, she grabbed her bottle of vodka from the top cupboard in the kitchen. It would have to do. Kneeling on the floor beside him, she touched his arm. "Rylan? I need to sterilize the wounds now. It's probably going to hurt a little bit."

He didn't respond and she dabbed a piece of gauze in the alcohol before gently wiping it across the edges of the wound. She gasped as Rylan's eyes shot open, his body tensing up. "Fuck!"

His hands shot out and gripped her biceps painfully. His chest rose and fell heavily as his eyes closed and she found her own breathing was erratic, hands trembling.

"Sorry," she said repeatedly, her voice squeaking. His hold on her arms didn't loosen and she hurried to finish cleaning the wounds. The circulation in her arms was being cut off but she didn't say anything. He was probably in more pain at this moment than she was.

When she was done, she tended to his eye and his body started to relax as her fingers gently applied an ointment she had found in her first aid kit which helped relieve bruising. His grip loosened and pins and needles tingled up her arms. With the remaining gauze, she covered the wounds and sat back feeling exhausted.

There was nothing more she could do until he was coherent enough to let her take him to a hospital. His breathing evened out and he fell asleep. Norah stared at him; his face gentled in sleep but the hard lines around his eyes and mouth told her he was still in pain. The thought of waking him to give him pain relief crossed her mind but she was hesitant to wake him. His hair was plastered to his forehead and not thinking, she brushed it aside, the dark strands cold and damp against her skin.

She saw the arm band tattoo around his bicep and brushed some dirt smudges underneath it. Even now, his skin was warm to the touch and she wondered if maybe he had a fever. Getting up, she grabbed a washer and some ice from the fridge before placing it on his forehead. He moved slightly when she placed it on but quickly resettled.

The bleeding appeared to have stopped and she sighed, resting her head on the coffee table. She stared at his face, still curious as to what he had been doing out in the forest with no clothes on. She was still trying to think of a reason as she drifted off to sleep, her hand stroking his arm gently in reassurance.

*   *   *   *   *

Ring ring.

The sound of the phone drifted through Norah's ears and she squinted as she glanced out the small front window towards the beach. Her body ached and she for a moment, she forgot why she had fallen asleep on the coffee table.

The phone clicked through to the answering machine and memories of last night came rushing back in. Head whipping around, she looked at the couch and froze. Rylan was gone. Glancing around, she saw the pile of clothes she'd grabbed were missing as well and a flash of annoyance coursed through her.

The bastard had left without as much as a thank you.

The answering machine beeped. Norah, you better pick up this phone right now before I come down there and –

"Hey Alice." She rushed over, tripping over her feet and picked up the phone before her friend got too carried away. She looked around for Rylan. "What's going on?"

"Norah Jacobs!" she screeched. "You don't talk to me for nearly two weeks and all you have to say is, what's going on?"

"Hey, I answered the phone, which says I'm alive." She stretched the phone cord, trying to see in her bedroom. "Although, I could have been killed and come back as a zombie, but then I probably wouldn't be able to talk –"

"Shut up!" Alice sighed heavily into the phone, knowing Norah hated the sound. "Tell me about Bellvale. Has everything been okay?"

Norah proceeded to tell Alice about her time there so far and the people she'd met, leaving out her discovery of a naked man and his subsequent disappearance this morning. She continued to pause as she looked around, expecting Rylan to suddenly appear from the bathroom or something.

"Norah?"

"Hmm?" She tuned back in after looking out the window to see if he had gone outside.

"I'm sorry, am I boring you?"

"What? No, I'm sorry, you just caught me at a bad time…"

A strange noise erupted from Alice's side of the phone and Norah winced. "Are you with a guy right now? Is he hot?"

"I'm with no one right now."

"Ah, but last you were with a guy, right?"

Norah rolled her eyes. "Alice…"

"Details!" she demanded.

"Not right now, I have to go."

"But I haven't even got to tell you about –"

"I'm sorry Alice, I really am. I just can't concentrate right now. I promise to call you back though. Tonight?" There was silence on the other end and Norah yanked the cord, knowing Alice would be dying to know what was wrong. "Please?"

"All right," she finally said. "But if I don't get a phone call tonight, I'm going to come down there and make you listen to my boring stories."

"It's a date. Love you."

"I love me too. Bye!" Alice hung up first and Norah placed the receiver back in the cradle.

Doing a quick run through of the house, she decided that Rylan was either a hide and seek champion, or he had really left. She started to feel peeved off that he hadn't hung around to let her know he was alright. After all the work she had done last night to help him, she deserved that much.

The feeling only intensified when she realised that both her linen and the jumper she was wearing were ruined. "Should have left that ungrateful bastard out there," she grumbled.

Clearing the coffee table, she noticed the blanked was folded neatly on the arm of the couch. Still ungrateful. There was a blood stain on the couch cushion and she scowled. "I need coffee before I can deal with this."

Walking to the bathroom first, she had a shower and tried to think of ways to get blood out of leather. Adam had only had blood on his skin, which had been easier to clean. The couch would be another matter though. She wondered if she typed, 'how to get blood out leather' into Google, what answers would come up? For some reason her mind just went straight to dirty websites and serial killer blogs. Not something she really wanted to look up at this time of morning. In the end, she decided that bleach was the best answer and she would simply flip the cushion over so it wasn't visible. Or place a rug over the top so it wasn't noticeable.

Her mood continued to darken when she saw the blood on her car seat. Sighing, she tilted the seat back so she wouldn't lean on it and headed for town. It seemed as though her life was filled with blood these days. Her mind still harboured a million questions about Rylan and why he had been naked in the forest. Her current top thought was that he was a nudist hippie just getting in touch with Mother Nature but that just seemed ridiculous.

She saw her notebook on the car floor and realised she had forgotten about her main intention last night. Picking it up, she headed for the café once she stopped the car in town.

"Norah, there you are!" Olivia rushed over and gave her a hug.

"Yes, here I am." Norah hugged her back awkwardly. "Did I miss something?"

"No, it's just I'm so used to you coming in at your usual time, I was worried something bad had happened to you! I've made your coffee four times while secretly hoping you weren't dead in a ditch somewhere."

"I only hang out in ditches when I've had a rough night with Jose, so it's all good."

"Jose?"

"Tequila!" Gail sang and hummed the tune as she took some empty plates back into the kitchen.

Norah smiled and nodded in approval before turning back to Olivia. "Sorry I worried you. I just had a rough night and needed a few extra z's."

"That's okay."

Norah grabbed her arm. "Actually, would it make you feel better if I gave you my phone number? I was just thinking about that last night."

"Oh sure! I can't believe I haven't gotten it yet." They exchanged numbers and Olivia frowned. "This is a land line. Don't you have a mobile so I can text you, too?"

"I don't have a mobile."

"You don't have a mobile?" she repeated.

"That's right. I don't think I really need one –"

"Of course you need one!" Olivia exclaimed. "What happens if you're out on a run and you get hurt? Who are you going to call with -?"

"Ghost busters!" Norah said before she could stop herself.

Olivia's frown deepened. "You have no idea how hard I want to laugh at that right now."

"I can kind of tell, actually," she poked Olivia between the eyes. "You're twitching."

She swatted her hand away. "Seriously though, Norah. You need to get a mobile phone. It's not safe to be out on your own without a way to contact someone."

"What if I use smoke signals? I'm not that good but I'm sure I can take an online class or something."

Olivia sighed and Norah grinned in apology. "Sorry. I'll think about getting one. In the meantime, if you want to contact me, I suggest you stick to the old fashion land line."

"Fine, but I'm not giving up on this."

"I'm not giving up on smoke signals either. I think they could really make a comeback in the next five years?"

Olivia went behind the counter. "Why five years?"

"Have to think in the long run, Olivia. It won't just happen overnight."

"You are being extra weird today," she muttered. "Go and sit down, I'll bring your coffee over."

"Thanks." Norah took her usual seat, thinking Olivia was right. She was feeling extra weird today. The whole incident with Rylan last night and then his disappearance this morning really had her feeling out of sorts. Acting weird was her defence against all the crazy.

The morning was getting on but the café was quiet save for a few tourists lingering. She scribbled a few notes from last night, crossing out Rylan's name when it suddenly appeared from the tip of her pen. In the end, she had more than enough for the scene she was stuck on, so at least it hadn't been a wasted effort. Every so often her mind kept drifting back to Rylan and she tried to push him from her thoughts, not wanting to deal with that right now. Olivia came over with her coffee and the aroma relaxed the tension from her body.

"Hey jerk," Olivia bounced over to the door after delivering Norah's coffee. Norah glanced up and her heart stopped.

Rylan stood in the doorway, grinning down at Olivia, his face fully healed. His white shirt was the same one she had collected last night and it held no traces of blood and no hint of any wounds or dressings beneath the thin cotton.

The cup in her hand trembled. What the hell?

6. Threat

Norah blinked, sure she had to be dreaming. Cup raised half way to her mouth, she watched Rylan follow Olivia back to the counter, thinking she was having some sort of mental break. Her eyes roved over him, desperate to find some sign that last night hadn't just been some crazy dream. There were no signs of pain in his expression, no stiffness in the way he moved and no bruising healed that quickly. A ball of nausea settled in the pit of her stomach.

He had been on the verge of death last night. No one had that much colour in their cheeks after losing so much blood. She squinted, trying to determine if he was wearing makeup, but it all looked natural.

"Where were you last night?" Olivia asked him as she prepared a sandwich for him.

If he knew Norah was burning holes into his back he didn't show it. "Nowhere. Just went for a run and then to bed."

"Whose bed? It wasn't yours," she accused, slapping some meat on the bread. "Luke said you were out all night."

"That's none of your business," she could hear the smile in his voice. "I will say one thing; she was good with her hands."

"Too much I –"

The sound of smashing china rang through the café as the cup slipped from Norah's fingers. The hot coffee sprayed her jumper and she shot back from the table as she felt it seep through onto her skin.

"Norah! Are you alright?" Gail and Olivia both headed over to her. "Did you burn yourself?"

She shook her head, pulling her jumper off. "I don't think so." Her skin felt hot but it wasn't burnt. "I'm sorry about the cup, I can pay for it –"

"Don't be silly!" Gail chided as she cleaned the mess. "It's just a cup."

"Oh my god, Norah what happened to your arms?" She followed Olivia's gaze to the bruises which were beginning to form on her biceps from Rylan's grip. She hadn't even noticed them in the shower this morning.

"Nothing," she muttered, covering them subconsciously. "I must have done it in my sleep or something." She picked up her book, feeling Rylan's gaze from across the room. She suddenly felt as if she were exposed, unnerved by the feel of his stare. "I'm going to go home and get changed."

"Let me make you another coffee," Olivia started to walk back to the counter.

"No, its fine, thanks. I'll see you tomorrow." She needed to get out of there. She kept her eyes lowered as she moved past Rylan, too nervous she would start screaming at him if they made eye contact. Once outside the café, she walked quickly down the street, one hand clenched over her chest to stop her pounding heart from breaking free.

Her mind was going in circles, trying to figure out how this was all possible. He should have been lying somewhere, in agony. Those slashes had been deep, or at least she had thought they were. Maybe the night had made them appear deeper – no! She had cleaned them, they had caused him pain, and the bruises on her arms were proof of that.

She was nearly at the wharf and came to a stop. She'd forgotten the damn bleach. Looking back up the street, she bit her lip. She didn't want to risk the chance of bumping into Rylan again. Turning up a side street, she went the long way around to the grocery store. There were few houses in the opposite and a small park where a few children were playing. She passed them by blindly, images of blood and wounds playing through her mind.

Forgetting her coffee stained clothes, she headed into the grocery store to buy the bleach. Again, another factor that proved she wasn't going mad. No matter how many times she ran through the events of last night in her head, there was just no way to explain his miraculous recovery.

Walking down the aisles, her body turned onto autopilot as she found the bleach and took it to the counter. Annoyance was slowly starting to creep in that maybe he hadn't needed her help, and he still hadn't bothered to thank her in the café but had blatantly teased her as if she wasn't there.

Jerk.

The cashier glared at her and Norah winced, not realising she had said it out loud. "Sorry, not you. Just a guy I was thinking about."

Her gaze became sympathetic. "I can relate there, honey. My own man is treading thin ice himself, at the moment. All men need some sense beaten into them at one time or another. Don't let him get to you though, that's the main thing."

"Yeah, you're right. Thanks Cara," she read her name tag. "Same to you, and I have baseball bat at home if you ever want to beat some sense into your man."

"Oh don't worry, honey. I've got a shovel that works just fine."

Norah paid her and walked back to her car, hoping Cara was being figurative, and thought about what she had to clean when she got home. The bleach would be fine for the couch because she could hide the mark, but it was going to stain her car seats which annoyed her. She took pride in her car, keeping it in good condition and now those marks would be a reminder of something she still couldn't explain.

The sound of a motorcycle starting made her shoot behind one of the large apple trees, heart thudding loudly in her chest. She felt like an idiot, but she couldn't bring herself to face him. She wanted answers, but at the same time, she wasn't sure she was ready for them. It drove by slowly, as if he was looking for her and she counted to fifty once the sound of the engine had faded before she was game to step out. It was stupid; she had no reason to fear him – apart from the fact that he appeared to have crazy wolverine healing abilities.

"Norah!" Jumping, she turned to see Brad running toward her. "Hey, what's with the bleach?"

Trying to calm her nerves, she shook the bottle. "Just making sure I have plenty of options at home should I decide to end it all."

"What?"

She saw the alarm on his face and patted his arm. "Just a joke, Brad. I'm cleaning the bathroom today, that's all. Do I seem like that type of person?"

"Of course not," he stuttered. "I would never – "

"It's okay, Brad. Breathe. Was there a reason you came over other than to say hello?"

"Oh, right. Well I was thinking I could stop by after work tonight –"

Norah felt a tension headache coming on. "Look, Brad. I know you're just trying to be nice –"

"Just as friends," he added quickly, sensing the imminent rejection.

"Still no," she said gently. "I've had a rough couple of days and I just want to go home and rest – by myself."

"Okay," he said in defeat. "But if you ever want to hang out, you know where to find me. I still want to be your friend, Norah?"

"Just my friend?" she asked, eyebrows raised.

He hesitated and she knew what that meant. Looking across the street, she saw Dark Thor talking to Dylan, Brad's apprentice which had her nerves fraying again. "See you later." Not waiting to hear his reply, she headed back to her car, hoping no one had seen the blood stains. She felt a little guilty about being so short with Brad but she honestly couldn't deal with his advances right now. She needed normalcy, a break from the mad reality she was currently living in and the only way she could do that was to dive into her writing without distractions, and so far all her problems were men based; Daniel, Rylan, Adam. She needed to get away from all of them, even the nice ones like Brad.

Turning the key, she looked across the street again and held her breath as she met Dark Thor's gaze. A chill ran down her spine as he held her eyes for a few seconds before turning to walk into the pub.

"This town is getting to me," she muttered to herself, as she drove home.

* * * * *

Sitting on the veranda, the sun had long set and she watched the sparkle of the moon on the water. It was slowly becoming her favourite way to relax. Just the sound of the waves crashing against the shore gave her a calming effect no anti-anxiety medication could. Her hands reeked of bleach, but all traces of blood had finally been removed from her couch and car. All the soiled linen had been tossed and she added it to her list for the next time she did a big shop. She hated buying towels, the good ones were ridiculously expensive and the new ones always left balls on everything. It took numerous washes to wear them in and she had no patience for stuff like that.

The air was starting to get cold and she decided to have an early night. Her body was still sore from the night before and she was keen to lie down in her bed. Locking the front door, she grabbed her laptop off the table and raided her movie collection before deciding on Footloose. Turning off all the lights, she walked in her room and shut the door as the laptop read the disk. Her body sank into the soft mattress and after making sure her knife was in her bedside drawer, she turned the movie on, feet tapping away to the beat of the opening song.

Footloose was one of her favourite movies, the original and not the remake. Kevin Bacon hadn't been a real looker, but he did bring the character of Ren to life. She had seen the remake but it wasn't the same. It didn't have the same spark, the characters didn't have the same life to them and it left her feeling disappointed. It wasn't just the characters though, it was the music too. It seemed to blend so much better in the original and the soundtrack was one of the reasons she loved the movie.

Her eyelids grew heavy and she drifted off to sleep as Willard was learning to dance, wishing her life was as simple as an eighties movie.

*   *   *   *   *

Crash!

Norah's eyes flew open and she shot up in bed. The room was pitch black, the laptop had put itself in sleep mode once the movie had finished. At first she thought it must have been her laptop falling off the bed, but listening closely, she heard the faint sound of footsteps in the other room and a ball of fear formed in her throat. What if it was Daniel?

Reaching over, she opened her bedside drawer quietly and grabbed the knife, the cool handle feeling reassuring in her grip. Standing up, she tiptoed to the bedroom door, heart pounding. Her stomach was doing back flips and she thought she was going to vomit. Placing her hand on the doorknob, she gripped tightly to try and mask the tremor of her hand. Be brave. You can defend yourself.

The doorknob creaked as she turned it and Norah cringed. In the silence it sounded too loud in her ears and she hoped whoever was out there didn't have super hearing. As she started to pull the door open, it flew open, hitting her face and she shrieked, stumbling back as a large figure rushed her. The intruder grabbed her hand which held the knife, twisting it so the knife clattered to the floor. She started to reach for it when a hand wrapped around her throat, shoving her against the wall, the force of her body making the picture frames rattle on their hinges.

Breathing heavily, she was on the verge of hyperventilating and tried not to scream. "What do you want?" she gasped.

His face drew close to hers, the smell of salt and liquor strong on his breath and she realised he was bare chested as her arm brushed against bare skin. "Stay away from the Montoya's," he snarled.

Olivia's flashed in her mind and she was confused. "What?"

"Stay away from them and their lackeys, or we'll be forced to get rid of you ourselves." His grip tightened on her throat, cutting off her air. "Do you understand?"

She nodded, hoping he would let her go and gasped in relief as the pressure vanished. She collapsed to the floor as he disappeared and a moment later she heard the front door slam on its hinges, the wood rattling from the intruder's strength.

Body trembling, she sat on the floor, gathering her breath. A sob got caught in her throat, the noise sounding strangled and she picked up the knife. She wanted to throw it for being so useless, but instead she held it against her chest, as if a small child being comforted by a teddy bear.

It took her ten minutes to regain some strength in her legs and rise to her feet. Still shaking, she flicked the light switch and her room was flooded in light. Walking out her door, she moved into the living area and stared at the front door. The lock on the door had been broken and it was swinging in the breeze. She stared at it briefly, the intruder's words echoing through her mind.

What had Olivia done to warrant such a threat?

His last warning flashed in her mind and her shoulders slumped, the knife dangling from her fingertips.

She was sick of getting death threats.

7. Debt

She was going to need a new lock.

The door was hanging wide open, moving gently in the breeze, and Norah sat in the middle of the floor, knife resting on her lap. She hadn't slept. Her body had shut down and for most of the night she had sat and stared at the broken door. It was an old door, made of dark brown wood and it had a single deadbolt lock. The connection on the frame was hanging by one screw, but the hole for the lock was practically intact. The guy had to be crazy strong to be able to be able to tear the lock out.

For the fifth time, Norah wondered if maybe she hadn't locked the door. She ran through her bed routine again from the evening before, hoping to remember everything but she couldn't remember for sure if she had locked the door. The sun was beginning to rise, the dark slowly turning grey and rather than calling the police, she was simply thinking of how to change the lock.

To be honest, Norah had had enough of the police. They had torn her home apart after Adam turned himself in and what could they do about a break in when the suspect had vanished? They could keep an eye on her, but she didn't want that. She hadn't got a good look at the intruder and she had no details to give them, so it was hopeless trying to catch him.

Her other option was to pack her bags and run, a thought which had crossed her mind more than once through the night, but a large part of her didn't want to run. After being terrorised by Daniel, this intruder's threat just didn't leave the same residual fear that Daniel's had. The initial fear had faded and she was simply left feeling tired, and over all the bullshit life kept throwing her way.

Looking at the ocean, she decided she would stay; she wanted to prove to herself that she was no coward. Bellvale was all about turning over a new leaf and that included not running from her fears. Standing up, she placed the knife on the table and got dressed in blue jeans and an old band shirt from her teen years. Grabbing her wallet, she headed out the door and wedged a piece of wood under the base to stop it moving.

Rather than drive, she chose to walk, hoping the fresh air would wake her up and bring her back to reality. She still felt a little numb but the crisp morning air was slowly taking effect and with it, her brain started pounding her with questions – why would someone consider her a threat? Why would someone tell her to stay away from Olivia? What had Olivia and her family done to be considered dangerous?

Norah hit the main road and walked on the bitumen, since the road was quiet. Norah had only ever met Olivia, she hadn't seen any of her other family, so it wasn't as if she had any ties to them. And she had only been in Bellvale just on a week now, so she barely knew anyone. Questions of Rylan still lingered, and she wondered if he had something to do with it but she put them aside. She wasn't sure if they were connected but right now she could only focus on so much crazy at a time.

The ten minute walk into town took longer as she tread a snail's pace. The morning fisherman were heading out onto the wharf and she waved blindly to them. She passed a few children running to the bus stop behind her. She hadn't seen many children in the town, and she wondered where the school was. Surely such a small town didn't need a school bus?

Instinctively, Norah found herself walking towards the café and she stopped in her tracks. The sign for the Twilight Café swung in the breeze, creaking on the old hinges and cursing her cowardly ways, she stepped away and crossed the road. Maybe it would be best if she stayed away today. She was getting braver but she wasn't that courageous yet.

Baby steps.

Continuing on, she headed for the hardware shop a block up from the café. There were no other customers at this time of morning and she looked for a sign which would point her towards door locks when she walked in.

"Can I help you, dear?" The owner and namesake - who Norah had met once - Paul Roker, greeted her from behind the counter.

"Good morning, Mr Roker, I hope I'm not too early."

"Don't be silly dear," he smiled. "What can I help you with?"

His voice was quiet and she saw a slight tremor in his hands as he reached for a pencil. "Um, I need a new lock for my front door."

"Oh my," he smiled. "Was Jack out there last night?"

It seemed Mr Roker knew who she was as well. He mentioned Jack, and she wondered if she should have told him. She didn't want him to know the door had been broken, afraid he would be angry. She'd rather pay for it herself.

"No," her voice sounded dead in her ears and she spit out the truth before she could stop herself. "Someone kicked in my front door last night and broke the lock thing."

"That's terrible, did they hurt you?" He put his glasses on to try and get a closer look.

"No, sir, he left pretty quickly when he realised I was there," she lied. "So, um, can you help me find a new lock?"

Paul looked at her for a long moment, not believing her lie before he nodded. "You wait here, I'll be right back." He ambled behind a few shelves and Norah waited patiently.

She stared at a small bell on the counter, deep in thought. The shock was still lingering and in a way, she was glad it was. Without it, she was sure she never would have made it out of the house. She wasn't sure if Paul would try to report her break-in to the police.

Maybe she should talk to him about keeping it to himself. She didn't want everyone knowing what happened.

"Norah?" A voice broke through the haze and she saw Brad standing beside her. "Are you okay?" He asked, concern in his eyes. "I've been calling your name."

"I'm fine," came the automatic reply. "Just tired, I guess."

"Ah, here we go." Paul returned with a few fittings in his hands. "Hello, Brad, I'll be with you in a moment." He handed Norah the lock pieces, so she could see them. "These will fit your door perfectly. I remember putting that door in back in sixty-three. Never forget my locks."

"Thank you, Mr Roker."

"You can call me Paul, dear."

"What happened, Norah?" Brad interrupted as she paid Paul. "Why do you need new locks?"

"Nothing happened, I just broke the lock last night by accident and need a new one." She glanced at Paul, hoping he wouldn't call her out on her lie and he gave her a small nod of understanding.

"How on earth did you do that?" he teased.

"Don't know, just did."

Thanking Mr Roker again, she walked out with Brad on her tail. She tripped as she walked out the front door and Brad caught her. "You don't seem alright, Norah. Let me drive you home."

"It's okay. It's not that far –"

"Not taking no for an answer this time, Norah."

Sighing, she let him lead her to his blue pick-up and climbed inside. Brad jumped in and started the engine, it was loud and rattly but she figured it had to be in good condition since he was a mechanic. They started down the main road and Norah was relieved when he opened his window. The cabin smelt of oil, sweat and dust; a typical man's truck but it was too stifling for Norah.

"So," Brad said over the engine. "How are you liking Bellvale so far?"

"It's good." *Apart from crazy healing men and random death threats.*

"That's good. You know," he said casually, "you should come into town and hang out with the locals more. Wednesday night at the Vale is more of a local's night and I'm sure you'd make some more friends."

"I have friends." *One that I've been told to stay away from.*

"I know, Wendy and Madison are good people, but you can meet –"

"You forgot Olivia." He hesitated and her eyes narrowed as her mind went into overdrive. "What's wrong with Olivia?" she snapped.

"Nothing," he said too quickly and she glared at him.

"Cut the crap, Brad. What are you dancing around?"

His shoulders slumped. "Well, around here, the Montoya's are known for being a bit...strange."

"Strange, how?"

"They live up in the forest and keep to themselves. It's known they keep wolves as pets, too."

"So what?"

He glanced at her. "And some people have heard that they perform strange gatherings at night in the forest."

Norah raised an eyebrow. "How does a gathering make them strange?"

"I don't know, it's like they think they have magic or something, it's just creepy." He shuddered. "I went to school with some of them, and Liam Montoya was a freak. He had the worst temper, you only had to look at him wrong and he would growl at you. I mean, literally growl at you like a dog."

Norah had to admit that was a bit strange. "But were they all like him?"

"No, his brother, Luke was almost normal." They turned into her driveway.

"So basically, you've condemned the entire family as freaks because one of them was a bit kooky in high school?" she accused.

He sighed exasperatedly. "Look, Norah, I know it sounds – what is he doing here?"

Norah followed his gaze, eyes widening. Rylan was sitting on his bike near her veranda. He was wearing a grey shirt today with the same faded black jeans. Hints of a smirk played across his features and Norah's defences went up.

"Who knows?" she muttered. "Thanks for the ride."

She started climbing out and Brad grabbed her arm. "Maybe I should stay and help – "

"It's fine, I've got it, Brad. Go to work." Shaking free of his grip, she climbed out and shut the door, heading towards Rylan. The truck idled for a moment before turning and trundling back up her drive.

Rylan and Norah stood facing each other in silence. Norah wasn't sure what to do. On the one hand, she wanted answers; on the other, she wanted to tell him to beat it.

"Is something wrong?" She finally asked.

"I came to fix the door." His voice had a soft edge and sounded different from the pain filled one she had heard two nights before.

"How did you know about my –" the light bulb clicked. "Why would Paul tell you?"

He stared at her, lips curving up. "Just because."

"Just because," she repeated, slightly annoyed. "Right, well you can go now then. I won't be requiring your assistance."

She went to walk past him and he grabbed her arm. "You know how to change locks then? Got all the tools?"

Damn.

He knew he'd guessed right and laughed softly under his breath. "Let me help, Norah."

She looked up at him his blue eyes shining with a quiet determination. "You're not going to leave if I say no, are you?"

"Nope," he grinned.

"Fine," she sighed, shoving the fittings at his chest. "Fix the door and then leave, please."

Her skin tingled as his fingers moved, lifting up the sleeve of her shirt and brushed against the bruises still covering her upper arm. His eyes flashed with regret. "I'm sorry I hurt you."

His eyes rose back to hers and there it was; a chance to ask him about the other night. His gaze told her he was expecting her to ask, he was giving her this chance to step into his crazy world. The questions leapt forth, sitting on the tip of her tongue and she bit them back down. *I've got enough crazy to deal with right now.*

"Fix the lock and we'll be even." She eventually spat out.

"Even," he said the word as if it was funny. "We are far from even." He took the bag and grabbed a bag of tools sitting near his bike on the ground.

She followed him inside and saw his eyes move over the knife still sitting on the kitchen table. "Did he attack you?" The gentle tone was gone, replaced with a sharp edge.

"What? No, he didn't touch me."

Rylan looked at her, his smirk slowly returning and he moved back to the door, crouching down and pulling out a screw driver. "You need to work on your lying. No one will believe that bullshit."

Her temper flared. "I'm sorry, but I'm pretty sure door fixing doesn't require talking."

"Consider it an extra." He started taking off the old lock. "So, how long are you planning on staying here?"

"None of your business."

"Got family nearby?"

"None of your business."

"Boyfriend?"

"Definitely none of your business."

He finished removing the broken pieces and started sorting through the new screws. "You don't seem to like me much, do you?"

She leaned against the table, arms crossed. "Haven't given me a reason to yet."

"Yet," he said softly and smiled. "I'm fixing your door, aren't I?"

"Doesn't count. You forced my hand with that." It infuriated Norah more that he seemed to be enjoying this conversation.

"Well, that's disappointing. Guess I'll have to try harder next time." He turned his back to her as he started attaching the new locks and she couldn't stop herself from glancing at him. His back seemed big from this angle, the muscles in his upper back shifting beneath the grey shirt as he worked. She watched them move, feeling hypnotised. He turned and she quickly looked away, naming the books she could see on the coffee table to try and distract herself. He looked away again and her eyes went to the couch, memories of him lying in pain creeping back in.

How?

Don't go there, she chided herself. Just focus on something else.

Her traitor eyes chose what to focus on and she found herself staring at his back again. Dammit.

He worked quickly and it felt like too soon he was standing up and dusting off his pants. "All done." He shut the door, twisting the lock to check it before opening it again. "Make sure it's bolted tight next time."

"Thank you," she said awkwardly. "You can go now."

He collected his tools and smiled. "See you next time, Norah."

"There won't be a next time," she muttered, following him out the door.

"Of course there will be, I still owe you."

"You don't owe me for anything."

He spun fast and she backed up, tilting her head up to meet his gaze. "Don't act stupid, Norah," he said, his voice serious. "You know exactly why I owe you."

She chose silence as her response and he turned, walking out. She watched him put the tools away and get onto his bike, starting the engine. It roared loudly and the bike drove slowly down the drive. Norah stared at the small trail of dust he left in his wake.

"You still didn't say thank you," she said to the wind.

*   *   *   *

That night, she triple checked every lock in the house before going to bed. She was exhausted after spending the afternoon cleaning the walls. She hadn't been able to write with everything on her mind and she had needed an outlet to stop thinking about the break in, about Rylan, Daniel…

Men were just screwing up her life.

It worried her that Rylan seemed determined to make it up to her. She had decided by the end of the day that she just wanted to pretend it had never happened. She wanted her life to get back to normal and the only way she saw that happening, was to put blinders on about the whole situation and forget about it.

She climbed into bed, hoping she didn't get another frantic phone call. News of the break in had spread against her wishes and she had received calls from Olivia, and Wendy who was with Madison. They had all offered to come and stay the night, after much screaming and dramatics, but she managed to dissuade them. She needed to deal with everything on her own. It was the only way she knew how to handle these situations; she was used to doing everything on her own.

The call with Olivia had felt awkward, Olivia hadn't noticed Norah's hesitation and rattled away about everything that happened that day. Norah had wanted to ask her about why the town didn't like her family. Instead she told her she had another call and hung up. Wendy had told her that Brad was annoyed she had lied to him. Norah felt a little guilty but she had her reasons for not spreading the truth of what happened and if he was going to pissy about it, then that was his problem.

She placed the knife on her bedside table, the blade felt silly now, after her failed attempt to defend herself, but she still felt safer knowing it was there. Laying down, she wasn't sure if she would sleep, but she needn't have worried; she drifted off as soon as her head hit the pillow, unaware of the creature watching her home from the cliffs above.

8. Revelations

"Hey, Norah!"

Olivia opened the front door and walked in, coffee cup in her hands.

"Hey, Olivia, what are you doing here?" Norah stood up from her spot in the middle of the floor.

"I haven't seen you for a couple of days, and Wendy said writers sometimes hibernate so I thought I'd bring the coffee to you." She placed a hot cup in her hands.

Norah's eyes closed, enjoying the smell. "Thanks, you didn't have to do that."

"Of course I did," Olivia leaned against the kitchen table. "You're the only customer I like and after your break in the other day, I was worried when I hadn't heard from you."

Norah didn't want to tell Olivia that one of the reasons she had been avoiding her was because of the break-in. She still liked Olivia, but her chicken nerves still got the better of her. "Sorry I kind of dropped off the planet. I just get in the zone sometimes and forget about everything else. Alice says I'm the most oblivious person she has ever met."

"Who is Alice?" Olivia asked.

"My friend from back home. Her husband co owns this place with Jack."

"Ah, okay! I think I can see what she means too, about you being oblivious."

"Why?" Norah asked nervously. "What have I missed?"

"Not much, just someone taking an interest in you," she said slyly.

"What, you mean, Brad? I've already told him –"

"No, I meant Rylan!"

Norah's whole body froze. "What?"

"Yeah, he's been asking how you are whenever I come home from work. I didn't even know you two had met, until he gave me this." She pulled out an envelope and passed it to Norah. "I couldn't help myself, I had a peek at the contents. What did Rylan do to your couch?"

Norah opened the envelope and found a wad of money and a small note. She opened the note - Sorry about the couch, hope this will cover it, R.

"He did nothing," she snapped and passed the envelope back to Olivia. "You can tell Rylan that I don't want his money."

"You want his body then?"

"What? No!"

Olivia laughed. "Sorry just had to check. So, there's nothing going on between you two?"

"Nothing at all," Norah declared and ran a hand through her hair, her fingers getting caught in the knots.

"If you say so." Olivia sang and looked around. "So, are you doing okay, since the break-in I mean?" Her voice had softened and Norah nodded.

In truth, she had been doing better. Her sleep had been broken the last couple of nights, every small noise waking her, but there hadn't been any more scary intruders, no more threats and no more weird nonsense. Apart from the wolf watching her on the cliffs. She had noticed him last night; all white, he had stood out on top of the cliffs, he was too far away for Norah to see properly but he looked quite large. She wasn't sure why the wolf was hanging around near the cliffs but she thought maybe there was prey nearby - as long as it wasn't her, the wolf could do what it wanted.

Olivia hung out for a few hours and Norah forgot all about the threats. Olivia had a personality that was hard to hate, and Norah couldn't understand why someone would tell her to stay away from her. Norah liked to trust her instincts, and Olivia didn't send off any alarm bells. After they finished arguing over who was the hottest Avenger, Olivia had to go home and Norah put on her running shoes and headed into town.

It was a busy afternoon, children were returning from school and running down the main street, candies in their mouths. She waved to Dylan who walked out of the pub and he gave her a quick nod before hurrying down the street. She wasn't sure what to make of him. He seemed like a sweet boy, but he was a little introverted. Not that Norah had anything against that - she was introverted herself - but his was more...odd.

She crossed the street and went into Dante's Emporium, secretly hoping to find a book to use for procrastination.

"Hey Charlie." She saw the big man standing behind the counter, a sullen look on his face. "Has Wendy got you on babysitting duty?"

He nodded. "My day off from the mill, and she has me selling stupid books."

Norah glared at him. "Don't take it out on the books, they never did anything to you."

"They made my sister into a book freak," he muttered and Norah sighed.

"Wait until I tell Wendy you called her a book freak."

His eyes shot up, fear glinting in them. "Don't tell her, she'll beat me."

Norah laughed, sizing him up. "I still can't understand how you're afraid of Wendy."

"If you had grown up with her, you would understand. The smaller a woman is, the scarier they are. A piece of advice my dad gave me when I was little. Mom had been a small woman and I can still remember my Dad folding beneath her icy glares."

"Wow," Norah murmured. "Your family sounds scary. So, where is Wendy? She said the other day she had a book she was saving for me?"

"She's with Madison," he said glumly and she grinned.

"So, you're upset because Wendy is spending time with Madison when you could be on your day off?"

"Yes - no! I mean..."

"It's all right, Charlie. You don't have to pretend in front of me. It's obvious you like Madison."

"How did you know?" he asked sheepishly.

She stared at him. "How could I not know? You look at her like she's the most amazing thing you've ever seen. The only one who can't bloody see it is Madison herself."

He sighed, running a hand through his hair. "Tell me about it. I think she might know though and is just pretending, because of Wendy, you know? I know Wendy doesn't want me to like her."

Norah leaned against the counter. "How do you know that?"

"She told me - screamed it at me more like it."

"Oh... Well maybe if Madison likes you back, Wendy will have to go along with it."

He looked at Norah, a silent plea in his eyes. "But how do I get her to do that?"

Norah couldn't help but giggle. He may look like a player but he was so innocent. "Excuse me for a moment." He looked confused and she reached over, squeezing his cheeks. "You are just too adorable!"

He shoved her hands away. "Stop it!"

"Sorry," she laughed. "I couldn't help myself. Look, you just need to show Madison that you aren't some little boy anymore. Show her that you're a capable man and you can look after her."

"It's not that easy, Norah."

"What do you mean?"

"Madison won't like me because she's still in love with Parker."

Norah was lost. "Who is Parker?"

Charlie pushed away from the counter, his eyes growing sad. "Parker was Madison's boyfriend in high school. They were a few years above me, but everyone knew who they were. They were known as the perfect couple. She was a cheerleader, and he was a football player, classic high school romance. They'd known each other since preschool."

"What happened to them?"

Charlie's voice grew quiet. "Parker committed suicide at the end of their final year. Jumped off the cliffs. They say he was depressed and couldn't handle it anymore. I can't understand why he was depressed when he had Madison."

Norah thought about how old Madison was. "That was eleven years ago, Charlie. Has Madison really not let go?"

He nodded. "Wendy told me, Madison used to say her and Parker were soul mates, and that there was no one else for her. When he died, she changed. She stopped eating, stopped laughing. She seemed to disappear within herself, it took months for us to bring her back. But she wasn't the same. A part of her died with Parker and she can't seem to live without that part of herself."

Norah felt a small pain in her chest. Poor Madison. She looked at Charlie, who appeared lost himself. Walking around the counter, she reached up and kissed his cheek. "Madison is lucky to have someone like you around, Charlie. Don't give up on her."

He smiled. "Thanks, Norah."

She left a note for Wendy and left Charlie to his moping. She knew he would be alright though. Charlie had a beautiful heart and she had a feeling he held a piece of what Madison needed to move on.

Brad caught her as she walked down the street. "Hey, Norah."

"Hey Brad." She knew he was still feeling a bit hurt since she'd lied to him and she sighed as he brushed passed her. "Are you free for lunch today?"

His turned to look at her, face guarded. "Why?"

"Well, I've been meaning to check out the restaurant on the wharf, and I always feel a bit weird going to restaurants on my own, so…"

He thought for a moment, and nodded. "Sure. Give us a minute." He ran up to the garage and returned a few minutes later in a clean shirt. "They wouldn't let me in with grease stains," he explained.

She nodded, looking down at her own attire. "Am I too under dressed?"

"No, you look pretty."

Norah snorted. She knew she looked like she'd just been for a run; her hair was knotted on top of her head and her shirt had a tear down the side. "I look like a mess, Brad. Don't lie to me."

They walked down the street together. "I thought most girls liked it when you fibbed about how they look?"

"I'm sure most do, but I'm not most girls. I know I look ratty."

"You definitely aren't like most girls," he murmured.

Brad led her onto the deck of the restaurant, choosing to sit outside. It had a beautiful view of the ocean; a few sail boats drifted by and the faint sound of Jazz music came from the speaker's situated outside.

Norah took a seat as a woman came by to take give them menus. She felt her eyes take in her clothes with disdain, and Norah stared at her. "Is there a problem?"

"No, ma'am," she said sweetly. She turned to Brad and smiled. "Is there something I can get you, Brad?"

"I'll just have my usual, Carla. Do you need more time, Norah?"

She shook her head. "No, I'll just have the prawn salad, thanks."

"Any drinks?"

"Water is fine."

The waitress went to place their order and Norah glanced at Brad. "She likes you."

"What?" Brad laughed. "No she doesn't, we're just friends."

"I wouldn't be so sure about that," Norah murmured as she poured herself a glass of water. "Friends don't look at your lunch date with disgust, unless there is something lurking beneath the surface."

"This is a date?"

She rolled her eyes, laughing. "That was all you took from what I just said? This is a lunch date, it's not a real date."

"Yes it is," he grinned. "It's real enough to me."

"Don't make me change my mind," she warned and he chuckled.

Although Brad didn't give up on his flirting, Norah did actually have a good time. He made her laugh with some of his old high school stories, he'd been a bit of a prankster; he was telling her about the time when himself, and Parker covered the principal's office in feathers when she interrupted. "You were friends with Parker?"

Brad nodded. "I was a few years above him. Our school wasn't big so we often had classes together. He was a funny guy."

"Charlie told me what happened to him."

"Yeah," he said softly. "No one really talks about him anymore."

"Because of Madison?"

"Yeah, she's a sweet girl and she took his death pretty hard."

"Everyone seems to have gone to school together here."

He grinned. "We're a small town, everyone knows everyone."

"Six hundred is still pretty big." Norah protested.

"Six hundred? No, there's probably only three hundred people in Bellvale."

Norah tried to remember the town sign. "I'm sure it said six hundred..."

Brad seemed to realise what she was talking about. "Oh, don't pay attention to those signs, they haven't been changed in years. Bellvale used to be pretty big, but people were finding it too expensive to live here. The town houses are big and cost a lost to upkeep. Now, a lot of them are empty most of the year and families only use them in summer."

"But many of the locals have stayed in the area, right?"

"True, there's a few who have left over the years, but many choose to stay in Bellvale. Growing up in such a close community, it's hard to just leave it unless there's a good reason."

The lunch passed quickly as Brad told her stories about the town and its inhabitants. Soon her plate was empty and it was time to head home and get some writing done for the day. "Thanks for lunch, Brad. I had a good time."

"Me too." He surprised her, leaning in and kissing her cheek. "See you soon."

She smiled. "Sure." She could have told him that the kiss was inappropriate, but she held her tongue, not wanting to end their lunch on a bad note.

* * * * *

Desire creates emotion.

Norah stared at the quote on her wall, the words blurring as she tried to figure out what she was doing. She had carefully plotted out this story from beginning to end, adding scenes and side stories as she went along, but suddenly the story had taken a huge unexpected turn, and Norah felt like she was lost in her story.

On one hand, she liked turn the story had taken, but if she continued on this path then the entire story would need a remodel, and just the thought of doing all that work again made her want to bury her head in the sand outside. Plotting the story out was hell. Norah had thought if she planned it all, it would be easier to write.

Yeah right. She ran a hand through her hair and looked at the clock; eleven pm. Maybe this problem would sort itself out on a night's sleep. Closing her laptop, she headed to bed, hoping the story would make more sense in the morning.

She drifted fitfully for a few hours, the story not letting her rest. It kept calling to her, demanding to know what she planned to do with it and she stared at the dark ceiling, huffing loudly.

"Annoying story," she muttered. Rolling over, she tried to force it out of her head, when the sound of a chair did it for her. Her heart stopped when she heard the sound of a chair leg scraping on the wooden floor and she remained still, listening intently for the noise again. The silence suddenly felt deafening and she bit her lip.

Maybe I imagined it?

Her stomach dropped as growling came from the kitchen, washing her with fear and she sat up. You've got to be kidding me, she thought. That better be a bloody Chihuahua.

Getting up, she grabbed her knife and walked out. She must have left the back door open, it was the only door she didn't check when she went to sleep. She'd been too busy thinking about the damn story.

The growling got louder and she turned the light on, ready to scare the creature but she shrieked instead. The kitchen was flooded in light and she saw two large wolves - one white and one dark - near the dining table, biting at each other. Their teeth were bared and their jaws bloody.

"What the hell?" she screeched. "Get out!" She reached for the phone, thinking to call the police or animal control, when the brown one lunged at the white one. They crashed into the floor in a flurry of limbs, the noise intensifying and she dialled the first two numbers, her fingers shaking.

As she was about to press the last button, a yelp sounded and the white wolf bit the neck of the other and she realised he must have bitten into his jugular, as blood poured from his body. He fell to the floor and the white wolf snarled, circling the body. It finally turned to look at her, its eyes piercing her own, and the phone slipped from her fingers. She knew those eyes.

Time seemed to slow down, and she looked away as the dead wolf moved, the sound of bones cracking echoed through her living room, and her heart pounded as the wolf disappeared, and dark Thor was left in its place, lying naked on her floor. A roaring sounded in her ears, her blood pumping loudly and she couldn't breathe.

The white wolf moved and she turned to look at him, her body trembling at what she had just seen. It started to step towards her and she stepped back, hands raised.

"S-stay away from me," she choked.

The sound started again and she watched the white wolf curled in on itself, body cracking and she dropped the knife, staring at the man crouched before her. He stood up, and she recognised his body, and the eyes watching her with wariness.

"Norah," Rylan said quietly. "It's all right, I won't hurt you."

She screamed.

9. Problems & Promises

Rylan jumped forward, covering her mouth. She tried to move away but his free hand moved to her hand, holding her gently. "Don't scream, Norah, I'm here to help you." She tried to fight his hold, and he made a shushing noise. "Listen to me; Tristan was sent here to kill you. I'm not the bad guy here. Now I need you to calm down."

He removed his hand and she stared at him, her breathing erratic. "Breathe," he whispered. His hand was still at the back of her head, his thumb moving in a circular motion. "Match my breaths, come on."

She stared into his eyes, trying to do as he said, her brain unable to think of anything else to do. Her breathing slowly changed as she mimicked his inhale and exhale, settling into a normal rhythm and she glanced past him, at the dead man. Her voice came out in a squeak. "Y-you were wolves, but h-how...?"

"Shh," he brushed her hair from her face. "I'll explain, I promise, but right now I need to get him out of here, okay?"

She nodded, and he let her go, moving to the phone she'd dropped on the floor. Once he moved, she had a clear view of dead Thor. Her eyes drifted over the pool of blood, reaching his lifeless eyes staring at the ceiling, and her legs buckled. She sunk to the floor unable to tear her eyes away.

"Aaron?" Rylan spoke on the phone. "Yeah, it's me. Got a problem at Jack's beach house."

There was silence and Rylan murmured. "Yeah, it was Tristan. She's pretty shaken up."

Silence again.

"No, she can come in the morning, just bring Logan for now. Later."

He hung up and there was a pause before he crouched down beside her. "Norah? Are you all right?" She didn't answer, and he sighed. "I'm sorry."

His words washed over her, she wanted to ask why he was sorry, but she couldn't speak, she could only stare at the dead man. Rylan moved in front of her, blocking her view. Her focus was now on his chest, and he tilted her chin, making her meet his eyes. "Are you in there?"

Her eyes moved lower and heat flooded her cheeks. "Naked."

"What?" He leaned closer to hear.

"You're naked."

"Oh, just realising?" She managed a weak glare, and he laughed lightly. "Not the time to joke, sorry. I don't have any clothes with me, so I suggest looking only at my pretty face."

Moving her legs, she curled them up to her chest and buried her head in her arms. She heard him laugh quietly and his hand touched her head. "Or that will work too."

They sat in silence, Norah because she was still in shock, and Rylan because he didn't know what to say. She kept replaying their transformations in her mind, trying to process if it was real or some cruel trick. A word kept flashing through her mind, but she refused to contemplate it, believing it to be too ridiculous. There's no way it can be that.

A truck sounded outside, the engine cutting off and she heard Rylan stand up. Footsteps sounded on the veranda and she heard the door open. "Hey - Jesus, Rylan, no wonder the girl's shaken up, seeing you naked would be enough to freak anyone out."

"Shut up, Aaron."

"Shit." Another voice sounded and she realised two people had come. They were silent for a moment and she heard a slap. "Sorry, Rylan."

Silence, then Rylan spoke. "Let's just get him out of here."

Norah kept her head down, listening to them move the man Rylan had called, Tristan from her house. They stayed outside afterwards, and she heard their muted voices speaking quietly. Cautiously, she looked up and saw her empty living room. The only reminder of the horror was a pool of blood. She stared at the puddle, her eyes drowning in red and it felt like it was taunting her, reminding her that her life was filled with bloodshed and trouble.

Unable to look at it anymore, she stood up and silently filled a bucket with hot water and bleach. Grabbing a scrub brush from under the sink, she took it all over to the puddle and sitting down, she began to scrub. The water quickly turned red, and soon the blood was gone, but she continued to scrub, her body becoming a robot as it went through the motions. She heard the sound of a truck driving off and feet appeared in her line of vision. When they didn't move, she scrubbed around them.

Rylan bent down, thankfully with a pair of jeans on, and grabbed her hand. "Stop, Norah."

She tried to move her hand, but his grip was strong. His refusal to let her clean, snapped something inside her, waking her from the stupor of the night's events, and her head shot up, eyes flaming. Wrestling her hand free, she threw the brush, satisfied when it hit him in the face. "What the hell?"

He looked at her calmly, as if he'd been expecting this reaction, which made her angrier for some reason. "What the hell, what?"

"What is going on, Rylan?" she hissed.

"What do you think is going on?"

Annoyed, she reached for the brush to throw at him again and he grabbed her hand. She looked at him hopelessly. "I don't know what's going on! I need you to tell me so I can stop thinking things that make me feel like an idiot."

He nodded. "Okay then. I'm a werewolf."

She laughed, the sound mingling with a sob. "Oh crap, I hate when my idiotic thoughts are real."

He smiled, squeezing her hand. "Me transforming in your living room wasn't a big enough clue?"

"It could have been magic," she muttered.

"You believe magic, but not werewolves? Strange girl –"

"Shut it!" She glared at him. "Please, just tell me what's going on. Why were you fighting in my house?"

His smile faded. "That's a very complicated question, Norah."

"No, it's not. Just be honest and tell me the truth."

"Maybe we should sit somewhere more comfortable?"

"Here is fine," she persisted. "Talk."

"That man was named Tristan," Rylan finally answered quietly. "Liam had him watching you since you helped Olivia the night you arrived."

"What? Olivia is...?"

He nodded. "She is a werewolf too. The Montoya's are all werewolves."

"Holy shit," she whispered. "But why tell me to keep away from them? I didn't even know what you guys were, I wasn't harming anyone!"

"They obviously didn't know that," Rylan explained. "The night you saved me, it added to their suspicion and they've been watching you closely ever since."

"But I'm no threat! I'm not a –" she shut her mouth, still unable to say the word. It still felt surreal to her.

Rylan lowered himself, sitting on the floor. He still hadn't released her hand. "You may be human, but there are many humans in the town who know of our existence. They keep our secret and many are friends with the Montoya's. Humans can still be a threat."

"So…" she tried to process what Rylan had told her. "Because I helped you and Olivia, I've somehow ended up in the middle of some shit storm between you and…Tristan's friends?" She tried to remember the name Rylan had mentioned.

"Shit storm is a, nice way to put it." He grinned. "Has Olivia told you about her brothers?"

Norah nodded. "She mentioned Luke, and I've heard of Liam."

"In our clan, the first born continues the line, taking charge of the clan and dealing with the bullshit politics of the pack. Luke and Liam however, are twins."

"Twins?" she repeated.

"Yeah. Their mother had a C-section when they were born, so it was impossible to determine who was meant to be born first. As the years went by, his father chose Luke to be his predecessor and, let's just say Liam wasn't happy with his choice."

"So what, they're having some sort of sibling spat and dragging innocent people into it?"

He sighed. "In a manner of speaking. The clan has been split because of Liam, we're fighting each other and losing friends because of his greed for power."

The memories of the night flashed through her mind and she remember something. "Was Tristan your friend? One of those guys, they apologised to you; was it because you had to kill him?"

Rylan's face closed off and he looked down at the stain on the floor. "We used to be friends, not anymore."

Not thinking, she reached up, cupping his cheek. He looked back up at her, surprised at the contact. "I'm sorry," she whispered.

She didn't have to explain why; they may not have been friends anymore, but it would still be a difficult thing to do. She felt him lean into her hand briefly, his eyes closing before he stood up, pulling her with him. "You should sleep. I'll explain more tomorrow. It's too late at night to explain everything and I'm not in the right head space for this talk."

She waited for him to walk out the front door, and was confused when he moved towards the couch. "What are you doing?"

"Going to sleep."

Her eyes widened. "On my couch?"

"Well, it would be too presumptuous of me to sleep in your bed tonight. But if you want me –"

"That's not what I meant!" she snapped. "You should be going home!"

He raised an eyebrow in her direction. "Someone just tried to attack you in your own home, if I hadn't been here, you wouldn't be alive right now. I will be staying until we sort this out. Now go to bed."

When she didn't move, he stepped towards her. "Do you want me to sleep with you?"

He hadn't even finished the sentence before she turned and ran to her room. Staring at the wall, she breathed heavily. She kept thinking of the mess on the floor, she wanted to go out and clean it, but she knew Rylan would still be awake. Thinking of the couch, she walked back out, stopping at her linen cupboard.

Rylan was lying on the couch, legs draped over the bottom. His arm was over his eyes but he heard her come in. "What are you doing?"

She threw the blanket in her arms over him and headed back to her room.

"Good night." She could hear the smile in his voice and muttered a quick goodnight before shutting her bedroom door.

* * * * *

Norah stared at her bedroom ceiling, her eyes strained from lack of sleep. The night had passed slowly, her sleep had been fitful, filled with gnashing teeth and rivers of blood. Not to mention the fact that a werewolf was sleeping on her couch.

Several times she had thought of climbing out of bed and shaking him awake, demanding he explain everything properly. The questions had started to pile up in her head, and she needed someone to answer them. The only thing stopping her was the thought that he said he wasn't in the right head space to explain it all. He'd just killed an old friend. She wanted to demand, to nag for an explanation, but she couldn't do that to him.

The sun shone through her curtains and her body started to twitch with the need to get up. Unable to wait any longer, she dragged herself out of bed, her head heavy with questions and exhaustion. Her problems had just increased in a way she couldn't comprehend.

She moved slowly into the kitchen, suddenly nervous and came to a stop; Rylan wasn't on the couch.

The blanket was folded neatly, like last time, and the mess she had left had been cleaned, and a towel placed over the stained wood. There was an extra addition to the room, and she looked at the table in surprise. "Olivia?"

Olivia stood up from the table, her hands folded nervously in front of her. "Morning, Norah. Did you sleep?"

"Not really." She looked at her warily. "Where's Rylan?"

"He had to go to work. He called me this morning and asked me to come and stay with you."

"I don't need a baby sitter."

"I'm not here like that," she protested. "Just as a concerned, and guilty friend. Rylan asked me to help explain everything."

Norah looked around, feeling awkward. "Are you one too?"

"A werewolf?"

She nodded. Rylan had said she was the night before, but she needed to hear it from Olivia.

Olivia bit her lip. "Yeah, I am. I'm sorry I didn't tell you." Her voice picked up speed. "It's just, we have to keep these things a secret, but when Rylan told me what happened to you last night and all the other times, I felt so awful. I mean it's all my fault –"

"Slow down!" Norah held up her hand, unable to understand Olivia's rushed words. "I need coffee before we talk."

"I'll make it!" Olivia started moving to the kitchen but Norah stopped her.

"I'll make it. You're my guest."

"But –"

"Sit!"

Olivia sat obediently and Norah moved about the kitchen, preparing two cups of coffee. "Do you take milk and sugar?"

"Yes to milk, and no to sugar."

The water boiled and Norah poured the drinks, carrying them over to the table. Olivia remained silent during this procedure and only spoke when Norah finally took a seat. "Are you mad at me?"

Norah took a sip of coffee, wishing she felt more alive. "I think I'm meant to be mad at you, but I'm not. I can understand you not telling me – you can't go around telling people you can change into a wolf, willy nilly." Olivia struggled not to laugh at the way Norah said it and she smiled. "I've told you I say weird things when crazy stuff happens to me."

"I remember. I really am sorry, Norah." Her voice broke and Norah patted her hand.

"Let's not talk about last night. I think you need to explain some other things to me before we get to last night."

Olivia nodded, leaning forward. "Anything you want, just ask away." Norah opened her mouth and froze. She didn't know where to begin. Olivia sensed her problem. "Should I tell you about my family?"

Norah nodded. "Okay."

"So my family, the Montoya's, we've been werewolves since the beginning."

"The beginning of what?"

"Since werewolves came into being." Olivia saw the worry on Norah's face. "I'll save that story for another time. Anyway, there are seven main packs in the world, and those are all broken into different branches. Our clan belong to the Blue Stone pack –"

"So, what you all descend from one main wolf?"

"In a way, wow this is hard, I've never had to explain this to someone before," Olivia laughed lightly. "So, the original leaders of the seven packs turned those humans loyal to them, and they were each given their own clans. It was basically a way to spread each packs power and worth across the country, and eventually the planet. Are you following me so far?"

Norah nodded. "I think so. Your family is part of the Blue Stone Pack?"

Olivia nodded. "The Montoya clan is one of the smallest at the moment. We only have twenty five or so, but as Rylan may have told you, we've been experiencing problems and the pack has split."

"Because of your brother, Liam?"

Olivia nodded, her eyes sad. "Dad always wanted Luke to be the next Varsk –"

"What's a Varsk?"

Olivia frowned. "I think the easiest way to explain it, would be that it's like a major. Just think of military rankings. The head of each pack is known as a Varsk, and the head of the entire clan, known as a Vuri, is like the General. Does that make sense?"

"I need more coffee," Norah muttered, taking another sip.

Olivia looked crestfallen and Norah waved her hand. "It makes sense, sorry. What were you saying about Liam?"

Olivia looked at her hands. "So, Liam wanted to be the Varsk, and my dad was against it. I overheard him telling Luke, that Liam wasn't fit to be a leader. I always thought dad was just favouring Luke, I think Liam thought that way too. When dad died last year though, I started to see what he meant," Olivia's voice grew quiet. "Liam grew cold, he started distancing himself from the clan and arguing with every decision Luke made. A few others agreed with him and –"

Her voice broke into a sob. "I don't even remember how it happened. I just know that one day, Liam walked in and declared he wanted to claim the right of Varsk. If he had been the oldest, it would be his by right, but because no one knew who was oldest and both Luke and Liam are matched in strength, the clan split, each choosing their respected leader and for the last nine months, they've been at each other's throats, trying to find ways to kill each other and take the Varsk position. Although in Luke's defence, it's mainly been Liam trying to kill people."

Norah reached over, holding Olivia's hand. She looked up, eyes filled with unshed tears. "I can still remember the way Liam looked at me, when I told him I was staying with Luke. I knew it was the right choice, but it still hurt. I love them both." Unable to keep talking, she broke down and Norah stood up and hugged her. "I'm so afraid one of them is going to die, and I don't want that to happen. I'm so scared I'm going to hate the one who kills the other. I don't want to lose both of my brothers."

Norah made soft shushing noises, rubbing her back as Olivia sobbed into her shoulder. She stayed like that until Olivia quietened and she moved away. Olivia sniffed, wiping her face. "I'm sorry. I'm meant to be comforting you!"

Norah laughed and Olivia smiled brokenly through her tears. "I don't need comforting, Olivia. I just need someone to help me make sense of all this madness. From what you've told me, your brothers are jerks for making you feel torn in the first place."

Olivia laughed, sniffing loudly. "Right? How dare they do this to their little sister?" They both smiled at each other, and Olivia reached out and grabbed her arm. "Thanks, Norah."

"You're welcome."

"And I'm sorry you got involved in all this. I know my brother, and Liam will definitely consider you to be an enemy from now on. I know it's stupid, but after last night, I know he'll think you're helping us."

"But that doesn't mean he's going to come after me. Rylan said last night there were other people in the town who knew what you guys are. Why hasn't he hurt them?"

"Murdering a local would raise too many questions. You've only been in town a few weeks. No one would bat an eye if you were to suddenly disappear."

A cold shiver ran down Norah's spine. "Right, so I'm an easy target."

"Not anymore," Olivia said, determined. "We'll keep you safe. I hope you don't mind our company, we'll probably be hanging around for a while."

Norah sighed. "I guess I don't have much of a choice, do I?"

"We'll keep you safe, Norah, I promise."

Norah nodded, wishing that promise extended to other more human threats she was hiding from.

10. Safe

The phone rang and Norah got up to answer it. "Hello?"

"Good morning, Norah. It's Brad, sorry to call you so early..."

She looked at Olivia, rolling her eyes. "It's fine, Brad, is something wrong?"

Olivia's eyebrows waggled suggestively as Brad continued. "No, I was just talking with some friends and we are going out tonight for drinks at the Vale. I thought you might want to come and meet a few of the locals, make some more friends and all that."

Norah bit her lip. "I don't know..."

"Come on, just as friends," he protested. "It will be good for you to get out of that house for awhile."

Brad was right. She did need to get out of the house and hanging out with some normal people might do her good, after all the madness of the last few days.

"Alright," she conceded. "What time do I need to get there?"

"Come by around eight. I can pick you up, if you want -"

"No it's fine, I'll walk there. See you tonight."

She hung up after they said their goodbyes and she thought of Rylan. If she was going out then there was no need for him to come to her house. Surely they wouldn't try to attack her twice in two days? They couldn't be that desperate to get rid of her.

"Hey Olivia, before you go do you have Rylan's number?" Norah grabbed a pen from the kitchen counter. "I need to call him."

"Oh sure." Olivia read out his number and Norah wrote it on a scrap piece of paper. "You going to ask him out?"

"Ask him to get out more like it," Norah muttered.

Olivia frowned. "Don't do that. I know he can be annoying sometimes, but it's better having him here. I'd feel better knowing you were being protected."

"I don't need protecting though."

"You kind of do, Norah. If you were up against a werewolf, you would lose, we are faster and stronger than you. Please reconsider."

Norah heard the concern in her voice and her shoulders dropped. "I'll think about it."

"Good! Now I have to get to work, Gail is going to kill me for coming in late." She waved goodbye and ran out the door, slamming it loudly and Norah waited two seconds before reaching for the phone. She had considered it, but the thought of some guy living in her house irked her.

The phone rang a couple of times before answering. "Rylan."

She jumped at his abruptness. "Hey Rylan, it's Norah."

"What's wrong?" he asked sharply. "Did someone come by the house?"

"No, only Olivia. I just wanted to -"

"Can this wait until I get home, then? I'm busy."

"No it can't," she blurted. "I don't want you staying here. I appreciate you saving me last night, but I think we're even now -" she broke off as he snorted and she heard the sound of a saw in the background. "What's so funny?"

"We are far from even, Norah."

She could hear the smile in his voice and her jaw clenched. "We are even -"

"See you tonight -"

"No you won't! I'm going out -"

"With who?"

"Brad and his friends," she ground out.

"Where, I'll meet you -"

"No thanks, I don't need chaperoning."

There was a moment of silence and then - "Fine. I'll pick you up afterwards. See you then."

"No you won't -" The line went dead and a noise of frustration broke past her lips. He didn't listen to a single thing she had said.

Slamming the phone down, she looked out the window and counted to ten. She kept going to twenty when the anger didn't fade and then thirty before she started to calm down. Needing a distraction, she picked up the phone and called Alice. She always knew how to calm Norah down.

She answered on the fourth ring. "What's wrong?"

"Hello to you too," Norah said wryly.

"Don't be snarky, you only ever ring when something is wrong. Dish." Alice demanded.

"Nothing is wrong, can't I ring a friend to see how she is going?"

"No! Because you don't do that."

"Dammit Alice, I rang you to calm down and you're just pissing me off more!"

She heard movement on the other end and Alice snorted. "You'll get over it. What's pissing you off?"

"Just things," Norah snapped.

"Oh," Alice dragged out. "It's not something, but some one?"

"No!" Norah said quickly and Alice laughed.

"It is! Who is the guy?"

"There is no guy!" Norah protested.

"Don't you try to bullshit me, Norah Jacobs! Only a guy could piss you off so much that you would call me. What did he do? Is he hitting on you?"

"No, there's nothing going on, he just doesn't listen -"

"I knew it!"

"Are you listening?" Norah snapped.

Alice giggled. "Oh I love when you get all defensive because of a guy. It's adorable."

"It is not adorable, I just tried to tell him I didn't want him hanging around, and he refused to listen and even tried to say he was picking me up tonight! I don't like being ordered around."

"Who are you going out with tonight?"

"A local guy and some of his friends -"

"Oh my God you've got two going at once?" Alice shrieked and Norah held the phone away. "I am so proud of you!"

"That is not what is happening! I am just trying to make new friends and - argh! Why did I call you?"

"Because you love me and miss me."

"I do miss you," Norah said quietly.

"I miss you too, Jacobs. Now, about these men -"

"No! There is nothing going on with these men. End of discussion!"

"But -"

"No!"

"Fine!" Alice huffed. "But if there is - you better tell me about it."

Norah pinched the bridge of her nose, shutting her eyes as she felt a headache coming on. "I promise to tell you."

"Good girl. I have to go back to work. Love your face."

"Love you too, bye, Alice."

"Bye honey."

She hung up and even though she was still annoyed, her heart was now homesick. She missed Alice and her old home. She hadn't felt right not telling Alice the truth. She wanted to blurt it out and ask her if she should let Rylan keep an eye out for her, but there was no way of telling her without mentioning all the werewolf drama that went with it.

Grabbing her notebook, she headed outside to kill a character. She needed to let off some steam, and unfortunately, her characters were going to be the ones that paid.

*   *   *   *   *

In its heyday, The Vale had probably been a beautiful building. The maroon coloured walls were faded to a light pink, the paint chipping along the lines of the ceiling. The bar was situated at the back of the pub and dark wood tables and chairs filled the empty space. Many tables had a single person, or two with their heads bent close in conversation. The jukebox played music from the seventies and while it was dark and a little dank, Norah liked it.

The owners, Todd and Marion were in their late sixties and the pub had been in their family for three generations. One wall was covered in photographs that dated back to the twenties at least. Flappers on the beach smiled in many images, their conservative bathing suits sure to have caused quite a scandal back then. Norah worked her way through the photos, eventually recognising some of the locals. She saw Frank, smiling out the front of his second hand store and Gail and Olivia laughing in The Twilight Cafe. Her eyes were drawn to the photograph of running wolves near the end, but she wanted nothing to do with wolves.

Not tonight anyway.

She saw an old photo of Madison, she appeared to be a teenager and her arm was linked with a tall boy with blonde hair. He looked familiar but she couldn't place him. Charlie, who had decided to join them walked over.

"Who is that?" She pointed to the boy with Madison.

Charlie's face fell. "That's Parker Roker. Her old boyfriend."

"Roker?" Norah asked. "As in Mr Roker from the hardware store?"

Charlie nodded. "Parker was his grandson."

Norah looked at the photo again, seeing Paul Roker in his grandson. "Does Paul have any other family?"

"His daughter moved away after Parker died," Charlie said quietly. "Said she couldn't live here anymore."

Norah could understand that. Her heart hurt for Mr. Roker, he was a nice man. She looked at Madison again, and noticed the subtle differences in her face. Her smile was brighter, her face filled with a happiness Norah had never seen her exhibit. Her eyes shone as she stared into the camera and all Norah could see was how in love she was. Now her heart was hurting for two people.

"Let's go back to the table," Norah suggested and Charlie followed. It was a small group of Brad's friends. Dylan was sitting quietly at the end of the table, he was still too young to drink so was sipping on water. A man with blonde dreadlocks, named Simon was Todd and Marion's son. He was in his late thirties and was learning the running of the pub. He had told her earlier that he'd spent most of his twenties travelling the world, but now he was ready to come home and settle down. He was a nice guy, and his girlfriend, Bella was sweet. Todd and Marion doted on her throughout the evening and Norah could tell they were hoping for a wedding in the near future. She just prayed they didn't put pressure on them. Parental pressure always seemed to have a way of pushing people apart.

Norah took her seat next to Madison, who had accepted Brad's invitation. She knew he had invited her so she had someone comfortable to talk with and Norah was grateful for that. Madison smiled and Norah couldn't help but see the differences from the photo. Her eyes weren't as bright, they were guarded with loneliness and pain. Norah's hands itched, wanting to reach out and hug her, but she restrained herself. It would be unkind to dredge up painful memories.

Looking across the room, she saw Jack sitting at the bar, his cheeks already red from alcohol consumption. He had looked at her before, but she doubted he had really seen her. Today must have been a really bad day if the amount of alcohol she'd seen him drink so far, was anything to go by. She hoped his fire habit wasn't needing to be fed tonight.

Simon's friend, Howie sat opposite Norah and he shot her a smile. "So, what do you think of our little town?"

"I like it," she smiled. "You really feel closed off from the rest of the world."

"It must be big difference from living in the city though." Bella leaned over Madison, her short black hair falling in her face. "Do you miss all the extra luxuries of big city life?"

Simon carried over a tray of drinks and Norah thanked him for her wine before answering. "I don't really. I lived in the suburbs and I rarely went right into the city, unless I had a reason. I prefer the quiet, so Bellvale suits me perfectly. What about you, Bella? How do you find quiet living after travelling with Simon?"

"I must admit," she looked at Simon as he sat next to Howie. "It was tough at first. When you have that wanderlust, it's hard to give it up. I guess you just need to find the right guy to give it up for."

Groans sounded across the table as Simon leaned over gave Bella a kiss. Madison and Norah smiled as the boys threw chips at Simon and he caught one, popping it into his mouth. "Thanks."

"So, have you got anyone special, Norah?" Howie asked and she shook her head.

"Only the characters in my stories."

"Wow, that sounds sad," Simon said and then table rocked as Bella kicked him under the table. "What?" He glared at her.

"It's okay," Norah laughed. "I know it is pretty sad. I'm just so focused on my writing at this point in my life, I haven't found anyone who can handle that, or has a big enough pull to drag me away from my characters."

"I'm sure you'll find that someone one day," Madison said quietly.

Norah nodded. "I will."

"Got any family back home?" Brad asked, joining in.

Norah felt her heart stutter. "Yeah, an older brother." The words felt strange coming out of her mouth, they were forced and almost alien. She had dreaded this question popping up.

"Is he coming down to see you? I'm sure there's a few ladies in the town who'd love to meet him." Bella grinned.

Norah plastered a smile on her face, hoping it didn't look as painful as it felt. "Unfortunately no, he's tied up with his own life at the moment."

"Aw that sucks," Bella pouted and glanced at Charlie. "We need to find someone for your sister, Charlie."

"I don't want to talk about setting my sister up," he muttered.

"Then how about we talk about setting you up?" Bella watched him panic and Norah tried not to laugh. Madison's eyes were lowered, and Norah saw her fingers curl into fists on her lap. She hoped all this talk of couples wasn't making her upset.

"Dylan," she called to the young man who hadn't said a word yet. "How do you like being a mechanic? Is Brad the tyrannical boss he appears to be?"

A small smile played on Dylan's lips and he nodded.

"I am not tyrannical!" Brad argued. "Dylan tell them."

Dylan looked up, cheeks flushed as the attention was on him and he said quietly, "I'll say he isn't, just so I don't get punished tomorrow."

The table broke into noise as everyone started harassing Brad and Norah laughed. The front door opened, a cool breeze seeping in, and Norah felt Madison tense beside her. She looked between Brad and Howie to see two men walking in.

The man standing just behind the blonde in front was of average height, coming up to the blonde's shoulder. His dark hair fell into his eyes as he glanced around calmly, assessing the atmosphere as the blonde one moved towards the bar. Sitting at a barstool, she saw him order a drink but his eyes weren't on the barman; they were on their table. Norah thought for a moment he was looking at her, his gaze was fixed, void of emotion. There was something familiar about him but she couldn't place it.

He continued to stare at the table and Norah wanted to tell him to stop when Madison stood up suddenly and Norah jumped. "Are you all right?"

She nodded. "I think I'll go home. I'm pretty tired."

Charlie shot up. "I'll take you."

Madison smiled gratefully and murmured her goodbyes to the table before leaving. Charlie followed close behind, and Norah saw the change in him. His shoulders were stiff, and he looked at the bar one last time before walking out.

"What got into Madison?" Bella asked. She jumped spilling her drink as a glass was slammed on the bar behind them. Turning, Norah saw the blonde walking back out, his drink barely touched. Norah thought it was strange, and Brad stood up, blocking their way. His face was serious but Norah caught a flash of fear in his eyes. "Leave her alone, Liam."

Her whole body jolted. This was Liam? She looked at him more closely, noticing a similarity to Olivia around the eyes. This was the werewolf who wanted her dead. She was suddenly so glad she was in a crowded pub.

Liam didn't stand down from Brad's weak threat, but rather stepped closer. He was larger than Brad, and his presence seemed to dominate the room. "Say that again, filth?"

Simon went to stand up, but Howie dragged him back down. The air in the room grew thick, and Norah felt a lump of fear form in her throat. Brad looked like he was trying to say something, but his mouth moved silently in fear. What if Liam killed him? She didn't know what he was like, but the look in his eyes said he wouldn't be against it. She saw his hand raise up, and she held her breath, afraid of what was to come when -

"That's enough, boy." Jack had miraculously crawled off his barstool and was standing between Liam and Brad, his hand resting on Liam's arm. His voice slurred slightly, but his eyes were sharp. Liam looked at him, trying to stare him down in the same way, but Jack was made of stronger stuff - or stronger alcohol at least. He returned the stare, his own sending a warning - back off. Norah didn't know if Jack knew what Liam was, but even she was scared of the drunk right now.

Liam ripped his arm from Jack's hand and stepped back. Without saying a word, he brushed past Brad, who stumbled, and stalked out the door. The other followed close behind, but his eyes met Norah's just once, and he winked. A shudder went through her as the door slammed shut, and the room was filled with silence.

"What the fuck was that all about?" Bella whispered. "Who the hell was that?"

"Liam Montoya," Howie said grimly. "One of the weirdos who lives up in the forest." Norah wanted to retaliate, but bit her tongue. "The other one was Blake, he follows Liam around like a shadow. Best to stay away from all of them."

Brad returned to the table, his face sullen and downed his beer in one shot. "Time for vodka," he muttered and stood up. A hand shoved him back down and a fresh bottle was slammed onto the table.

"Way ahead of you." Jack took the empty seat next to Norah and took a swig from the bottle, as if it were simply water. "They aren't all weirdo's too, Howard Newitt, you'll do best to watch that tongue." Howie's gaze lowered and he look ashamed. "Blake's father used to babysit you and your sister every Friday while your mother worked the late shift. And that family took in Rylan White after his fucked up mother swept through town - you'll do right to remember they aren't all bad people."

Norah ears perked up. "What happened to Rylan?"

Jack took another long drink from the bottle. "His mother was a drug mule, got herself in a bad way with the wrong people, and was on the run. Dumped him on the side of the road when she passed through Bellvale with nothing other than the clothes on his back."

"Perhaps she was just trying to save him from the trouble she was in," Bella suggested.

Jack shook his head. "I met her when she came through. Only interested in her own safety. If anything, she probably felt Rylan was slowing her down and needed to ditch him."

Brad reached for the bottle of vodka and took a drink, choking and couching on the strong liquid. "Let's not talk about the Montoya's," he muttered. "They're a bunch of freaks."

Norah glared at him and she felt Jack stiffen beside her. The tension started to build again and Howie, thankfully intervened. "So, Bella, tell me about Amsterdam again."

Bella took the hint. "Not much to tell when you can't remember!"

The conversation slowly drifted to menial topics, and Brad moved over to the bar for another drink. Norah thought he should stop, but something told her he wasn't going to listen.

Jack nudged her arm. "How's the house?"

"It's fine, the lock on the front door broke the other day so I replaced it." She decided to tell him part of the truth, in case he somehow noticed on one of his more sober days.

"How much?" She told him the cost and he nodded, his eyes beginning to droop. "I'll send you the money in the morning."

"Oh no that's all right -"

"I'll send you the money," he growled.

She shut her mouth and nodded. "Thank you."

"Don't mention it."

She watched as it took a few attempts for Jack to get to his feet. He raised the near empty bottle in a mock salute. "Night all."

Todd walked over to take the bottle and Jack snatched it back, holding it close to his chest. "Come on, Jack, you know I can't let you take it," Todd smiled.

Jack turned away and Norah watched in fascination as he sculled the rest of the bottle like it was nothing. Smacking his lips loudly, he passed the bottle back. "There ya go."

"Thanks," Todd said wryly. "Night, Jack."

Jack stumbled out the door, and Norah shook her head. She hoped he got home all right.

The rest of the night passed quietly as Norah listened to Bella and Simon tell stories about their travels. Soon it was closing time and they all went their own ways. Howie was staying with Simon and Bella, so Norah helped Dylan drag a very inebriated Brad out of the pub.

"Please let me drive you home, Norah. I promise I won't try anything," Brad slurred, leaning heavily on her.

She smiled and pushed him towards Dylan. "You aren't driving anywhere, Brad. Go home and go to bed."

He stumbled into Dylan who smiled apologetically. "Sorry, he's going to regret this in the morning."

"I can tell," she laughed. "Take care of him. Goodnight."

"Night, Norah." She heard Brad shouting her name as she walked down the Main Street and shook her head. She don't know why he had to drink so much after Liam left, she guessed it was some macho thing.

Brad's shouts eventually faded and the night had become eerily quiet. The only sound she heard was her footfalls on the cement and the crashing of the waves ahead. She looked around, suddenly feeling ill at ease as a chill went down her spine. There was no one around, but she felt like someone was watching her. She thought of Liam and Blake, worried they might have hung around. Part of her thought that was stupid, she was nobody, but once the thought entered her mind, it stuck like glue and refused to leave.

Walking quicker, she made it to the wharf and the sound of the ocean flooded her ears. She jumped as she heard a growl come from behind her and she looked around. It was darker down by the wharf, the main light was out and her heart thudded painfully against her chest.

It's nothing, I'm just paranoid after last night, she tried to reassure herself but it wasn't working. She was an idiot, she should have asked Dylan to drive her home.

A light flashed behind her and she spun around in relief, hoping it was Dylan coming back for her. At this point she would have taken drunk Brad. A single light approached her and she recognised the sound of a motorbike.

Rylan came to a stop beside her, his eyes guarded. "Get on."

"Where's your helmet?" she asked.

"Don't need one. Now get on."

Not in the mood to argue, she climbed on behind him, resting her hands gingerly on his waist.

"Hang on," he growled, and the bike took off. She gasped, leaning forward and buried her head in his back. The air was colder as they surged forward and she tried to hide her whole body behind him, which wasn't that hard.

He shifted slightly and she felt him grab her hand, yanking it forward and putting it in his jacket pocket. He started to reach for the other, but she beat him to it, too cold to fight him. With her hands in his pockets she was pressed closer against him and she closed her eyes, listening to the gentle roar of the engine.

His jacket smelled of leather and pine and she couldn't stop herself from inhaling deeply. It was an oddly comforting smell, and she unconsciously pressed herself closer, desperate to hold onto that feeling of safety.

It had been some time since she'd felt safe. It unnerved her somewhat that she should feel safe with a man she barely knew, but she was too tired to question it. She hadn't felt this way since Adam had shown up on her doorstep that fatal night, and she wasn't ready to let go of the feeling; not yet.

The ride was over in record time and Rylan pulled the motorbike to stop, sitting back on the seat. Norah hadn't moved from her position, her body had fallen into a state of relaxation and Rylan grabbed her hand through his pocket. "We're home, Norah."

She nodded against his back and climbed off, her hands and face protesting against the cool air. She didn't look back, knowing Rylan was going to follow. He'd made it clear he was staying here tonight on the phone earlier and while she didn't want a babysitter, she found she didn't want to be alone either after being spooked in town.

Unlocking the front door, she started to walk in when Rylan pushed past her. "Hey!"

He didn't respond and stood in the doorway for a moment, as if assessing, before stepping aside. "After you."

She pushed past him, glaring as she did so and made her way to her room. She passed the bare couch, a frown forming and she made a detour to the linen cupboard. Rylan was sitting down when she came back, arms full of linen. She dropped them on the couch beside him "Stand up."

"Why? What are you going to do to me?" He wiggled his eyebrows and she rolled her eyes. Reaching down, she grabbed his arm and attempted to pull him off the couch. He stood quickly and she wasn't prepared; her body flew backwards and his hands shot out, grabbing her arms and yanking her back to him. She hit his chest and stepped back, trying to put some distance between them.

She stared at his chest. "Step aside."

He didn't respond, and she felt his fingers move slightly on her skin. She refused to think about the roughness of his fingertips and the gentle way they brushed her arms. Taking a breath, she looked up at him.

He was staring back down at her, a playful smile on his lips and she scowled. "Let go, I'm tired and want to go to bed."

"I can -"

"You are not sleeping with me," she finished for him.

He grinned and stepped aside. "Very well, my offer still stands though."

Norah muttered obscenities under her breath as she made up the couch. He was still too big to fit on the small piece of furniture, but it was still better than the floor, and she wasn't going to think about the other option, he was always keen to suggest.

Once she was finished, she turned around and leaned back; Rylan was standing in her personal space, and she nearly fell back. Her arm shot out behind her, stabling herself on the back of the couch.

"What are you doing?" she stammered.

He reached out and she froze as he grabbed a strand of hair, tucking it behind her ear. "Good night, Norah," he said softly and moved back.

Pushing away from the couch, she made it to her room, calling out goodnight as she shut the door. Leaning against the wooden frame, she inhaled deeply. What the hell had that been about? He was trying to mess with her head. She didn't know why he seemed to enjoy annoying her, but that crap had to stop. Norah was suddenly regretting her moment of weakness earlier and not wanting to be alone.

She thought his mother, and her anger faded a little. She couldn't imagine something like that happening to her as a child. If the Montoya's had taken him in, then she couldn't see why everyone thought they were bad people. Apart from Liam, she thought. He had scared her, she hoped she never ran into him, anywhere.

She walked over to her cupboard and pulled out some pyjamas, hoping this whole thing blew over quickly and she could have her house back to herself. Rylan was doing something nice, but she didn't want people having to protect her. Especially someone who left her feeling annoyed and confused all at once.

11. Grief

Norah lay in bed, listening to the sounds of the ocean. With each crash of a wave, she told herself she would get up and go out to tell Rylan to go, and when each wave came, her body tensed, but she didn't move.

She'd been listening to see if he was awake, but she hadn't heard the front door open or close; the house was silent. Sleeping on it, she had had time to think about everything that happened last night and the night before.

Would it really be so bad if he stayed for a few days?

She didn't like the idea of needing someone to look out for her, but thinking of Liam and Blake and the vibe they had, it gave Norah comfort knowing someone else was in the house with her. Even if he did act like jerk eight times out of ten.

The waves crashed once more, and Norah sat up, deciding she wouldn't make him leave today. She would wait a few days and see what happened. Hopefully Liam's little group would forget about her, and she could go back to her boring life.

Throwing on a large dark blue sweater, she padded silently out into the kitchen. She looked at the couch, Rylan was still fast asleep, and she wondered what he did during the day. She remembered hearing the sound of a saw during their last phone call and she guessed he worked at the Montoya's Mill. She'd come home late last night, and she wondered if he'd had to stay awake and keep an eye on her.

She grabbed some bread and put it in the toaster as the kettle boiled. His legs were twisted, hanging over the top of the couch and she stared at his feet, thinking of how this would work. It had been so long since she had lived with someone, she didn't know if she should make rules or clear a shelf for him in the fridge. He's only staying for a few days, she reminded herself.

But he was meant to be protecting her so she should make his stay comfortable...

The kettle popped and she poured the tea and buttered her toast before spreading her favourite raspberry jam. She glanced back at Rylan, he still seemed to be asleep and instead of sitting at the table, she stepped out onto the front veranda, worried she would wake him.

It was a cool morning, the sun hadn't broken through the grey clouds so the air had a bite to it. Sitting on the top step, she ate slowly staring out at the ocean. She wondered what her main characters would do if a werewolf suddenly started sleeping on their couch. Joseph, her male protagonist, would be bewildered, at a man sleeping on his couch. His first action would be to call the police and then hide in case the guy tried to kill him.

Norah took a sip of tea, enjoying the warmth spread through her body. She really needed to help Joseph become more manlier. Tasha, her female protagonist would be fascinated by him, especially if she got to see him without his shirt on. She would sit and stare at his chest, fingers twitching with a strange desire to trace the contours - wait!

Norah shook her head, her face burning. Was that really Tasha who wanted to do that?

A familiar truck rolled down the track and she finished her toast, standing up. "I wasn't expecting you to be alive at this time of morning," Norah called as Brad stepped out from the truck.

He smiled ruefully and walked over to stand on the bottom step. "I've dosed myself so I can be functional for work. I think Dylan might be doing most of it though today."

"Ah, the joys of being the boss," Norah teased. He ran a hand through his hair and she could see the shadows under his eyes. His skin was pale and she didn't think he'd be doing anything for the day.

"I just came over this morning to apologise. Dylan filled me in on some of the blanks and I feel like an idiot."

"Alcohol does that to you," Norah finished her tea and put the cup on the railing. "It's okay, I know you didn't mean any of it."

"I know, I was hoping perhaps, you and me could do something like that again, but just the two of us?"

She sighed. "Brad, I -"

She heard the front door open and turned slightly. Rylan walked out with only his black jeans on and her eyes started roaming against her better judgement.

"Morning." Rylan stretched his arms above his head and Norah turned away, not prepared for such a sight this early in the morning. She looked back at Brad and flinched.

His eyes had grown cold. "So, this is why you've been turning me down."

"What? No, Brad -"

"It's fine, I get it. Should have known you would be into the weird ones," he muttered. He turned back to his truck and Norah felt a flash of anger rip through her.

"Hey!" She spun his shoulder around. "You have no idea what is going on right now. Insulting me and insulting them is just childish and I would never date someone who judges someone as quickly as you. You know what? I'm glad you got drunk last night, at least now I know what type of person you really are. Go to work and suffer through your stupid hangover."

Brad looked guilty but she didn't give him time to respond, instead turning and heading back inside. She brushed past Rylan who was staring at Brad. She grabbed her cup on her way in and moved to the sink, rinsing it out. If he was going to act like a child then she wanted nothing to do with him. He had no idea what was going on with her. To judge her, and judge them so quickly, it made her so mad -

"Norah."

She looked to her left and Rylan was leaning against the sink, watching her calmly. "You scrub any harder and you'll wash the paint off that cup."

She looked down at the cup, which was completely clean and sat it in the sink, breathing deeply. "I just don't get what his problem is. I've shut him down that many times and he doesn't get it! He didn't even ask if there was something else happening, he just assumed -"

"Well it's a pretty easy assumption to jump to," Rylan folded his arms. "What would you have done in that situation?"

Leaning on the sink, she closed her eyes. "Probably the same thing." She bit her lip and opened her eyes. "Should I apologise to him?"

Rylan snorted, eyes moving from her mouth to her eyes. "No, let the idiot sulk for a few days. He's never liked the Montoya's, never really bothered or cared to find out why. Got any more toast floating around?"

"Uh yeah, there should be some bread in the cupboard."

She went to move but Rylan grabbed her arm. "I can make toast, got my toast making licence and everything."

She rolled her eyes. "Go ahead then."

He let go of her arm and she leaned back as his hand moved to her face. Before she could ask what he was doing, he brushed toast crumbs from the corner of her mouth. His thumb moved gently and her heart stuttered.

"Been driving me mad since I stepped outside," he muttered. Once he was finished, he moved over to the cupboard to grab the bread. "You always eat like a pig?"

Any confused feelings were replaced with anger. "I do not eat like a pig!" she snapped.

"Only pigs leave messes," he said in a matter of fact tone, and she bit the inside of her cheek.

"Are you always going to be an annoying ass?"

He put the bread in the toaster. "I'm not an annoying ass, I'm an adorable ass." Before Norah could stop herself, she snorted loudly and Rylan looked at her in shock. "Even snorts like a pig too," he said to himself.

She glared at him. "Shut up. Don't you have somewhere to be?"

"Not for a little bit. Plenty of time to rile you up some more." She moved past him and grabbed her laptop from the coffee table, taking it to the kitchen table. "What are you doing?"

"Getting some writing done," she muttered.

He nodded and didn't say anything else. She opened the document of her recent chapter and started plotting out the next scene, trying avoid thinking about the shirtless man making toast in her kitchen. She heard him moving around as she started typing and the tension started leaving her shoulders as the words appeared on the screen.

Norah had written two pages when she felt a breath on her shoulder and she jumped. Rylan was leaning down behind her, looking at the screen. "What are you writing?"

"Your death warrant," she slammed the screen down. "Do you mind?"

"Sorry, I didn't mean to distract you," he sounded sincere but she didn't believe him. She half turned in the chair and saw he was fully dressed. "I'm heading off to work. Put your number in my phone so I can call you if anything comes up and I'll give you mine."

She put in her number silently, wanting to get back to her chapter, and handed the phone back. There was a pause and he sighed. "Funny, Norah. Give me your mobile number too."

"I don't have one." She had the screen open halfway so she could keep typing but he couldn't see what she was writing.

"What?"

"I don't have one, got rid of it before I came here."

He moved her hands, putting the screen back down. "Are you an idiot? Why would you get rid of it?"

"None of your business," she said defensively. "I just did." He loomed over her, pale blue eyes boring into her own and she could see him trying to figure out what was going through her head. "Just use the house number, I'm home most of the day."

He shook his head. "Get a mobile phone, today."

"No."

"Please, get a mobile phone."

"Just use the house phone!" She argued and a flash of annoyance crossed his features.

"I'll be coming back tonight, you better have one by then," he said shortly. "And I'll be coming back whether you want me here or not -"

"I do," she said over him and he looked surprised. Her cheeks flushed and she looked out the window, finding the view easier to talk to. "Just for a few days anyway, until this mess calms down. But you don't have to stay every night, I'm sure Olivia can stay one night -"

"No. I'm the one that owes you."

"You already paid me back, Rylan!"

"Not yet," he murmured. "See you tonight - and for Pete's sake, stay away from the forest and come home before dark."

"Yes dad," she said sarcastically. "I'll be a good girl."

"You better," he said as he walked out the door. "Or I'll have to spank you - actually -"

"Just go!" she shouted, knowing what he was going to say.

Opening her screen again, she heard the motorbike start up and she tried to get back into the storyline. She looked at the last line she had written.

Joseph's pale blue eyes widened in surprise -

She rested her head on her hand, sighing in annoyance. Joseph's eyes were brown...

* * * * *

Norah didn't know why, but she had always held a strange fascination for cemeteries. There was a deep silence about them that seemed to clear her head, leaving her with a sense of melancholy.

After trying to sort her characters for two hours, she finally gave up. Her focus was scattered, and she kept writing a certain someone's name by accident. Leaving everything at home, she wandered up to town and started walking through the small side streets until she came across the town's cemetery. It was a large block and the grass was a vibrant green, neatly mowed and well kept.

In the centre was a line of trees which cast a shadow on either half of the cemetery depending on the time of day. Currently, the shadow was cast on the right side and it gave that part a darker, more haunting vibe. Norah walked down each aisle, many of the headstones on this side were old and crumbling around the edges. She looked at the names and dates they had lived and died, wondering what their lives had been like.

Had they travelled the world, been a part of something incredible in history? Had they simply stayed in Bellvale, content with the lives they had lived or had they been full of regret? Regret was something Norah didn't want. She wanted to live her life doing what she wanted. Writing a novel wasn't necessarily at the top her list, but it was pretty high. She wanted to travel, get a tattoo, get married, have children...

They weren't big dreams, but she wouldn't be satisfied until she'd achieved them all.

A movement past the trees caught her attention, and she moved closer, standing behind a large oak. Madison stood in one of the rows on the brighter side, a single yellow tulip in her hand. Norah tried to slip away unseen, but she tripped on a root and made herself known.

Madison's lips moved into a smile as she saw her, but her eyes were filled with sadness. "Hi Norah."

"I'm sorry," she said quickly. "I didn't mean to intrude."

"It's alright, I was just stopping by on my way home."

Norah hesitated before moving closer. She stood beside Madison and saw the name on the tombstone; Parker Roker.

She glanced at Madison, who hadn't stopped looking at the stone. Another yellow tulip was sitting on the earth in front of the headstone and Norah put two and two together.

"I come here every day, to put a flower here," Madison said weakly. "Yellow tulips were our flower; Parker said yellow tulips meant you were hopelessly in love. It's silly, right? I know everyone thinks I'm silly -"

"It's not silly," Norah said quietly. "I don't know much about him, but I can tell how much you loved him and that's not silly."

Madison bent down and picked up the other tulip, replacing it with the fresh one. "They say the pain is meant to fade with time," Madison whispered. "Why does it feel like the pain is just getting worse?"

Norah didn't know what to say. "Have you talk with Wendy about this?"

She shook her head. "I can't, I know it sounds strange, but I know what she's going to say. Everyone treats me like a fragile doll, too afraid to ask me how I feel. No one talks about him anymore, which just hurts more."

Her voice broke into a sob and Norah crouched down beside her, placing her hand over Madison's. "Tell me about him. How did you two meet?"

Madison hesitate and Norah nodded, giving her encouragement.

"We'd known each other since preschool." A watery smile spread across her face. "The first thing I can remember is we faced off against each other. The girls wanted the swings, but the boys wouldn't let us, so we had a challenge to see who could eat the most worms; whoever ate the most won, and I was chosen to represent the girls."

Norah laughed quietly. "Who won?"

"I did; I ate ten worms and Parker ate nine before he threw up." Norah giggled and Madison laughed breathlessly. "He didn't even hate that I had beaten him. He told me he thought I was cool, and after that we started playing together and became friends."

They sat on the grass and Madison told Norah everything she could remember. It was as if she had been keeping it all bottled up for years, afraid to talk to anyone, and now it was all pouring out with no way to stop it.

Norah listened patiently; she laughed and cried at the moments Madison had had with Parker, and she grew silent as Madison talked of finally falling in love.

"I don't even remember how it really happened," she laughed. "I was sitting in class and dropped my pen. Parker always sat beside me and he bent down and picked it up for me. All he said was - 'Your pen, milady', and I felt something snap inside me, making me see him in a whole new light. I was lost from that moment."

"Nothing like some elegant language to make you fall in love."

Madison smiled, looking at her hands. "I couldn't tell him, I was so shy and terrified he wouldn't be interested because we'd been friends for so long. It took him two weeks, and a little help from Wendy, to realise the way I felt."

Her eyes watered again. "I still remember that day so clearly. I was walking home behind the back of the school and he seemed to appear out of nowhere. I didn't even have time to ask him why he was there. He just grabbed me and said - 'Took you long enough', and then he kissed me. It is still the best kiss I've ever had."

Madison looked Norah in the eye. "Have you ever had those moments where you were just so incredibly happy, it felt like nothing could go wrong?"

Norah nodded. "A few times."

"With Parker, it felt like one long moment of happiness. We had our bad days, but it was never something so bad we couldn't fix it. We were madly, hopelessly happy," her smile faded. "Or at least, I was."

Her eyes grew red as tears fell against her will, and Norah squeezed her hand. "It's okay."

Madison sniffed loudly, looking to the sky. "I don't know what happened. He never mentioned being sad or depressed. I never saw any signs." Her gaze shot down and she looked at Norah imploringly. "Why didn't I see them? I was closer to him than anyone! If he was so depressed, why did he ask me to marry him?"

She gasped, slapping a hand over her mouth. Norah felt just as shocked. "He asked you to marry him?"

She nodded. "I've never told that to anyone, not even Wendy." Hands trembling, she reached beneath her shirt and pulled out a fine silver chain. A silver ring with a small white diamond hung from it. "We were secretly engaged for three months. That's why I can't understand why he would do it. What could have possibly happened in those three months to make him -" her voice broke off, unable to say the word and her hand tightened on the ring.

"He didn't talk with his friends?"

She shook her head. "They were just as confused as me. No one saw it coming, but if someone did, it should have been me! He didn't even leave a note or say goodbye," her voice warbled and the tears fell faster. "Why didn't he say goodbye?"

With no more words left, Madison broke down. Norah pulled her close, hugging her as she cried it out. She clung to Norah, sobbing into her shoulder and unconsciously, Norah started rocking, her own tears falling quietly.

She didn't know how long they sat there, but they didn't move until Madison's sobs quieted, her tears finally spent and she pulled herself away. "Oh God, Norah I'm so sorry."

"Don't be sorry. You obviously needed that, and sometimes it's easier to talk to a stranger than a friend."

"You're no stranger," Madison smiled, wiping her face. "Not anymore."

They stood and Madison touched the headstone briefly before following Norah out. They stopped at the gate to the cemetery and Madison crushed Norah in a hug. "Thank you. I...I don't know what I feel right now, but I know it's better than what I've been feeling lately."

Norah returned the hug just as fiercely. "If you ever want to talk, you know where to find me."

Madison pulled back, more tears threatening to fall. "I think I need to get home before people see what a mess I am."

Norah laughed, wiping her own tears away. "Me too. I'm going to see Wendy tomorrow to get a new book, I'll join your weekly lunch date."

Madison smiled. "I'll see you then."

Norah watched Madison walk away, feeling drained. It was no wonder Madison had been so sad; keeping so much bottled up for so many years would wear anyone down. Just listening to her pain had made her feel exhausted for Madison. She was glad she had opened up though. Her eyes had been sad, but after talking, there was a hint of something more there; peace.

Norah headed back home, thinking a glass of wine and a bubble bath was in order.

12. Panic

Norah hadn't used the small tub for a bath yet, but she was thinking it was going to become a regular thing.

Her skin stung, the water too hot and Norah clenched her hands, breathing sharply through her nose as she waited for her body to become accustomed to the water. The lavender scent of her bubble bath filled the room and her body started to relax as peace stole over her.

The sound of her laptop playing music drifted through the closed door and she closed her eyes, enjoying something she hadn't done in a long time. Gradually, thoughts started drifting in and she processed them slowly, her fingers playing with the bubbles.

Norah felt terrible for Madison. The girl had obviously been head over heels and with no one to talk with, it was any wonder she hadn't gotten over him yet. They all treated her like a porcelain doll that would break at the slightest mention of Parker.

Norah opened her eyes, looking at the ceiling. She was only a doll because they had made her that way. The phone started ringing and she ignored it, knowing it would go to the answering machine. She wanted to help Madison get through this grief that had been eating away at her for nearly ten years. Grief was paralysing, and Madison would never be able to move on with her life until she dealt with it and to deal with it, she needed someone who wasn't afraid to show a little tough love to get her there.

She heard the beep of the answering machine and zoned it out, sinking lower into the tub. She would have to have a talk with Wendy about helping Madison. She knew they were best friends and she was sure she could convince Wendy to help. Feeling satisfied with her decision, she blocked out all other thoughts, allowing herself to simply enjoy the water.

Every now and then her characters would start playing on her mind, potential scenes drifting through her head and she allowed them to play out, sometimes changing a moment or two, or ditching the scene when it didn't properly reflect her character's personalities. Eventually the water started to cool and Norah climbed out, her skin beginning to wrinkle. Grabbing her towel, she padded through to her bedroom and quickly dried off, slipping into a pair of black shorts and purple singlet. The air was beginning to grow cold so she threw on her large grey sweater which hung down to her knees and pulled on a pair of pink and white bed socks. Her outfit was completely mismatched but she didn't care. Comfy clothes didn't have to match, that wasn't their job.

Feeling warmer, she went out to the kitchen to make herself a cup of tea before grabbing her computer. As the kettle boiled, the song changed to, 'Fly me to the moon' and Norah felt her heart twist. Leaning against the counter, she stared into space as she smiled softly.

She hadn't listened to this song since her father had died. And before that, when her mother died. It had been her mother's favourite song. Norah had so many memories as a child, of sneaking down the stairs long after her bed time, and watching her parents dance in their living room to this song. She used to poke her head around the corner, fascinated at the sight of her parents dancing to such a pretty song. On several occasions she had gone back to her room and tried to imitate their steps with a teddy bear as her partner, but it was never the same.

She had often longed for the day she was old enough to dance with someone like that. Now that she was old enough though, she had no one to dance with.

Norah's smile faded as the kettle whistled and she poured her tea, wondering if she would ever find that someone special to dance with. The flashing light of the answering machine caught her eye and she pressed the button, moving across to the table to grab her laptop when her insides turned cold.

"Hey, Norah. It's Alice. Now listen, don't get freaked out, but Daniel stopped by today. He was trying to be subtle about finding out where you were the little shit, but I managed to scare him off. Ray said I shouldn't tell you.."

The rest of the message fell on deaf ears. The cup slipped from her fingers, clattering to the ground and smashed to pieces. She didn't bother trying to clean it up, her mind was only focused on one thing;

Daniel was onto her. If he had started hovering around Alice, it was only a matter of time before he figured out where she was.

Panic crept through her being slowly and started to hasten as her mind went through different scenarios of Daniel finding her. A little piece of her sanity told her that she was still safe, she hadn't been found, but the rest was determined that he was on his way here now.

Caught in her fear, she spun around and dashed to her room. The knife was still sitting in her bedside drawer and she clutched it tightly, hands trembling. *Idiot! It won't help you,* the sane part of her mind argued, but Norah wasn't listening. She couldn't see past the fear clutching at her chest, making it difficult to breathe and she stumbled into the bathroom, shutting the door behind her. She managed to lock it and slid down onto the floor as a panic attack set in.

Breathe. Norah had had a panic attack once before; during her final year of school, her English Lit exam had been a killer and the night before she'd suffered a full blown panic attack. Except back then, Adam had been there with her, his voice a soothing anchor, calming her worries and easing her through it. Right now she was all alone.

Breathe, she instructed herself. Her chest tightened painfully, her breath coming in short audible gasps that pulled at her lungs. With each pull, her panic grew and tears blurred her vision as she rested her fist against her chest. Closing her eyes, she tried to recall Adam's face, his gentle tone telling her it would be all right. *Just focus on your breathing, Norah, don't think about anything else. Just in and out.*

She focused on those words, forcing her body to follow their instruction. Minutes passed and the tightening in her chest began to fade. Her breathing gradually began to even out and then finally, it was over. Her body trembled with exhaustion and she curled her legs up, burying her head in her knees. Her eyes drifted shut and she continued to focus on her breathing, only one thought passing through her mind.

I wish you were here, Adam.

*   *   *   *

She was running, she didn't know why or where, but her feet kept moving forward, the panic in her chest warring with confusion. What was she running from?

"Norah, come out and play..." The words were light and accentuated, causing the panic to heighten and her breath to quicken.

Daniel.

"You know what I want, Norah. Just give me the diamonds and then we can have some fun..."

Her feet moved faster, arms pumping and looking around, she realised where she was - Bellvale Forest. She wasn't completely sure, but she hadn't been in many forests in her life and it was the first one that came to mind.

She wanted to turn, to see if he was getting closer, but her head refused to move to look behind. She heart footfalls, keeping pace with her own and her breath started coming out in short gasps, fear overriding her common sense that this was a dream.

"Norah."

The voice came from right behind her and shrieking, she fell to the forest floor. Her body finally turned and she backed herself against a large tree, the bark cold against her back and she finally came face to face with her nightmare.

Daniel looked the same; sometimes people would appear more evil, or darker to signify a person's fear of them in a dream, but he hadn't changed. Did that mean he was terrifying enough as he was? He crouched before her, leaning back on his haunches and his mouth was stretched from ear to ear.

"Dear, sweet Norah," he shook his head in mock disbelief. "You can't escape me."

"This isn't real," she whispered. A wolf howled in the distance and a strange hope flared through her - Rylan?

When he didn't appear, her hope faded and she jumped as Daniel touched her knee. "What's wrong?" he chuckled. "Are you afraid of the big bad wolf?"

Daniel lunged at her, his mouth elongating, teeth sharpening and he growled as suddenly it was a wolf, biting her throat -

"Norah!"

Her eyes flew open, she was surrounded by white and a large figure sat in front of her. Not thinking, she shrieked, "No!" And shoved her knife at her attacker.

A hand grabbed her own, stopping its advance and she met a pair of shocked pale blue eyes.

"Rylan." Her mouth opened in panic, opening and closing as her eyes moved lower to the kitchen knife protruding from Rylan's chest.

"Norah," he winced. "Calm down. That noise you're making is going to rupture my ear drums."

Small shrieks continued to make their way from her throat, she was too shocked to absorb Rylan's words. "O-Oh my god, I'm so sorry -" she tried to move the knife out and he hissed, holding her hand tighter.

This only made her shriek more and she released her hold completely, hands covering her mouth as tears started pouring down her face. "I have to get you to a hospital!"

She tried to move, but Rylan pushed her back against the wall. "It's all right, Norah."

"I stabbed you!" she cried, and he rolled his eyes.

"I got that part, trust me." Gritting his teeth, he pulled the knife out in one quick movement and she sobbed as the knife clattered on the floor. "Norah," his voice was gentle. "Look at me."

She raised her eyes from the blood covering his shirt and met his eyes. They were calm, with no fear. "Trust me." He reached down and tore his shirt open until the wound was fully exposed. Her breathing increased in tempo, and Rylan grabbed her trembling hand, covering it with his own. "Just watch."

Her eyes were glued to the wound, unsure of what she was meant to be waiting for, but it only caused her panic to grow as the blood continued to ooze out. She wiped her eyes angrily as tears blurred her vision, and Rylan eventually reached out with his spare hand and started brushing them away as they fell.

Norah didn't pay attention, her focus only on his chest. She was ready to drag him to a hospital before he bled to death when her breath caught in her throat. The wound began to stop bleeding and edges appeared to be getting smaller. Mesmerised, she watched as the wound continued to grow smaller, her breathing beginning to slow and the tears eventually stilled. Rylan's hand continued to stroke her cheek, his eyes solely focused on her.

Her breath hitched as she found herself staring at bloodied skin, the wound completely gone. Shaking, she reached out with her free hand and felt his chest. It was smooth, the skin only stained with blood, and her fingers kept moving over the spot, trying to make sure it was completely gone.

His stroking had ceased and his thumb pressed into her jaw line gently. "Norah." His voice was deeper, and she finally managed to tear her eyes away from his chest and meet his gaze. His eyes were warm, and strangely close.

She suddenly realised what position they were in but she couldn't bring herself to move. "I'm so sor-"

"Shh." He shushed her apologies, his fingers gently brushed her cheek and leaving a trail of fire across her skin. "Norah," he murmured. He moved closer, and without realising, her breathing stopped completely, their noses almost touching and her eyes started to close - "Why are you hiding in the bathroom with a knife?"

If ever there was a way to wake Norah from the daze Rylan had her in, that question did it. She moved her head back, hitting the wall and yanked her hand from his, removing herself from his touch.

"It's nothing," she lied, reminding herself to delete the message on the answering machine. "I was researching wolves and I heard a howl and freaked out. I came in here and fell asleep."

Her lie was mixed with truths, but the look in Rylan's eyes said he didn't believe one word of it. "You want to stop feeding me bullshit and try again? Why were you -"

"I told you! I just got freaked out. Now can we drop it, please? I need to move, my lower half has gone numb." She started to stand, and Rylan beat her to it, wrapping one hand around her back and the other under her knees, picking her up. "What are you -?"

"Shut it," he said shortly. Moving from the bathroom, he carried her to her room and dumped her on the bed. "You should sleep."

"But I have to make -"

"I ate earlier." He said coldly, reading her thoughts. "Get some rest."

She grabbed his shirt as he tried to turn and her eyes travelled back to the gaping hole. "I'm sorry."

The words were whispered, filled with defeat. She was sorry she had stupidly hurt him, sorry she couldn't tell him the truth, and sorry because he knew she was lying. He walked out, and she stared at the door, unsure what to do.

He returned moments later and threw a small object at her. It hit the mattress beside her and she looked down. "You didn't get one, did you?" She shook her head, quietly picking up the mobile phone.

"My number is already in there," he explained. "Don't lose it and keep it on you at all times."

She looked up to say thank you, but the words died on her lips. His face was closed off, and she didn't know what to say. She wasn't sure why she cared that he didn't like her lying.

In the end, she nodded and looked away. Rylan walked out to the kitchen and she heard the front door open and close. Her fingers moved over the edges of the black phone, she pressed button on the side and the screen lit up, a picture of a white flower the background image.

She hated lying, it had never been something she was comfortable with. Normally, she could push the words past her lips and that was the end of it. But she found she didn't want to lie to Rylan. In the short time she'd known him, he'd done more for her than most people she'd met, and she could see why he would want to know about the knife. But telling him about her brother, about Daniel... she just wasn't ready for that can of worms to be opened yet. She'd already involved Alice and Ray in her mess, she couldn't keep dragging people in.

Her thoughts drifted to his ruined shirt and she frowned. Standing up, she put the phone in her pocket and moved to her closet, searching through a box at the bottom. She threw the clothing on the floor until she found what she was looking for - a large black shirt of Pink Floyd's, Dark side of the Moon. She walked out through the kitchen and stepped onto the veranda.

Rylan was leaning against the railing, looking out at the ocean. "Aren't you meant to be sleeping?"

Norah laid the shirt beside his hand on the railing. "I thought you might need a new shirt," she said lamely.

He grabbed it, lifting it up and his eyes narrowed. "Bit big for you, isn't it?"

She looked out at the ocean, the wind blowing through her hair. "It's my brother's," she said quietly.

"You have a brother?"

She nodded, hands clenching the railing tightly. "Adam."

"Older or younger?"

"Older." She heard Rylan move, changing shirts and she kept her gaze fixed ahead, though her eyes continued to threaten to drift sideways.

"Is he going to come down and visit you?"

She shook her head, her mouth replying automatically. "He can't."

"Why not?"

She didn't want to say, she wanted to keep her problems private, but something inside her was forcing her to tell him, as if it could make up for what she couldn't say. "He's in prison."

She felt him shift and knew he was surprised. "Would not have guessed that. What's he in for, rob a bookstore for you or something?"

She knew he was trying to make light of the situation but it only made her feel worse. "Attempted murder."

She felt him stiffen. "Fuck, that's heavy."

The ball of nerves that had been sitting in her throat slowly started to unravel and she felt the tension leave her shoulders. After saying the words, she felt strangely relieved that someone here knew part of her secret. Rylan stayed silent and she took that to mean he was uncomfortable with the way the conversation had gone.

"I'm going to bed," she said finally when the silence became unbearable. She turned to leave and Rylan grabbed her arm.

"Your brother being in prison - it has to do with what you won't tell me, doesn't it?"

She tried to tug her arm away but his grip was strong. "Maybe," she whispered. She glanced up at him and saw the gears turning in his head.

He let go of her arm and gently pushed her towards the house. "I won't ask anymore tonight, but just remember this, Norah; you can trust me. Whatever the problem is, you don't have to run from it, I'll face it with you."

You have your own problems to deal with, she thought. Instead, she nodded and grabbed the door handle. "I'm used to dealing with my own problems," she murmured before heading inside.

Walking through the kitchen, she didn't hear his last words carried away on the wind. "Not anymore."

13. Dinner

"Norah, are you paying attention?"

Norah lifted her head from her notebook, the world rushing back in. "Sorry, what were you saying?"

"I was telling you about this new vampire book I read, and you completely zoned out," Wendy complained.

"Sorry, I'm just trying to sort something out." Norah glanced at her book again, tapping her pen on the paper.

She'd been stuck on this chapter for a week now. Since Rylan had unofficially moved in with her and taken her knife away, her writing had taken a dive. Every time she tried to write, her brain came up with nothing and her frustration wasn't making it any better.

To be fair to Rylan, he wasn't the problem. He kept out of her way when she was writing, and didn't bother her. She only ever saw him at night and he spent a lot of time watching TV - something he had dragged into the house on the second day. The block she was experiencing, she didn't know why it was happening, but she didn't think it was over something as simple as Rylan invading her personal space.

"What's the problem, Norah?" Madison leaned over the table, looking at her notebook.

Norah glanced up, sighing loudly. "I don't know, I'm just stuck in a rut."

"That sucks, don't worry, I'm sure you'll overcome it."

Norah smiled, hoping Madison was right. The day at the cemetery had strangely brought them closer as friends. At Madison's begging, Norah hadn't mentioned anything to Wendy yet. Madison wanted to be the one to bring it up when the time was ready. Wendy was still dealing with issues with her ex, and Madison didn't want to pile on her problems.

They were sitting in the Twilight Cafe and Olivia came over with a bottle of water, taking the seat next to Norah. "Hey, can you tell remind Rylan about dinner tonight? Mum will kill him if he doesn't show his face. You're invited too of course."

Norah's death glares were lost on Olivia and she braced herself, feeling two pairs of eyes beaming into her skull.

"Why do you have to remind Rylan?" Wendy asked slyly.

Olivia winced, muttering something about dishes before running off. Thanks Olivia, she thought sourly.

"I thought I saw Rylan's bike in the distance at your house the other night," Madison whispered excitedly. "Are you two -"

"No! There is nothing going on, he's just staying there since the break in. As a favour to Olivia."

"But there's only one bed!" Wendy jittered on her seat. "Where is he sleeping?"

"I have a couch, Wen," Norah muttered, sinking further into her chair.

Madison and Wendy looked as though this was the most exciting thing to happen in years. "Have you ever caught him coming out of the shower?" Wendy asked.

"I hope he doesn't track grease through your house,' Madison worried. "Bikers are notorious for grease stains -"

"You could always shower together, save water. We need to be more environmentally friendly -"

"Enough!" Norah snapped loudly. She felt a few heads turn their way and leaned forward. "There is nothing going on between us. He is just a friend doing another friend a favour!"

Wendy frowned. "You should at least get some sexual favours -" she closed her mouth at Norah's glare. "All right, I won't pry any more. I'm just saying, if a fine looking man like that was staying in my house, I would be dropping hints left right and centre."

"Oh god," Norah's cheeks flamed.

"You should at least let him sleep in the bed with you, isn't your couch tiny?"

Norah shook her head. "The couch is fine." She was having enough trouble sleeping lately without having a distraction like that lying next to her.

Since the knife incident in the bathroom, her dreams had been plagued with wolves and Daniel. He was always chasing her and no matter how far she ran, she couldn't escape. Then Liam would appear before her, his cold eyes freezing her feet and Daniel would catch up. Just as he killed her, the dream would end and she would wake, covered in sweat.

She hated feeling so weak. It was bad enough she felt pathetic in real life, but now she was worse in her dreams. Madison knocked on the glass and Norah jumped. Brad was walking by and he smiled at the girls. When his gaze drifted over Norah, the smile faded and he walked off, his mouth in a hard line.

"Wow, Brad is pissed with you," Wendy sipped her iced coffee. "What crawled up his bum?"

"Nothing, I just snapped at him last week and he's still sulking I guess." Norah had been right in thinking Brad was like her past boyfriends. They knew how to hold a petty grudge. She had tried to apologise for snapping at him, but he brushed it off, using work as an excuse and Norah gave up, not in the mood for his immaturity.

Norah could see the girls weren't going to give up their line of conversation so she quickly excused herself, using her writing to escape. Walking back home, she moved slowly, looking at the plotted chapter again. She'd written it and rewritten it so many times in the last week, her notebook was nearly full with just this chapter plot alone. Reaching the house, she made it to the veranda and sat down, chewing on her pen.

She was writing a scene with the gypsy woman in the past and her research had left her unprepared for this chapter. She knew the basics of what she needed to write, but her mind couldn't wrap itself around it. She kept trying to make it harder than it should have been and in the end, the never knew where to begin. She continued to stare at the page, trying to create different scenes and openings in her mind when a foot kicked her leg.

"Shit!" Gasping, she clapped a hand over her mouth.

Rylan stood above her, a wry look on his face. "Hello to you too. Didn't realise I was that scary."

"You're not," she said defensively, "you just snuck up on me, that's all."

He glanced back at his bike. "Kind of hard to sneak up here on a bike, Norah." He grabbed her paper. "What's got you so sucked in?"

"Nothing!" She jumped up, trying to grab the paper but he put it out of her reach. "Give it back!"

"A gypsy?" He frowned, pushing her away by her forehead. "Why would you want to write about gypsies? Aren't they all mysterious?"

"Dammit, Rylan, stop being an ass and give it -" Her sentence ended on a shriek as she jumped and landed on the edge of the top step. Her ankle bent and she started falling backwards. Her eyes shut as she anticipated the pain to come. Arms wrapped around her and she was shoved against a firm chest before she hit the ground. Her legs hit the bottom step and she winced. The pain was jarring but it would only bruise at most. A hand rested behind her head so the fall hadn't hurt that much but the weight on top of her was crushing.

"Ow."

"Christ, Norah are you alright?" Rylan shifted, leaning over her and she opened her eyes to his concerned face. They were rather close and unconsciously she held her breath.

"Yeah I'm fine, thanks." A moment passed; Norah could hear her heart beating in her ears and she didn't know what to do. Rylan stared at her and she lost herself in his blue irises. She felt his fingers move in her hair, tense and hesitant. She wondered if she should say something when Rylan's phone rang.

The moment shattered and Rylan rolled off her. Norah quickly sat up, inhaling deeply. Rylan frowned as he looked at the screen and let the phone ring.

"Who is it?" she asked, trying to sound normal.

"No one important," he stood up and held out his hand. She took it and he pulled her to her feet. He passed the piece of paper back and she quickly smoothed the crinkles.

"Uh, Olivia said to remind you about dinner tonight."

He nodded. "I remembered. You'll have to change your clothes. We'll head off now."

She looked down at her dirt covered pants. "I wasn't really planning on going -"

"Yeah you're going, Cassie wants to meet you."

"Who is Cassie?"

Rylan walked inside and she followed. "Cassie is Liv's mom. She's been nagging me all week to bring you by so you have to come or I won't hear the end of it."

Norah went into her room to get changed. "Why does she want to meet me?" she called.

"Well, she's heard a bit about you, and I think she feels guilty about what's been happening with Liam and the others. She might try to bring it up, if she does, can you not make a big deal out of it?"

Norah walked out in a pair of black jeans and a loose fitting white dress shirt. "Of course. I'm sure she's probably stressing herself out enough with everything that's going on with her sons. I wouldn't add onto that. Is this too underdressed?"

He shook his head. "No, you look good. It's only a casual dinner."

"Are we taking your bike?"

"We can take your car if you want." he offered.

She was slightly disappointed, she had been secretly hoping to go on his bike again, but she didn't want him to know that. "Sure."

Norah tied her hair up quickly and grabbed her wallet before reaching for the wine cupboard. "Does Cassie like red or white wine?"

"White, why?"

She reached up on her tip toes, grabbing a bottle of Riesling. "I can't show up with nothing, it's rude. It's good wine, she should like it, I hope."

Norah came back down, making sure she had the right bottle and froze when she felt Rylan standing behind her. His hand moved over her hair, pulling it out.

"What are you doing?" she whispered.

"You missed some hair." His voice was soft and she didn't move as he pulled her hair gently into a ponytail and retied it.

"I could have done that myself," she tried to sound annoyed but she liked it when other people did her hair.

"I know. Come on, we better head off."

Heading out to her car, she quickly adjusted the towel which hid the blood stain. Rylan climbed in, adjusting the seat for his long legs and lifted the towel as she turned around. "Do you want some money to fix the upholstery?"

"And where would I take it?" She rolled her eyes. "I think Brad would be pretty suspicious of a blood stained car seat, don't you think?"

"You could take it out of town, Brad isn't the only mechanic around, you know."

She started the engine and reversed out. "Let's just pretend it doesn't exist like I have been for the last few weeks."

"I can take it up to -"

"I think car time should be quiet time," she demanded. "Don't distract me while I'm driving."

"I can distract you in other ways." His fingers brushed her arm and she jumped, slapping his hand away.

"Do you want me to crash? Just tell me where to go and keep your hands to yourself." she stuttered.

She hoped he wasn't looking at her and didn't see the red tint warming her cheeks. She could feel his gaze every now and then kept her eyes on the road. Her emotions had been scattered over the last week and Norah wondered if maybe it was Rylan's fault that she had writer's block. Rylan didn't say anything else, other than to direct her to the Montoya's home.

Norah finally turned onto a dirt road and Rylan shifted in his seat. "All right, we're nearly there. There's a few things you should know before you go in."

"Why are you only telling me now?" she demanded.

"You wanted quiet time," he said innocently.

"Tell me," she seethed.

"Okay, well because there is a bit of a division at the moment, some of the family have split as well. Aston - who is Olivia's uncle - his son, Nick has sided with Liam. They haven't talked to each other in months, so don't be upset if Aston isn't in a good mood. He hasn't been since this mess started."

"Got it," she tried to remember the names. "Who else?"

"I don't know how much Olivia has told you about her family, but you know that her father recently died which is why this started. Her grandfather, Holden is still alive but because of his age, he is in no condition to lead the clan anymore. He comes across as a gentle old man but don't piss him off, and don't mention Liam."

"Okay, don't make the scary grandpa angry, anything else?"

They reached the house and Rylan shook his head. "The others will fill you in on the other stuff, but those are the main points so far. Liam is pretty taboo at the moment so if someone brings him up, try to change the topic before people start throwing their plates."

Norah looked at him, trying to determine if he was joking and he shook his head. "Gone through four sets of china in the last two months. Cassie has not been happy about it."

"Okay then," she said weakly.

Rylan surprised her and reached out, squeezing her hand. "You'll be fine. If things get to hectic I'll get you out of there, okay?"

She nodded. "Okay. Do we need a codeword?"

He smiled, his fingers moving against her palm. "How about, gypsy?"

She removed her hand from his and slapped his knuckles. He chuckled and opened the door. "Gypsy it is."

Norah got out as well and slammed the door shut. The sun was beginning to set, casting an orange glow through the forest. The Montoya's home was massive. Made of large grey stone, a white railed set of stairs led up to the veranda with matching railing and arches. The roof was a darker grey and the large windows on the left side of the house caught the rays of the setting sun, casting a shadow over the rest of the house. There was no extravagant garden, only a few rose bushes and some Daphne creeping along the right side of the house.

"How many rooms does this place have?" she whispered.

"Thirteen, the place isn't completely full at the moment, but there are many houses on the land Holden owns so they get used as well when people decide they need some privacy."

The front door opened and an older woman stepped out. She had bright golden wavy hair which was cut in a bob. Her green eyes shone brightly as she sighted Norah and Rylan. "You're here! I thought you had forgotten."

Rylan walked forward and caught the woman as she jumped at him from the top of the stairs and gave him a hug. "I never forget when you're cooking dinner, mom. Highlight of my week."

She beamed as he put her down and she shoved past him towards Norah. "You must be Norah, I can't tell you how thrilled I am to finally meet you. Between this guy and Olivia, I feel like I already know you."

She crushed Norah in a hug and she bit back a yelp. It had been a long time since she'd been hugged by a mother but she figured it was like her dads. There was the occasional squeeze, as if assessing if she had been eating enough, something her father used to do all the time.

"Norah, this is Cassie, Olivia's mom." Rylan grinned.

"And yours, Rylan," she chided. She stepped back and looked Norah over. "Aren't you a pretty thing. I hope Rylan hasn't been giving you too much trouble?"

"Just a little, ma'am," she said calmly and Rylan winced as Cassie turned on him.

"What did you do to her? The poor thing probably isn't eating because you're stressing her out with your silly ways."

"I'm eating -"

"She's so thin, don't you check to make sure she's been eating?" Cassie demanded, ignoring Norah's protest, hands on hips.

"She can feed herself," he mumbled, which earned him a smack across the head.

"Don't talk back like that," she snapped. "You look after her properly, after everything she's been through because of us -" she broke off, her voice quaking and she looked away from Norah. Rylan squeezed her shoulder and Norah quickly stepped forward.

"Cassie, would you mind showing me around your home? It looks lovely -"

"Of course," she smiled, wiping her eyes. "Come on, Rylan can go and hang with the men while I show you around. Olivia is helping Annie in the kitchen, she'll be so happy you're here."

Cassie linked her arm through Norah's and dragged her away. Norah looked back and saw Rylan watching them, he grinned giving her a wave and mouthed, 'Gypsy' before heading inside.

Cassie showed Norah around the outside of the house first before stepping through some open French doors that were painted a pine green. The room they stepped into was painted much the same with light brown furnishings and a small fireplace. Herbs hung from the ceiling and Norah's nose wrinkled as she fought a sneeze.

"This is my room," Cassie smiled. "The men don't generally come in here because I don't want them breaking anything. Olivia uses this room when she needs to study too. If you ever stay with us, feel free to use this room too."

"Thank you, I love the colours, it's beautiful."

Cassie smiled. "Roger's mother, Jenna picked out the colour scheme. I'm quite fond of it myself. Sadly she's in New Orleans at the moment with Meegan, Luke's fiancé."

"Oh, I didn't know Luke was engaged."

"It was only recent," Cassie said quietly. "Luke sent her away until this situation has been sorted out. He didn't want her getting caught in the crossfire. He tried to make Olivia leave too but she refused. I know my daughter, she would have worried herself sick if she left."

Norah nodded, sensing they were heading into dangerous territory and tried to change the conversation. Cassie took the hint and led her through the rest of the house. She didn't see the bedrooms, though Cassie seemed to find it important to point out which room was Rylan's - the first on the right at the top of the second floor.

There was a large sitting room on the second floor, painted in the same green with the wooden beams contrasting for a natural feel. One wall was covered in old photographs of the family and Norah tried not to spend too much time looking at them. She saw a photo of Olivia and the twins, and Cassie was hugging a man two times her size who had dark hair.

"That's my Roger," she looked at the photo, touching the glass fondly. "He passed away nearly six months ago now. It's scary to think so much has happened since he's been gone."

"I'm sorry for your loss," Norah said quietly. Cassie looked at the photo, her eyes filled with sadness and Norah tried to change the topic again. "Should we go and help Olivia in the kitchen?"

"Soon, I still have so much to show you!" Cassie showed her the rest of the house, the dining room was on the bottom floor with large open windows letting in the light and another sitting room in the front which they didn't enter. She could hear men laughing and Cassie rolled her eyes.

"They always make so much noise, rowdiest bunch of creatures I've ever met."

"We can hear you mom!" A male voice called that Norah didn't recognise and Cassie grinned.

"The fun of being a werewolf - you hear everything."

"Wouldn't that get frustrating, with so many people living in the house?"

"No, the bedrooms are all sound proofed and so are the dining room and top sitting room. We do have privacy when we need it and everyone gets along very well. If we start to tire of one another, some move to the cottages ten minutes down the road."

They walked down a corridor and into a large kitchen. The stone work from outside lined the outer wall and white and cream beams and doors matched off perfectly. There was a large island in the centre of the room with a black stone bench top that was covered in food and dirty bowls. Olivia sat on a stool, mashing a large bowl of potatoes. There was another bowl next to her, just as large and Norah's eyes widened. The amount of food she could see was terrifying.

"Hey, Norah!" Olivia waved a masher in her direction. "How did you like the tour?"

"It was good, you have a beautiful home."

"It's not bad," Olivia kept mashing. "Pull up a stool. Sorry about today too. I didn't know you hadn't told the others that Rylan was staying with you."

"That's okay. I just didn't want them to get the wrong idea."

"I guess you can't tell them the truth."

"No," Norah sat down and watched Olivia. "Can I help?"

"No, you're the guest! If I made you help, mom would chuck a fit."

"I would not chuck a fit," Olivia, her mother said from across the counter. "I would just be very disappointed."

"That's how she chucks her fits," Olivia muttered.

Cassie glared at her daughter and Norah smiled. A woman sat beside Cassie and she guessed this was Annie. She had similar blonde curls to Cassie but they were longer and Annie was more curvier.

"Norah, this is my sister, Annie." Norah reached over the island to shake her hand. "Her sons Aaron and Logan live with us. Her daughter Chloe lives in town though."

Olivia rolled her eyes at the mention of Chloe and Norah guessed she wasn't a fan. Annie smiled. "It's nice to meet you Norah. We have something in common already." Norah looked at her confused and Annie grinned. "We are the only humans at this dinner."

"Oh! I thought you were a werewolf."

"No, believe it or not, I'm actually the younger sister. Perks of being a werewolf, you don't age as fast. One thing that bugs me about Cassie."

"But your children are werewolves?" Norah asked.

Annie nodded as she tossed the salad. "It was their choice to be turned and I wasn't going to stop them. I'd been through it all with Cassie, and I knew the risks and choices. Roger's family have been good to me and the children since my husband passed. I know they'll take care of them."

"You didn't want to?"

Annie shook her head. "I'm happy as I am."

Cassie smiled and hugged her sister. "Annie keeps us all grounded, I'd be lost without her here. There's too many men in this house!"

"You've got me mom!" Olivia protested.

"Yes, but you won't be here forever, your life is only just starting. Soon it will just be me, Annie and the men. I need another woman to help keep the men in check."

Norah listened as they spoke about silly things, avoiding the big elephant in the room that was the feud and she joined in as they prepared dinner, speaking of her own family and her parents. When Cassie heard that both her parents had passed, a look crossed her face and she came to stand beside Norah, resting her hand on her shoulder from time to time.

Soon dinner was ready and they moved all the food into the dining room. The table was large but all the dishes still couldn't fit and Cassie placed the extras on the long table against the wall. Then she whistled a large shrilling noise through the door and Norah jumped.

"Dinner's ready!"

The reaction was immediate. The door opened down the hall and the men filed in, talking loudly amongst themselves. Norah recognised Rylan, and Luke, from his similarity to Liam, but his face didn't have the same hardness as Liam's. His eyes were softer and his features showed that he smiled often. Two older men walked in and then a large man came in last. He was large compared to the others, his peppered hair was the only thing that signified his greater age. There was a slight limp to his walk and Norah tried not to shrink into Olivia.

"Norah," Luke stepped forward and grasped her shoulders as the others took their seats. "We meet at last."

"Hi," she smiled awkwardly. "Thank you for inviting me to dinner."

"That was all mom," he smiled at Cassie. "I was a bit concerned you might not want anything to do with us, but she was adamant about meeting you and no one says no to Cassie Montoya."

"Damn straight they don't," the younger man of the group said. He had light brown hair and his hazel eyes sparkled. "I'm Aaron. You probably don't remember me, but I came to your house that night."

Norah didn't have to ask which night he was talking about. "Well it's nice to meet you officially."

They took their seats and Rylan directed Norah between himself and Aaron. Olivia sat on the other side of Aaron and she sent Norah a wink as she sat down. Holden and Luke both took the heads of the table and Norah noticed another woman sitting opposite her.

"Hi, I'm Emma," the red head introduced herself when she saw Norah's confusion. "I was in with the men. My talents are wasted in the kitchen."

"The only talent you have is poisoning everyone," Rylan teased and Emma stuck her tongue out. "I don't know how you haven't killed Peter yet."

Norah looked down the table at the other man, wondering if that was Peter. He had black hair and familiar blue eyes.

"That's Aston," Rylan murmured and Norah nodded. "Peter is out on watch, tonight."

Now that she knew everyone's names, she had to remember them. Everyone grabbed at the plates and bowls, piling their plates with everything they could reach. If they couldn't, they shouted down the table for bowls to be passed. Annie walked around the table, offering gravy and dressings which were all gone by the time she did one full round.

Norah could only sit back and watch in amazement. She had never seen something like it before. Unsure of the protocol, she waited patiently for everyone to finish grabbing their food.

"Help the poor lass, Rylan," Holden's deep voice rumbled down the table. "She'll starve if she doesn't grab something soon."

Norah sent Holden a smile of relief, and Rylan grabbed her plate and started piling on food. She tried to stop him when it became a small mountain. "I won't eat all that!"

"Don't worry about it." He put the plate back in front of her and Norah sighed. There was silence as everyone ate quickly, desperate to put more food on their plates. Norah watched them with a strange fascination as she ate slowly. Annie saw her looking across the table and shot her a knowing look. She had a normal amount of food on her plate and Norah wished Annie had dished up her serving.

It didn't take long for the food to vanish and Norah didn't even consume a quarter of hers. She noticed that Rylan was finished and quickly swapped plates with him, hoping no one would notice.

Groans sounded across the table and she jumped. Aaron stared at her plate with longing.

"I was going to ask you for that."

"Oh, sorry." She turned to give the plate to him but Rylan had nearly demolished it already. She turned back, shrugging her shoulders. "Sorry, Aaron."

"It's okay, I'll know to be quicker next time. So, Norah how old are you?"

She frowned. "Twenty four...why?"

"Just curious, I thought you must have been closer to Olivia's age."

"How old are you?"

"Thirty two. Still look in my early twenties though, don't I?"

She bit back a smile. "I was going to say late thirties but I can say early twenties if it makes you feel better?"

"Ouch," he laughed. "Way to kick a man down."

"Please," she scoffed. "You're a werewolf, right? Like I could kick you down."

Rylan finished her food and she jumped when his hand rested on her thigh. Something passed through Aaron's eyes and he chuckled, turning away. Norah turned to glare at Rylan but he was taking a drink of beer.

Everyone started leaving the table and Norah looked around, confused. Luke smiled. "We'll move into the sitting room now. It's a bit more comfortable in there."

"Oh, okay."

Everyone left and Norah started grabbing plates to take them back to the kitchen. Rylan grabbed her hand. "You don't have to do that. They'll clean up later."

"I've done nothing all night," she whispered. "I have to help clean up at least." Shaking his hand off she kept piling on plates.

Rylan sighed and started grabbing plates and bowls too. He followed her into the kitchen and it took them three trips to clear the dining room. Norah started filling the sink and searched for the detergent. Rylan passed it to her and she frowned at him.

"What was that back there?"

"What was what?" He grabbed a tea towel.

"I was talking to Aaron and you grabbed my leg. Why?"

"He was flirting with you."

"No he wasn't," Norah laughed.

"Trust me," Rylan said seriously. "He was."

"He wasn't being serious though," she protested. "I think he was just trying to make me feel more comfortable."

"He was being an ass," Rylan muttered and Norah turned the water off.

"What did you say?"

"Nothing."

They did the dishes in silence. Rylan stood close, their hips brushing against each other and Norah didn't say anything, not wanting to break the silence. She tried to focus on the dishes and not the hidden meaning behind Rylan's actions earlier that her brain demanded she over analyse.

She was saved from analysing when Olivia came looking for them. "Here you are! I thought you must have snuck off home. Why are you doing dishes?"

"I felt like I needed to do something." Norah explained. "You all made dinner so you shouldn't have to clean up."

Olivia came over and pushed Norah out of the way. "Let me at it."

"Hey! Did you not hear a thing I said?"

"I did," Olivia passed a plate to Rylan and bumped him with her hip so he would move away. "But you are still the guest so your argument is invalid."

Norah took the tea towel from Rylan and told him to start putting everything away. They worked quickly and had the kitchen clean in record time. Olivia grabbed the tea towel from Norah and threw it on the bench. "Come on, Gramps said he was going to tell you a story."

"A story?" She looked at Rylan who followed behind, shooing her on.

"Yeah, I asked him to tell you about our origins, since you don't know much. It's a good story."

"It's your favourite story," Rylan pointed out and Olivia turned to glare at him.

"So what?"

They walked into the sitting room and Olivia plopped down on the floor, dragging Norah with her. Rylan took the seat behind them, next to Aston and Norah leaned back against his leg.

"We're all here, you can tell the story now, Gramps," Olivia said.

Holden smiled down at his granddaughter. Emma and Aston weren't in the room and Norah was going to say something but she figured they had their own things to do. She got comfortable and ready to listen.

"You know you could tell this story yourself, Olivia," he said calmly.

"Yeah, but you tell it the best," she waved her hand at him. "Tell it!"

"Very well...

In the beginning, the only creatures to roam this earth were man and beast. Those who possessed greater power lived in the stars, observing those inferior beings from above. Many knew of their existence, praying for a healthy crop or to survive the next Winter. If they were worthy enough, the Gods would answer their call, if not, they were left to perish.

This story is of seven men who worshipped Lupa; Goddess of the moon and wolves. Those who hunted in her forest, prayed for her guidance and protection. Amongst these hunters were seven men, who craved to be more than their worth. They planned a gathering on the full moon, begging for Lupa to bless them with her presence, to prove that she was protecting those who loved and adored her. They lied, crying to the heavens that many were losing faith, as food was sparse and so many prayers were left unanswered. We know now that this ceremony was during winter, which is why food was possibly sparse, but back then, everything came down your God's will, and they believed they were punished for something they had not done. So, they felt Lupa must be punished also.

Lupa, unable to bear the cries of her followers no more, descended from the stars and appeared before them, wanting to assure them they had her love. Many tales have been told of Lupa's beauty; of her white hair, white than the moon that flowed about her body, her alabaster skin which drove mortal men into a frenzy of desire. Her eyes though, that is something everyone remembers. They were a perfect black, the moon reflected within them and if you stared too long, you would go mad.

"I have not abandoned you," she spoke, her voice soft and pleading. "The seasons grow harsher with each year and alas, I have no control of that. You are strong, sturdy men, for I have helped you be so, and when the ice thaws and sun shines once again, there will be food for all."

As she spoke, the seven men put their plan into action. They had created strings of silver, for it was said to be Lupa's weakness and they wrapped them about her, holding her taut on the ground.

The surrounding men who knew of their plan, cheered and celebrated their success. The oldest stepped forward to face his Goddess. "We cannot wait that long, our people are dying and the only way to save them is with your power. Grace us with your light so we may provide for our families for aeons to come."

Lupa, shocked at this betrayal, looked at him sadly. "What a fool I am; you have never worshipped me, only my power."

As she spoke, seven tears escaped her eyes. As each fell to the earth, they morphed in the light of the moon and shaped into seven different coloured stones. "You crave power?" she cried. "Then you shall have it but know this; I shall never heed your call ever again."

She looked amongst them all, eyes defiant. "No longer shall I be your guardian! I shall be your curse!"

She stood tall, the strings snapping beneath her power and in a flash of light, she vanished from this realm, never to be seen again.

The seven men grabbed a stone each, disregarding her final warning and as they gazed at their treasures in wonder, a strange thing happened. Pain ripped through their bodies, their bones cracking, causing them their spines to bend, their nails to grow.

They collapsed on all fours, their hair growing rapidly and their screams of agony becoming howls of anguish as they cried to the moon. Lupa did no listen to their cries but she had listened to their pleas. Her curse would provide for their families for aeons to come.

Holden sat back, finished and Norah glanced at Olivia. "Is that true?"

"Of course," she said. "Each pack is named after a certain stone, remember? Our clan belongs to the Bluestone Pack."

"So, do they still have the stones?"

Holden nodded. "Aye, I have seen the Bluestone for myself, when I was a young lad. The Whitestone pack died out in the early 1950's and the there are only thirty or so members left of the Bloodstone pack. They live in Greece now, away from the politics."

"Whitestone..." Norah looked at Rylan and he grinned shaking his head.

"No relation."

"So, it's passed down each family line, or something, but then what about those like Rylan, they are just turned?"

Cassie leaned forward on her elbows. "The curse is passed down from the oldest child, no matter if they are girl of boy. If Olivia was to bless me with a grandchild, it would not be born a werewolf. Only Luke's would....we think."

Holden growled and Cassie quickly moved on. "Olivia was born a wolf because Roger was first born, but she can't produce them herself, does that make sense?"

"Can we stop talking about me having babies?" Olivia muttered.

"I get it, thanks Cassie. So you can, 'turn' humans though, right?"

"Yes, but we never do it unless it is their decision. If someone is turned against their will, then it is taken before that pack's council. For instance, our council now resides in New Orleans."

"Where Meegan is?" Norah bit her lip, wondering if she should have said that.

Luke nodded. "That's right, that's why I sent her there; it's the safest place for her to be right now."

Norah nodded. "Okay, I think I understand everything...maybe."

Cassie smiled. "It's a lot to take in. If you ever have any questions, feel free to drop by and ask me."

They said their goodbyes not long after that. Many of them had to work in the morning and Rylan took Norah's keys. "I'll drive."

Cassie caught her in a bone crushing hug as she said goodbye. "I meant what I said before. Come by anytime. I'm happy to have you."

"Thanks Cassie, same to you."

As the house faded in the night, Norah turned to Rylan in the car. "Did you ask to be turned?"

He nodded. "That family has done right by me since I was little. I'm going to do everything I can to protect them in return."

Norah closed her eyes, feeling tired and sent a silly prayer out to Lupa that her dreams wouldn't be plagued by werewolves that night.

14. Coward

The forest grew thicker as she ran. Norah desperately wanted to wake up - she could hear Daniel's laugh all around, echoing through the trees and she tried to move faster but her feet wouldn't listen. She moved as if out for a morning jog and the sound of footfalls grew closer

"Norah."

Liam appeared before her and she gasped, running straight into him. He grabbed her, forcing her around and Daniel was there.

"Surprise," he grinned, reaching for her throat -

Norah gasped, shooting up straight in bed. Breathing heavily, she looked around her room, closing her eyes in relief. It was over for another night.

She shrieked as the bedroom door shot open and Rylan burst in. "What is it?" he asked sharply.

"What?" she tried to regain control of her breathing.

"You called out like you were being attacked." He looked around. "I can't smell anyone."

"It was no one, just a bad dream."

Rylan stood at the edge of her bed, his outline barely visible in the darkness. "How long have you been having bad dreams?"

"I don't know, over a week now maybe."

"Shit, Norah, you should tell me these things." He sat on the edge of the bed and she crossed her legs automatically.

"And what can you do about a bad dream?" she snapped.

Silence.

"Are the dreams about what you won't tell me?"

Norah looked out the window, unsure of how to answer. Rylan muttered to himself and shifted closer. "Why won't you tell me?"

"Because it's foolish and it's my problem." Norah had decided the night before on the drive home that she couldn't tell Rylan about Daniel. He was so wrapped up in his own problems, hers just seemed silly in comparison. She wasn't about to dump more on his lap. Her only problem now was trying to stop him from prying.

A hand touched her knee and she jumped slightly. "Fear is foolish," he said softly. "But it can still paralyse us if we let it. Let me help."

She moved his hand away reluctantly. She wanted nothing more than to lean on someone, to have someone share her craziness with, but she just couldn't.

"How about I make you a deal?" she said quietly. "When I'm ready to face my fears, you'll be the first one I ask for help. I'm just not ready now, I can't do it. Does that sound fair?"

She heard his hand running across his stubble and he scratched his head. "I guess I have to settle for that, don't I?"

"You do."

He got up to leave and Norah leaned over to turn the lamp on. He turned back, eyes squinting in the light. "What are you doing?"

"Reading."

"Go back to sleep."

She shook her head. "Not yet."

Rylan shook his head and she buried her nose in the book from her bedside table. She hadn't even read one line when it was snatched from her hands. "Hey, what are you doi -"

The words died on her lips as Rylan turned her lamp off and lay on the bed beside her. "Rylan! Get the hell out."

"Go to sleep."

"I said I wanted to read, get out now before I kick you out." She yelped as he grabbed her, dragging her back down and then he rolled, lying half on top of her. He was larger than her, and half his weight alone was enough to pin her down. She tried to kick him but his leg on top of hers didn't budge. His breath ruffled her hair and a small noise of annoyance erupted from her throat.

"Go to sleep."

"Get off of me!"

"Don't worry," he said sleepily, "I'll keep the nasty monsters at bay."

"Gee, I feel so much better now," she said sarcastically. Getting one hand free, she slapped his chest. "Move, now."

"Nope." He captured her hand and pinned it on her stomach. "Go to sleep, Norah."

She lay stiffly, her heart pounding painfully in her chest, with what she told herself was anger, and listened to Rylan's breathing. His body was warm and though he was holding her still, he wasn't gripping her tightly. He lay in just the right position so they...fit together perfectly.

Norah's eyes widened at the thought and brushed it aside. Idiot, don't think like that. Of course it was hard not to with an attractive man lying on top of her.

Slowly, Rylan's breathing deepened out as he drifted off to sleep and Norah waited patiently for the right moment. His body began to relax and slowly, she started lifting his arm off her stomach and inch by inch, began to slide out. When she finally had her legs free, she grabbed her book, thinking she would have to sleep on the couch. Swinging her legs off the bed, she bit back a shout as Rylan's arm shot around her waist. He rolled, taking her with him and resettled in basically their original position.

"Go to sleep dammit," he mumbled. "I have work in the morning."

She huffed in annoyance and stared into the darkness, trying to think of ways to best a werewolf. Annoying jerk. As she started listing off ways to get back at him, she drifted off to sleep in his arms.

The sun woke Norah the next morning and she rolled over staring at the open window. *I didn't leave that curtain open last night...*

Memories flashed in of her nightmare and Rylan refusing to leave her bed. Cheeks flaming, she hid her face in her hands. "Oh god," she mumbled. "He must think I'm really pathetic."

Sitting up, she forced herself into the bathroom to have a shower. His scent still lingered on her - and while she didn't necessarily mind - it would be weird if she could smell him on her all day. Plus she had to get coffee and if Olivia sniffed her and realised, she wouldn't hear the end of it.

Once she'd showered and dressed, she put some toast on and grabbed her laptop, flipping it open. Her blank document lit up to greet her and she frowned, thinking of the scene she'd been struggling with. As she went through the scene again, her eyes widened as something strangely clicked into place and the whole scene made sense. Instead of congratulating herself, she slapped her cheek. "Idiot."

The morning passed by slowly and she managed to write half of the chapter after adding and deleting a few scenes. She still wasn't satisfied but she decided to take a break and get some coffee. Grabbing her book, she walked into town to do some reading at the cafe.

She chose to walk along the beach this time, taking off her shoes and enjoying the sand between her toes. She used to love digging her toes into the wet sand, she would pick up the sand in her toes and throw it at Adam when they had beach days. She had many fond memories of the beach with her family, but the last one made her smile fade. Adam had been in his final year of school, and already hanging with the wrong crowd. In the middle of the night, she received a drunken phone call from Adam telling her to come and pick him up. Angry, she drove down to collect him but he wanted her to take his drugged out friends with her. That was where she put her foot down. She had just gotten her licence and she was terrified of getting caught.

Her refusal had resulted in one of their biggest arguments and in the end, he left her alone on the beach, saying he would find his own way home. Blinded by tears, she had driven home, wondering what had happened to her brother when a branch fell across the road, hitting her car. She had only suffered whiplash and a few minor injuries, but it had been enough for Adam to wake up and apologise.

Norah kicked the sand, passing a few beach goers. He had behaved himself for a little while - until his friends returned and continued to steer him away from her.

Stop thinking of the past, she reminded herself. It's not worth the heartache.

As she reached the pier, she waved to the men who were fishing over the edge but they all averted their gaze, muttering in response.

That's weird, she thought.

Brushing it aside, she walked up the main street and headed to the cafe. The need for coffee overrode everything at the moment. Slipping in quietly, she took her usual seat and waited, knowing Olivia would come when she was ready.

"Hey Norah," Olivia sat opposite her, tea towel in hand. "Did you have fun last night?"

"Yeah it was nice, you have a great family," Norah smiled.

"Sorry about my mom, she can get a bit full on sometimes."

"No don't apologise, she was lovely." She looked around, noticing the stares and frowned. "Why are they all staring at us like that?"

Olivia quickly glanced around. "They probably heard about you and Rylan."

"There's nothing happening between us though!"

"Isn't there?" Olivia drawled. "You guys were so cute at dinner last night, I could see my mom planning the wedding already."

"Don't be stupid!" Norah snapped. "We've been living together for a week and I barely see him as it is. You know he's just doing this because he thinks he owes me or something."

Olivia burst into laughter and Norah glared at her. "Sorry! It's just that anyone could be watching out for you. Hell I even offered, but Rylan wasn't having any of it. He kept making up excuses as to why it should be him and trust me, they weren't well thought out. He's there because he wants to be there, Norah. He's into you bad."

"Again, we've only known each other a week," she pressed.

"So what? He's not going to profess his undying love to you or whatever. I'm just saying he's interested, and if I didn't know any better, you're interested too."

"Am not."

She flushed and Olivia grinned. "I call bullshit. You better let me be a bridesmaid."

"Olivia -"

She got up laughing. "Who am I kidding? Mom will be planning the wedding, of course I'll be a bridesmaid."

The front door opened and a beautiful blonde woman walked in as Norah started banging her head on the table.

"Hey Olivia," the blonde stopped in front of Olivia whose smile vanished.

"Chloe." She said shortly.

Gail walked out with a tray of coffees. "Olivia take these down to the restaurant, would you?"

Olivia took them, eyeing Chloe warily as she walked out. Norah heard the chair shift again. "Hi, you must be Norah."

Norah looked up and her face heated in embarrassment. "That's right. Sorry you had to see that."

"I'm Chloe," she said simply, as if Norah should know immediately who that was. It took her a minute to remember the name.

"You're part of the Montoya clan, right? Annie's daughter?"

She nodded, flicking her hair back. "I couldn't help overhearing your talk with Olivia about Rylan."

Her voice grew hard and Norah frowned. "Didn't you just come in - oh right, werewolf powers and all that. Anyway, sorry about that. Olivia was just -"

"He's my mate, you know."

Norah froze, a ball of unease dropping into the pit of her stomach. "What?"

"Surely you must know what a mate is?" she asked coldly.

Norah nodded, feeling numb. She's read enough fantasy novels to know what that meant. "I don't understand though, I thought -"

Chloe snorted, folding her arms. "Please. He doesn't actually like you. He's just playing around because he's trying to fight his fate. In the end though, he'll come running back to me. He won't be able to help it."

Norah could see why he would want to get away from her - she was a bitch. But still... "I'm sorry, I didn't know -"

"No, you didn't," she said sarcastically. "Don't tell him I told you either. It will only make him annoyed and I'm not in the mood for his theatrics." Standing up, she grabbed her bag, and shot Norah a fake smile. "It was nice meeting you!"

Norah stared at the vacated seat, listening to the door open and close.

Rylan belonged to someone else.

This was perfect, now she didn't have to clarify that there was nothing between them. She guessed Olivia didn't know or she would have mentioned it already. She should have been thrilled but -

Her heart hurt.

She wasn't supposed to care, but it was suddenly difficult to breathe.

She hadn't really liked him, had she?

He'd been an annoying jerk, always trying to pry into her life, funny, steadfast, kind - She shook her head and stood up, the chair scraping loudly. She couldn't think like that.

She left money on the counter, forgetting she hadn't ordered a coffee yet, and rushed out as her feelings started to make themselves known.

Oh crap. She had liked him.

"When did that happen?" she said out loud.

Walking home, she pulled out her phone and dialled his number. This wouldn't do. She had to get rid of him before her feelings got worse.

He answered on the fourth ring. "What's wrong?"

"Oh, hey Rylan. How are you?" she stammered. Be cool, dammit!

"No time for small talk, Norah. What's the problem?"

"Nothing," she said quickly. "I was just wondering what time you would be home, I need to talk to you about something."

There was silence for a few breaths and then - "I'll see you in twenty."

He hung up.

"Twenty," she whispered. "I only have twenty minutes to prepare for this?"

She took off running, passing a white car as she turned down her driveway. Now that her emotions had made themselves known, her stomach fluttered with nerves. Why was she freaking out so much? She started rehearsing her argument in her head. She would tell him that she was no longer in any danger and he didn't need to stay anymore. If she needed to, she would use her writing as an excuse.

Rushing inside, she grabbed the bottle of Tequila from her liquor cabinet and had a quick shot for courage. It burned and she coughed, breathing heavily.

"Stay in control of the conversation," she said calmly. "Make him hate you, Norah."

She didn't want him to hate her though.

"Stupid feelings!" she snapped. "Go away!"

She heard his motorbike rumble up the drive and had another shot. Slamming the bottle down, she breathed deeply. Let's do this.

Norah watched Rylan pull up and a ball of nerves fluttered in her stomach. Why did she suddenly feel like a school girl trying to talk to her crush for the first time?

He took his helmet off and walked over to her. "Hey, what did you need to talk about?"

"I wasn't expecting you back until later," she said breathlessly.

He shrugged his shoulders. "I took an early lunch. What's wrong?"

The nerves threatened to tear her body apart and she said the words before she chickened out. "You need to move out."

His smile faltered. "What's brought this on?"

She took a small step backwards and his eyes narrowed as she started to use her prepared argument. "People in town are talking, and they think we're together –"

"And?"

She stared at him, not prepared for a comeback so soon. "And what?"

"And what does that matter? It's just gossip. You and I both know the truth so who cares?"

"I care!" she exclaimed. "I don't want people believing false things about me."

"Bullshit."

"I beg your pardon?" she said darkly.

"Don't act like you don't know," he said, running a hand through his hair. "You lie about everything else, Norah, why should this matter?"

"I do not lie about everything," she snapped. "I barely know these people, why should I tell them my life story? I'm allowed to keep my life private!"

He snorted. "There is a difference between wanting privacy and hiding who you are."

"I don't hide anything -" she tried to defend herself but Rylan snapped.

"Everything about you is false, Norah! You keep everything real hidden behind those walls and refuse to let anyone in. God knows I've tried to break through, but you are the most stubborn woman I've ever met."

"I don't need to let anyone in," she retorted. "There is nothing there for them to know."

He took a step forward, closing the distance between them and she held her breath. "You're wrong," he growled. "That's where the real Norah Jacobs is and everything I want to know is behind that wall."

Her heart pounded in her chest and she tried to take control of the situation. "You don't need to know anything about me," she stammered. "This is just a job for you, one that I'm tired of. I want my life back and, you aren't needed."

Those words felt wrong in her mouth and she watched his eyes darken. Her heart rate increased but she kept going. "I haven't been approached in over a week, they aren't interested in me and I doubt they ever would be. So you don't have to stay anymore."

She hadn't realised they were moving, he continued to walk toward her and she tried to keep the distance between them until she hit the side of the house.

"What brought this bullshit on, Norah? I left you this morning and everything was good. Who did you meet today that fucked with your head?"

"No one!"

"Stop lying!" he shouted and she flinched, pressing harder into the weatherboards. "Would it kill you to tell the truth for once? That you do have some problem you're hiding from the world, that you like having me around or that you had the best sleep last night because you were in my arms? Stop bullshitting me Norah and tell me the truth!"

Tears threatened to fall and she clenched her fists. "You want the truth? Fine, I do have a problem – it's you. You've pushed yourself into my life and I've had enough of it. You don't get to decide what I share with the world, only I make that choice and trying to push your way in was a stupid thing to do. Oh, and you were wrong. I didn't sleep well last night, quite the opposite in fact."

Listening to herself speak, even she could hear the lie in that last part.

"Coward," he muttered, stepping away.

"What?"

"You're a bloody coward, always pushing everyone away and trying to do it all on your own. How do you think you ended up in this shit in the first place? Because, instead of facing your problems head on, you just keep running away from them and hoping everything will magically sort itself out. Wake the fuck up, Norah. This isn't one of your stupid stories."

She flinched.

"Leave, now," she whispered.

"Gladly," he laughed bitterly, moving away. "I always pick the bloody messed up ones."

"Go on," he said louder. "Run away again, eventually there will be nowhere left to run though, Norah and then what will you do?"

"Get your womanising ass off my property!" she snapped, her nerves close to fraying. His words were like knives; they cut and slashed until she had nothing left but anger that he was right; she was a coward.

"Womanising!" he spun around. "So it was a woman who messed with your head today. Who was it?"

"Chloe," she muttered, too tired to lie.

"Chloe," he growled. "Well, I guess I should thank her for showing me the fucking light. In fact, I might go and see her right now. Anything I left in there, give it to Olivia."

Norah's heart wrenched painfully at the mention of Chloe and she tried to remind herself that she didn't care, that Chloe was his mate or whatever that entailed. The motorbike roared to life and her arms wrapped around her stomach as she watched him drive off. This was the right thing to do, she thought. She couldn't let him stay with the way she was feeling, especially when he had Chloe. This was for the best, she wouldn't drag him into her mess.

"Fucking coward," she whispered to herself.

Walking back in, she kicked the door and it rocked on its hinges. She'd done the right thing, it would only end in heartache if she ventured down that path. She just wished Olivia had told her about this mates thing in the first place. Why had no one mentioned it?

She stared at the Tequila bottle, wondering how long it would take to finish the bottle. She didn't hear the car pull up until it's owner was knocking on her front door. She turned around, thinking Rylan must have come back.

"Would you just -"

The words died on her lips.

Her breathing sounded loud in her ears, drowning out the frantic beating of her heart as she stood frozen in fear.

"Hello, Norah," Daniel smiled.

15. Fight

Daniel stepped inside and Norah bolted for the back door.

She heard fast footsteps behind her and shrieked as fingers grasped her hair, yanking her away from the door and into the wall. Daniel pinned her, one hand wrapped around her throat and he stood close, leaving no room for her to fight back. His eyes were bloodshot and the light sheen of sweat on his skin suggested he wasn't as fit as he made out to be.

"Oh, Norah," he smiled, breathing heavily. "How could you leave without saying goodbye? I thought you had better manners than that. Then again, your brother is a murderer so it is to be expected."

"He is no murderer," she snapped. "It was all your fault that it happened."

His fingers tightened on her throat and she closed her eyes as it got difficult to breathe. "Now you know that's not true," he laughed. "I never touched that man, the only one who laid a finger on him was poor Adam. He must be feeling quite lonely in jail, you haven't been in to visit him once. Not very sisterly, don't you think?"

"I've had other things on my mind," she wheezed.

"Ah yes," he stepped back, brushing her hair from her shoulder. "I never knew you liked to play hide and seek. You gave me a good run around, I'll give you that. Now, let's get down to business, shall we? Where are my diamonds?"

"I don't know."

Her legs buckled as Daniel punched her in the stomach. She coughed, the air rushing from her lungs and she bent over but Daniel's hand, still wrapped around her throat, shoved her back against the wall.

"Wrong answer, gorgeous. I suggest you have another think before I have to rattle your brain and make you remember."

"I honestly don't know!" she cried. "Adam never had diamonds on him when he came to my house that night!"

"Don't lie!" He threw her down the corridor and she landed near the entryway to the kitchen, banging her hip on the door. She winced, tears stinging her eyes as she tried to crawl away. She heard footsteps and then a foot was digging into her lower back, pressing her into the floor.

"I know Adam had those diamonds that night," he said softly. "I went back after he left and the diamonds were gone." He rolled her over and dragged her in front of the kitchen sink. The cupboard door knob pressed into her back and she fought back as he grabbed her hands. "Calm yourself, Norah, you're being silly."

When she didn't stop resisting, he slapped her across the face. Her head snapped sideways under the blow and the world blurred. Something wrapped around her wrists and she groaned as it tightened painfully. Glancing down, she saw her hands bound with rope.

He grabbed her chin, making her face him and she breathed through her nose, glaring at him defiantly. "Now that you're comfortable, we'll start our next game of hide and seek. You hid the diamonds, and I get to find them. Doesn't that sound fun?"

"Fuck you," she murmured, twisting her head out of his grasp.

He chuckled, patting her cheek gently. "If you play your cards right, you just might."

Her body ran cold at the thought. She felt her mobile pressing against the hip that had connected with the door and welcomed the pain, hoping it hadn't been broken in the fall. Standing up, Daniel dusted off his pants. "You just sit there and rest those injuries while I have a poke through your house. This one isn't as big as the other thank god, shouldn't take too long."

He disappeared into her bedroom and she closed her eyes, head tilting skyward.

He'd been in her home.

It made her feel sick knowing he had gone through all her personal belongings. All those memories and objects tainted by his evil hands. She heard the cupboard being open and something crash to the floor.

Trying not to think about it, she shifted slightly and reached into her pocket. The jeans she wore were tight fitting, making it difficult to grab the phone out. She shifted lower, arching her back to reach the slim object and nearly cried in relief when it finally slid out between her fingers. Biting her lip, she whimpered at the cracked screen.

Pressing the button at the top, the screen lit up and she sighed in relief and started searching for a number. Her fingers moved automatically and she froze, realising whose number she was finding.

Rylan's name came onto the screen and she wondered if she should call him. What if he didn't answer because he was still mad?

"Police," she whispered. Hands trembling, she started dialling the three numbers. She started to press the call button when a foot came from nowhere, connecting with her hand. She screamed, the phone flying from her hand and Daniel crouched down.

"Why couldn't you just sit there quietly and wait for me to finish? Now I have to punish you."

Before she could ask what he meant, his fist connected with her head and the world disappeared.

*   *   *

The first thing Norah noticed was the world was moving. She opened her eyes, trying to figure out where she was. Everything was dark and for one stupid moment, she thought she'd gone blind, before she realised she was looking at the night sky. She shifted, and felt the rope around her hands tighten. Remembering what had happened, consciousness returned sharply and she sat up, nearly connecting the dashboard of the car she was in.

"Hey there, sleepy head. Finally awake?"

The voice made her want to cry.

Daniel sat in the driver's seat, fingers tapping on the steering wheel. "Where are we?" she croaked.

"Just doing a little sightseeing," he said calmly. "After having no luck in your house, I thought we could use some fresh air. I did sit back and wonder if I should wake you and ask again before we left, but then a voice said to me, 'No, Daniel. You know she won't tell you where they are.' I realised the voice was right, it was pointless trying to make you tell me. So I'm going to give you a little more...incentive to tell me. Otherwise I'm just going to kill you."

Norah buried her hands between her legs, her right one throbbing with pain. Slowly, she started to twist her hands against the rope, trying to loosen it enough to slip her hands through. Daniel hummed quietly, driving slowly through the town. It was quiet and Norah no one would be able to see her in the car anyway.

A sense of resolve Norah didn't know she possessed seeped through her. She knew what he planned to do and where he was going when he took a familiar turn towards the far cliffs. She would not die today. Rylan's voice calling her a coward kept playing through her mind and she wanted to prove him wrong. Just once, she wanted to be brave and stand up for herself. Even if she was doing it alone.

The car bumped along the dirt road and Norah felt the ropes beginning to ease around her wrists. Worried Daniel would look down and see, she started talking. "Why don't you just go and ask Adam where he hid the diamonds? If he tells you where they are, you can have them."

"Ah, so you want me to go into a prison in the hopes I'll be caught, is that it?"

"What? No, I'm just saying Adam can tell you -"

"He won't tell me, Norah. He went to so much trouble to keep them from me, he won't reveal his little secret now," Daniel said, slowing down over a large puddle in the road. "He knows how to hold a grudge, your brother. It's not my fault he killed that man. If he'd just ran none of this would have happened."

"Adam doesn't run," Norah said quietly. "He stayed because he actually has feelings and emotions you seem to lack."

The brakes slammed and Norah flew forward, the seatbelt catching her before she hit the dashboard. Daniel grabbed her shoulder, twisting it painfully. "You know nothing about me, little Norah. I suggest you shut your mouth before I have to shut it for you." He laughed, his demeanour changing in an instant. "Of course I plan on shutting it anyway, can't have you blabbing to the authorities about my little visit. Why don't we stretch our legs? The air in this car is starting to get a little thin."

Daniel climbed out first and Norah quickly struggled as he walked around the car. Come on!

The door opened and she was yanked out. Stumbling to the ground, she felt the ropes give way and nearly cried with relief. Holding them together, she let him drag her up the track, waiting for the opportune moment.

"These cliffs are beautiful," he said loudly over the wind. "I wonder how many people have ended their lives up here?"

The sound of the waves crashing against the rocks below was muted by keening of the wind and Norah stumbled as the light from the car faded. It was overcast, the moon hidden and there was little light to show the way. Daniel kept pushing her forward, his breathing growing heavy with the incline and Norah knew the moment was coming. Her head throbbed from the earlier beating and the world blurred slightly as the pounding grew heavier with each step.

They reached the top and Norah looked around. The lights of Bellvale could be seen to the right and she wondered if anyone had seen them go up the cliffs. Will they find my body tomorrow on the rocks? A voice whispered in her head and she squashed it down. Stay positive.

"Now," Daniel stood beside her, grinning madly. "I've never been good with goodbyes so how about we skip them and get straight to business?"

Now.

Norah kicked him in the shin and he cursed, stumbling forward. "Bitch!"

He swung wildly and she tried to duck but his fist connected with her temple and everything spun, a ringing starting in her ears and she gasped as he pinned her to the ground.

"Stupid Norah," he snarled, hands finding her throat in the dark. "You had to take the hard way." They started to tighten and her hands scrambled in the dirt, desperate for any sort of weapon.

Her fingers traced over a rock and she grabbed it, raising it up and smashing it into his head. He roared in pain, his hands loosening and she tried to throw him off her. They rolled together, Daniel refusing to let go and still holding the rock, she hit him again, feeling his nose being crushed beneath the stone. A strange gurgling came from his mouth and she pushed him off her, breathing heavily.

Her throat hurt, her head pounded and she knew she had a concussion. She felt discombobulated and turned her head, wondering why Daniel hadn't attacked her again. In the dark, she couldn't see him and reached out with her hand, feeling for him - her hand hit the edge of the cliff.

She stopped breathing.

Sitting up slowly, she waited for the world to stop spinning, before leaning forward and peering over the edge of the cliff, already knowing what she would see. It was dark, but she just could make out the waves crashing against the rocky cliffs and the white of a shirt lying awkwardly on the high rocks. She covered her mouth, a strange shrieking passing her lips as reality sank in.

She hadn't -

She didn't mean -

Turning her head, she vomited the contents of her stomach all over the ground. It couldn't be real.

Time slipped by as she sat atop the cliffs, her body going into shock. She didn't care that she practically sitting in her own vomit. It didn't seem that important when she thought about what she had just done. The pain in her head reminded her that it was real, that it had happened and finally, she stood on shaking legs and walked away.

She walked past the car, its doors still open, lights still shining in the night, continuing down to the beach, feet sinking into the sand and her body started to turn, to see if he was still there, but she stopped herself.

Don't do it.

She kept walking, as though lost in some horrid nightmare. The pier came into view, the one light shining and she continued along the beach, slipping back into the darkness until she reached her house. There were no lights on, the door was closed and rather than wonder if anyone had noticed she was missing, she just walked inside. Stepping over the mess he had made, she made it to her room and sat on the bed, staring at the wall.

"Not real," she whispered. "Please, it can't be real."

Murderer, the voice whispered and a sob tore from her chest.

Lying back, she started crying, her body wracked with sobs until the pain in her head finally pushed her into the darkness.

16. Senseless

The phone was ringing.

Norah could hear it in the kitchen, the shrill tone sounding like a marching band parading through her head. She tried to open her eyes but they were stuck together with sleep and tears.

Her head continued to pound and she decided against opening them in the end. The thought of light was enough to make a whimper pass her lips. The memories of last night scattered in her head, refusing to piece together and she caught snatches, unable to determine what it was that had happened. As the phone finally stopped ringing, she started to wonder why Rylan hadn't just answered it and froze.

Rylan was gone, and Daniel was -

As one, the memories surged forward, crashing together in one large cluster and she was bombarded with the horror that had been the night before. Her chest tightened and pushing through the pain, she opened her eyes. The daylight shone dimly through the curtains.

It was enough to make the throbbing in her head hurt more, but the pain no longer seemed important.

Daniel was dead.

She had killed someone.

She didn't know what to do. She felt detached from the events, as if she were no longer the same person. Numbly, she sat up. The world swayed and she held her head, stumbling to the bathroom. Running the shower, she stripped off her clothes, the smell of salt and dirt clung to them and she gasped when she saw her reflection in the mirror. Bruises lined her stomach and ribs, from Daniel's fists; they were an ugly red and purple that marred against her pale skin.

Looking higher, her face was a mess. Covered in dirt, she saw a bruise along her hairline above her left temple. The skin around her eye felt tender as she touched it, but it wasn't swollen. She was lucky in that aspect.

Stepping into the shower, she let the water run over her. Even though she knew the night before had happened, it felt like nothing more than an awful dream. She didn't want it to be real. Scrubbing the dirt and grime from her battered body, she knew what she had to do - she had to turn herself in. She had made Adam do it, and she had to follow her own example. Daniel had been a monster, but murder was wrong and she couldn't live with the guilt of knowing she had ended someone's life.

When she finished showering, she got changed and arranged her hair to hide the bruising. First, she would go to the cliffs. She knew she should go to the police station first, but something inside her needed to see - needed to know that it hadn't all been a dream. That she had become the monster.

Grabbing a pair of sunglasses, she downed two pain killers and trudged outside. The air was warm, it was going to be hot day. Norah didn't like that. When a protagonist had done something wrong in a book, the day should be miserable, rain pelting down on the ground to symbolise their grief and despair.

This isn't one of your stories, Norah.

She flinched as Rylan's words came back to haunt her. He was right. This wasn't one of her stories, if it was, she could simply go back and rewrite that whole scene, pretending it had never happened. There were no rewrites in real life.

Climbing in her car, she breathed deeply, her head still causing her grief. The pain killers hadn't kicked in yet, and she hoped they did soon. She didn't think she would get anymore once she turned herself in. The town was already bustling with tourists as she drove through. She wondered if the word had spread that a body had been found - she assumed they had found the body by now. Someone had to have seen the car lights last night. She hadn't turned them off - she hadn't done anything other than push a man off a cliff.

Her grip on the steering wheel tightened.

The track came into view and she thought she would start panicking, that the flashing of police lights would meet her - but there was nothing. She reached the spot where the car had been left and stopped, climbing out.

The white vehicle was gone. There was no police - no yellow investigative tape, just....empty space.

What...

She walked up the hill, confusion slowly being replaced with fear until she was running, trying to run from the panic that threatened to break free. Reaching the top, she looked around, breathing heavily.

Still nothing.

Her blood roared in her ears as she stepped towards the edge, hesitating before she looked over, to the rocks below -

"No no no."

She stepped back and bolted down the hill, all rational thought fading. It wasn't possible. Her sandal slipped off but she didn't stop until she reached the bottom. All was quiet apart from the crash of the waves against the cliffs. Climbing over the rocks, she started hyperventilating as she found the spot where he had fallen. She knew because it was still dry - too high up for the tide to wash a body away - and blood stained the spiked stone.

A strange hiccupping noise reached her ears and she realised it was herself, the panic starting to set in. Where were the police? Why was no one hanging around and collecting evidence?

She glanced at her watch. It was only early in the morning, they couldn't have finished an investigation this early on.

"I'm going mad," she whispered, staring at the blood stain.

God she hated blood.

The hiccupping sobs eventually stopped and like a zombie, she made her way back to her car.

"This can't be happening," she whispered, hands trembling as she turned the key in the ignition. She decided they had to have finished their investigation and had just packed up early. She would just go to the police station and turn herself in.

A strange calm settled over as she drove back into town, parking in her usual spot outside the Twilight cafe before she realised. Hopping out, she stared at the people walking by, listening to their conversations in hopes of hearing something that would prove she wasn't going mad.

A man spoke of walking his dog, another the wrong bait resulting in no catches for the morning. A young girl screamed for ice cream -

No one was gossiping about a potential murder.

"Norah!" A hand grabbed her shoulder and she was spun around. Olivia glared at her. Norah didn't think she had ever seen the young girl so angry before. "What the hell is your problem? Rylan told me all that crap you threw at him yesterday. He has saved your life countless of times and this is how you repay him, by being a bitch? I thought you were a good person, Norah. Boy was I wrong."

The words rolled off her, she felt guilty about Rylan but that guilt couldn't break through the shock.

"Has there been any police about today?" Her voice sounded strange, almost detached from her body and Olivia jolted.

"What? No, only the sergeant who gets his morning coffee."

"Did he talk about anything happening at the beach?" she pleaded.

"No, only about the amount of tourists - what the hell is wrong with you? Where is your other shoe?"

Norah glanced down and saw she had forgotten her shoe. It was still up on the cliffs - but she couldn't go back there.

"So there's been no accidents reported," she whispered.

Olivia stepped forward, concerned. "No, Norah what are you talking about?" Her eyes moved over her glasses and the different hair style. "What happened?"

"Nothing, I just drank too much last night or something, I have to go." The panic was starting to creep back in at what all this could possibly mean.

"Norah -"

"Bye Olivia." Getting back into her car, she quickly pulled away and headed home. "I'm not mad," she whispered.

The bruises proved she hadn't imagined it. Still, mad thoughts started creeping in and she let them, too afraid to chase them away with reason. No one could survive a fall like that, the amount of blood had been life threatening. And yet... No police investigation. No body. No Car.

Irrational fear won.

Getting home, she flew from the car, only one thing on her mind. Run.

She stumbled through the disarrayed kitchen and into her bedroom, grabbing whatever she saw and shoving it into a bag. She was a coward. There was no escaping that. She knew he couldn't be alive - but what if he was? What if he was some strange creature, like the Montoya's?

Going out into the kitchen, she heard a crunch as her foot landed on something and looked down. Reaching down, she picked up her phone, the cracked screen lighting up as she clicked the button. Unsure why, she dialled the now familiar number and waited as it rang. When he didn't answer, something inside her wilted. He hated her.

"This is Rylan. You know what to do."

The voice mail beeped and she hesitated, suddenly unsure of what to say. "Rylan...it's Norah. You were right. I'm such a pathetic coward." Her voice broke. "I'm sorry I was such a stubborn idiot, but it's for the best. I couldn't get you involved in the shit I'm in. And I can't stay. I just can't. You're right, all I do is run from my problems. It's all I know how to do. Thank -"

The tone beeped, signalling she'd run out of time and she stared at the black screen, placing the phone on the counter. If he ever decided to listen to it, she hoped he would forgive her.

It took her ten minutes to pack the car with what she needed. She'd call Ray and tell him Jack could burn the rest for all she cared. The house phone started ringing again and she left it, picking up her laptop when it changed over to the answering machine.

"Norah? Are you there?"

She froze.

"Look, I know you don't want to talk to me but -"

"Adam?" She picked up the call and heard his sigh of relief.

"Thank god! I've been so worried about you."

"How did you get this number?"

"Alice told me," he said simply. "She threatened to break into jail and kill me if I told another soul."

"Did you?" Norah whispered, her fingers white around the phone cord. "Did you tell Daniel?"

"What, no of course not! I'd never tell him where you are. Just tell me you're all right."

"No, I'm not all right. He...he knows where I am."

"Oh fuck. Look, get out of there and find somewhere else to lie low for awhile. He should leave you alone -"

"He won't leave me alone, Adam," she laughed darkly. "Not until he gets those stupid bloody diamonds."

"Well he's not getting them -"

"Why not! Are jewels more important to you than your own sister?" she shouted. "He is ruining my life - YOU are ruining my life, all because of some shiny stones!"

"Norah -"

"No! Just tell me where the fucking diamonds are and if I see him again, I'll tell him where to find them." She still didn't know if she would see him again, but her gut told her this wasn't the last of him.

"I can't do that, Norah."

"Of course you can't," she snapped. "So bloody selfish -"

"No! Norah, I can't tell him where the diamonds are because... you have the diamonds."

Her heart stopped. "What?"

The silence between them became deafening, a ball of rage started to build in the pit of her stomach, making it difficult to see.

"That night," he said quickly, sensing her anger. "While you were on the phone with the lawyers, I hid the diamonds in your jewellery box. You know the one that used to belong to mum with the secret compartment in the back?"

"This...whole time," her entire body shook with the effort not to shout. "Those diamonds were on me - the one thing that would have made Daniel leave me alone - and you're just telling me now?"

"Norah, I couldn't let him -"

"WHAT THE FUCK?" she screeched. "What the hell were you thinking? You destroyed my life because you didn't want him to have them? Fuck you!"

"Norah please -"

"No, I am so mad right now, I'm going to say something I'll regret so you need to shut up. Don't call me again, I don't want to know you right now."

She slammed the phone down. Unhappy, she then picked it up and threw it across the kitchen. The cord grew taught and it crashed to the floor.

That arse! Storming into her bedroom, she grabbed the jewellery box which hadn't been packed. It was small white box, a fleur de lis painted on the top. Her mother had gotten it when she was a child and always told Norah how much she loved it.

Hands trembling, she found the latch at the back and pulled the compartment open. Shoved inside was a small blue pouch. She couldn't believe it. All this time, the cause of her torment had been hiding in her bedroom.

If Adam ever got out of jail, she was going to kill him herself.

Holding the pouch in her hand, her fingers clenched into a fist, wanting to rid the world of their existence. She flew around, walking outside with the mindset that like that jewel in the Titanic movie, they would fit in at the bottom of the ocean.

A bang to her left made her jump and she spun, shoving the pouch into her shorts pocket. "Luke?"

Luke strode over, his smile guarded. "Hey Norah, what's going on?"

"What are you doing here?" she asked, ignoring his question.

"I'm here as a favour I owe." His eyes roamed over her before glancing at the house. "Everything all right?"

"Fine," she said slowly. "Who told you to come here?"

He walked over to her car and pulled out the keys she'd left in the ignition.

"Hey!" Closing the doors, he locked it and tucked the keys in his pocket. "What are you doing?"

"Returning a favour," he said simply. "I'm going to keep these until you calm down."

"I am calm," she ground out. "You're not helping by stealing my keys."

He stepped back as she took a step forward. "Hey don't shoot the messenger. Look, Norah I don't know what trouble you're in, but it must be heavy for you to be trying to hide those bruises. Is the guy still around?"

She jumped before remembering Luke would be able to smell him. "No."

Luke heard the uncertainty in her voice and frowned. "I'll remember the scent in case he shows up again. Until then, I suggest you go and lay down. You look like crap."

"Give back my keys, I need them."

"No you don't," he smiled. "And besides, if I let you go, Rylan will kill me. I'll talk to you later."

He jumped back in his truck and Norah watched dumbfounded as he drove away, brushing over the fact Rylan had sent him. Her one vehicle of escape had been stolen from her - or at least the keys had.

God dammit!

The pouch pressed against her pocket and she pulled it out, wondering why she'd hid them from Luke. He didn't know what they were from.

"Right, time to see how well you guys swim." Turning, she walked into the water, pushing against the waves until she stood waist deep. Opening the pouch, she poured the rocks out and they glistened in her palm. They were tiny, their shape perfect and Norah couldn't help but be momentarily mesmerised by their allure before she remembered all the heartache they had caused her.

Diamonds were definitely not a girls best friend, she told herself.

She stared them, willing her hand to move and drop them into the water, to be forgotten forever. Something held her back. What if Daniel did come back? He would be beyond pissed, and he would want the diamonds. Norah wondered if she should hang onto them - just in case he did come back for them.

Even if he does, he'll kill you anyway, the voice of reason whispered in her mind and she sighed. Just throw them away and be done with it. Her hand tilted slightly to the left, the diamonds starting to roll against the skin -

A whistle shrilled behind her.

By reflex, her fingers curled, grabbing the diamonds and she spun in surprise.

"What the hell are you doing?" Rylan stood at the shore, one foot already in the water.

She shoved the diamonds back into her pocket. "W-what?"

She wanted to ask why he was suddenly there but words failed her. He motioned for her to come back to shore. When she didn't move, he waved his hands in annoyance. "Are you really going to make me come in after you?"

Her body started moving back to shore, stopping cautiously a few feet away from him. "Why are you here?"

"What, did you think you could just leave a message like that and I'd do nothing?"

"No, I didn't think you'd get it until..."

"Until you were gone?" He finished her sentence. He walked out, meeting her in the shallow waves and she would have moved back but her feet had sunk in the sand. His eyes scanned her face, they were hard and laced with anger. "Who's been here?"

She opened her mouth to lie and flinched as he gently grabbed her chin, fingers moving up her face, removing her sunglasses. She squinted in the bright light and heard a low growl in his chest.

"One fucking night," he muttered under his breath. "What happened?"

"Nothing worth mentioning." She knew from his expression that was the wrong answer. He started to turn away and without thinking, she grabbed his arm, stopping him. "Someone I know - someone I was hiding from found me and...this happened."

"Where is he now?" Her mouth opened but no sound came out. She couldn't bring herself to say it. She didn't even know if it was possible. Rylan cupped her face, thumb brushing the tear that escaped down her cheek.

"You were right," she whispered. "I'm just coward."

"You're not a coward, Norah. No coward would have saved my life in the forest or stuck around when she discovered he was werewolf."

At the mention of werewolf she remembered Chloe and pulled herself out of his grasp. "I shouldn't be doing this. It's not fair to Chloe -"

"Chloe is not my mate," he said flatly.

"What?"

"She made the whole thing up. We did date for a little while, but she has a few screws loose and I dumped her. She heard I was chasing you and this was her way of getting back at me. I went and saw her last night and told her to back off."

"So, she isn't your mate?"

"No, there's no such thing. It's all made up. If you were to mate with someone, it only like a marriage. You do tie yourself to them - it's not something to take lightly, but it doesn't mean you're destined for each other or anything. That's just a load of crap."

She nodded and looked through her lashes. "Why did you come back though? You said I was crazy as well."

He sighed. "You are crazy, but in a good way. I was just pissed off when I said that because you were keeping all this crap from me. I trusted you with my biggest secret but you couldn't trust me with yours. Of course I was going to insulted."

Norah flinched. She'd never thought of it that way. "I didn't want to tell you because I didn't want to pile on top of the problems you already have with Liam and the leadership and all that."

"I was asking you to tell me, Norah. If I couldn't handle your drama I wouldn't have asked in the first place. I only wanted to help."

"Only because you felt like you owed me for saving your life."

A languid smile stretched across his face. "That is not the reason why, Norah."

She looked up at him. "Then why would you want to help me?"

He laughed under his breath. "Hopeless."

Before she could snap at him, he stepped forward pressing his lips against hers.

Norah's eyes widened, hands coming up to grab his shoulders as he stepped closer, hands resting on her waist. Eyes closing, she let herself fall into the moment, hands wrapping around his neck and Rylan pressed her closer, lips moving softly against hers. They pulled apart, foreheads resting against each other.

"That's why," he grinned. "If you haven't figured it out after that, then I'll need to get more creative."

"I've figured it out," she said quickly.

His hand moved up, brushing her hair from her face and she winced as he touched the bump made by Daniel. He felt her body jerk and stepped back, cursing as he revealed the sore area. "Where is the bastard? I'll kill him."

"I-I don't know. Honestly!" She added when saw the disbelief in his eyes. "I don't know how to explain it..."

Tears threatened to fall and she stepped back, only to be brought straight back against Rylan's chest. "Right, here's what is going to happen; we are going to go inside, take a look at that head of yours and then you are going to tell me everything. No negotiations."

"Don't you have work?"

"I took a personal day. Now, inside."

Too tired to argue, Norah let him lead her inside, his hand curling around hers. It felt warm, sending tingles up her arm and she didn't know if she deserved whatever this was. Not after what she'd done.

Walking inside, she heard him growl as he took in the state of her main room. He took her to the couch and sat her down. "Wait here."

She sat quietly, staring at the broken cup on the coffee table as Rylan looked around for something. The cup had been one of her favourites. It had a good handle and she loved the image of the shells on the side. *I wonder what else is broken?*

Rylan returned with her emergency kit and sat on the coffee table in front of her. He scooted closer and lifted her hair away to inspect the area again. She hissed when he dabbed it with a cool cloth. His care was gentle though, and he cleaned the area meticulously.

"Cassie has got a good remedy for bruising, we'll put some on it tonight when we go home."

"What? Why can't I stay here?"

"You're not staying here until we get this place sorted out. You're attacker messed this place up pretty bad, a lot of the small furniture is broken."

"I'll have to invite Jack down for a bonfire," she said weakly.

He took her hand, encasing in his large ones. She watched his fingers move against her skin, finding comfort in their small movements. "Tell me what happened, Norah."

Her hand trembled in his as the words tumbled forth and she told him everything about Adam, and about Daniel and what happened the night before. Rylan lifted her hand, lips brushing her knuckles as her breathing grew panicked. "Norah, don't panic. If he had been found, the town would have heard about it by now. He might not have died."

"But he fell from the cliffs! How could he not?"

Rylan shifted, sitting on the couch beside her and he moved his hand through her hair. "I'll go out later and do a sweep to see what I can find. Tonight you're staying with me though at the main house. I'm not leaving you alone again. One fucking night and this is what happens."

"What do we tell them?"

"About Daniel? We'll just keep it -"

"No, I mean what do we tell them about us? I get that you like me and all that, but...what exactly is this?"

"Jesus we haven't even started and you're already trying to define us."

"Sorry -" he kissed away her apology.

"I'm into you, you're into me - obviously I mean why wouldn't you be - so for now, we're just two people getting to know each other - and hopefully that will include all the benefits that go with it."

She glared at him and he laughed. "I know, I should shut up. Or you could make me."

His eyebrow raised and she laughed weakly at his attempt to cheer her up, before placing a quick peck on his lips.

17. Protection

The air was starting to cool, the warm day coming to an end and Norah tried to hide herself in Rylan's back, escaping the roaring wind.

Rylan had wasted no time dragging her out of the house, she had wanted to stay and grab some things but he promised they would come back tomorrow. At that moment, he just wanted to get her somewhere safe.

Before they left, she showed him what she'd been hiding in her pocket. Rylan had glanced at the diamonds, as if looking at scrap metal. "Do you want to me throw them out?"

Her hand hesitated, fingers unconsciously curling around the stones. "What if he comes back?"

Rylan kissed her forehead, moving his hand over her fist and pressing it closer together. "Keep them for now if you want, but that bastard won't be getting close enough to you to get his hands on them. If it stops you worrying though, I don't care if you hang on to them."

She nodded and had put the diamonds back in her pocket.

Rylan's hand reached down and squeezed her own which were clinging to his waist. He didn't have a jacket on, otherwise she would have put her hands in his pockets. His body was warm, despite the wind, and she spread her fingers across his abdomen, trying to absorb the warmth.

The bike bumped, turning onto a dirt road and she shifted her head, watching the trees blur past. The morning felt like a strange dream. One she'd rather forget. They pulled up in front of the house, the engine cutting off and Rylan sat back. Norah moved with him, her head still resting against his back. She didn't want to go in there and face everyone, to explain everything all over again. She'd rather just drive around and try to forget everything.

"Norah? You letting go anytime soon?"

She shook her head against his back and he chuckled softly, pulling her arms from around his waist. "Do I have to carry you in? Because if I do I have to tell you, I'm not against this plan."

He twisted, pulling her off the bike and standing with her. He reached over to pick her up and she slapped his hands away. "I'll walk."

They both stood still, one waiting for the other to move. When Norah's feet refused to move, Rylan grabbed her hand and pushed her forward.

"They won't bite," he murmured. "Unless they're eating and you try to take their food, because then all bets are off."

Her lips curled at his attempt to make her smile and he seemed satisfied that he got a response from her.

"Do you want me to tell them what happened, or do you want to do it yourself?"

She looked up, mouth opening to take his offer but paused. It was her problem, she knew she should do the right thing and explain it herself, rather than make Rylan do everything. An exhaustion had seeped through her during the ride and rather than play the stubborn independent card, she took his offer to share the load.

Making a decision, she answered, "can we do it together?"

Somehow, this seemed to make Rylan happier and he grinned. "Together then."

Cassie met them at the front door, worry and concern pouring from her face. "What's happened? Lucas told me to expect you."

Rylan squeezed Norah's hand. "Norah was attacked last night."

Cassie's face paled and Norah had a feeling the direction her mind was taking and quickly added, "It was someone I used to know, it wasn't a local."

She didn't use his name, but she knew Cassie had been thinking of Liam and the relief was instant. She masked it but Norah had seen it.

They headed into the kitchen and were met by the older Montoya's; Holden, Aston, Annie and a dark featured man Norah hadn't met yet.

Holden stood up and she felt his gaze move over her. "Who attacked you, Norah?"

His voice filled the large kitchen and though she knew he was a good man, his intimidating presence made it difficult to keep his gaze. "It was someone I knew back home, a man who got my brother into trouble."

Holden stepped forward and took her free hand. Norah had no choice but to let go of Rylan's as Holden guided her into his vacated seat. He turned to Rylan. "Get her a drink, son. Preferably something with a kick."

Rylan moved to the next room and appeared a moment later with a glass and bottle of scotch. Norah opened her mouth to protest but Holden silenced her. "It'll calm those nerves you're trying to hide."

Norah took the glass from Rylan and took a sip, the liquid burning all the way to her stomach. It was a comforting sensation and she took another sip before placing the glass on the counter.

Cassie watched her from the other side, clearly anxious to ask a thousand questions but restraining herself. Aston stood up and moved to stand beside Cassie. "What happened?"

Together, Norah and Rylan recounted the events of the night before and that morning. Norah did her best to explain everything, but every now and then her voice would falter and Rylan would take over and explain what he could while she composed herself.

They listened in silence and Cassie had slowly moved around the counter as they spoke, finishing right beside Norah and she took hold of her hand when they finished. "You poor thing, all this time you've been hiding something so dark as that in your heart. You can stay here as long as you like, you're always welcome here."

Holden growled and she started. "Werewolves, Vampires - they are nothing compared to the monsters of man. His disappearance is somewhat unsettling."

A look passed between Holden and Aston, as if they had come to an understanding. Rylan leaned against the counter, eyes on Norah. "I'm going to go out to the cliffs and take a look around, see if I can figure out what happened. Would you mind giving me a hand, Pete? Everyone else is still at the Mill"

The other man nodded, standing up. "No problem."

Holden moved with them towards the door. "Aston and I will go and ask some questions." He faced "Norah, you'll be safe here, lass. Cassie's tougher than she looks."

Cassie squeezed her hand and Norah sent her a smile. The men walked out and Rylan waited back. Cassie took the hint and left the room.

"Are you all right?" She nodded, looking up at him as he stepped closer. "I'll be back later, I'll let Olivia know what's happened and tell her to come home straight after work."

Norah remembered their interactions that morning and knew they would both have apologies to make.

"Do you need anything from home?"

She thought for a moment and shook her head. "Nothing that can't wait until tomorrow."

He nodded, his fingers brushing her hair behind her ear. "Get some rest, and don't let Cassie drill you too much with questions because

I know she's listening right now, probably with that stupid grin on her face -"

"It is not stupid!" A voice called from the dining room and Norah released a breathy laugh. Rylan kissed her once more before he left and Norah stood up as Cassie returned. Her eyes were shining brighter than before and Norah knew she was bursting to ask about her and Rylan.

Her eyes darted back and forth, fingers twitching as she restrained herself and Norah smiled. "It's okay, you can ask."

"Oh thank god!" Cassie rushed forward and took the seat next to her. "I know I should be taking care of you and offering you tea, but I'm so happy this has finally happened!"

Norah started to stand. "I can make us some tea -"

"Oh no, dear, sit down. I'll handle that. How do you take it?"

"Just black, thank you."

Cassie set about boiling the kettle and turned to face her, teabag in hand. She stared at Norah, who was starting to get uncomfortable before she shook her head. "I'm sorry. I'm just so relieved Rylan found someone like you. He rarely brings girls home and when he does, they are never 'relationship' material. I wish you'd both met under kinder circumstances but I am glad you saved him in the forest that night."

Norah flushed. "He told you about that?"

She nodded. "He told me about it last night. Came home in such a foul mood, I made him tell me what was on his mind and before I knew it he'd told me all about you and how frustrating you were."

She smiled fondly, setting the cups on the counter. "Even though he was angry, I could still see his affection for you. I was a bit upset that you were pushing him away, but deep down I knew you must have had a reason for doing it. When I met you the other night I could tell there was something you were keeping from us."

Norah started. "How -?"

"I have my ways," Cassie grinned, tapping her nose. "Call it a mother's instinct. We know when you are keeping secrets from us. Anyway, I knew it wouldn't be long before he went back to you, I didn't imagine it to happen so quickly but I'm not complaining!"

Norah accepted the warm cup, tracing the rim with her finger. "I'm not sure how to distinguish what our relationship is, but I must admit it is a nice distraction from everything."

Cassie leaned against the counter, eyes sad. "Have you heard from your brother since he was put away?"

Norah and Rylan had left his phone call out, not wanting to explain the diamonds and Norah felt their weight in her pocket when he was mentioned.

"One phone call," she admitted, "but I hung up on him. I didn't want to talk with him."

Cassie nodded, taking a sip of tea. "I hope there comes a time when you can talk to him, I'm sure he never meant to hurt you, it just sounds like he got mixed up with the wrong people. Siblings shouldn't fight."

Her voice grew soft and Norah knew she wasn't thinking of her and Adam anymore. Not wanting her to be sad, Norah agreed to try and talk to him in the future.

Feeling tired, Norah finished her tea and asked Cassie if she could lie down for a little while. "Of course! How terrible I completely forgot that you've been injured. I'll put some ointment on your bruises before you lie down."

She followed Cassie out of the kitchen and up to the second floor. Cassie opened the second door on the right and motioned for her to wait inside. "This is Rylan's room, wait here and I'll be back."

She hurried down the hall and Norah stepped inside, looking around. It was a standard sized room, a double bed sat against two medium sized windows with deep blue curtains half open. A rumpled blue striped doona rested on side, two white pillows rumpled at the head of the bed. A dark wooden desk stood opposite, magazines and books scattered across it. Clothes were all over the floor leading to the built in cupboard on the left side of the room, and Norah resisted the urge to pick them up. The room held his familiar scent and she instantly felt comforted.

Cassie walked in, a small tube in hand and looked about with displeasure. "Sorry about the mess, I refuse to clean up after these boys, you have no idea how messy they all are, I could strangle them some days! I'll speak to Rylan about cleaning up later."

Norah wondered if she should say something about staying in Rylan's room. "I don't mind the mess, I can always stay with Olivia if you would prefer...?"

"Oh no! Don't be silly, we aren't so conservative in this house. We're all adults - apart from Olivia, if she tried to bring a boy home her grandfather would be smacking her hide!"

Norah grinned and Cassie mirrored her expression. "Sit down Norah and show me those bruises."

Norah let Cassie see all the bruises she had accumulated the day before, noticing her worried expression and the way she bit her lip to stop from commenting. Her touch was gentle and Norah found her eyes closing, her body relaxing and Cassie finished helping her put the cream on and gave her a motherly kiss on the head. "Get some sleep, dear. We'll wake you for dinner."

Leaving Norah, she closed the door quietly on her way out. Norah lay back on the bed, head resting on Rylan's pillow and closed her eyes, wishing that when she woke up it would have somehow blanked out all the bad things that had happened in the last twenty four hours.

* * * * *

Norah woke slowly, her head beginning to ache dully as the painkillers had worn off. She felt another weight on the bed and opened her eyes as she recognised the faint smell of floral perfume.

Olivia lay beside her, watching her anxiously. "Did I wake you?" she whispered.

Norah shook her head. "Didn't even hear you come in."

Olivia buried deeper into the spare pillow. "I'm so sorry about this morning, I should have known something was wrong -" Norah reached over and covered her mouth with her hand.

"I know and I'm just as much to blame for not telling you about my problems. Let's just call it even and forget it, okay?"

Olivia nodded, mumbling against Norah's hand. "I called you a bitch though so you get a free bitch to use at any time."

Norah smirked, moving her hand away. "I'll save it, for a rainy day." She looked around, noticing the sun had faded. "Has Rylan come back yet?"

"Not yet, they should be home soon, dinner's almost ready and the men in this family aren't ones to miss a meal. So, you and Rylan, huh? I totally knew it."

Norah couldn't stop the smile stretching across her face. Olivia grinned in return. "So getting married."

"Olivia!" she hissed. "Don't say stuff like that! People can hear you."

"No they can't, the bedrooms are all soundproofed, remember?"

"Oh right. Well, still no talk of marriage. I'm barely wrapping my head around suddenly finding myself in a relationship without thinking of marriage."

Olivia nodded, though Norah could tell she hadn't heard the end of it. "I'm going to head down and give mom a hand with dinner. Did you want to come down?"

Norah nodded and made a detour to the bathroom before following Olivia downstairs. She tried to fix her hair, but it had become a knotted mess and she settled for tying it in a bun. Small shadows underlined her eyes and her skin was still pale. Splashing some water on her face, she hoped it would make a difference, though it probably only accentuated how crap she looked. Not in the mood to care much about her appearance, she gave up and headed downstairs.

The front door opened as she reached the bottom step and Luke and Logan walked in. Norah started to say hello and froze as Charlie followed them in, pulling his shirt on like the two men before him. Putting two and two together, her eyes widened. Charlie looked up in horror at her, knowing she had figured it out. Luke stepped in before Norah could drag Charlie away for an explanation.

"How are you, Norah? You look better since this morning."

"I'm fine, I'll be better when I have my keys back." She stared at him pointedly and he laughed.

Digging into his pocket he pulled out her keys and placed them in her hand. "You're not going to run again, are you?"

Her fingers curled around them. "Not anytime soon. Thank you for today."

He smiled. "Anytime. If you'll excuse me, dinner is calling."

He walked away towards the dining room and Norah grabbed Charlie as he tried to slip by with Logan.

"Norah -"

"Does Wendy know?" she demanded.

He shook his head. "And she never will if I have anything to do with it."

"Do you really think you can hide this from your sister?"

"I can try," he said weakly.

Norah sighed, letting him go. "I hope whatever reason you have for this, it was worth it."

"It was," he said quietly. "You won't -"

"I won't tell her," Norah finished. "But I plan on being there when she finds out, because I have no doubt she will and I look forward to watching her kill you."

"She won't be able to kill me," he laughed lightly.

Norah stared at him. "Wendy is obsessed with werewolf lore, she probably knows on the subject that you. Trust me, she'll be able to kill you."

Charlie's face paled as Norah walked passed him and she released the smile she had been holding back. It amused her that a werewolf was afraid of his human sister who was half his size. Olivia met her at the kitchen door, a knowing smile on her face and Norah grinned. "Do you need a hand?"

"Nope, we're all set. Head on into the dining room."

They went in and met the others who were already seated. Holden and Aston were back, Norah was tempted to ask what they'd found out but she held her tongue. Holden enquired after her health and she assured him she was feeling better. She sat next to Aaron and they started talking about a movie he'd watched the night before while Cassie heaped a plate of food and put it in front of Norah.

"I call dibs on Norah's leftovers," Aaron suddenly said, eyeing her plate.

Everyone groaned, Holden included and Norah laughed quietly. The door opened she sat up taller as Rylan and Peter walked in. Their faces were flushed from running and any sort of appetite vanished in wake of a need to hear what they had discovered. Rylan took the empty seat on her other side and Peter sat opposite her, sending her a grim smile.

Her heart sank.

Rylan touched her leg gently before grabbing his own food and Aaron touched her arm. She looked at him and he mouthed 'after dinner', knowing what she wanted to ask. Everyone had heard what had happened to her by now and she knew it would be rude to ruin their dinner so she waited, hands buried in her lap.

Dinner was a loud affair, everyone talking of their day and the problems at the Mill. Holden spoke of an old friend coming to visit in the coming weeks which had Olivia excited. Apparently it was a Vampire by the ridiculous name of Daddy.

"Daddy?" she asked dubiously.

Olivia nodded. "His real name is Dada or something, he's the head of the Lubau coven, one of the oldest in existence. He comes from Mesopotamia, how awesome is that?"

"Mesopotamia? He must be really old."

"For sure, he's one of the oldest known vampires in existence. Him and Grandad used to work together when Grandad was young. I met him once when I was really little. Rylan met him too, though he didn't know at the time he was a vampire."

Rylan nodded through mouthfuls of food, his eyes on Norah's plate. "Scared the hell out of me he did, one of the largest men I've ever met."

"How does he go...drinking blood?" Norah asked hesitantly, trying not to insult Holden's friend.

"He probably uses donors." Peter joined in.

"What are they?"

"Donors are people who offer basically offer themselves as meal tickets to vampires. The Liberex states that a vampire cannot feed off a human unless they are a donor and then there's a whole other set of laws just for donor's themselves."

Norah started to feel lost, there was so much she still didn't know. Her head still ached and she put off asking more questions about this Liberex until her head could handle it. Olivia and Peter continued to talk about Daddy and what they remembered of him. Rylan nudged Norah and pointed at her food. "Eat something."

She shook her head. "I'm not hungry."

Finishing his bite, he pulled out his phone and typed something, showing it to her below the table -

Try to eat something. Cassie's been staring at you for the last ten minutes.

She stopped herself from looking across the table at Cassie, but now she was aware of her eyes boring into her. She picked up her fork, trying to find something that would be easy to swallow past the lump of worry resting in her throat. Rylan typed something again and she glanced back down -

I can feed you if you want? ;-)

Rolling her eyes, she smiled shrewdly at him. 'Idiot' she mouthed at him and he sent her a wink, grinning.

Finally settling on the cauliflower, she picked at the small pieces, eating slowly until she'd managed to finish both the cauliflower and half of the peas on her plate. The majority of food was still untouched and she started pushing it towards Aaron.

A noise of indignation erupted to her left and she found Rylan looking at her plate in horror. "Why are you giving it to Aaron?"

"Because I called dibs, brother," Aaron grinned pulling the plate towards himself.

Rylan reached over Norah, grabbing at what he could before Aaron snatched it away. "I call dibs on your leftovers for every night from now on."

"You can't call dibs for multiple nights," Logan interrupted, eyeing the full plate with equal disappointment. "You know the dibs rules."

Rylan muttered under his breath and Norah patted his arm in mock sympathy. Rylan had finished his meal and started talking with Logan and Luke about things at the Mill. His hand found hers under the table, their fingers entwining on her lap and she covered his hand with her other, a blush covering her cheeks. Butterflies fluttered in her belly, it had been a while since someone had been so affectionate with her.

It wasn't much longer until all the food was gone and Olivia and Logan started clearing the table. Cassie headed into the kitchen to help and Norah started to rise, intent on helping but Rylan stopped her. Her stomach filled with dread.

"Did you find him?"

Rylan shook his head. "We didn't find him, but we did find evidence of others being there. Others we are more familiar with."

She looked around, wanting to know what was going on. "Liam was there?"

Peter nodded. "We could scent Liam and Nick. They were all over the cliffs and Daniel's scent left with them."

Norah struggled to breath, her grip on Rylan's hand tightening. "Does that mean he's alive?"

Holden cleared his throat. "Aston and I went to pay my grandson a visit and ask him about it. Stubborn lad wouldn't answer us but we could scent another man there, one we weren't familiar with. We traced his scent back to the cliffs you mentioned and I believe it is the same man. We have no other reason but to believe that he is alive."

She breathed deeply through her nose, trying to remain composed. "So, should I leave -"

"No," Rylan growled.

She slapped his hand. "I mean, I don't want to bring any trouble into your family -"

"Norah," Holden said quietly. "I don't think you understand yet. You told us this Daniel fell from the cliffs, that you believed him dead when you saw him. No human could have survived that fall without supernatural help."

Norah thought over his words, chest tightening as she realised their meaning. "They've turned him into a werewolf?"

The room was silent but their answer was deafening. Her body trembled and Rylan inched closer. "Wonderful," she whispered.

"You won't have anything to fear," Aston said gravely. "With the injuries he sustained it will be sometime before his body is fully healed and then they will need to teach him how to control his abilities. If they let him go rogue, which I doubt they will, it will bring not only the Blue Stone Council, but the Council of Nine upon them."

"Council of Nine?"

"The Council of all Supernatural beings," Rylan murmured.

Holden stood up, chair scraping loudly on the floorboards. "It looks like your trouble is now officially our own. If there's anything else we should know tell us now."

Norah shifted uncomfortably. "There is one thing."

She pulled out the diamonds and placed them on the table. Everyone's eyes sharpened and she told them about the stones and Daniel's lust for them. When she was finished there was a pause as everyone stared at the diamonds, slightly allured to their shine before the silence was broken.

"Do you want to hold onto them, Norah?" Holden asked. "We have a safe in the study if you would prefer to keep them there."

Norah nodded, relieved to put the diamonds out of her sight. "That would be great, thanks."

She gave the diamonds to Holden who left the room immediately to be put them away. Everyone started to drift away, doing their own thing for the night and Norah decided to head back to bed. They had had a late dinner and she was still exhausted.

Rylan followed her upstairs and they said goodnight to Olivia as they passed her on the stairs. Closing the door, Rylan grabbed something beside the door. "Your shoe, Cinderella."

Her missing show was held out before him and she took it, smiling. There were teeth marks along the sole and she raised her eyebrow. "Were you chewing on my shoe?"

He chuckled and started searching through the mess that was his cupboard. Pulling out a black shirt, he threw it at her. "Wear this for tonight. We'll get your clothes tomorrow."

Norah hesitated, looking at the shirt. "Can't I borrow something from Olivia?"

"Nope, only clothes you wear in this room are yours or mine."

Norah flushed and turned away, changing into the large shirt which fell just above her knees. Keeping her shorts on, she stood awkwardly at the foot of the bed. It had been alright sleeping on it before when it was just herself. Now, she was more self conscious.

Rylan had stripped down to his briefs and was already climbing onto the bed. Norah sat on the edge. "Don't let me distract from your normal routine. If you want to watch or read something go ahead."

Rylan shook his head. "It's been a mad day, I'm ready for some shut eye. You planning on sleeping at the foot of the bed or you hopping in?"

She hesitated just long enough for Rylan to reach over and grab her arm, dragging her onto the bed. He got up to get the light and she glared at him. "I was getting there," she said hotly.

He rolled his eyes, flicking the light off. The mattress lowered as he climbed back into bed and she pulled the covers up to her chin, rolling away from him to the opposite side of the bed. His arm wrapped around her waist, pulling her back against him and she elbowed him. "Stop dragging me around, dammit."

"Stop being so stubborn and I won't have to," he murmured into her hair.

Not wanting to argue, she closed her eyes, hand curling around his which rested on her stomach, and fell asleep to Rylan's whispered promises of protection.

18. Storms Eye

Birds chirping outside the window were the first thing to drag Norah from sleep and for a brief moment, she forgot where she was. She felt a hand on her waist and yesterday came rushing back in, bringing with it a sense of fear and peace, the emotions warring against each other.

Peace slowly won - it was difficult to feel afraid in Rylan's arms - and she tried to disengage herself so she could go to the bathroom. As soon as she started moving, Rylan's grip tightened and she felt his face bury into her shoulder.

"Where are you going?"

"Bathroom."

He let her go, rolling away and she crawled out, stumbling over to the door. The mess on the floor was dangerous with limited lighting and her OCD for a clean room started to kick in. It was quiet out in the passage, and she quickly went to the bathroom. Her hair was in a mad bird nest and no matter what she did, it wouldn't tame down.

Splashing some water on her face, she went back to Rylan's room to get dressed.

Upon entering however, Rylan proceeded to drag her back onto the bed. "Let me go, I need to get dressed."

"Not yet," he murmured. "Too early."

"It's seven thirty, aren't you late for work?"

He shook his head, the morning light sneaking through the curtains highlighting that his dark hair was just as messy as hers. "I took the day off so we can sort out your house."

"Is it all right for you to take so many days off?" she asked worriedly.

He grinned, kissing the tip of her nose. "It's not very often I ask for a day off and Aston wasn't going to say no."

"Is it Aston who runs the mill? I didn't know that."

Rylan made a noise of agreement. "Holden passed the job onto him a couple of years ago, decided it was time to slowly retire."

Norah bit her lip. "How old is Holden?"

Rylan's hand brushed her hair behind her ear. "How old do you think he is?"

She thought of his strong features, the grey hair and wrinkles which were more distinguishable when he spoke. "Maybe seventy something?"

Rylan chuckled. "He's ninety one."

"What?" She shot up. "Get out."

Rylan laughed, pulling her back down and rolling so he lay half on top of her. "It's true. Holden and Jenna had their kids late in life because they were involved in a few movements during the 1900's.

Cassie is close to sixty herself. It's part of being a werewolf, we age slower than humans."

"How long do you live?" she squeaked.

"The oldest werewolf I've heard of was about one hundred and eighty, he was in the Sun Stone pack. You should ask Holden though, he probably knows others who are older."

"Holy crap," she whispered. Her mind was in overdrive thinking about the aging and how she would get older before him. It was a vain thought, and deep down she knew that it shouldn't matter, but being young, it was an automatic response she couldn't stop.

Rylan, sensing her way of thinking proceeded to distract her. His lips brushed against her own, her hand came up, touching his cheek. The stubble felt rough beneath her fingertips and she traced it along his jaw line, coming up to his hairline as he deepened the kiss. His body shifted, covering her own and his hand rested on her waist, lifting her into him so the space between them was minimal.

Her free hand wrapped around his chest, resting lightly on the middle of his back and her other moved further into his hair. Her body felt hot, a familiar ache settling in her core and she was surprised when Rylan moved back. "What's wrong?"

"Nothing," he said huskily. "I just don't want to rush you after everything that's happened."

She slapped his chest, rolling her eyes. "That's very gentlemanly of you, but trust me, I'd rather be distracted than think about it."

He grinned. "Back to distraction then."

His lips claimed hers once more, this time with more hunger and less gentleness. It was a pleasant distraction and she lost herself in his touch, discovering him with her own.

Knock knock

Rylan groaned, moving to the side and burying his head in her hair. "Olivia," he muttered.

"How do you know it's her?" she whispered breathlessly.

"No one else would be knocking on my door so early in the morning. She'll want you."

"I thought the rooms were sound proof. How can we hear her knocking?"

"Don't know. Some sort of faery wood Holden says. You can't hear anything if you are standing outside but inside, you can others if they make a noise on the wood."

Sitting up, she started to move towards the door but Rylan grabbed her. "What are you doing?" she asked.

"Hoping that if we ignore her she'll go away."

Norah raised her eyebrow. "Does that sound like something Olivia would do?"

He shook his head. "No, she'll just get more demanding."

Sure enough, the knocking sounded again, this time more forceful, as if worried they hadn't heard the first ones. "Let me go."

"This sucks," he muttered.

Norah almost agreed with him but she knew there would always be another chance. Opening the door, Olivia waited on the other side, grinning widely. "Morning! Sorry to wake you."

"No you're not," Rylan muttered and she poked her tongue out at him.

"Do you need some new clothes for today?" she asked Norah.

"I should be all right with my own -"

"No, don't be silly, you had to sleep in those clothes, you should have come and borrowed some pyjamas from me."

Norah glanced wryly at Rylan. "That thought did cross my mind ..."

Olivia grabbed her arm, dragging her out. "Come on, I have the perfect outfit for you."

"Olivia!"

Norah was dragged down the passage and she had forgotten that Olivia was a werewolf too and just as strong as the others. They passed Annie, who'd been out the night before and she smiled, greeting them before Olivia opened a door, shoving her into her room.

Olivia's room was full of colour. The bed linen and curtain matched with white and pale pinks, the walls a pretty cream and covered with photos and pictures from magazines. Olivia moved straight to her wardrobe, which was neater and well kept compared to Rylan's.

"Here." She pulled out a pair of jeans and a plain deep purple shirt. "I know you have to do some cleaning but don't worry about getting them dirty, I'm not fussed."

"I can always change when I get home -"

"No! Just leave them on, why dirty two pairs of clothing in one day? Anyway, I'm coming to help as well, so I'll order Rylan to do everything."

Norah grinned, slipping her other clothes off. "That would be nice, but I'd get too OCD about the things he moves around. I'd rather do it myself."

She heard a small noise of distress and turned, the clean shirt halfway over her head. "What's wrong?"

She followed Olivia's eyes to the bruises on her ribs and quickly lowered the shirt. "Does it hurt?" Olivia said softly.

"No, I'm tougher than that," she smiled. "They'll disappear soon enough."

"Rylan must have been pissed when he saw them last night."

Norah's brows furrowed as she pulled the jeans on, thinking about the night before. "I don't think he saw them. We changed at the same time and I had my back to him."

"Maybe he didn't say something, I'm sure he must have tried to perv on you though. He is a man."

Norah snorted. "I don't know if I feel comfortable discussing Rylan with you. You're his sister after all."

Olivia rolled her eyes, sitting on the bed. "Please, I'm not a child. As long you don't mention any bed action I'll be fine."

Norah laughed, rearranging her hair into a neater ponytail and walked back out. "I'll keep that in mind. Don't you have to work today either?"

Olivia bounced after her. "Nope, Gail gave me the day off. She's training a new girl and she finds it's better when she's on her own. When I'm there she says I try to help them too much and they don't learn how to do it themselves."

They walked into the kitchen and Rylan was already leaning against the counter, drinking a coffee. He pushed two cups towards the girls. "What do you want to do for breakfast?"

Norah opened her mouth to say she didn't mind but Olivia bet her to it. "Let's go to the cafe! I want to ask Gail about her date last night."

"Who is Gail seeing?" Norah asked curiously.

Olivia was beaming. "She's been going out with Paul for the last two weeks. I know she's really into him and Paul feels the same way."

"Of course he does," Rylan muttered, "if he didn't like her, you'd be hounding him like an annoying little pest."

Olivia giggled, drinking her coffee, acknowledging that Rylan was right on the mark. Finishing their drinks, they left a note for Cassie who was still asleep, letting her know where they were going. Olivia offered to drive her car and Norah slipped into the backseat, considerate of Rylan's long legs.

The drive into town consisted mainly of Olivia and Rylan bickering about people they knew and a book they'd both read recently. They passed her driveway and she turned to look back, anxious to see her house again.

Pulling up in front of the cafe, Norah was eager to get out and take a break from the sibling argument. Though they weren't related by blood, it was obvious Rylan and Olivia were brother and sister.

Norah thought Olivia lucky to have two older brothers who were so reliable. The other...well she felt she could relate to her when it came to a bad brother.

Gail smiled, talking with Olivia as they walked in and Rylan and Norah took a seat at her favourite table since the place was still empty at this time of morning. Her thoughts were still on Olivia's brothers and she worried for her friend. Though Liam was going down a dark road, did he still care for his little sister?

"Norah?"

"Hmm?" She found Rylan staring at her.

"Are you all right?"

She nodded, knowing not to bring Liam up. Thought she had only been the Montoya's home twice, she had seen the looks on their faces when his name was even hinted at, and though she was curious about him, she knew better than to pry and ask questions." Just thinking about today."

Rylan reached over, giving her hand a squeeze. "It'll all work out. Now, what do you want to eat?"

Norah browsed the menu, mentioning French Toast and Rylan voiced his disappointment. "That won't be enough. You should get the breakfast stack."

She smiled. "We both know I won't eat all that."

"I know," his eyes gleamed. "Leftovers!"

Olivia walked over with the new girl, Juliet who was a pretty black haired girl with large blue eyes. She took their order hesitantly, writing and scribbling as she made mistakes. Olivia stood next to her, whispering advice, only to quickly sit down when Gail snapped at her to stop helping.

"She won't learn if you coddle her Olivia!"

"I was just offering a suggestion," Olivia called out, sending Juliet a wink.

The young girl smiled gratefully, obviously terrified of her red haired employer. Once she had got their orders set - and some more advice from Olivia - she set off to get the drinks organised. Olivia looked at Rylan's hand on Norah's, a stupid grin resting on her face and Norah elbowed her.

Olivia's grin widened as she looked out the window and Norah turned, biting back a shriek. Wendy and Madison stood on the other side, eyes narrowed onto the hand holding.

"Oh crap," Norah muttered.

Rylan looked up, giving the ladies a nod before returning to the morning paper he'd grabbed from the table over. They disappeared and Norah didn't have to look behind her to know they were coming inside. The door tinkled open and she braced herself. She tried to pull her hand from Rylan's but his grip tightened.

"Just suck it up and get it over with," he said calmly.

Wendy careened into the seat next to Rylan and Madison stood calmly at the head of the table. Wendy's eyes beamed at Norah. "When did this happen?"

"Yesterday."

Wendy squealed, jittering in her chair and Madison placed a hand on her shoulder, like a mother trying to calm an excited child. Wendy turned and slapped Rylan's arm. "About time you opened your eyes and found a decent girl. All the others have been loco."

"Don't count your chickens yet," Rylan said. "Norah's got a fair bit of crazy in her I recon."

The table jolted as Norah kicked him. She knew it wouldn't harm him, but she felt satisfied when her foot connected with his shin. Gail came over, bringing chair for Madison. She spoke quietly in Madison's ear, her voice tinged with concern and Madison nodded, smiling in reassurance. Gail didn't appear satisfied but moved back to the kitchen.

Olivia face was guarded, and she knew Rylan and Olivia had heard the interaction. Rylan was preoccupied joking with Wendy but she figured he had to have heard it. Norah didn't know how they could handle it, listening to everyone's conversations. It would be useful, but terrible at the same time. Wendy and Madison joined them for breakfast, the former asking twenty questions about their current relationship status and where Rylan should take her on a date.

The latter was silent, listening quietly and smiling every now and then. They didn't tell Wendy and Madison what they were doing that day and fortunately they left them after breakfast. Wendy had to open the shop - after threatening Norah with bodily harm if she didn't come in soon - and Madison was working down on the beach. Three times a week she worked as a lifeguard and the rest worked in the towers as a secretary of sorts. According the Madison the men were terrible at keeping up with the paperwork and would be neck deep if she didn't keep it organised.

By this point Norah was anxious to get home. She wanted to get everything cleared and back to normal.

Pulling up out the front of her house, they were surprised that someone else was already cleaning for them.

"Jack." Rylan hopped out first, clearly surprised. "What are you doing up here? Norah is still living here you know?"

Jack glared at him, throwing a broken chair onto his small pile. "I ain't stupid boy, I know she still lives here. Got a call from Holden this morning. He told me what happened and thought I'd come down early and fix it up for the girl."

His eyes moved over to Norah. "You should have told me you had trouble on your heels. Would've looked out for you. Though I hear the wolves have been doing a good job of that."

Norah's eyes widened. "You know about the werewolves too?"

He nodded, reaching over the bottle of whiskey sitting on the veranda. "When you've lived in this town as long as I have, you pick up a few secrets along the way."

"Thank you, for helping, Jack. I'm sorry for any damage to the house. I'll pay of -"

"No you won't," he growled. "This wasn't your fault. I ain't expecting you to pay for this. I'll sort out a deal with Frank on my way back through town to replace the furniture that was broken."

"Jack," Norah said uncertainly, "that doesn't feel right -"

"Let me burn what's here and we'll call it even."

"Done," Rylan interjected. "Norah won't be staying here tonight so you can do it then."

"Right," Jack said, pausing. "All sorted then. I'll leave you to the rest."

Thankfully, he hadn't driven over and he ambled off down the beach, the bottle raising to his lips every now and then.

"I guess we better get started then." Norah said quietly.

They stepped inside and the place was neater than the day before. Everything that had been lying on the floor was stacked neatly on the table and Norah decided to buy Jack a good bottle of Whiskey to say thank you.

Olivia found Norah's laptop and put some music on while they cleaned. Rylan cleaned up the broken glass in the kitchen and Norah and Olivia set to putting her room back together. Daniel had torn it apart looking for the diamonds and everything was on the floor. Once she was finished, she packed a bag to take with her to the Montoya's.

They were done by mid afternoon and Olivia left them to lock the place up. Aston wanted her to come and collect some letters from the Mill and take them to the post office.

Once she was gone, Norah rested against the sink, looking at the main room. Three chairs were broken, and they had decided to throw out the coffee table when they discovered one of its legs had been kicked in and didn't sit right. The damage wasn't as bad as Norah thought it to be, but she still didn't feel easy.

Rylan leaned over her, hands resting on either side of her on the sink. "What are you thinking about?"

"Just wondering if I need new furniture. There's enough here for me to live with."

"I don't think Jack would be happy if you turned down his offer."

She bit her lip. "You're probably right. I was just going to get him some whiskey though. Wouldn't that be better?"

Rylan's eyes were focused on her lips. "What did you say?"

She slapped his chest. "Pay attention."

He shook his head. "Can't. Need a kiss, that might kick start my brain back into action."

Grabbing his shirt, she yanked him forward and kissing him lightly on the mouth. Rylan refused to move back, unhappy with just a light peck and kissed her again. It turned into a slow, languid kiss, the sensation causing a pool of heat to slowly boil in her core. He lifted her up onto the sink and she wrapped her limbs around him -

A phone started ringing. Norah recognised the tone, as Rylan groaned in annoyance.

"You should answer it," she murmured.

He nodded, muttering obscenities and answered the phone. "What? Yes Luke, I'm pissed. What do you want?"

He planted a kiss on Norah's head, walking outside to take the call and Norah grabbed the rest of her things. Grabbing her laptop, she quickly checked her emails and noticed one on the list which killed her good mood.

Adam Jacobs: PLEASE READ NORAH.

Slamming the lid down, she jammed it into its case and walked out to her car, not ready to open that can of worms yet.

19. Hope

Norah woke to an empty bed and knew Rylan must have left for work. Her body still thrummed from the activities of the night before. Rylan had attempted to be a gentleman for as long as he could, but when she crawled into bed in her summer pyjamas, apparently that was the straw that broke the camel's back and she hadn't had them on for five minutes before he was taking them off again.

She stretched and rolled over, reaching up to pull the curtain across. Her bruises ached slightly, but they weren't painful. She knew Rylan had been angry when he'd seen them, but he'd been careful to avoid them and touch them gently if he couldn't avoid it.

Looking at the bedside table, she squinted in the light and saw a note lying on its surface. Picking it up, she grinned as she read it.

Norah. You. Me. Date. After work. Dress casual. Rylan. Ps. Stay safe.

"Is he trying to speak in Morse code or something?" she laughed. She would have to teach him the finer points of writing a letter.

Grabbing her journal, she slipped the note between its pages and rolled out of bed. Picking out some new clothes, she slipped across the hall to the bathroom, saying good morning to Logan as he rushed past, obviously late for work.

"Morning Norah," he ran past her.

"Run Forest, run!" She heard him chuckle as he ran down the stairs. The Montoya's bathroom was two times larger than her own and she was slightly envious of the larger shower head. It was like a waterfall. She showered quickly, trying to keep her mind occupied and failing.

Adam's email continued to enter her mind and try to tempt her to read it. Last night during dinner she had struggled to keep her mind in the moment, it continued to drift to the email and because she wasn't eating, Luke and Rylan were arguing over who got her leftovers because they thought she was finished. In the end she had halved her plate and though they both weren't satisfied, it shut them up.

She could have stayed in the shower forever, but she was conscious that this wasn't her home and she didn't want to waste water. Drying her hair, she slipped on a white and blue striped shirt and blue denim shorts. Norah enjoyed the warm weather but she was beginning to miss the rain. It was one of her favourite smells; rain on a cold morning. Leaving her hair out to dry some more, she made her way down to the kitchen for breakfast.

She heard quiet voices talking and one stopped just before she walked in. Cassie and Annie were standing near the sink, faces visibly distressed.

"Good morning," Norah said awkwardly.

Cassie muttered a reply before slipping out, eyes red with tears. Norah looked at Annie. "I'm sorry, I didn't mean to interrupt -"

"No dear, it's all right." Annie wiped her eyes which were red as well.

"Is everyone all right?"

Annie hesitated. "Last night, Liam confronted Holden at the Mill. They were arguing about the leadership and Liam refused to leave. They got into a fight."

"Is Holden all right?" Norah stepped forward, anxious.

"He'll be fine, it will take more than a cocky youth to bring him down, as he would say," Annie gave her a watery smile. "He's got a few injuries but they'll be healed by tonight. Being a bit older, his ability to heal isn't as good as it used to be."

Norah had a feeling Annie was playing his injuries down but she didn't say anything. "What about Liam? Was he okay? Is that why Cassie -?"

"No, Liam was fine, a couple of minor injuries I believe Aston said -"

"Aston was there?"

She nodded, biting her lip. "He was stopping his own son, Nick from joining in with Liam. Nick's a strong boy, but he would never attack his father."

"Poor Aston," Norah said quietly.

"It's a difficult situation for everyone," Annie turned to busy herself at the sink so Norah wouldn't see her tears. "Family fighting against each other, it's painful on the heart, especially on Cassie's. She's a gentle soul and having everyone she loves at each other's throats is slowly eating away at her. Holden refuses to let everyone speak of Liam in the house which Cassie finds difficult to do. She has already denounced him as our future leader, which was a difficult choice for her to make. To never be allowed to speak of him, or see him - it's breaking her heart."

Norah reached over, touching Annie's shoulder. "What about you? They're your family as well."

Annie turned, attempting to smile. "They are, and it does pain my heart, but someone needs to be strong and during these hard times, that role has fallen on me. Luke will follow what his grandfather orders at this stage. I know this separation from his brother has been equally hard on him, but he won't say it. The boys all tend to clam up and believe they are doing what is right. Olivia smiles and puts on a brave face, but she loves her brothers dearly and this is affecting her more than she lets on. Everyone is hiding or drowning in their emotions, they need someone to help keep the family together, and when Cassie has days like these, that responsibility falls to me."

Annie turned back to the dishes. "I don't mind, I like to help where I can, and if this is all I can do for them, then I will work my hardest to give them what happiness I can."

Not thinking, Norah gave Annie a quick hug. "They're lucky to have you and Cassie looking out for them. So much testosterone needs a couple of clear headed women to put them in order."

Annie patted her hand. "We're lucky to have them, and Rylan is lucky to have you. He was good friends with the boys growing up and I know he's been keeping his feelings on the matter well guarded."

Norah stepped back, looking around the kitchen, suddenly wanting to do something for all of them. "Can I do anything to help you this morning?"

"No dear, I'll just be doing some tidying up and talking with Cassie. When she gets this emotional she can be quite difficult to handle. I'd recommend you get out of the house and get some fresh air, let everything calm down. I hope you don't feel like I'm pushing you out -"

"No, not at all. I've been meaning to catch up on some reading and writing. I might head down to the cafe and see Olivia." If Cassie was feeling like this, then Olivia would need someone too.

"Oh that's perfect. Olivia did a run to town this morning and I think she'll need her car to get home. It's meant to rain early this evening. Would you mind driving it in for her? I can come and pick you up later -"

"No that's fine. I'll be back early this afternoon, I don't mind the walk."

"All right then." Norah left her in the kitchen and grabbed Olivia's keys from the rack out front. Her car was more modern than her own, and she marvelled at such a comfortable drive. She loved her own car, she'd had it for so long now, but it was nearing its last days and she knew it was probably time to start looking for a new one. She was living in the past with that vehicle. It was time to step forward.

She knew Olivia liked to park her car around the back in the parking lot for the grocery store and she pulled in there before heading for the cafe. It was full of tourists, who had come down to enjoy the last few warm days of summer. Their children ran around the cafe, screaming and shouting for their parents to pay them attention. The noise of yelling and chatter was deafening, and Norah managed to find an available table near the back where it was a bit quieter.

Juliet hurried past, hair frazzled from working her first busy period. Gail could be heard shouting from the kitchen and Olivia snapping back, unafraid of her boss. It was too busy to try and talk to Olivia, so she decided to wait, thinking at least Olivia was being kept distracted from any unhappy thoughts.

Norah pulled out the book she had grabbed before she had left, Sense and Sensibility by Jane Austen. She'd read it a few times in her life, and with everything that had been happening in the last few weeks, she needed something old and familiar to lose herself in. Something that would bring comfort.

Juliet came over, a coffee already in hand and placed it down with a rushed smile. "Olivia said to give this to you. Do you need anything else?"

"No I'm fine. Are you all right Juliet?"

She nodded frantically, appearing on the edge of a mental break down. "I'm fine." She rushed off.

Poor girl, Norah opened her book. The sounds of the cafe slowly dimmed as she became immersed in the story of the Dashwood girls. She had always loved the comparisons between Elinor and Marianne.

They were so different in their personalities and their approaches to life and love, but it was still so painful to see the hardships they went through. Elinor with the awful Miss Steele and her affection towards Edward, and Marianne's affection for Willoughby while Norah had always wanted her to be with Colonel Brandon, regardless of his age.

It made Norah wonder which Dashwood she would be. Sometimes she felt she was both. She would try to be like Elinor, hiding her emotions so the world didn't know she was suffering, then there were days she felt like Marianne, wanting to be free to express her feelings without caring what others thought.

Every now and then, Adam's email slipped through the cracks in her mind and distracted her from the book. It continued to plague her, demanding attention and she wondered what he would want. To sell the diamonds and give him the money one he got out? Reason with Daniel? Had he met a new BFF in jail and wanted her to help him out with something?

She had read the same page three times before putting it down in defeat. Why couldn't Adam just leave her in peace? She loved him, but just the thought of him made her so frustrated -

"Norah?"

She jumped. Madison sat opposite her, a wry smile on her face. She hadn't even noticed her sit down. "You nearly look as frustrated as Wendy when I left her just now."

"Sorry, is she all right?"

Madison frowned. "No, she's on the phone to Dante, arguing over the shop again."

"Dante needs to just let her, and the shop go. He's the one who walked away from that relationship, right? He has no one to blame but himself."

Madison nodded. "I think Wendy was trying to explain that to him, though not in such pleasant words."

Norah laughed lightly. "How are you, Madison? Have you talked to Wendy yet?"

"No," she said quietly. "Dante is still a big problem for her, I should wait until she has it resolved."

"I have a feeling you're going to be waiting a long time for that ship to sail."

"True. Are you all right, Norah? You've seemed a bit stressed the last few days?"

"Just family problems coming back to bite me in the arse," Norah muttered.

Madison looked at her for a moment, seeming to come to a decision. "Why don't we go for a walk? The cafe isn't the best place to relieve stress at the moment."

Norah agreed and got up to pay for her coffee. Olivia was busy and Norah managed to pass her the money and keys for her car before she was swamped by other customers. She didn't look upset though her eyes had a hint of stress about them, Norah couldn't determine if it was from work or family problems.

"See you tonight!" Olivia called out and Norah gave her a wave as she stepped out with Madison. She would try and talk to her later, and make her sure she was okay after everything the night before.

Madison turned left, heading up the next block before turning left again and heading down a side street. Norah still hadn't explored Bellvale properly so she didn't know all the side streets. It just looked like any other suburban street. The houses were all creams and whites, made of sandstone and brick. Many had their windows open, curtains playing in the breeze.

They passed a few young kids playing a ball game in the middle of the road but other than that it was quiet. Everyone stuck to the main streets and the beach on a day as nice as this. They walked in silence, neither having much to say, when Madison spoke first.

"How are things with you and Rylan?"

"Going well, I think. It's all still pretty new so I don't want to oversell it."

Madison smiled. "He's obviously very smitten with you."

"I don't think he'd like the word smitten used to describe himself." Norah grinned.

"I suppose not, he's quite a card though."

"Card?" Norah teased. "What century are you from again?"

"It's from Gail," Madison laughed. "I often wonder what century she is from myself, sometimes she uses the most unique words. She's very new age, I think."

Norah remembered Gail's concern for Madison. "Are the two of your close?"

"Yes, my mother died when I was a young teenager and my step dad pretty much left town the day after her funeral. Gail took me in and helped me finish school. She was there for me after Parker died too. She's basically been a second mother to me."

"I'm glad you had someone like her around for everything." They reached the end of the street and Norah looked at their destination in surprise. "The old High school?"

Madison stood next to her. "It's all locked off," Madison explained, "but what I want to show you is around the back."

They slipped through a hole in the gate, meant to keep trespassers out and Norah chastised her. "I never would have pinned you for a law breaker."

"I have my wild streak, it's just not so wild as everyone else's," she protested.

The building was quite dilapidated after years of neglect. Norah wondered why they hadn't torn it down or done something else with it. The town was small but surely they could use the land for something? The lawns were still maintained, but the garden ran wild. Weeds and tree trunks poking through cracks in the bitumen were telltale signs of how long it had been since the school had been closed.

They walked around the back of the school and Norah stared in amazement. The back wall was made of red brick, and stretched the length of the tennis court adjacent. The red brick was faded, and difficult to be seen with the coloured writing covering every available space.

"We called it the Hope Wall," Madison explained. "I don't know who started it, the janitor used to try and clean them off, but the student's hopes just kept coming back and in the end he gave up."

"It's amazing," Norah whispered. Walking along, she read a few different coloured words. Peace, love, success - so many dreams covered the wall, Norah felt stunned into silence.

Madison stopped about halfway down, fingers touching a small space. Her eyes were glazed with longing and Norah read the words - To be happy.

No words could define that moment. Norah stood silently beside Madison, reading the hopes of hundreds of students and wondering if their hopes had come true. The word power, stood out near Madison's written in bold black paint and it unnerved her, that someone would write something so vain.

"Here." Madison pulled out a permanent marker and handed it to Norah. "You should add yours."

"No, I wasn't a student here -"

"You don't have to be," Madison smiled. "It's become more than that. I know many people who never attended this school who have written their hopes on the wall. You're a part of this town, Norah. Your hopes deserve to be up there with ours."

Norah looked at the marker in her hand. "Why did you have a marker in your pocket?"

"I grabbed it at the cafe on the way out. I'm not weird and just carry around a marker all the time."

"Sure sure," Norah teased.

She walked away, looking for a space to add her own hopes, and found a small space near the bottom of the wall. She crouched down, thinking of what she wanted to write. Many thoughts filtered through her mind, many of the words she thought of were already spread across the wall, she wanted to add something different. One word stood out above the rest and after looking across the wall and not seeing it, she added it to the wall. She wrote the one word, tracing the lines repeatedly so it wouldn't get washed away by any future rain. It wasn't just a hope for herself; but a hope for everyone she had come to care about in Bellvale.

Safe.

20. Date

Not long after she'd left Madison, Norah headed back to the Montoya's, stopping in at her house on the way. Everything had been cleaned, the furniture had been replaced, save for two of the kitchen chairs, but they weren't necessary.

Norah wasn't sure what Rylan had in mind for a date, but she didn't think it would be anything to elaborate, so she grabbed a clean pair of jeans and a light cardigan to wear with a singlet she had at their house.

Walking up the long road, she felt a bit nervous being out on her own again. Normally she enjoyed her time alone, but after everything that had happened, she was feeling nervous of walking around so close to the forest. The trees loomed to her right, and unconsciously she moved to the other side of the road. Her cell phone started ringing, giving her a fright.

"Hello?"

"Norah!" Alice's familiar voice eased the tension from her shoulders.

"Hey Alice, how's everything?"

"The same, but what about you? We haven't seen Daniel in a few days - I think it might be safe to come home -"

"No..." She started to say more but kept her mouth shut. If Alice knew that Daniel had found her, she would freak out and drive down to drag her home. "I haven't heard from him, but I think it's a bit early to head back yet." I suppose," Alice said uncertainly. "How's the boy you're hiding from me?"

She rolled her eyes. "He's fine, I'm heading to his house right now."

"So things are getting serious?" Alice demanded. "Are you wearing appropriate underwear?"

"I'm wearing comfortable underwear if that's what you mean."

"No! God, you are the un-sexiest woman ever."

"Thank you?" They spoke about proper dating attire and Norah tried to remain evasive. Alice had a bad habit of getting too involved whenever Norah started dating. She would try to primp her into a girly girl with lace underwear and dresses which did nothing to cover her modesty.

The Montoya's driveway came into view and the brown fallen leaves crunched under feet as she hit the dirt. "I have to go Alice, it's been good catching up."

"It has, you better come home soon, I miss your face. Also..." her voice grew quiet. "Adam got in touch with me and I gave him your email address."

"I know, he sent me an email a couple of days ago."

"You're not mad?"

"Yes and no. I haven't read his email yet. I'm not in the mood to be listen to his excuses."

"I know you Norah," she could hear Alice's smile. "You're angry now but you one day you'll realise that you still love that stupid head and you'll be ready to listen."

"I hate when you're right," Norah muttered. They hung up as the house came into view and Norah hesitated at the front door, wondering if she should knock first or just walk in.

"Come in," Holden's voice sounded from the sitting room to her left and she jumped. Pushing the door open, she met Holden in the entrance way. His face was grey and for the first time, he looked closer to his actual age. His eyes were sunken, dark circles under them and he leaned against the door.

"Are you all right, Holden? Should you be out of bed?"

"Never better," he growled. "Damn women trying to keep me in bed all day, I'll go mad."

"It's only because we're worried about you." Norah looked around for Cassie or Aston. "Where is everyone else?"

"Cassie is in the kitchen, and everyone else is out."

"I think you should sit down," Norah said suddenly as Holden slouched more. She could see the white of a bandage beneath the collar of his shirt. He started to argue, but Norah, feeling brave, grabbed his arm and started dragging him back to the armchair placed near the window. "I know you're a big tough creature of myth, but even they need to rest to recover...I think."

Holden sat down, glancing at her wryly. "You remind me of Jenna."

"Your wife?" Norah remembered.

He nodded, letting Norah adjust the pillow behind his back. "You have the same temperament. Quiet and polite, but deep down you have a hidden strength that surfaces when those around you need protecting."

"Um, thank you," Norah replied.

"Rylan better not stuff this up with you. First decent girl he's bloody brought home."

Norah burst into laughter. "I hope not either."

After extracting a weak promise from Holden to rest, Norah headed into the kitchen. The door was closed and she opened it cautiously. Cassie stood near the sink, scrubbing a large pot. "Hey Norah," she didn't look up. "Take a seat."

Norah was already heading towards her and she grabbed a tea towel and started drying the dishes.

"Oh you don't have to do that," Cassie tried to pull the tea towel away from her but Norah jumped back.

"I want to. You are letting me stay and I need to feel like I'm pulling my weight somehow or I'll feel guilty."

Cassie let go of the tea towel, a soft smile playing on her lips. "Okay then. After this I need to shell some peas for dinner, would you mind helping?"

"Of course." Norah explained that she may have to leave early with Rylan, but Cassie was delighted.

"Do you know where he's taking you?"

"No clue, his note was very abrupt this morning."

"I'm sure it will be lovely, he's a good boy."

Norah placed another dry plate in her growing pile. "Rylan's lucky you were all took him in."

Cassie paused, hands in the sink. "His mother's actions were wrong, but in a strange way," she lowered her voice, "I'm glad she left him here. Rylan is my child, now and forever and if his birth mother ever tried to come back and lay some sort of claim over him, I'd send her packing."

"You talk as though he's still a child."

"To me, he always will be. It doesn't matter how old our children get, Norah, we always see them as our children who need protecting. One day, when you have children you'll come to understand that. And I agree with Holden too," Cassie added. "Rylan better not stuff this up."

Norah grinned. "You were listening?"

"Just a little bit," she admitted. "I'm more keeping an ear out in case Holden tries to make a break for it." She spoke the last part louder, so Holden would hear clearly and Norah laughed. She heard a door shut down the hall and Cassie grinned.

"Are you okay, after this morning?" Norah asked uncertainly.

"Yes, I'll be fine." Cassie brushed the matter aside and Norah could see the tension in her shoulders. They worked in silence for a little while, each asking a question every now and then. Norah found herself telling Cassie about her home and Alice and Ray. They started unshelling peas, and Cassie told Norah a few embarrassing stories about Rylan when he was younger. She made sure to tuck them away should she need them for future teasing.

The tension around Cassie's eyes hadn't faded though, and Norah spoke up one last time. "Cassie, I know I may be out of line here, but if you ever need to talk about anything, I'm happy to listen. I know everything that is going on can't be easy for you."

Her smile faded, and she played with the green shell in her hands. "I'm just being silly, I know, but I'm worried about the Gathering coming up."

"Gathering?"

"It's like an anniversary of our creation. A few packs get together and we just have a party, before doing a midnight run. It's a yearly tradition...one Liam has never missed."

"Are you afraid, something's going to happen?"

She nodded. "What if he tries coming and starts another fight? I won't know what to do, I couldn't bear to watch -"

Norah grabbed her hands. "I don't know Liam that well, but he sounds like he has some common sense," Norah spoke carefully, not wanting to upset Cassie further. "I doubt he'll do anything with so many people - err, werewolves in one place. It isn't logical."

Cassie nodded. "You're probably right." She brushed the unshed tears away and sat taller. "Rylan's home. You should go and get ready."

Norah hesitated, not wanting to leave Cassie in such a vulnerable state. Cassie saw her concern and smiled. "I'll be fine, dear. Even better when you come back and tell me if that son has a romantic bone in that body of his."

Leaning over, she gave Cassie a kiss on the cheek and headed out. She met Rylan in the entranceway and he grinned. "How's your day been?"

"Interesting." She smiled, feeling more at ease in his presence.

"You ready to head out?"

"What should I wear?"

He looked at her. "Less, you should wear less."

Rolling her eyes, she hit him. "Be serious."

He chuckled. "What you're wearing is fine, though wear some sturdy shoes."

She went and grabbed her runners while Rylan checked in Holden and Cassie. She waited outside, enjoying the quiet of the surrounding forest. There was no wind, and she closed her eyes, enjoying the warmth from the sun. If there wasn't some slightly power crazed werewolves running around beyond the trees, she might actually like to live here; away from civilisation and the worries of the world.

Gravel crunched beside her and she opened her eyes to Rylan's lips on hers. "Finished day dreaming?"

"No, you interrupted."

"Oh well, you don't have to dream about me anymore, the real deal is here."

"Oh god," she groaned. He grabbed her hand, pulling her past the motorbike and she frowned. "I thought we were going somewhere?"

"We are." They headed towards the forest and Norah dug in her heels.

"We're going in there? B-but there's..." She didn't say anymore, worried Cassie might be listening and Rylan stepped closer.

"You're safe with me, and there won't be any danger where we are going." Norah knew he meant Liam's little pack and frowned.

"Are you sure?" He kissed the tip of her nose. "Positive."

She let him drag her into the forest, the temperature cooling slightly in the trees and she pulled her jacket closer around her. "So, where are you taking me?"

"Somewhere nice and secluded."

"To kill me?"

"Damn," he grinned. "Figured me out already, huh?"

"If you're going to kill me, at least bury me somewhere pretty, like...under that tree." She pointed to a large oak with bright green leaves.

He groaned. "That sounds like work, I was just going to drop you over the cliff."

Norah flinched, memories of her fight with Daniel resurfacing and Rylan paused, realising his error. "Shit, always saying the wrong bloody thing."

"It's okay, I know. So, Cassie was telling me about this Gathering coming up."

He cleared his throat. "Yeah, it's basically an excuse to get drunk and party. You're invited of course."

"Ah, already trying to get me drunk?"

He grinned, climbing on top of a fallen tree. "Nothing wrong with loosening up every now and then."

"Especially if it means making it easier to get my clothes off?"

Rylan crouched down and lifted her up as though she weighed nothing more than a baby. They stood on top of the trunk, Rylan smirking. "I do like you better when you're naked."

Annoyed, she pushed him and he fell to the ground. "Hey!"

"You'll be fine," she muttered. She tried to get down herself, but the tree was large and she slipped. Rylan moved fast, grabbing her before she hit the ground.

"Should I just carry you the rest of the way?"

"No thanks, you'd enjoy that too much. I can't have you too over stimulated, I won't be able to handle it."

Rylan put her down, reclaiming her hand. "Just being with you is overstimulating."

"Oh come on!" She laughed, hiding her face with her free hand. "That is so cheesy, I can't bear it!"

"Come on, girls love all that cheesy stuff." He protested.

"What sort of girls do you date that enjoy that?"

"The normal kind."

She frowned. "So, I'm not normal?" She tried to pull her hand away in mock indignation, but Rylan pulled her closer, gripping her hand tighter.

"You're better than normal. You're part crazy, part weird and part frustrating. My type of girl. How's that for cheesy?"

Norah couldn't help but grin. "I'll allow the cheesiness, for now."

They walked on, Norah told him about seeing Madison and visiting the Hope Wall. She asked him if he'd put something up there. "My last day of school, Luke and I added our own words to the wall."

"What did you write?"

"Family."

"The Montoya's?" Rylan nodded, they moved to single file as the gap between the trees narrowed.

"Have you heard anything about my past?"

"Yes, bits and pieces."

"The story going around town is relatively true," he explained, "with a few important factors taken out." His voice became hard. "My mother was addicted to a substance called Pixaine. What's that? It's a supernatural drug, though most people know it as Euphoria. It's basically a concentrated dose of Pixie dust and morning dew. To the supernatural, it gives you a little kick, kind of like Speed. To humans, it's more like crystal meth. Your sense of reality fades and everything supernatural is suddenly more clear. I don't know how my mother got hooked on it, but it slowly ate away at her. She could barely look after herself, let alone me. Eventually, her supplier came searching for her when she failed to pay and things started getting out of control. We jumped on a train and ended up in Bellvale.

"I had no idea my mother planned on abandoning me," he stopped walking. "I knew we were running from bad people, but I always believed I was the one thing she couldn't live without. She told me to hide in the woods and that she'd be back soon. I was there all night."

Rylan still held her hand, and his grip tightened. "The Montoya's found me early in the morning. I didn't know anything about werewolves or the supernatural back then, only bits and pieces I picked up from my mum, so when two wolves suddenly turned into two naked men, I freaked out. Ironically, that turned out to be the best day of my life. Cassie has been the best mother I could ever ask for."

"Do you ever wonder what happened to your real mother?"

"Sometimes."

The density of the forest thinned out and Norah grabbed Rylan's arm. They stood in a small clearing, near the cliffs and the sound of the waves became more prominent once they were out of the trees.

"You really weren't joking about throwing me off a cliff," she said weakly.

Rylan chuckled and pulled her forward a bit more before sitting down. "Don't worry, I would never do something foolish like that - not while I still have use of your body, anyway."

"Ha ha," she smacked his arm but didn't let go, still nervous.

Rylan pried his arm free and wrapped it around her shoulder. "I used to come here all the time growing up."

"Really?" Norah glanced across at him.

"Yeah, back then, I struggled to fit in with the others and I still missed my mother. I found this place one day and I would keep coming back, whenever I felt alone."

"And you wanted to share it with me?" Rylan coughed, muttering under his breath in agreement and Norah smiled, resting her head on his shoulder. "Apart from the proximity to the cliffs, I love it here. Not bad for a first date."

"What's my reward?"

She elbowed him. "Is not my lovely presence enough?"

"I guess it will do," he muttered dejectedly.

Norah grinned and turned her head, kissing his jaw line. "Better?"

He kissed her forehead in return. "It will do for now. My feelings may need more appeasing soon though so you better pick up your game."

Rylan started talking about having to go on watch that night, and Norah picked at a hole in her pants, wanting to ask something that she'd been curious about. "Can I ask...when you change into a werewolf, does it hurt?"

"Not as much as it used to. When I first changed I thought my body was being torn to shreds, now it's a...familiar pain, I guess. Nothing I can't handle. I'll show you."

He stood up and Norah reached for him. "What are you doing? Now?"

He started taking his clothes off and Norah covered her eyes. "Rylan put your clothes back on!"

"You've seen me naked, Norah. More times than I've seen you naked, which I'm not too happy about by the way."

"You'll get over it," she snapped.

"Just open your eyes." Moving her hands away, she stared at his face, though her eyes were demanding their attention was needed lower. He crouched down and she jumped when she heard a large snap.

"What - ?"

"Don't freak out," was all he said. He looked down and she watched, mesmerised as his body seemed to ripple, the muscles twisting and white fur appearing everywhere. Bones cracked, making her curl inward and then she blinked, and a white wolf sat in front of her.

"Holy crackers, that looked awful," she whispered. He crawled forward, touched his nose to her own and then hung his tongue out like a fool.

She snorted, looking at him. "Does it feel weird, being like that?" He shook his head and she laughed. "Oh god, this feels so weird, talking to a wolf."

He touched her hand with his paw and then nuzzled his head against it. Hesitantly, she reached up and touched his fur. Under his neck, it was soft but on his back it was coarser. She traced the outline of his muzzle, finding it all fascinating, when Rylan pounced and she fell backwards. She heard the bones cracking and then a very naked Rylan lay on top of her.

"Was jumping on me really necessary?" she complained.

He nodded, eyes hazy. "Can't have you running away after seducing me like that."

"What?" she laughed.

"Groping my body like that, there's only so much a man can take, you know."

"Oh come on, I was not groping you, and you wanted me too! I think."

"Of course I wanted you to, what man doesn't want his woman to grope them, why should the man do all the work? Now, no more talking, it's my turn."

He kissed her, silencing her argument and it wasn't long before they were both naked and the sun had set before they had any thought of putting them back on.

21. Fangs & Fur

They returned to the house in time for dinner and it was a small group tonight. Aston was busy at the Mill with Paul, and Logan and Aaron were on perimeter watch. Norah was surprised to see Charlie sitting at the table.

"Why are you here?"

His face was dark, and he jabbed at his vegetables savagely. "Wendy's in a bad mood."

"Oh, is that because of her ex? Madison was telling me -"

"When did you see Madison?" His eyes lit up and she refrained the urge to roll her eyes.

"Calm your jets, lover boy. I saw her earlier in town. And no, she didn't talk about you."

"I never asked that," he snapped.

"You didn't have to," Rylan spoke between the food in his mouth, reaching for food on Norah's. "You're pussy whipped."

"Language, Rylan!" Cassie snapped from the head of the table, shocking Annie next to her. Luke and Holden looked up from their conversation, amused and Rylan bowed his head.

"Sorry, Cassie." Olivia grinned playfully and Rylan stuck his tongue out. "Anyway, you are, man. Just ask her out already and be done with it."

"What, like you did with Norah?" Charlie scoffed. "You were worse than me, always hanging around her, finding excuses why it should be you staying at her place -"

Rylan kicked him under the table and Norah glanced at him wryly. "You sound like a stalker."

"I prefer determined scallywag," he muttered, taking a huge chunk of meat off her plate.

"So," Olivia got Norah's attention. "What did you two get up to this afternoon?"

Norah's cheeks reddened and she focused on her food. "Nothing big, just went for a walk in the forest. Rylan revealed how he's going to kill me in the future - that sort of thing."

"If he kills you," Olivia glared at her brother. "I'll avenge you. Charlie will help, won't you?"

He nodded. "Definitely. I already have the perfect plan in mind."

"Oh, tell me more!"

Norah listened as Charlie told Olivia his devious plan of ending Rylan's life. It was a strangely entertaining conversation and Norah laughed as Rylan vehemently protested the use of a blow torch, arguing that electrical torture would be more effective, when the room fell silent.

Norah's smile faded, watching the way their gazes sharpened, as if listening to something elsewhere. "What -?"

They all shot up from the table, rushing from the room and Norah looked at Annie in shock. She smiled apologetically, though her eyes revealed her concern. "It would seem something has happened. Come on, dear."

Norah followed Annie out to the foyer and caught Annie as she collapsed, crying in shock. Logan crouched in the doorway, covered in blood and Aaron lay unconscious in his arms. Luke knelt beside them, eyes burning with fury. "Liam?"

Logan nodded. "I'm sorry Luke, they came out of nowhere - we were outnumbered - "

Luke slapped his shoulder, gripping it tightly. "It's okay. You did well getting Aaron back here. How bad is the damage?"

"A few stomach wounds," Logan stared at his brother with worry, "and I think his spleen might be damaged."

Holden stared into the night, a low growl emitting from his throat. "Cassie, take the boys inside and take care of them with Annie."

"I want to stay," Cassie cried. "I want to see -"

"Now!" Cassie turned away, eyes red with unshed tears and helped her sister with Logan and Aaron. Olivia trembled beside Norah, and unconsciously grabbed her arm.

"What's wrong?" Norah whispered.

"He's here," her voice shook.

The four men went on guard, Rylan moving in front of the girls as five figures melted from the shadows. Four were large wolves, their muzzles matted in blood, their teeth bared, glistening under the waxing moon. In the centre was a familiar figure, though unclothed. Unabashed at his naked appearance, Liam stepped into the dim light emanating from the house, eyes blazing.

"What are you doing here?" Luke growled.

Liam's lips curled. "Why brother, is that any way to welcome me home?"

"You're no longer welcome here," Holden's voice was deceptively calm. Norah could see his hand shaking with fury.

"Do you think you can stop me?" Liam glanced his grandfather as if he were nothing more than an ant. "Your attempts last night certainly proved that impossible."

The sound of bones snapping filled the foyer and Norah grabbed the back of Rylan's shirt, beginning to wonder why she was here. She wanted to turn tail and hide, but Olivia's grip held her in place. Norah felt Liam's eyes land on her as he perused the group, the blue irises honing in on her.

"I see you have a new whore, Rylan."

He growled, Norah's grip on his shirt stopping him from moving forward. Liam smiled. "I have a new friend who is just dying to be reacquainted with you."

Her heart stuttered.

Rylan immediately stepped back, reaching around to grab her free arm. Olivia's grip tightened and she stepped closer.

"Enough, brother." Luke stepped forward, putting himself between Liam and the Montoya's. "Do not do this. This is between you and me."

"It is between all of us," Liam hissed. "By causing our family to choose sides, you made it about everyone. Those of you who chose the wrong side, must bear the punishment."

Olivia's grip vanished and she slipped past Rylan before he or Norah could stop her. "Liam," she whimpered, standing beside Luke. "Please don't do this."

For a moment, Liam's expression faltered and Norah thought she could see a hint of guilt in his eyes. But before she could blink, it was gone and his face was a wall. "I'm sorry, Olivia. But this is the way it has to be."

In a flash, the wolves howled and Liam lunged forward, shifting mid leap. Luke shoved Olivia behind him, Norah heard bones snapping as the others prepared to join in. Rylan shoved her away.

"Go and find Cassie -"

The growl cut off, replaced with a yelp.

Peering under Rylan's arm, Norah's eyes widened. A large man stood in front of Luke, his tanned skin glowing in the moonlight. He held Liam - in wolf form - one large hand around his throat. Liam's legs kicked and fought to break free.

Another man stood in the shadows, watching the other wolves. The monster man turned slightly, his soft brown eyes landing on Holden. "Greetings, friend. Have I interrupted?"

His voice held a faint trace of an accent - maybe something European. Holden's body relaxed, his body returning to normal. "You haven't interrupted anything, old friend. My grandson here was just leaving."

"Grandson?" He looked at Liam, lip curling with disgust. "Where I come from, you respect your family, not attack them. Had you been my grandson, you would be dead already."

He threw Liam, and Olivia gasped as he hit a tree, yelping in pain. The other wolves slowly backed away. Norah could feel the power radiating from the two newcomers. It was cold and powerful, making her heart beat increase and her skin shiver.

They stood in silence, watching the wolves melt away into the darkness and it was only when the large man turned around did Norah breathe again.

"Come in," Holden said quietly. He stepped inside, the other man close behind. He had similar dark hair to the large man, though shorter and smoothed back from his face, which was whiter in comparison to the big man. His blue eyes took them in calmly, unaffected by what had just happened. There was a stillness about them that was unnatural, and Norah had a strange urge to run away.

"This is an old friend of mine, Gregori, of the Kammani Coven," the large man introduced his friend. Gregori introduced himself to Holden politely and the head of the family introduced them all in turn.

"Everyone," he said finally, "this Dada Lu-bau of the Lubau Coven."

"Daddy is fine," the large man said to them all. Norah saw the look of wonder on Olivia's face, and had a feeling it mirrored her own. It wasn't that long ago she had met werewolves, now she was face to face with her very first vampire - and she couldn't determine who terrified her more.

Holden invited them in, the tension in the entryway slowly receding. Rylan released his grip on her arm and she rubbed it unconsciously. It was likely going to bruise, but Norah didn't care.

Daddy and Gregori brushed past them, following Holden and Norah suppressed the urge to shiver. There was a strange coldness that surrounded them, she felt Gregori's eyes pass over her and she tried not to shrink away, not wanting to be rude.

Rylan turned around and grabbed her hand, his warmth a welcoming comfort. "You all right?"

She nodded. There was a strain around Rylan's eyes and she touched his temples when Olivia returned to the dining room, trying to smooth them away. "Are you?"

He breathed deeply, grabbing her hands and kissing them lightly before pressing them to his chest. "Later."

She nodded again, letting him lead her back to their cold dinners. Daddy sat at the head of the table, Gregori on his right, Holden on the left. Rylan took the spare seat next to the vampire, and Norah sat next to him, opposite Olivia, who still hadn't stopped staring. Charlie returned from the kitchen.

"Aaron's recovering. Cassie's keeping an eye on him." Holden nodded, motioning for him to take a seat.

"I wasn't expecting you for another day," Holden spoke to Daddy.

The vampire nodded, his head moving subtly. "Time is of the essence. Troubles are arising in the Kimmani Coven and Gregori will need to return to settle matters."

"I would offer you our services, but I am afraid we have our own problems right now."

"I understand," Gregori said calmly. "We have Lupi allies in Australia whom I can call on, but if possible I would like to deal with it myself. Of course, it would be better if I could return with Ali, but that is seeming like a fading dream."

"Your leader?" Holden asked.

"Aye, and my oldest friend," Daddy said gravely. "She's been missing for near on a century now, and I fear she is treading dangerous waters. I thought she had come to this country, in search of answers, but if she has, she is long gone."

"We were waylaid in the East, with two other warring covens," Gregori said quietly, "and I fear we may have lost the trail because of it."

Norah listened quietly as they spoke of trying to find their friend, watching Olivia from the corner of her eye who was fascinated by their appearance. Charlie elbowed her, but she paid him no mind, too enraptured by the two creatures at the head of the table. It was as if the meeting outside had never happened. She could still see the tension in their gazes, but they were remaining calm for appearances' sake.

Norah sat close to Rylan, letting him pick the leftovers that were on the plate in front of her. Absentmindedly, she pushed the plate closer to him and the china clinked, making her jump. Gregori glanced at her, as Daddy and Holden continued their conversation.

"I apologise," he said quietly, "if we frighten you, my dear."

"N-no," she stuttered. "I'm not afraid, just...a little overwhelmed."

Rylan explained her recent introduction into the supernatural world and Gregori frowned. "I am sorry it has been so difficult for you, Norah. I think you are in very capable hands however. Daddy speaks very highly of the Montoya's and I am sure they will keep you safe."

She thanked him, trying hard not to avert her eyes in case he thought she was rude. She started when he smiled, his white teeth shining brighter than his skin. "You remind me of a new friend I made before I left Australia. Entirely new to our way of life, but fitting in as if you were born to it."

"Me? Fitting in?" Norah laughed shakily. "I don't think so."

Rylan reached under the table, his hand resting on her thigh as Gregori's face softened. "Tonight you have seen werewolves try to attack your friends, rather than run you stayed, knowing it can't have been easy for them to see someone they love attack them. You've met two vampires, one who you are bravely talking to - a normal human would have ran away long ago, yet, here you are. You're braver than you realise."

Rylan squeezed her knee. "See? You are brave."

"I recall you calling me a coward," Norah muttered.

Olivia's eyes finally left Gregori and snapped to Rylan. "You called her what? You pig!" The table banged as Olivia tried to kick him. "Why would you do that?"

"I didn't mean it," he protested. "I was just angry, it was in the moment -" he turned to Norah, exasperated. "Why would you bring that up?"

She shrugged her shoulders. "I didn't realise it was meant to be private."

Olivia threw a piece of broccoli at him and Rylan twisted, catching the flying vegetable in his mouth. Norah laughed as Olivia rolled her eyes. "You're such a weirdo."

Daddy asked Gregori a question and he turned back to their conversation. Norah started collecting all the plates, and carried them in to the kitchen. Olivia followed, standing next to her as she filled the sink. "What do you think of them?"

"They're...interesting."

"Aren't they? I heard Daddy saying they were heading off tonight. I wish they'd stay longer, I want to ask them so many questions!"

"I'm sure they won't be the last vampires you ever meet."

"True, but who knows how long it will be until I meet another? Man, if I was in New Orleans with Meegan, I'd probably meet hundreds of them!"

"How is Meegan going? Luke must be missing her." Norah asked, thinking of Luke's pregnant fiance.

Olivia nodded. "He does. I know he's worried about the baby. She's due in three months, but if things haven't settled down here, he's going to make her stay. I know Grandpa is missing Grandma as well. This is the longest the two of them have been separated since they married."

Norah put all the plates in the soapy water. Olivia grew quiet, playing with her hands and Norah, not wanting to put her wet hands on her, leaned over and rested her head on her shoulder. "I'm sure everything will calm down soon."

"I hope so," she whispered.

"Why don't you go and check on your mum and Annie? Make sure they are all right?"

Olivia nodded and headed out upstairs. Rylan met her at the door, scruffing her hair as she passed.

"Dork," Olivia muttered, smiling wryly.

Rylan took Olivia's spot and watched Norah. "You know," she said, after a few minutes while scrubbing a plate. "You could help me, rather than watch."

"There's no fun in that. But if you insist." He shifted, standing behind her and put his hands in the water, holding her own.

She sighed. "You really are a dork."

"A lovable dork," he helped her scrub the plates, his head resting on her shoulder and rather than argue, she let him have his way. It had been a tough night for everyone in the Montoya family and if this was how she could help Rylan, then she would do it.

They finished the dishes in silence and Rylan kissed her before heading back into the dining room. Norah told him she was going to see how Cassie was, and then head to bed.

Once the kitchen was clean, she found Cassie and the others in Aaron's room near the end of the hall upstairs. A sheen of sweat covered his still, pale skin, and he remained unconscious. Logan sat beside him, cleaned up, and a bandage wrapped around his neck. Annie was asleep beside Aaron on the large bed, her hand resting on his chest. Cassie and Olivia sat on the floor beside the bed, both asleep. Norah quietly slipped out and headed back to Rylan's room.

She wished there was more she could do for them. Seeing them like that, she felt a pang of envy. She wished her relationship with Adam had been like that. The love these people had for each other was beautiful, and she wanted some of it. She wanted to know what that felt like. She got changed into her pyjama's and grabbed her laptop, turning it on.

She found Adam's email and the mouse hovered over the message. She bit her lip, clicking the mouse pad once and the message opened -

Norah,

I know you probably want nothing to do with me and you'd have every right. I've been a horrible brother over the years and I've dragged you down every dark road I've travelled. You were right to make me turn myself in. My lawyer says I can get early parole with good behaviour so I'm doing my best to try and steer clear of those dark paths, though there's so many in here, it's hard. I want to prove to you that I can change, that I have some redeeming feature.

I don't want to sound selfish but - I need to see you. That last phone call is keeping me awake at night, hearing how much you hated me...I've been beaten a few times in my life, but those three words hurt more than any of it. I want to talk to you about everything, but face to face. I know it could be the last time I ever see you, and I can accept that, but just once, please come and see me once and I promise I'll never bother you again if that's what you want. I'll check my email everyday for a week. If you haven't replied by then, I'll know your answer.

Love Adam.

Norah read it again, and then again before slamming the screen shut and pushing the laptop away. She knew as soon as she read it she would be sucked back in. If she didn't go to see him now, she'd be ridden with guilt.

Sleep on it, she thought. If she replied now, the annoyance she felt would come through. She needed time to think out her answer and come to terms with the fact that he was basically guilt tripping her into seeing him.

She lay down, arm over her eyes and breathed deeply. Sleep came in snippets, her arm became sore but she didn't move it. The next time she woke, she was on her side and Rylan lay beside her, his hand resting on her waist.

Norah rested her hand on her cheek, watching Rylan in the dark. The light of the moon outlined his frame, making him seem larger. His scent of ocean and pine drowned her senses. The combination was strange but oddly comforting. Heat seemed to roll off him and she moved to kick her bed socks off, her feet getting too hot. His hand fell from her waist as she moved, and she stifled a gasp as it shot back out, his arm dragging her into his chest.

"Go to sleep," he murmured. "You're keeping me awake."

"Then sleep somewhere else," she mumbled half heartedly.

He curled around her, his leg draping across her own. "Like it here," he sighed into her hair. "Sleep, Norah. We'll argue in the morning."

22. Normal

Norah headed to the cafe early the next morning, an idea in her head for a scene to write. It felt like it had been so long since she'd written anything, her fingers were twitching with the need to put words to paper. She jogged into town, needing the exercise after all the eating she was doing at the Montoya's. She was happy she was going home tonight, and could eat what she wanted. Her notebook under her arm, she walked through the front door, bumping into Brad who was on his way out.

"Oh sorry," she exclaimed, brushing the drops of coffee that had spilled as their bodies connected.

Brad glanced at her coldly, and she guessed he still wasn't happy with her being involved with the Montoya's. "No problem."

He moved past her and she rolled her eyes. If he was going to be petty about it then fine. She would have been happy to be friends, but obviously Brad was incapable of being mature about the situation.

"Men," she muttered, sitting in her usual seat.

Gail walked over, placing a muffin in front of her. "Man troubles, Norah?"

"Not specifically, its more just men in general."

"Ah, I see. That's too heavy a subject for this time of morning." Gail pulled a red strand of hair back behind her ear. "Give us a shout if you need anything. Olivia should be in soon."

"Sure." Gail headed back to serve another customer and Norah opened her notebook, reading over her notes and the scene she had finished on. The scene she had in her mind, didn't follow on from her last point, but she felt it would be a good way to finish the story. The only problem was trying to find her way to that scene. Sometimes she would think of scenes that would be amazing, but she could never get the story to move in the right direction so the scene would fit in.

She started scribbling down ideas for different plot lines which could help her. A coffee appeared in front of her and she murmured a quick hello to Olivia, recognising her perfume. Olivia disappeared and she kept writing, filling three pages back and front with ideas. A general plot had started to form by the time her coffee was finished and she reached for her muffin, but it was gone. Glancing up, she saw the last of her muffin being eaten by the man now seated opposite her.

"Is no food sacred?" she snapped.

Rylan grinned, licking his fingers. "Gail makes the best muffins in Bellvale. Don't tell Cassie I said that."

"What are you doing here?"

"I was hungry." She raised an eyebrow and Rylan chuckled. "Doing the coffee run for the Mill. I volunteered after Gail mentioned to Aston that you were here."

"How are they doing?" she asked quietly. "Are Logan and Aaron alright?"

He nodded. "Both back to their normal annoying selves. Aston's given them the day off though so I'm going to be working late tonight."

"Can I still go home tonight?"

He nodded. "I've asked the boys to keep an eye on your place until I get home. There's no chance they'll stay in the house all day and I'd rather they do something productive than go off and find trouble."

"Is that necessary?" she asked.

He reached over, grabbing her hand. "It's more of a precaution at t this stage. Last time I left you alone that stalker of yours got to you. I know you like your privacy, but humour me this once, okay?"

She consented to the boys keeping an eye on her house only because she wanted to go home. She loved the Montoya's, but she missed her own things, and her own space. It had been a mad week and she needed some normalcy.

Olivia called out that his order was ready and he gave Norah a quick kiss and headed out. She turned to a new page, and thought of what to buy for dinner tonight. If she was going to be feeding him from now on, she was going to need to increase her food budget.

"Norah?"

She glanced up. "Hey, Madison. Are you all right?"

Madison stood over her, looking more distressed that Norah had ever seen her. Her face was pale, and her hair was sticking out on all ends like she had just gotten out of bed. "I'm fine, but I could use your help."

"Sure." Norah grabbed her stuff and followed Madison outside. She hadn't known Madison for long, but she knew she wasn't the type to ask for help unless it was something important. She jumped into an old white sedan and Norah followed suit. "What's going on?"

"I just got a call from Dante. Wendy is over at his house causing havoc. Or at least I gather she is judging from the screaming I could hear in the background."

Oh crap. "What exactly do you need me to do?"

"Well, I need to get Wendy out of there, and I could use the extra hands."

"Why didn't you ring Charlie?"

"He's busy with work, and I didn't want him to know. He hates Dante and I was worried if he came with me, they would get into a fight."

"I'd still rather have a strong guy with us." Norah muttered.

"Dante wouldn't hurt us."

"It's not Dante I'm worried about."

The drive took half an hour, heading towards Cavenden, where Dante now lived. Norah hadn't been this far out of Bellvale and with the forest behind them, the land become more open, and livestock grazed in the fields. The road was busy with tourists heading back towards to the larger cities as the holiday season approached its end.

Madison was still pale and Norah kept an eye on her, concerned there was something else going on.

"Are you sure there isn't anything else the matter?"

Madison sighed, her knuckles white on the steering wheel. "The anniversary of Parker's death is this week."

"Oh." Norah didn't know what else to say.

"I usually go to visit Parker's mother at this time of year, but..."

"You're worried about leaving Wendy alone?" Norah guessed.

Madison nodded. "She's normally very understanding, but she's been so caught up in this argument with Dante, I think it must have slipped her mind or something."

"Then we will have to remind her," Norah said firmly.

The town came into view and Madison took a few turns, heading into suburbia. The fact that she knew her way told Norah volumes. "This isn't the first time you've had to intercept a fight, is it?"

She shook her head. "I wish I could say this was a rare occurrence, but this is the fourth time this year."

"Bloody hell."

Madison pulled up in front of a red brick home. The garden was minimal with a neat lawn and a bed of white roses which were in desperate need of pruning. The only sign of trouble within was a chair lying on its side in the doorway.

"Do we have a plan?" Norah asked.

Madison turned the car off and got out. "Just to get her out before blood is spilled."

"Right," she replied weakly. They headed inside and Norah spent the next twenty minutes in hell.

Wendy was tiny, but her strength was terrifying. They entered to her and Dante in a shouting match. Wendy was too busy throwing objects to notice they had arrived and Madison took the lead, grabbing her arm and attempting to drag her out. It was almost comical trying to get Wendy out of the house. Voices were raised on all sides, Norah had to duck twice to avoid flying hands and on one occasion Wendy's leg connected with her shin, making her double over in pain.

Dante offered no help, only continuing to rile her up and Norah felt her patience wearing thin. She was on the verge of hitting the man herself when they finally managed to shove Wendy out the front door. As soon as they were out, Dante slammed it shut and Wendy started kicking it.

"Stupid bastard!" she screeched. "Like he needs my bloody money, he should just get it from his whore girlfriend!"

"Wendy! Quiet down," Madison hissed. "People can hear you."

"I don't care! I want to kill him!"

They managed to get her into the car and Madison handed Norah the keys to Wendy's. "Would you mind driving her car home?"

"Are you sure you'll be right on your own with her?"

Madison nodded. "I'll try and have a chat with her."

"Good luck."

Norah climbed into Wendy's car, a black four door hatchback, and followed Madison down the road. She took deep breath, the moment feeling surreal. After dealing with all the supernatural problems in the last few days, something completely normal suddenly felt unfamiliar.

She stared at the white car ahead, What would Madison and Wendy think if they knew of the creatures living in their town? She knew Wendy would most likely be thrilled, though she couldn't be too sure how she would feel about Charlie. When it came to family, everything was different.

Speaking of family... Norah attempted to compose a response to Adam as they reached the outskirts of Bellvale. She continued on, after dropping off Wendy's car and went to buy some food, changing her response again and again. Her first few attempts were harsh, thinly veiled threats of bodily harm. She moved blindly through the grocery store, grabbing all the food on her list as she muttered to herself. The woman behind the counter stared at her strangely but she ignored it.

By the time she was unlocking the front door and stepping inside her house, she had it cut down to something short and simple. Rylan had dropped off her bag that morning, and she pulled out her laptop, firing it up. She bit her bottom lip, her palms sweating as she suddenly became nervous. As she opened her web browser, all the feelings of anger and hate faded away, leaving an ache in her heart. She wanted to see him. She didn't know for sure if she would try to hurt him, or scream at him when she did, but she still loved the stupid idiot. Finding the email, she hit reply -

Tomorrow. Morning visiting hours. Norah x.

A tension she didn't realise she had been carrying eased from her body as she hit send, closing the browser tab. She still wasn't sure she had made the right decision, but she felt better, knowing she would be able to see him and hopefully put some closure on all the crap between them.

She put on some music - settling for The Beatles - and started fixing up the house. Everything was tidy, but she gave it all a once over, just to be on the safe side. The sun had set by the time she finished, and she had a quick shower, rubbing her bruised shin.

Pulling out the food for dinner, she started preparing meat and salad for tacos. In a normal situation it would have been enough to serve near on eight people. Instead, it was enough for one human and one werewolf - or at least she hoped it was.

The sound of Rylan's motorbike sounded as she placed the cooked meat on the table. "Hi honey, I'm home."

He strode in like he owned the place, a large grin in place. He was covered in dirt and oil, and she prayed he didn't get any on anything now that she had cleaned up. He kissed her and she squirmed away, rubbing dirt from her cheek. "Go and wash up, you smell disgusting."

"Crap, I don't smell at all."

He tried to grab her again and she scooted around the table to evade him. "If you can't smell yourself, then your werewolf senses must be on the fritz."

He pouted. "Fine, I'll wash up."

She grabbed some drinks, putting them on the table while he was in the bathroom and sat down to put a taco together. It would be best to get in now in case she hadn't made enough food.

Rylan came back in with a clean shirt and water droplets falling from his dark hair. "Better?"

She glanced up, pretending to assess him. "You may be seated."

Taking the seat opposite her, he tucked in. Rylan told her about his day, ands she told him about the drama with Wendy and Madison. Norah finished her first taco by the time Rylan had finished his fifth, and she watched him eat, marvelling at the werewolf appetite. She was going to have to contact Cassie to figure out how much she should be purchasing to keep him from starving.

"How many have you had?"

"Hmm?" She glanced up from the empty plates, distracted.

He motioned to what was left on the table. "How many have you had?"

"Oh just the one."

Rylan grabbed the rest of the food, enough to fill one last shell and passed it to her. "Here."

"What?" She stared in surprise. "Are you full?"

"Norah," he grinned. "I'm not going to eat all the food on my own. Have the last one."

She laughed under her breath, taking the shell from his hand. She hadn't seen any of the Montoya men give up food while she had stayed with them. This was a big deal.

"Are you sure?" she asked. "I'm not that hungry."

"Eat."

She consumed half of it, knowing he was still hungry, and returned the rest to him. Rather than argue, he ate it in two bites.

"You're so charming," she muttered, grabbing the empty plates.

"Nice of you to finally notice, and here I was thinking you only liked me for my body."

"I like the wolf one," she teased. "Your human one, not so much."

"You wound me, woman."

"You're tough, you'll get over it."

Norah filled the sink and started washing as Rylan grabbed a dish towel. "So the Gathering is two nights from now."

"Your werewolf night, right?"

He nodded, grabbing a plate. "Cassie has been wanting to cancel it, but Holden is adamant. It's tradition and he feels the area will be secure with the two other packs who will be there."

"So, is 'have fun' an appropriate response?"

"It is, as long as you come with me, otherwise it'll be boring."

Norah's hand slipped on a cup. "Why would you want me to go? Won't you be running around on all fours and howling at the moon and stuff? What will I be doing? Offering treats to the best looking wolf?"

"Wow, someone's crabby tonight. There will be other humans there you know. And we don't run around as wolves all night. Only at midnight when we do the Luna run."

"Oh, so I should go?"

"Yes," he said firmly. "And if I find out you've been giving treats out to anyone except me, I'm going to be so mad."

"But what if there is a better looking wolf than you?" she asked innocently.

The dish towel fell around her shoulders and Rylan pulled her close. "That's impossible. I'm the best looking wolf out there."

"We'll see." Rylan leaned in close, kissing her gently. Her eyes closed, her hands coming up to cup his face. He grunted and moved away. "What?"

She opened her eyes and laughed. Her hands had left soapy suds on his cheeks. He wiped them away. "Damn woman, stop trying to clean me."

"I wasn't cleaning," she grinned. "I was just trying the mutton chop look on you."

"Mutton chops, huh?" He stroked his chin in thought. "I'll consider it."

They finished cleaning up and Rylan put a movie on. Norah grabbed a book, wanting to read and they sat together on the couch in comfortable silence.

Thoughts of tomorrow kept creeping in and Norah knew she needed to check the train times so she could organise the next day. She thought of telling Rylan, but she needed to do this on her own, and she knew he would want to come if she told him.

Halfway into the movie, she put her book down and using the bathroom as her excuse, sneaked off to check the times on her laptop. After looking at the times, she surmised it would take her a few hours to get home by train, and she would have to get the early one if she was to make it in time for visiting hours.

"What you looking at?"

She jumped, slamming the lid shut. "Nothing, just confused about something in the book I was reading."

Rylan raised an eyebrow. "If it's too confusing, you should try The Hungry Caterpillar. It's a nail biter but it might be more to your standard - oomph!"

Norah elbowed him in the stomach. "Bloody standard my ass. I'm going to bed."

"Oh what a good idea."

"Uh uh you sleep on the couch, like always."

Rylan stumbled. "What?"

She stifled a grin. "Oh man, I wish I had a camera to capture the look on your face right now. So gullible."

She squealed as Rylan grabbed her, throwing her over his shoulder. "You are going to pay for that one, Jacobs."

For the first time in over a week, Norah forgot about the monsters and went to bed feeling happier than she had in some time.

23. Visit

Stepping off the train, Norah pulled her handbag closer to her side. People swarmed the platform from all sides, the smell of metal, sweat and smoke over powering her senses. For the last few months she had been spoiled with the fresh air or the sea and the forest. To come back to the city so suddenly, her body wasn't prepared for the onslaught of noise and smells.

Surely it hadn't been this bad? She didn't remember it being so hectic. Pushing her way through the crowd, it took her fifteen minutes to leave the central train station and already she was covered in a light sheen of sweat.

"Goddammit," she muttered, wiping her brow. She walked over to the taxi rank, queuing up to wait. Unconsciously, she pulled out her phone and looked at the screen. No new calls or messages. She didn't know why she was expecting a message from Rylan, telling her he knew what she was up to. Butterflies fluttered in her stomach, and she realised she didn't like keeping secrets from him. The last time she'd kept secrets from him, it hadn't ended so well and parts of her body still ached in remembrance.

Her turn came and she climbed in to the back of the taxi, giving the driver the name of the prison. She saw his eyes narrow in the rear-view mirror and she resisted the urge to glare at him. Just because she was going to the prison didn't mean she was a criminal. Bigoted people. Her fingers traced the outline of the phone as she watched the city go by.

The skyscrapers soon shrunk to normal size buildings as they reached the outskirts of the city and her grip on the phone tightened as they turned into the Prison's visitors car park. It was large, and relatively empty of cars save for three. Norah couldn't help but wonder why they would think they would need such a large car park. Visiting people in jail was nowhere near the top of her list of things to do on a quiet day.

Paying the driver, she stepped out and stood nervously, listening to the car pull away behind her. The whitewash stone building still didn't remind her of a prison - except for the large steel gates and wired fencing surrounded the facility, it looked more like the entrance to a high school than a prison full of deranged criminals. Part of her mind told her to exclude her brother from that group, but she was happy to bunch him with them for the moment.

Stepping forward, she started the long process of getting inside. She spoke to guard after guard, went through searches, bag checks, ID checks and lastly, signing a ledger. She felt like she had some sort of sign on her back that said 'suspicious, potential criminal'.

To be fair, she frowned, she had pushed a man off a cliff, essentially killing him until a lunatic werewolf raised him from the dead. Somehow, even if she did come clean with that horrible truth, she had a feeling they would lock her in a mental asylum, rather than a prison.

She kept quiet, entering the small room with the two way glass. Black phones hung from either side of the glass, and Norah sat down. It still felt like she was in a movie when she came in here. This place was highly old fashioned with some of their equipment, she wondered where all the tax payers money was going if not into improving the facilities.

A door opened on the other side and two guards walked in, Adam between them. In the months since she had seen him, he'd lost a little weight, his face more drawn and the shadows under his eyes telling her he wasn't getting much sleep. A light beard covered his cheek bones and his hair was pulled back in a messy knot.

His eyes lit up when he saw her and he grabbed the phone eagerly. Norah followed suit, though more cautiously. "You came!"

Norah felt a bit guilty at the joy in his voice, but she tried to remain aloof. "I said I would. What do you want?"

Adam remained oblivious to her attitude, her appearance, blinding him to anything bad. "I wanted to see you, it's been so long since you came, and I've been so worried that that bastard had hurt you. Have you seen him?"

Norah shook her head, unable to voice the truth. Adam's face melted into relief, the strain around his eyes easing somewhat. "That's good. Hopefully he's given up and backed off."

If only you knew, Norah thought wryly.

Adam started talking about his time in lock up, about the people he had met and how his lawyer said if he continued to stay out of trouble, he could have an early parole for good behaviour. Norah listened quietly, letting him get it all out. If he asked her what she'd been up to, she wouldn't know what to say. Everything involved some form of the supernatural, and he would think she was going mad. Eventually Adam fell silent and Norah snapped out of her daze.

"You're still angry with me," he said quietly.

She sighed. "Of course I am, though the urge to kill you has faded."

"That's a good sign," he smiled nervously. He touched his hand to the glass. "Norah, I am so, SO sorry for everything I have put you through. Not just this mess, but everything that happened before it. I've been a horrible brother and I don't know how you've put up with me."

She saw the unshed tears in his eyes and felt her heart soften. "You have been a real jerk to put up with, but you've never been a bad brother when it counts," she said softly. "You always looked out for me, and tried to keep me safe. Unfortunately you are easily guiled into foolish escapades. In some ways, this is my fault, for years I've been wanting to pull you up on all the bad things you do, but I was afraid you would run away, and then I would be alone."

"Norah," he whispered. "I would never leave you alone. You're my sister, I love you, even if I never show it."

She placed her hand on the glass over his, ignoring how cliché it was. "I'm sorry."

"I'm sorry too." He sighed, tapping the phone against his forehead. "And about those stones," his voice lowered. "Just throw them away. They've given us both nothing but trouble and I won't have you in danger anymore."

Norah felt something like pride spread through her chest. A guard stepped forward, signalling their time was up and Adam's face fell.

"Will you come again?" Adam begged as he stood up.

She nodded. "I'll try to come again soon. Stay safe, Adam."

"You too, Norah." She watched as he walked back through that large door and felt her eyes begin to sting. She had known he would break her, but now she didn't care. She still loved the stupid idiot, and she knew she could never erase him from her life - it wasn't who she was.

Stepping outside, she called the cab service to come and collect her and waited in the empty parking lot as the doors locked shut behind her, a sense of relief spreading through her body.

"Norah Jacobs?" She jumped, turning around. A man leaned against a car to her left, causing warning bells to start ringing in her head. Dressed in all black, he staggered over, his eyes roaming her body.

"N-no," she stammered. "My name is Madison." She blurted out the first name that popped into her head.

He chuckled, stepping closer. "I got a picture of ya from Daniel. Now where are those diamonds?"

You've got to be kidding me! She stepped back, wondering if she screamed would the guards hear her. Why was no one posted outside for God's sake!

"Don't even think about it, missy -" She shrieked as someone grabbed her shoulder and a fist connected with the large man's face, blurt spurting from his mouth. He went down hard, and Norah tried to break free.

"Norah calm down!" She froze at the familiar voice. Rylan stood beside her, eyes blazing with anger. Too caught up in the moment, she hit his chest.

"What the hell? We're at a prison!"

"It wasn't going to stop him," he growled. A taxi entered the car park and Rylan dragged her forward, shoving her in the back seat before the car had even stopped. "Central Train Station."

The taxi took off and Norah closed her eyes, heart beating wildly. They remained in silence until they reached the outskirts of the city. Rylan's anger faded, and he knew better than to try and raise the matter with her until she was ready.

Norah opened her eyes, staring at the sky. The clouds had become dark and overcast, and the smell of rain drifted through the driver's open window. Rylan reached over, grabbing her hand and she sighed, knowing he wouldn't wait forever. "When did you know?"

"Last night, when you tried to hide your laptop from me. I knew it would either be porn or something important, and since you have me, I knew it had be something other than porn."

She snorted, trying not to smile. "You didn't have to follow me."

"I was curious to see what you were doing. I wasn't going to make myself known, but when that prick approached you, I couldn't just stand back."

"So you were just going to stalk me?"

"Well, I knew this was something you needed to do on your own, I was just making sure you were safe - and before you get angry, just know, I'm always going to be concerned about your safety. If you had told me this is what you were doing today, I would have understood. I still would have stalked you, but I would understand."

She squeezed his hand. "It's hard to stay annoyed at you," she muttered.

He grinned, lifting her hand kissing her thumb. "Part of my charm."

"I don't know if I would call it charm." He shook her hand in mock indignation and she smiled. The taxi pulled up at the train station and Rylan paid before she could pull out her wallet. They made their way to the platform, forced to stand in the open since the shelter was crowded.

Norah leaned against Rylan, his arms wrapped around her waist. It was almost unnatural how easily they seemed to fall into these moments. It normally took her some time in a relationship before she was comfortable with PDA, but for some reason with Rylan it felt right, no matter where they were.

Norah crossed her arms across her chest, a cold shiver going down her spine as the clouds finally tore open and the rain started to fall. The train was running late. She brushed her hair from her face to stop the water which was beginning to drip in her eyes. Rylan was always warm so she knew he wouldn't be bothered by the rain. At times like this she almost envied his supernatural abilities.

Movement sounded behind her, hands leaving her waist and a shadow formed above her. Looking up, she saw a jacket hovering over her head and turned around. Rylan was holding his arms up, holding his jacket over her.

She looked up at him, his dark hair was already sticking to his scalp, the water running into his eyes. His clothes were soaked in such a short time and she tried not to look at the way his shirt clung to his body, knowing it would only fuel his ego. "What about you?"

"I don't mind a little rain," he smiled.

Not comfortable with him getting wet after everything he'd done for her today, she stepped closer, reaching up and clasping his forearms gently as she moved his arms so the jacket covered them both.

Her heart thudded at their close proximity and she immediately wondered if turning around had been such a good idea. Rylan shifted closer, his front pressing against hers and dropped his arms. Eyes widening, she grabbed the jacket to stop it falling on them. "What are you doing?"

"My arms were getting tired."

She laughed in disbelief. "Yeah right."

He grinned. "They were, I'm not as strong as I look you know."

"I doubt that," she muttered.

He reached around, one hand resting on her lower back, the other between her shoulder blades, stopping any form of escape. She tilted her head up to meet his gaze and as she did, the sounds around them faded away. The only sound she could hear was her pulse pounding in her ears, the noise fast and irregular. She could feel his own heart beating against her chest, mingling with her own to create a tangled beat and she lost herself in the blue of his eyes. She saw specks of dark brown mixed in with the blue and she found it strange she had never noticed that before. Neither one was willing to look away and Norah didn't know what was happening but the strange thing was, she didn't want it to end.

A faint horn sounded in the distance, breaking the moment and she turned her head in the direction of the noise. "The train..."

Rylan's hand pressed harder into her lower back, the other moving up and capturing her chin, turning her back to him and lowered his mouth over hers. There was no desperation or need in his movements, they were slow and languid, his lips moving gently against hers, kissing her again and again. Her eyes closed in pleasure and she reached up on her toes to close the small distance between them. A small noise escaped her throat and his hand pressed harder into her back, the small space between them becoming miniscule. His hand moved from her chin, tracing gently along her jaw line, leaving a hot trail before moving through her hair to cradle the nape of her neck.

Not thinking, she lowered her hands, running her fingers through his hair, the wet strands clinging to her skin, causing the jacket to fall on top of his head. Breaking away, she laughed and reached for the jacket. Rylan grinned, beating her to it and moved it out of the way before claiming her mouth once more.

The train horn sounded again, louder this time and Norah jumped in shock. The train had arrived during their kiss and she felt slightly embarrassed knowing the passengers had probably been watching. Uncaring, Rylan grabbed her hand. "Come on."

He led her onto the train, shaking the excess water from his jacket before boarding. Leading her down the aisle, she felt eyes on her but kept her gaze on Rylan's hand in hers. Once they were right at the end of the carriage, Rylan gently guided her into the seat next to his and placed his jacket on the floor before sitting down.

They sat in silence as they waited for the train to depart, hands still entwined. Rylan's thumb moved across her skin, sending tingles up her arm. Feeling his eyes on her, she didn't dare look up and she heard a faint shout from outside, indicating the train was ready to leave. With a shudder, the train began to move and Norah hoped the journey home would be a fast one. It felt strange, calling Bellvale her home now. She had never wanted it to be home, just a place she could hide in until Daniel left her alone. Even with the thought of him out there somewhere, she didn't want to run anymore. Being with Rylan, she felt safe and she didn't want to leave him and her new friends.

A shudder shook her body as the cold began to seep through her clothes, now that she was in a dry place, her body began to thaw and shiver. The jacket hadn't kept her completely dry and her skin raised in goose bumps, her complexion turning pale. Freeing her hand from Rylan's she tried to rub her arms to warm up.

"Here."

Rylan reached over and placed his arm around her, pulling her against his side. Normally, Norah wasn't too comfortable being in this position in a carriage full of prying eyes but his body was a natural heater and she couldn't resist sinking against him, wrapping her arm around his waist and resting her head in the nook of his shoulder.

"You know," he murmured, "I would be enjoying this a whole lot more if I knew you weren't just using me for my heat."

"Shh," she whispered, burying her face into his shoulder as her eyes began to get heavy. "Heaters don't talk."

His body shook as he chuckled and shifted into her so he could hold her closer. "Get some sleep. I'll wake you when we get home."

Norah didn't hear him, she was already asleep.

24. Preparations

Norah finished the last of her coffee, watching Olivia run around the cafe like a mad woman. She'd promised her she would wait around and drive her home to help prepare for tonight. Apparently the Gathering was a very big thing for them. The Mill had been closed for the day, and all the boys were out in the forest, doing perimeter checks and greeting the other packs which were arriving that day.

Rylan had left early that morning, he'd told her to be ready by six o'clock and he would come back to pick her up. She had no idea what she was meant to wear to this sort of thing. Was it fancy, semi-formal, or casual? She didn't want to look like an idiot in front of all those werewolves.

Olivia rushed over, grabbing her cup, her hair beginning to stick out on odd ends. "I'm sorry, Norah. I'll be five more minutes, I swear!"

"It's okay," Norah called as she ran off again. Norah wasn't the one in the rush. She knew Olivia was meant to have been home nearly an hour ago, but the cafe had been so busy and Olivia refused to leave Gail alone to deal with it all herself. The lunch rush was beginning to quiet and Norah gathered her books together, knowing she truly wouldn't be much longer.

The front door opened and Charlie walked in. Spotting Norah he quickly came over. "Hey, have you seen Madison?"

Norah shook her head. "No, not today. Aren't you meant to be out helping the others in the forest?"

He nodded. "Yeah, but I came to get some stuff for Cassie –"

"And thought you'd stalk Madison while you were at it?"

He glared. "No, I just haven't seen her today and I was concerned. Normally she has lunch with Wendy today but she wasn't there."

"Was Wendy concerned that she wasn't there?"

"No, but –"

"And isn't it this time of year that she goes to visit Parker's mother?" Norah remembered Madison mentioning it the other day.

He nodded. "Well, yeah –"

"Then perhaps she has headed off, don't you think?"

"But surely she would have told –"

"Charlie, she's a big girl, she can look after herself. She doesn't need to tell everyone every little thing she does. She'll be back soon, so don't worry and go and get Cassie what she sent you for. If she's anything like Olivia today, I can't imagine she is going to like being left waiting."

Charlie nodded, still unappeased but he walked out, shoulders hunched. Poor boy, she thought. He needs to find another girl.

Olivia sat down beside her, bag in hand. "I'm ready!"

Norah took in her frazzled appearance. "Are you okay?"

She shook her head. "I freaking love the Gathering, but the lead up is such a bitch. Mom turns into such a cooking monster. I'm almost happy Gran isn't here this year. If she was, it would be ten times worse."

They walked out to Norah's car and she mentioned Charlie. "Oh he is like this every year," Olivia rolled her eyes. "I think he expects her to tell him every year or something, and when she doesn't he thinks the worst."

"Poor Charlie." They headed out of Bellvale and Norah asked Olivia about the dress code, making her laugh.

"Just wear whatever you feel comfortable in. It's going to be a warm night, even with the bonfire so I would say wear something light."

Norah took mental notes. "Do you want me to help with anything today?"

Olivia grabbed her arm. "I would love it, if you could hang out for a few hours. Maybe if your there mom won't be so crazy."

"That's fine, I'm happy to help."

Olivia grinned. "You won't be saying that in a few hours. You'll be looking for the nearest exit within two hours, trust me."

"Don't freak me out, I'm trying to help you!"

"Sorry, just trying to prepare you. But don't worry, you're going to love the Gathering. I'm so excited Rylan is bringing you."

"Why is it exciting?"

"Because!" Olivia's eyes gleamed. "Humans are only invited to the Gathering if they have a strong attachment to someone in the family. Don't you see what this means? Rylan is crazy into you!"

Norah's heart leapt, but she kept her cool. "I think you might be reading too much into this. I mean, our relationship is still relatively new, and there's still a lot of challenges we have to face."

"Challenges?"

"Well," Norah gripped the steering wheel tightly. "What about the whole, werewolf and human factor? What if he asks me to make the change?"

"You wouldn't want to?"

"I don't know, it's a big decision..."

"Norah, you don't have to become a werewolf to be with Rylan. He would never make you do something you wouldn't want to do."

They pulled up out the front of the Montoya home and Norah turned the engine off. "But it would make things easier if I did, right?"

Olivia remained silent and Norah had her answer. It would be easier.

She climbed out, surprised when Olivia didn't get out too. "Uh, Olivia?"

"I'm coming," she whined. "I'm just preparing." After taking two deep breaths, she hopped out and followed Norah inside.

The inside of the house was chaos. Cassie had full charge of the kitchen, every hot plate and cooking utensil seemed to be in use and already a large assortment of prepared meals filled the table in the dining room, ready to be packed and taken to the Gathering site. The smell of food was amazing, there was a combination of everything and Norah's mouth watered. Cassie looked just as frazzled as her daughter, but there was a tension about her that made Norah concerned.

"Oh good, you're here!" Cassie grabbed Olivia, practically throwing her into the dining room. "I need you to start taking some of these dishes down to the site. Annie is there setting up with some of the guys. Norah, can you help her? Once you guys are finished I'll get you to give me a hand with some of the furniture."

Norah decided silence was the best answer, and she followed Olivia, grabbing what she could carry of the food and loaded the car. Once they were at capacity, they headed up the road, the site was deep in the forest but there was a walking track near the top of the hill that was easier to walk on with all the food.

Norah thought over their previous conversation as Olivia drove. She knew her feelings for Rylan were strong, not just because of everything they have been through together. She knew a relationship with him was long term, and she didn't want to stuff it up. The ageing factor frightened her a little bit. She knew it shouldn't matter, but she was scared if things got...serious serious, she would need to take that next step, and she didn't know if she could do it. She didn't wanted to grow older faster than her partner. It was a scary thought.

Norah shook her head, trying to dislodge the awful thoughts and glanced at Olivia. "Is your mom usually that stressed?"

Olivia shook her head. "It's a tough day for her. She's basically in charge of all the preparations and she likes everything to be perfect. Gran is usually here to help, but this year she's on her own." Olivia's eyes reddened. "This is the first year our family has been separated like this, and also our first gathering since Daddy died."

Her voice broke and Norah touched her shoulder as they pulled into the rest area. "Are you okay?"

Olivia nodded, and then immediately shook her head. "I'm so worried something bad is going to happen. It's like a horrible feeling in the pit of my stomach that won't go away. Liam has been quiet for a few days and Grandpa thinks everything will be fine, but..."

"I understand," Norah spoke quietly. "I wish I knew what to say to make you feel better. All I can say is that I'll keep all my fingers crossed that tonight goes smoothly."

Olivia nodded again and they carried the food through the forest in silence. Norah felt a little green, walking through the forest without Rylan, but she reminded herself that nothing bad was going to happen so she had to remain positive.

It took them fifteen minutes to reach the clearing. In the centre was a large bonfire, the size of a large house and consisted mainly of tree trunks, rather than twigs and branches.

"Holy crap," Norah muttered. "Jack would have a field with this."

Olivia laughed. "He came to one a few years ago and I swear, it was like watching a kid at Christmas. It was the first time I'd seen him smile in a long time."

To the left there was a hut, a safe distance from the fire, and Annie met them at the entrance. "Hey girls, just put the food in the refrigerators."

They placed the food in one of the three large refrigerators lining the back of the cabin. Olivia checked the generator which was running the electricity before they headed back to the car. On their second trip, Logan and Aston were carrying another tree trunk into the clearing.

"Hey girls," Logan's head turned towards the food. "You sticking around?"

"No," Olivia pulled out a large padlock, swinging it around her finger. "But don't get too excited. The food will on lock down until tonight."

Norah tried not to laugh as both Logan and Aston's faces fell. "Isn't there something we can give them?" Norah turned to Olivia and Annie. "I mean they are working…"

"Nope, Cassie would have my head if I let them have some now." Annie explained.

Both men groaned, throwing the trunk down in dismay and Norah jumped as the sound reverberated through the forest.

"Sorry Norah," Logan looked at her sheepishly.

"It's okay, I know food is an emotional subject for you guys."

They headed back to the car for the final load, leaving the men to their dissatisfaction.

"So, how many packs are going to be here tonight?" Norah grabbed the last plate of food from the car, kicking the door shut.

Olivia followed behind, her arms laden with two times the amount. "There will just be three packs. Each are part of the Bluestone pack. Every year, we take it in turns performing the gathering. This year is our turn."

Norah opened her mouth to mention the obvious, but Olivia continued on. "I know it seems irrational, with everything that has been happening, but Grandpa doesn't like to show weakness, even amongst other packs in link with our own. I don't know the specifics about his past, but Grandad used to be quite high up in the Bluestone hierarchy during the civil wars."

"But he's retired from all that now, right?"

Olivia nodded. "You know the old saying though – old habits die hard."

Norah fell into silence, worried that she seemed to keep unconsciously bringing up Olivia's family problems. It was like rubbing dirt into an open wound over and over again. They finished their last delivery, checked the food was locked up tight and then headed back home, taking Annie with them.

Olivia drove slowly and Norah knew she didn't want to head home. The tension around her eyes told her this was taking its toll on the youngest Montoya.

"Do you want to come back to my place?" Norah offered as they pulled up out the front of the Montoya home. Annie jumped out of the backseat and headed inside straight away to help Cassie. "You can help me figure out what the hell I'm meant to wear to this thing."

Olivia smiled weakly, leaning back in her seat. "Thanks Norah, but I better stay here and help mum. There shouldn't be much left to do, except get the boys organised and she's going to need help getting their asses in order I'm sure."

"Do you want me to stay?"

"No, you head home and get organised. I'll see you later on tonight. We can handle the rest."

"Okay." Norah headed in and grabbed her keys. Olivia headed into the kitchen and Norah called out farewell before going back to her car.

Paul and Rylan pulled up as she opened her door. "Hey," Rylan walked over and gave her a kiss. "Heading off already?"

Norah nodded. "I had a feeling you were on your way, so thought I'd escape while I can."

"Why must you hurt me?" He pouted.

She poked her tongue out in response and climbed into her car. Rylan quickly raced around the vehicle and jumped in. "Hey!"

"I'll see you later," he called out to Paul. The man grinned, waving before heading inside. Norah noticed his smile didn't reach his eyes and frowned as she reversed out.

"Is Paul okay?"

Rylan's good humour faltered. "It's a hard day for everyone. Paul's worried about what Liam and Nick are doing."

Norah remembered that Nick was Aston's son and grimaced forgetting that it wasn't just Olivia and Cassie who were suffering. "My foot in mouth disease is running rampart today."

Rylan reached over, taking her hand, their fingers automatically entwining. "It's okay."

They drove in silence, Rylan's thumb moving gently across her skin in a slow rhythm. Norah glanced over occasionally. His eyes remained closed. Norah couldn't help but notice the worry in his face too. They reached her house and she turned the car off.

Neither of them moved. Norah rested her head against the seat, watching Rylan. She twisted sideways, reaching out with her free hand to touch his cheek. His eyes opened on contact, finding hers instantly. They didn't say anything; no words were needed. Norah knew Rylan was having a hard time too, and rather than talk about it, she just wanted him to know she was there for him.

They stayed like that for a few minutes before finally moving inside to get ready. As they walked through the front door, Rylan picked her up from behind, carrying her to the couch.

"Shouldn't we be getting ready?"

He sat down, taking her with him. "Not yet," he mumbled into her back. "We don't have to head up to the house for a few more hours."

"But I need to get ready –"

"You look good now."

She rolled her eyes. "I smell disgusting after trudging food through the forest."

"Food?" His voice perked up. "What type of food?"

She went through all the food she'd carried until his stomach started rumbling and she laughed. "I think I better stop now."

He shook his head the movement rubbing against her shoulder blades. "I can wait until later. Not even food could make me want to move right now."

"Wow," she leaned back and he shifted, his hands curling around her stomach as she rested her head on his shoulder. "That's quite a declaration coming from you."

He chuckled, his hold on her tightening. "I'm full of charming one liners."

"I didn't say it was a charming declaration."

"You didn't have to, I know you're only trying to keep my ego in check."

She laughed in disbelief, twisting around to face him. "Your ego is too big for even me to keep in check."

"Crap," he kissed her nose. "You're the only one who can control it. The only one I would ever let control it."

She smiled, resting her forehead against his. She knew there was a deeper meaning to those words, but she wasn't ready to open that barrel of fish yet. She chose to remain ignorant. Rylan sighed, his fingers curling into her hair. "I have another charming one liner for you. You ready?"

She pretended to prepare herself, and felt his lips curve upwards against her lips. "I'm ready."

"I'm glad you're here."

She smiled, kissing him lightly. "I'll allow that one."

"Good." His lips moved lower, brushing over the curve of her neck. Her nerves tingled.

"I don't think we have time for this," she murmured.

"We've got a couple of hours," his head moved lower. "And I think this will help downsize my ego."

"Inflate it more like it." He didn't respond and the time was soon forgotten, the sun's last rays their only alert that they were going to be late.

Norah rushed to get ready, brushing her teeth furiously. Her body still thrummed from the afternoon's events but it was put on a side burner to her annoyance. She hated running late to anything. She shoved a white sundress over her head, cursing Rylan's ability to distract her.

Grabbing a denim jacket, she walked out to the kitchen, running her hands through her hair. Rylan was already waiting outside, the sound of the car engine running reached her ears and she grabbed her turquoise scarf from the kitchen table. She hadn't had a chance to shower properly and she was worried the perfume wouldn't be enough to cover up that fact. Still, she had no other choice, and secretly prayed they would all be too busy stuffing their faces and doing other Gathering –like activities to notice.

She locked the front door, rushing out to the car. Rylan leaned against the driver's side, eyes travelling her frame appreciatively.

"Is this okay?" Norah asked nervously. Rylan had simply changed his shirt to a plain black v neck. "If I'm too overdressed, I can change –"

"No, don't change. You look good." His hands brushed her waist and he kissed her slowly.

She tried to break away, but found herself melting into him instead. "We need to get going."

"We do," He groaned, "but it's hard to think of anything else when you look like that."

"Just think of the food waiting for you." Norah teased.

"Well if you put it like that," he turned away and hopped in the car, leaving her to walk around and climb in herself.

"It's amazing how food works on you," she pulled her seatbelt around and Rylan grabbed it, buckling it for her. He grabbed her hand, pressing his lips to her fingertips.

"Food is definitely a motivator, but that dress is working so much better. You better not take it off later."

"What, you want me to wear it forever?"

"Of course not," he grinned. "I just want to be the one to take it off you."

They pulled out onto the main road, Norah's heart doing backflips. It was a quiet drive as Nora's thoughts drifted back to her earlier musings. She knew she'd only known Rylan a few months, but she was extremely close to being in love with him. She didn't want to stuff it all up by bringing up things better left unsaid, but the words were bursting forth before she could stop them.

"Do I have to become a werewolf for us to stay together?"

Norah's body lurched forward as Rylan slammed on the breaks. She steadied herself on the dashboard, heart in her throat. Before she could scream at him, he spoke first –

"Why'd you ask something like that? Of course you don't have to."

"I just –" Norah faltered. "I mean, if we stay together, and things keep going the way they are, it would make sense if we were both the same…species. Otherwise, we wouldn't age the same way, and we couldn't do everything together –"

Rylan grabbed her chin, leaning over and kissing her into silence. He didn't let her up for air until she had melted against him. "I've been waiting for this, you know? A woman with your tendency to overthink everything would naturally start thinking about this stuff."

Norah felt sick, the ball in her throat making it difficult to breathe. Curse her stupid mouth! She knew it was a bad idea to bring this up –

"Human, werewolf, Jedi Knight, I don't care what you are. As long as we're together, I'm happy. If you should decide you want to make that choice, then it has to be your decision. Don't choose to change because of me. It's your life, and you need to live it in a way that makes you happy – not others."

Norah felt her eyes sting. "I'm stupid for bringing it up, aren't I?"

He chuckled, stroking her cheek. "You're not stupid. Its in your nature to question things like this. Don't ever be afraid to ask me stupid questions. I'm an expert in all things stupid, so I'll be able to answer them. If you want answers to things like politics and the state of the economy, you'd be better off asking Holden."

She laughed, sniffing slightly. "I'll keep that in mind."

"Good. Now let's get going. I'm hungry and the sooner we get through the Gathering, the sooner I get to take that dress off."

25. Gathering

The walk to the site was quiet. They parked at the house and followed a trail lit by wooden torches. The flames glowed a pale orange, and Rylan explained they were covered in a special oil which would keep them burning until sunrise. Norah kept close to Rylan, every noise making her stomach tighten. She had no fond memories of the forest at night. It was eerily silent, the full moon was high in the sky, casting an ethereal glow on the forest. The air was cool and she shivered, pulling her jacket closer about her. Olivia had promised the fire would be enough to keep her warm though so she walked faster in anticipation.

They had been walking for ten minutes before the sound of voices reached them. Norah could make out the flames thought the trees and she started to feel nervous.

Rylan's hold on her hand tightened in reassurance. "It's going to be fun. Don't stress."

"Right," she muttered. They entered the clearing and Norah's eyes widened.

The large bonfire was alight; the heat rolled through the clearing and most of the gatherers stood along the outskirts, unable to get close the huge flames. Norah guessed there had to be at least fifty or so people there. Nearly everyone had some sort of food or beverage in their hand and everyone was chatting animatedly. Norah didn't recognise many of them, but knew they had to belong to the other clans of the Bluestone pack.

Norah let Rylan lead her across the clearing towards the food hut where Annie and Cassie were rapidly emptying out the stored fridges. They managed a quick hello before being swamped by men wanting more food. Old arm chairs and couches were arranged outside the hut in a crooked line, people hanging off them in small groups. Norah spotted Charlie and Olivia talking to a young guy with a large black Mohawk she didn't recognise.

The Montoya's were spread out across the clearing and they slowly made their way around to everyone. Rylan introduced her to everyone they met, and Norah shamefully forget their names within moments. The amount of introductions was overwhelming and she was relieved whenever they came across a familiar face. Aston and Logan dragged them over to their small group and Norah's smile faded when she noticed Chloe amongst their number. Her attempts to fool Norah were still fresh in her mind and she plastered a fake smile on her face.

"How are you enjoying the night so far?" Logan asked her.

"It's good," Norah's smile turned genuine as she turned to look at him. "I am a bit overwhelmed by the amount of people, but I do love the atmosphere."

"Why even bother coming?" Chloe muttered, turning away.

Rylan wrapped an arm around Norah's waist and she bit back a retort. Aston glared at his niece but she was moving away before she could feel its full effects. There was a moment of awkward silence the Montoya men felt embarrassed by her behaviour.

"Don't worry about her," Aston sighed. "She still hasn't grown up yet."

"It's okay, I can handle her," Norah murmured.

"You'd be the only one," Rylan muttered and Norah elbowed him.

Logan grinned. "You're one to talk; I don't know how you handle him, Norah."

"What are you talking about?" Rylan snapped. "I'm a catch."

"You are?" Norah asked innocently. "Since when?"

"Dammit woman, you're meant to be on my side defending my honour!"

"I thought I was meant to be keeping your ego in check?"

"Not when we're with other people!" He whined. "How else are they going to realise how awesome I am?"

Aston, Logan and Norah exclaimed with false astonishment at the news that he was awesome, and Rylan started pouting and walked away.

"Where are you going?" Norah called through her laughter.

"Somewhere I am appreciated!"

Logan mouthed, 'Cassie' and Norah laughed. She left the boys, finding a seat near Charlie on one of the couches. He was sitting on his own, watching the flames with a glum expression. "Hey, Charlie. Having fun?"

He glanced across at her. "I guess."

"Oh my God, are you still moping about Madison? Just man up already and tell her!"

"It's not that easy," he growled.

"Yes it is! You just walk up to her when she comes home, grab her close and tell her you're into her!" Norah grabbed Charlie by the shoulders, showing him the actions he needed to make and stared at him determinedly. "You got it?"

"Do I want to know what is happening right now?" Rylan had snuck up behind her and she jumped, falling onto Charlie.

"You left me so I'm mingling," Norah said calmly, wrapping an arm around Charlie.

"Dude, it's not what it looks like," Charlie shoved Norah off of him.

"Of course it's not." Rylan stepped over the back of the couch, sitting between them. He wiggled, forcing them both to move as he settled in. "Like anyone would ever cheat on this."

He wrapped an arm around Norah while motioning to his own body. Norah snorted and Charlie struggled not to laugh. He got up, moving away before he could and Norah slapped Rylan's chest. "That ego of yours is in full swing," she grinned.

"What can I say? I thrive in a crowd."

"We may have to limit your interactions in the future," Norah said seriously, snuggling against him. "If your ego gets any bigger, I won't be able to control it."

"Of course you will," he murmured, his hand stroking her arm gently. They fell into silence, watching the others run around them, raised voices and laughter filling the night air.

"Is everyone having fun?" Norah asked quietly.

"Hmmm," he mumbled into her hair. "Yes and no."

Norah saw Holden watching them from across the clearing. He looked happy, but there was a worry in his eyes which unnerved her. Somehow, seeing the matriarch on guard filled her with a ball of unease. Norah looked around, and was surprised to see Dylan sitting with Chloe near the food hut. "Isn't that Dylan, Brad's apprentice?"

Rylan frowned. "Yeah. Poor bugger, getting sucked into her web."

"Be nice," Norah murmured, though she secretly agreed. Dylan felt her gaze and their eyes met. He smiled, waving nervously and she waved back. He seemed like a nice guy, she just hoped Chloe and Brad hadn't filled his head with bad things about her. Brad was avoiding her which still annoyed her. She didn't like having bad air between them. She just hoped he got over his stupid moping and found someone else.

Olivia came and sat beside Norah as Logan and Aaron sat at their feet. Norah listened as they talked about the past gatherings and the games and tricks they had played. Olivia's father was mentioned often and Norah liked getting to know more about the man they had all loved and admired. When Rylan spoke of him, she could hear the respect he had had for the man had ultimately been his surrogate father. She wished she had met him.

The bonfire began to die down and everyone moved forward. Luke made his way through the people, standing on a chair before releasing a shrill whistle. The crowd fell silent and all eyes fell on him. Luke looked confident, but his shoulders were tense. Rylan had told her this was his first time leading the run, and she knew he must be nervous.

"I'd like to thank you all for coming tonight," he began. "You are all aware that our pack is not at its strongest right now, but your support and continued loyalty gives us the strength we need to keep going. Family has never been about blood to our kind. You make your own family in life, and I am honoured to meet all the newcomers to the Braxton and Quiotta clans. You are now our family, as I hope we have become yours. This year we lost someone loved by all, my father. He loved these Gatherings. It was my father who taught me my family beliefs and told me that a true leader does not discriminate by blood. This is my first Gathering without him, and though his presence is missed, I know he is here in spirit."

There was a moment of silence, and Norah held Rylan's hand, his fingers trapping her hand tightly in his own.

"It is now time for the midnight run," he grinned. "Finish your food and prepare to run."

Everyone stood up, Rylan pushed Norah back down as she moved to follow him. "You stay here. Annie will still be here, she'll keep you company."

Norah felt a flare of panic as she realised all the werewolves were leaving. She resisted the urge to grab Rylan and beg him to stay. She knew this was important to all of them. Her cheeks flamed as one by one, everyone started removing their clothes. Modesty was no factor here and Norah closed her eyes, feeling embarrassed. Rylan leaned down and kissed her forehead. His lips were soft and the sentiment relieved some of her pent up nerves.

"We won't be long," he murmured, his voice getting lost in the myriad of cracking bones as the shifting began. "Norah."

She opened her eyes. His voice sounded different. She looked up, his mouth was open like he wanted to say something, and she realised he was nervous. "Rylan?"

"I...I'll be back soon." Norah nodded, watching as he shifted, his white coat standing out in the sea of black and grey. A large grey wolf stood to her left and howled, nose pointing to the sky. The others followed suit and a shiver ran down her spine as one, they took off into the forest. Within a few moments, they were gone and only the humans remained. There was ten of them and they all smiled knowingly at each other from their seated points. Those who had been to a gathering before started merging towards each other small cliques forming on either side of the fire.

Norah saw Annie sitting near the hut and walked over to join her. "What did you think?" Annie asked as Norah sat down.

"It was pretty cool, though I had my eyes closed during the change." She admitted.

Annie laughed. "Oh I used to be like that. I remember the first gathering Cassie took me to. This large man just stripped down in front of me, and I swear I had never felt so mortified! I like to think it was the mortification which caused my excessive staring at his....nakedness."

Norah burst into laughter. "That sounds like a, 'how I met my husband' story."

"Oh no! I met my husband in a sports bar. I used to waitress when I was younger and this man copped a feel as I walked past him. I hit him – quite hard – with my service tray and the rest is history."

Norah giggled. "That sounds almost sweet."

Annie smiled fondly. "It was, after he apologised of course."

"Did he become a werewolf?"

"No, he died when Logan was just a baby. We knew of their existence, but he had leukaemia, and it just wasn't meant to be."

"Sorry, Annie."

"Don't be sorry dear. It's nice to remember those we have lost. Not a day goes by that I don't think of him."

Norah smiled softly. "You'll have to tell me more about him sometime."

"I'd like that," Annie smiled. She stood up. "Well I might starting clearing out the hut and take some things back to the car." Norah offered to help but Annie refused. "Rylan will be worried if he comes back and you're not here. I've been watching the way he looks at you and I have to say, I'm happy you came to Bellvale, even though it was under sad circumstances. Seeing the look in Rylan's eyes when he looks at you – it's worth it."

Norah's stomach fluttered as Annie walked away. Could that mean what she hoped it meant? Looking at her knees, she tried to control the stupid grin trying to break her face.

"Hey, Norah." Dylan sat down beside her.

"Hey!" She smothered her grin miserably. "I was surprised to see you here. I didn't know you knew..."

"Yeah," he laughed awkwardly. "I found out last year after hooking up with Chloe."

"Ah, so are you two...?"

"No!" He replied hurriedly. "Just friends...with benefits," he mumbled the last word and she patted his arm.

"It's okay. I won't ask about it. Does Brad know you mingle with his arch enemies?"

Dylan smiled. "No, if he did I doubt I would be working there. He really doesn't like them, it's almost toxic. You won't mention it will you?"

"Mum's the word."

"Oh good!" He looked relieved. "I've been avoiding Logan and Aaron all night too. I know they suspect about Chloe and I, but I'm too nervous to face them on my own."

He looked around nervously, his leg twitching and she wondered if he was worried that they would come back early. Norah jumped as a wolf ran into the clearing, followed by two more and she grabbed

Dylan's arm as he shot up, thinking it must be Logan and Aaron. "It's okay. It's probably not them."

"It's not them," he said calmly. The sudden shift in his tone made her wary.

"How do you know?" Dylan turned to look at her and her stomach dropped. Gone was the state of nervousness and a cold calm spread across his features.

"Sorry, Norah. You were always nice to me and I wish it didn't have to be this way."

By this point, Norah had risen to her feet and was slowly backing away. Annie entered the clearing, having returned from the car and gasped as she stared at a large black wolf. "Nick?"

The wolf growled, lunging forward and his jaws clamped around her leg.

Annie screamed.

More wolves appeared from the darkness, attacking those left behind. Norah moved to run and screamed as Dylan jumped, bones cracking and he shifted, his paws shoving her onto the ground. She froze, heart pounding as her eyes remained focused on his sharp teeth, inches from her throat. "You're a werewolf too? Dylan what are you doing?"

He growled, teeth snapping and she tried to sink further into the ground, heart beating wildly.

"That will do, I will take it from here."

Norah's body turned cold at the familiar voice. Dylan stepped off her, remaining close and she turned her head, body trembling. A naked man stood to her left. A large scar covered half his face, though Norah would still recognise him anywhere.

Daniel walked forward. "Miss me?"

Those words set her into motion and she turned away, trying to run. Something hard connected with the back of her head and she fell, the world fading into darkness.

26. Truths

Cold.

The first thing Norah thought was she was cold. Her body felt tired, she moved her fingers experimentally and they stung like they would on a cool winter morning. The aroma of meat was the second thing she noticed. The smell was quite overpowering and she breathed through her mouth trying to accumulate to the scent.

Norah's eyelids fluttered, her other senses returning slowly. The pain in her head was numbed from the cold surface she lay on. She managed to open her eyes enough to focus, and after half a minute she realised she was looking at a metallic wall. She could make out the bolts rising vertically in the dark. A sliver of light came from somewhere above her, the light casting a dim glow on the small room. She moved to look, and immediately groaned, the noise echoing in the confined space.

The pain in her head intensified from the small movement and her eyes flew shut. Whatever Daniel had hit her with had possibly given her a concussion. She would be lucky to have any brain cells left if Daniel kept giving her concussions.

"Mmmhmm."

Her eyes flew open. The muffled voice behind her stiffened her spine. Moving slowly, she rolled over, fighting the nausea as the room spun slowly. Her spine bumped along something thin and hard, the sound of metal scraping along the floor. She reached for it, hissing as she touched something sharp and brushed it to the side. She saw the outline of someone sitting against the far wall and she squinted in the dark, eyes widening as she finally realised who it was.

"Madison?"

The young woman tried to move towards Norah, her cries of distress muted by whatever was covering her mouth. Norah struggled to her knees, the world spinning some more. She bit her cheek, fighting through it as she stumbled over to Madison.

Norah had thought she was cold, but when she touched Madison's arm, it was like ice. They were obviously in some sort of freezer. Listening closely, she could hear the soft hum of an engine from beyond the walls and she wondered if it was a portable freezer, judging from the size. Reaching up, she found a cloth covering Madison's mouth and felt around until she found a knot behind her head. It took her over a minute to untie the knot. Her fingers were numb and she continued to slip on the difficult tie.

"It's okay," she whispered, finally loosening the knot. She pulled it away from Madison's mouth and heard her take a shaky breath.

"Norah! Oh my God I can't believe Liam got you too!"

"I don't think it was Liam who was after me," Norah said softly, afraid of who was listening. She remembered the way Daniel had looked at her in the clearing. Like he had already won.

"Is anyone looking for me?" Madison whispered hopefully.

Norah shook her head, the motion making her head flare in pain. "We all thought you had left early to see Parker's mother."

Norah heard Madison whimper and immediately felt guilty. Charlie would be kicking himself when he realised the truth. If he realised the truth.

"Norah," Madison sobbed. "Liam killed Parker."

"What? How do you know?"

"He told me!" she cried. "He said he couldn't risk me being with someone else."

Norah frowned, confused at the madman's logic. "How long have you been here?"

"I don't know," she answered brokenly. "A few days?"

"Madison, I'm so sorry we didn't realise." Norah tried to find the ropes around her wrists. They were tighter than the cloth and she rested her head on Madison's shoulder as she worked.

"Norah, Liam is insane," Madison's voice was barely audible. "He comes in here and just sits in the doorway, staring at me."

"He doesn't talk to you?"

"He did at first. He kept asking me about my parents and my family line. He also made sure to rub in the fact that it was him who killed Parker. It was mad, Norah he kept insinuating my parents were werewolves!"

"What?" She tugged on the rope in surprise. "Why would he think that?"

"I don't know! I didn't think werewolves were real, and then suddenly he-he changed into a huge beast...and - oh Norah I must sound just as mad."

Norah paused, closing her eyes. "Not as mad as you might think." She quietly told Madison about the Montoya's and the supernatural shit war she had been dragged into.

"You're not joking are you?" She replied when Norah fell silent. "This isn't some make believe story he's made up, he hasn't drugged me with hallucinogens. Oh my God!"

Madison cried silently as Norah kept working on the knot. She managed to make it worse when she untied the wrong part and she nearly started crying herself.

A creaking sounded from outside and they both froze.

Norah shifted, sitting in front of Madison. The door opened, creaking loudly on its hinges and a light was flashed in her face. Squinting, she turned away from the light, the pain in her head beginning to throb painfully, threatening to crack her skull open. and the door closed shut sending them back into moderate darkness. Norah looked back to the door, her heart sinking.

Daniel stood over them, a flashlight in his hand which he placed in the corner of the freezer. Fortunately he had some clothes on and Norah squared her shoulders, trying to look brave. I'm not afraid, I'm not afraid, she chanted in her head, eyes never leaving his face.

"So, Norah. I bet you weren't expecting to see me again." He crouched down to her eye level. She kept her face blank, determined to prove she wasn't a coward anymore. Rylan's face flashed through her mind and she focused on his face, trying to absorb what strength she could from his image. "Thanks for the scar by the way. I'm still getting used to it, but it's proved to be quite intimidating."

"Screw you -"

Whack! Daniel's hand came out from nowhere and she tumbled over. Madison screamed but Daniel covered her mouth, muffling her cries for help. He shifted, retying the cloth over her mouth.

Norah's face, already numb from the cold, now felt nothing at all. There was a small throbbing through the centre of her face and the metallic taste of blood in her mouth. Those were the only indications she had that he had done any damage. Sitting up, she glared at him.

He laughed. "You look so cute when you try to be intimidating," he cupped her chin and she spat blood all over his face. He shoved her away, kicking her in the ribs. "Don't test me, Norah. I'm much stronger now. I should be thanking you, really. If you hadn't pushed me off that cliff, none of this would never have happened. Unfortunately, I still need more from you."

He grabbed her by the hair and she cried out as he dragged her up. He shoved her against the wall, her spine hitting a bolt and the pain reverberated through her body, her nerves tingling. "Where are my diamonds?"

"In the ocean," she lied. She knew it didn't matter if she told him or not, but she didn't want him to have the upper hand. He would never get his hands on them and if she ever got out of this alive, the first thing she did would be to throw those diamonds right in the ocean.

He slapped her again and the freezer grew dimmer. Madison's cries sounded like they were far away and she tried to remain conscious. She couldn't black out and leave Madison alone with him.

"Where are they?" he snarled.

"I told you," she choked. "I threw them in the ocean the day after you fell from the cliffs -"

His hand moved to her throat, tightening, and she spluttered, trying to fight him off. It was no use. She was too weak to loosen his hold. The cold and fresh beatings had taken their toll and all she could do was pathetically slap at his hands. Madison's voice faded in out, slowly becoming softer until all she could hear was the pounding of her heart in her chest.

Somewhere, she heard a door creaking and then his hands were gone. She fell to the floor, her body no longer supported by his hold. She breathed raggedly, trying to fill her oxygen deprived lungs. Her heart pounded loudly in her ears, blood rushing through her body and she curled into a ball.

"What do you think you are doing?" A new voice sounded somewhere above her. There was no anger in his tone, just a cold steeliness which made Norah shiver.

"I'm questioning her."

"Without my permission?" Norah looked up and saw Liam standing in front of her, Daniel opposite him. It was still strange seeing those features which were soft on Luke's face, hard and emotionless on his twin's.

"She's my prisoner," Daniel snarled.

"No," Liam stepped towards him. "She is my prisoner and you don't question her until I say so. Now get back to your post."

"But -"

Liam's hand shot out, gripping his collar. "Don't make me say it again."

Daniel growled, stepping back. He sent Norah a menacing glare before turning on his heel and stalking out the door. Liam turned, looking at Norah from the corner of his eye. "You better tell him next time or he might just kill you."

"What do you care?" She rasped, rubbing her throat.

"You're right. I don't care. But I need his head on straight and that's impossible when all he wants to do is wring your neck for those pathetic rocks."

Norah looked past Liam, seeing someone else standing just beyond the door. She hadn't seen him before, but she could tell from his features whose son he was. "How can you do this?" she called out to Nick, Aston's son. "Don't you realise this is wrong? You even hurt Annie! She's innocent!"

She saw a flash of guilt in his eyes before Liam moved, closing the door. It clicked shut and as he turned, he kicked out, connecting with her stomach. All the air she had managed to draw back in rushed out and she lay on the floor, wheezing. Liam looked at Madison, his stare intense. "Have you decided to believe me yet?"

She looked at him, eyes filled with fear and glanced at Norah. Norah pushed herself up to a sitting position. "I told her the werewolves were real. Why does it matter if she believes you?"

"Because, I need her."

"What for?"

"Years ago, I discovered the reason why Holden moved to this shit hole of a town. He was here to help protect Frank and Andrea Walker."

"Walker?" Norah glanced at Madison. Her eyes were wide with recognition.

"Frank and Andrea Walker were the last two surviving members of the Whitestone pack. In their day, the Whitestone pack were a force to be reckoned with, their line was strong, their heirs harnessing unbelievable strength and power. When Madison was born, she was the last heir to a once strong pack."

"What happened to her parents?"

"They were killed," he said simply. "Their enemies caught up with them and my grandfather was unable to protect them."

"What does this have to do with Madison?" Norah pushed herself into a sitting position, the pain slowly numbing again with the cold.

"She is their first born, a werewolf of pure blood," he stared at her, eyes hungry. "I don't know the full details, but I know some sort of lock was put on her shifting abilities long ago. She was raised away from the Montoya's so everyone would believe the Whitestone's were truly extinct. With Madison's help, I plan on reviving the pack which once brought others to their knees in respect."

He moved closer to Madison as she tried shrink away from him. Norah's mind was trying to put all the information together. She had thought that Liam was only after the seat of power amongst the Montoya clan. Why would he search elsewhere? Unless...

"You're not the firstborn," she said the words out loud. Liam froze, head whipping towards her.

"What?"

"Why else would you go after Madison? You've known for years about her, and she was your back up in the event you weren't really the firstborn. It's why you killed Parker, you couldn't risk her having a child with him, because then her so called power would go to that child."

Liam turned back to Madison, stroking her hair. "That was basically my plan. The Montoya's will be weak under my brother's rule. He may be first born, but his heart is soft. Once I have reinstated the Whitestone pack's power, incorporating it as my own, it will be child's play to place them under my rule."

"Why do this?" Norah asked.

"Because!" He snarled. "I should have been first born! I am more deserving of the power my brother was born with."

"I doubt that. Luke is a born leader. It's not all about power -"

He hit her leg and she cried out. "If you want to keep your tongue for a bit longer, I suggest you keep it still. Once we figure out who in the town put the lock on Madison's werewolf, we'll be ready for the next stage."

"What makes you think they are still around?" Norah shrunk back, cursing her mouth.

"They're still around, I know it." He stood up and walked out. "The run should be almost over. It's time for us to move before they return and find their precious humans slaughtered."

Norah's insides twisted. "You killed Annie?"

"All for the cause." He walked out, shutting the door and Norah lunged forward kicking the door.

"She was your Aunt!" she screamed. "She was innocent!"

Tears stung her eyes and she closed them tight, sobs racking her body. Madison whimpered behind her, reminding Norah she wasn't alone. Turning back, she crawled over to Madison and undid the cloth around her mouth.

"Norah," she whispered. "What are we going to do?"

"I don't know," she whispered. She went back to work on the knots on Madison's wrists.

"I'm sorry about Annie," Madison spoke softly.

Norah nodded. A sob was sitting in her chest, wanting to break free but she held it in. She couldn't mourn for Annie yet. She had to keep a clear head otherwise they would never get out of here. Even that thought was a hopeless one. Norah wondered if Rylan had noticed she was gone yet. Had they discovered Annie, seen what had happened to the woman they all loved? One knot came loose and she started working on the other.

"I'm sorry about Parker," she said eventually, her voice hoarse.

Madison nodded, leaning her head on Norah's and breathed deeply. "My whole life has been a lie."

"When we get out of here, I'll make sure Holden explains it all to you. You deserve that much." Norah said, feeling a small sense of triumph as she finished untying Madison.

She moved her arms, rubbing her wrists. "I don't think we are getting out of this Norah."

"We are," she said angrily. "I am not letting a monster like that win. He's not getting you, and he's not getting the Montoya's. Not without a fight."

She knew there was nothing she could do personally to stop him, but she wasn't going to sit in here and do nothing. She searched around, finding the thin metal hook she had felt earlier on. She felt along the edge, finding a sharp tip and knew it must have been a meat hook. They obviously weren't worried about two human girls or they would have tied her up and removed any potential weapons.

"Can you stand?" She mouthed to Madison.

Madison stood, watching her warily. "What are you going to do?"

Norah positioned herself near the door, the meat hook pressed close to her chest. She looked at Madison, glad the cold of the freezer had stopped any telltale trembling she knew she must be feeling.

"Get ready to run."

27. Turning Point

Norah waited anxiously, her heart pounding a frantic tempo in her ears. She didn't know how long Liam would leave them there, but it couldn't be for long. The others surely had come back to the clearing by now and realised what had happened. They had to have seen the massacre - seen Annie. Norah bit her lip, a tear escaping. How could they do this to their own family? They would be looking for her - she hoped - and they should be able to track her scent.

She hoped.

Standing for a few minutes, Madison came to stand beside her. Her fingertips were a faint blue and Norah wondered how long she'd been in the freezer. Surely they hadn't kept her in here for the last couple of days? Norah grabbed her hands, folding them in Madison's jacket. Madison shot her a weak smile.

The sound of a chain rattling clanged against the outer wall and both girls tensed. Norah lifted the meat hook high, desperately putting all her remaining energy into her arms. They trembled slightly but she stood strong, relying on the adrenaline she was sure was running through her to give her the strength to do this. There was a good chance this would fail, but she had to try.

The door opened and for a brief moment, her heart stopped, her entire being focused on the task at hand.

Once the door was open enough, she swung the meat hook, gritting her teeth as she felt it connect. She turned, pushing it harder and came face to face with Nick. His eyes were wide with surprise. He was too strong and resisted her, it was difficult to push the meat hook through his body - it was blunted from years of use - and she felt a sliver of despair.

Madison suddenly came up behind Norah, her hands covering her own and helped her push. Nick grunted, falling to the ground and the girls fell on top of him, helping to push the hook all the way through his chest. He gurgled, hands reaching for them but Norah slapped them away, scooting away from him.

"Quickly!" Norah hissed. She rushed to stand, attempting to drag Madison. Madison was trying to pull the hook out of Nick and she swatted her hand away. "Leave it, there's no time!"

Grabbing Madison's hand, Norah looked around. There was a light through the trees to her right and she guessed there was a house there. Not that way. She turned to her left and rushed into the forest.

The light of the moon was enough to show them the way, but she stumbled on unsuspecting branches that lay fallen on the forest floor. There was no sound behind them and she wondered how long they would have. It wouldn't take them long to realise they were gone.

"Where are we going?" Madison huffed.

Norah pulled her along. "I don't know. As far away as we can."

Norah's chest was tight with pain. The beatings had taken their toll and after running through the forest, her body was beginning to warm and the pain was making an unwelcome return to her limbs. The side of her face throbbed painfully and she felt her vision blurring every so often. The kicks to her chest made it difficult to breathe and what should have been an easy run for her was excruciating.

Madison lagged behind and she knew the poor woman had to be weaker than her after being tied up for so many days. Still, she didn't complain and she pushed herself to match Norah's pace, neither of them very keen to get caught once more.

Howling tore through the night air and Norah felt tears sting her eyes. They'd been discovered. "Run faster!" She cried, knowing their time was running out. She wanted to scream for Rylan, for anyone for help, but if she did it would only give them away to Liam and Daniel quicker.

Oh, how she wished it had been Daniel who had opened that door! She would have stabbed that meat hook through his body repeatedly until he could never move again. Of course then she would have been caught and it would all be for naught. Maybe it was better he hadn't been the one who opened the door.

They kept running, both knowing it was only a matter of time before they were caught. The sound of Madison's wheezing breath filled her ears and she pulled her along, her grip on her hand painfully tight. Growling sounded behind them and her body trembled, the adrenaline coursing through her making it impossible to think.

As the noise gradually began to get closer, Norah stopped, knowing it was pointless to keep running and reached on the ground until she found a firm feeling branch. Picking it up, she held it tightly. Madison collapsed to the ground, sobbing quietly. "It's over."

"It's not over yet." Norah stood in front of her. "You should keep running, I'll hold them off for as long as I can."

Madison gripped her leg. "I'm not leaving you alone, Norah. They'll tear you apart!"

Norah knew it was true, but she wasn't going down without a fight. She didn't know where this courage had come from, but she wasn't about to question it. She just hoped it didn't leave her when they appeared.

The sound of wolves drew closer and the branch began to tremble in her grip. Her fingers tightened, the skin digging into the bark, surely drawing blood. Her mind went blank and she stared into the darkness, waiting for their impending death.

"Norah," Madison whispered. "Over there."

Norah looked where she was pointing and her heart stopped. A pair of eyes twinkled in the dark of the trees and she bit her cheek, stopping a sob from breaking forth. One by one, wolves started stepping out from the trees and Norah knew they were done for.

She had thought Liam's group only small, maybe ten at the most. She counted at least fifteen to twenty and a memory reminded her that there had been rumours of Liam recruiting wolves from other packs. It would seem they were true.

Liam shifted, his eyes filled with a cold fury. Norah glanced at a wolf to his left, seeing a large scar on his face.

"You are not a smart girl," Liam said quietly. Norah raised the branch and Liam laughed. "You have fire, I'll give you that. I'm going to have fun snuffing it out."

He stepped towards her and she moved back, her legs pressing against Madison. Liam stopped, turning to look to his left. He growled, his body shifting and Norah jumped as another wolf ran out of the forest, grabbing his neck.

Norah gasped, other wolves appearing and she caught a flash of white.

Rylan.

Relief seeped through her and her grip on the branch loosened. Help had arrived. Norah cried out as the wolves merged on one another in a mêlée of fur and blood. She crouched down, trying to grab Madison so they could make a run for it. "Come on, we have to go -"

A sharp pain lanced through her ankle and she screamed.

"Norah!"

Madison looked behind her and Norah turned. The wolf with the large scar had his jaw clamped tightly around her ankle. His eyes glared at her knowingly, a sense of triumph flashing through them.

His teeth pressed deeper and Norah screamed again. Her leg moved involuntarily to get away only causing her more pain. The pain started to burn up her leg and she tried to hit him with her fist, anything to make him left go.

Madison reached for the branch and hit Daniel on the head. He didn't let go, but only clamped down tighter and Norah was sure he was going to bite her foot off. A flash of white rushed past her and tackled Daniel. He yelped as they tumbled away and the pain in her foot heightened as the blood began to flow freely. Madison crawled forward, trying to apply pressure to the bite marks. The blood was flowing too quickly and she couldn't stop it.

Norah felt lightheaded. A strange feeling of euphoria spread through her body and she slowly sunk to the ground. The pain in her foot became a numb throbbing and the world seemed to fade.

"Madison," she whispered. Her voice sounded like it was coming from the end of a tunnel. "I think something's wrong."

"It's all right Norah," Madison was shouting, Norah could tell by the look on her face but to her ears it was a faint whisper. "Keep your eyes open, stay with me!"

Norah looked around, her head lolling to the side. The wolves were slaughtering each other. Her vision blurred, coming in to focus with each throb of pain causing the wolves to look like one large ball of fur. She saw three wolves attacking the one. Two of them looked frighteningly similar and she couldn't tell if they were the same or her vision playing tricks on her.

She tried to move her head, to look away as they tore the creature apart, but her head wouldn't move. She tried to speak to Madison, to tell her something really was wrong, but her mouth wouldn't obey her commands. She started to panic.

A cold spread through her, starting from her legs and her breathing began to shallow. Was she dying? She had heard you went cold when you were. She tried to remember where she had heard it from and then wondered why she was wasting her time trying to remember pointless things.

"Norah!" Her head was moved and she found herself looking up at Rylan. Blood covered his skin, a large wound covered his entire shoulder and she wanted to reach up and try to stop the bleeding. Her body refused to do anything though but breath and stare. She saw his eyes glance down, his face turning whiter than his wolf fur. The words 'toxic' and 'bite' formed on his lips but she didn't know what that meant.

Holden appeared to her left. She saw his hand reach down and knew he had to be touching her leg but she couldn't feel it. From the look on his face, she knew the prognosis wasn't good. She looked away and kept her eyes on Rylan, wanting him to be the last thing she saw.

The darkness slowly started closing in and she wished she could say something, anything to take the frightened look off his face. His lips moved one last time before the world went dark and she thought she knew what words they formed but before she could decipher it, she knew no more.

She was lost in darkness.

Voices faded in and out. Some she recognised, others were strange to her. Her body felt heavy. At first the pain had been agonising. She had had moments of consciousness but they were filled with nothing but agony. Her body felt as though it were on fire, her limbs taut and heavy. She remembered flashes of Olivia and Logan holding her down, Cassie brushing her forehead and murmuring softly in her ear. She didn't know what was happening but something told her it was not natural.

She was aware of time passing slowly, and the moments of pain and consciousness receded until she was forever in the dark. The pain was gone, but so was everything else. Norah had an awareness of there being people around her, but she couldn't awaken.

There was a sense of peace in the darkness that gave her comfort. Peace from the pain and troubles of werewolves and dangerous men - she sometimes thought it would be nice to never wake. The voices were comforting and she recognised Olivia and Cassie's the most - but there was one voice that she did not hear which she longed to. The lack of his presence left her feeling afraid.

Was he all right? Did something happen to him after she had fallen unconscious? A part of her wanted to wake and discover if he was there, but the other part was afraid that if she did, he would be gone and she would be alone.

She drifted in the darkness, waiting for some chance, some sign that she should find a way out. She waited to hear his voice telling her everything would be all right.

As the time passed, her sense of her surroundings became more focused, the voices sharper and she could feel when people touched her hand, her forehead - a desire to live spread through her and she clung to it. He may not be there, but she had to wake up. She had to know for sure.

Eventually, she felt someone press their lips lightly against her own, the gesture sparking a sense of familiarity in her.

"You need to wake up, Norah." The voice filled her with relief and happiness. He was alive. The voice itself sounded sad and she tried to reach for it. "My ego is running wild without you here to keep it in check," he joked lightly. He kissed her again and she felt him grab her hand. "Please come back to me."

The darkness started to clear and she welcomed the light, her fingers curling around Rylan's as she returned to the world.

28. Ready

"..it's not normal for someone to be out this long, is it?"

"Give her time, she went through something quite traumatic."

Be quiet. Norah spoke the words in her mind. The voices sounded as though they were right next to her head, shouting as loudly as possible. Her eyes scrunched tight - the noise was too much - and groggily, she opened her eyes to tell whoever it was to go away. It didn't take her eyes long to adjust; she was lying in a strange room. The curtains were pulled closed and a small amount of light trickled through. Common sense told her she shouldn't have been able to see so vividly in the dark. She turned her head, looking for another light source but there was none. Her breathing increased painfully.

What was going on? As she inhaled , she gasped, bolting upright. As assortment of scents invaded her senses. Rain, earth, sweat, perfume - she covered her nose, gagging at the overdose.

"She's awake!" A voice shouted eagerly to her left and she scooted away from it, hitting a wall. The sound of her body connecting with the wall sounded like a gunshot and she gasped, beginning to hyperventilate.

Olivia and Cassie rushed in, eyes filled with relief. "I'm so glad you're awake!" Olivia smiled.

Norah winced and covered her ears, allowing the scents to rush in once more. "Why are you shouting?" she whimpered. Olivia stepped closer and her perfume started to make Norah nauseated. Cassie's scent of baking and flour mixed in with it and Norah's chest began to tighten. "Why can I smell you? What's happening to me?"

The sound of her own voice made her eardrums ring and she buried her head in her knees as she started to have a panic attack.

"Go and get him." Footsteps pounded away from her and she flinched as Cassie touched her back. She knew it was Cassie because her scent still remained. But she didn't know why she knew that.

"Breathe, Norah." The voice sounded softer and she tried to obey, wishing the tightness in her chest to fade away. The footsteps returned and Norah could hear two sets. "Quietly," Cassie said.

Another hand touched her shoulder and the bed lowered as someone sat beside her. The smell of pine tinged with earth and sea helped the tightness in her chest recede. She knew that smell. "Norah?"

She knew it was spoken quietly, but it was still too loud. She found she didn't care so much this time though. It was a voice she needed to hear. Looking up, through tear soaked eyelashes, she saw

Rylan watching her nervously. She sensed the others leave and Rylan reached over, covering her ears.

"What's wrong with me?" she whispered, at least she thought it was a whisper.

"Nothing, it's just - Norah, I'm so sorry." His eyes were pained. "This isn't how I wanted it to happen."

Memories of the Gathering flashed through her mind -Annie, Madison, Daniel biting her - chest started to get tight once more. "What did Daniel do to me?"

Deep down, she already knew the answer but she didn't want it to be true. Not like this. Rylan didn't say anything but he didn't have to. His eyes spoke more than enough. Sobs wracked her body and Rylan pulled her close, kissing her head as he rocked her gently back into oblivion.

The next time Norah woke the room was completely silent. No voices could be heard, no footsteps pounding through her skull. Rylan's scent lingered and she knew he must have been here recently.

She didn't open her eyes. This couldn't be real. And yet, it was. Her body felt different; every nerve and sense felt alive. Every breath, move and sound was amplified. She looked around. The room was dark. There was no sun shining through the curtain and she guessed it was night time. The room wasn't as clear as it had been earlier - whenever that was - but her sight was still better than it should have been in the dark. No one was in the room, and she stared at the ceiling, trying to remain calm.

"Hello." The sound was quite loud and she repeated the word, trying to make it softer. It was a test she used to do when she little. She would see how loud she could speak without waking her parents. It had been a strange experiment, one that often got her into trouble. She tried to figure out her vocal range and settled on what she felt was normal. It didn't sound too loud in her head and she strain on her vocal chords felt normal.

Sitting up, she was surprised at how agile she felt. Every movement felt fluid and she stood up, expecting to be weak after lying for so long. Instead she felt invigorated. It was as if she had simply had a good night's sleep. Bouncing on the balls of her feet, she headed for the door and hesitated. She knew she had to be in the Montoya home from the soundproofed room and the thought of all the noise on the other side scared her. Bracing herself, she opened the door slightly.

Noise filtered in; people talking, plates clattering. The smell of roast drifted in and her stomach growled. The noise was not as horrific as her last waking experience and she wondered if maybe she getting more accustomed to her new…abilities. She tiptoed out to the landing of the stairs and sat down, listening to the chatter.

"How did the meeting go?"

"The perimeter was clear…"

"Gail and Madison are stopping by tomorrow…"

Norah took it all in, letting her ears get used to the cacophony of sound. A door opened behind her and she jumped. Olivia stepped out of her room, eyes wide with surprise. She opened her mouth and hesitated. Norah stood up and offered a timid smile. She felt slightly ashamed of how she had acted when she woke up before. She must have looked so childish.

"Are you okay?" Olivia whispered.

Her voice sounded normal and Norah smiled in relief. "I think so."

There was a falter in the chatter downstairs and Olivia hugged her fiercely. "I know this must be so weird for you. Can I do anything for you?" Norah didn't know what she wanted but her stomach answered for her. Olivia grinned. "So it begins. Come on."

She led Norah downstairs past the dining room and into the kitchen. Cassie was standing at the sink when they entered. She smiled, rushing forward to give Norah a kiss on the cheek. "I am so glad you pulled through. Your ankle looked terrible. For a while there, I thought..."

She drifted off and Norah glanced down at her leg. There was a red scar along the outer part of her ankle and she reached down to touch it. "I'm afraid that scar will be there forever," Cassie said quietly.

Norah rubbed it for a few moments, trying to remain calm before standing back up. "What happened?"

Cassie's smile faltered and Norah's heart sank. Olivia's eyes reddened and she turned to away to prepare Norah a sandwich. The kitchen remained silent and Norah regretted asking anything. She was trying to think of a way to fix the situation when she heard the front door open. A comforting scent drifted towards her.

By the time she had turned around, Rylan was already through the kitchen door, sweeping her into his arms. She wrapped her arms around his waist, inhaling deeply. She had always liked the way Rylan smelled, but now it was different. Now, it was something that made all the troubles of the world seem to instantly melt away.

"Are you okay?" he murmured.

She nodded. "I think so." She had a thousand things she wanted to ask, but was too afraid to voice them in case she upset Cassie and Olivia again. The latter passed her a plate of five sandwiches. "I'm not that hungry," she protested, though her stomach rumbled appreciatively.

"You'd be surprised," Olivia said weakly. "Well, I'm off to bed. Night."

Rylan still had a hold of her and she looked up at him. "Do you mind if I eat these in your room?" She didn't feel ready to face the others yet. Not without knowing more. She turned to Cassie, motioning to the dining room. "Will they...?"

Cassie shook her head. "They understand."

Rylan kissed her forehead. "Head on up. I'll be there in a minute."

She gave Cassie one last hug - feeling as though she needed it - before she took her food upstairs. Rylan's room hadn't changed which gave her a strange comfort. She flicked on the lamp and started eating. The bed was unmade and she smoothed the pillows, suddenly feeling ill.

When Rylan came in he would surely tell her what had happened. Was she ready to hear it? To hear of those who were gone, of the pain and grief they were all experiencing? Butterflies prevented her from eating anymore though she was surprised she had consumed four of the five sandwiches. Crossing her legs, she didn't have to wait for long.

Rylan walked in a few minutes later, closing the door behind him. He sat beside her, brushing a few strands of hair from her face. "Is it better?"

"What?"

"The sound, the smells - they can be pretty overwhelming when you first..."

Norah tensed. Neither of them had said it out loud. As if afraid it would change everything.

"He turned me, didn't he?" Norah whispered. "I'm a...werewolf." Norah had said the word at least a hundred times before, but this time the word felt think on her tongue.

Rylan moved away, standing near the desk. "I was too late," he growled. "I was so focused on protecting Luke, I didn't get to you -"

Norah crawled over the bed, standing behind him. She wrapped her arms around his waist. "Don't ever blame yourself for this," she murmured into his back. "It was madness out there -"

"I should have gotten to you sooner!" He slammed his fist on the desk and she jumped. He spun around instantly. "Sorry, I just - I nearly lost you, Norah. If you hadn't have accepted the change, you would have died."

She caressed his cheek, seeing his inner turmoil. She knew that Rylan had always wanted the option to change to be entirely her own. That had been taken from her and he felt guilty. On the other hand, he was relieved she was still alive and the two emotions were warring with each other.

"Rylan, I know it wasn't my choice," her voice trembled, but she knew the words were true, "but if it means I get to be with you then I don't care what I am. I have you now to help me through this and I know it won't be easy, but I believe we'll get there."

He kissed her roughly, the sensation causing her body to respond more acutely than ever before. She was still freaking out, but she tried to keep internal, not wanting Rylan to feel any worse that he already did. She knew as long as she had him, everything would be okay. She forced herself up for air, trying to remain positive. "Look, I'll admit, I did have my heart set on Jedi Knight, but I'll learn to adapt."

He chuckled, claiming her mouth again. He lowered her onto the bed and they lay together for some time, touching and memorising everything about the other. After nearly losing each other, there was a need to remember every minute detail about the other, as if afraid they would never get to see it again.

When Rylan's hand brushed her ankle, she froze. He stroked the skin softly. Norah sat up, heart in her throat. "What happened that night?"

The words rushed out of him in a huge burst. They had returned to the clearing in horror. Apparently there had been guards posted to protect them - Liam had killed them all. Norah hesitantly asked about Annie when he fell silent.

"It broke Cassie," Rylan said quietly. "I've never seen her like that before. Everyone loved Annie and for Nick to do that -"

He broke off and Norah shifted, sitting beside him. He kissed her cheek and continued. They had tracked Norah through the forest only to be sidetracked by a scent bomb. They were made to eradicate smells and prevent werewolves from tracking. They had thought all hope was lost when her scent had suddenly reappeared. As he mentioned the battle, he slowly fell silent once more.

"Who?" she whispered.

"We lost Peter and five others from the Braxton and Quiotta clans. Aaron was badly injured, but he has recovered well."

Norah remembered seeing Peter around. He didn't stay up at the house so she hadn't known him well. Still, it hurt to know Rylan had lost a friend. "What about Liam?"

"Luke finished him. He was never going to be taken alive," Rylan spoke bitterly. "Nick and Dylan have been sent to face judgement before the Council. There was minimal losses on either side. We should consider ourselves lucky, but it feels like we've lost so much more."

"What...what about Daniel?" She finally asked the question she had been most anxious about.

Rylan wrapped his arms around her. "I tore him limb from limb. No way was that bastard living past that night."

Norah rested her head on his shoulder, letting it sink in. Daniel was dead. She knew she should feel elated, but instead there was nothing. It was hard to feel emotion for someone she had detested so much. Not wanting to think about him, she asked about Madison.

According to Rylan she'd been in to visit regularly and was adjusting well. Holden had spent a few days with her telling her about her family and his regrets at not being able to protect them.

"She came to see you a lot," he explained. "She was really worried."

"What about the block on her werewolf...thing? Did they find out who did it?"

"It was Gail."

"What?" Norah hadn't suspected her. "Are you serious?"

"Yeah, apparently she's a faery. She was friends with Madison's parents and promised them she would protect her."

"Holy crap, she's a faery, that is so cool."

"You weren't this excited when you found out about werewolves," he grumbled.

Norah patted his chest. "As I recall, you were fighting another wolf in my living room and suddenly changed into a naked man. I doubt a faery would scare me like that."

He muttered under his breath about saving her and Norah smiled. Shoving him down, she lay her head on his chest. His hands came up holding her closer. The beat of his heart was reassuring, the sound more distinct than it used to be.

"Rylan?" she whispered.

"Hmm?"

"Is it hard being a werewolf? What if I'm not good at it?"

Rylan rolled, lying half on top of her. "It's been one day, Jacobs and you're already freaking out."

"Shut up," she mumbled. "You know I worry about stupid stuff."

He kissed her languidly. "I know," his lips moved against her own. "It's one of the million things I love about you."

Norah's breath caught at the four letter word. He stared into her eyes, his own filled with emotion. "I love you, Norah."

"I love you too," she said breathlessly. "Ego and all."

Rylan claimed her mouth and set to work proving just how much he loved her.

The next day was easier on Norah's senses. Every sound and smell was less extreme. Rylan told her it would take at least a week for her senses to settle down. They would still be stronger than a human's, but she would learn to control them. The mood in the Montoya home remained sombre. Everyone was still in mourning for those they had lost. Aston spent most his time at the Mill. Olivia told her he was taking Nick's punishment hard. He felt responsible for Annie and had been avoiding Cassie. Cassie knew it wasn't his fault, but no one could convince him otherwise.

A funeral had taken place for all those who had died the week before. Their bodies had been cremated and ashes scattered through the forest. A tree had been planted and on the third day she had been awake, she slipped out after lunch to see it. She knew it wasn't exactly a tombstone, but she wanted to pay her respects to Annie and the others.

The sapling stood in the centre of a small clearing behind the house. It would grow to be an oak tree if it survived the years and Norah wondered if she would be around to see it grow. Footsteps approached her from behind.

"How are you, Norah?" Holden stopped beside her.

"Still processing, still adapting." They stood in silence, watching the baby tree sway in the wind.

"I am sorry the choice was not yours to become one of us," Holden voice rumbled in the silence.

"It's okay."

"Rylan was concerned -"

"I know, but he doesn't have to be." She intervened. "And neither does anyone else. I know I'm only new to your family, but I love you all and I'm not upset. I always thought I would be, but I think a huge part of me is relieved at the thought of having a family again, as weird as that is. Not that I'm trying to force my way in!" she added hastily. "I mean, if you guys don't want me stay after everything that has happened, I understand -"

Holden chuckled. "Rylan was right. You do worry over strange things."

Norah blushed.

He grabbed her by the shoulders facing her to him. "You became a member of this family long before Rylan first brought you home. That boy is mad about you and if he is, then so are we. You do love him, I hope?"

"I think I'm just as mad as he is," she mumbled.

"Good," he smiled. "I know my Jenna will be keen to meet you."

"Is she coming back?"

He nodded. "She is bringing Meegan home. Luke needs her here. He's struggling more than he lets on."

Norah and briefly seen Luke that morning and she had to agree with Holden. To be forced to kill your own twin must have taken a heavy toll. Surprising herself and Holden she gave him a hug. "I'm so sorry."

He hugged her back quickly before stepping away. "Before I forget." He pulled out a familiar pouch and passed it to her. "Now that your stalker is dead, you can do as you please with them."

Norah's fingers closed around the velvet pouch. "I know just what to do with them."

The next few days passed in silence. Moods were lifting slowly and Norah did what she could to comfort. Olivia and Cassie were often together and she knew they have done so much for her while she was unconscious and so she did what she could to return the favour. She cleaned, cooked, washed and leant them a listening ear. Mother and daughter were grateful for her company and on more than one occasion, Olivia told Norah how happy she was that Norah would be staying with them.

Rylan was kept busy with the Mill which continued to run, and he stayed with Luke who they were all worried for. Norah hoped his fiance returned soon to help his mood. The only time they saw each other was at night and they would stay up to all hours, talking of anything that popped into their heads. Norah encouraged Rylan to talk about what was on his mind, not wanting him to dwell on painful things. Liam had been his friend once and she knew he had to be hurting as well.

There was no more talk of Norah's change, but she didn't mind. She had grown accustomed to her new senses and she knew now was not the time to make a big deal out of it. There were more important things to worry about.

Madison came to see her on the fifth day and there was a sense of peace about her that Norah had never seen.

"I'm so glad you're okay," she smiled, sitting beside her in Cassie's private sitting room.

"Same goes for you. How are you taking it all?"

"I admit, it was a little daunting at first," Madison laughed breathlessly. "I wanted so badly for it to be some rotten dream. Then I spoke with Holden and he helped me come to terms with everything."

"And you didn't have the block removed?"

Madison shook her head. "Gail offered but I refused. I don't want to create anymore madness by continuing my family line. Gail promised me the block will stop the werewolf gene from passing onto my children - should I have any - so I am safe."

"I didn't realise faeries were so powerful."

"I don't think they are really. Gail said the spell took a lot out of her and even now she hasn't fully recovered."

"And you're okay with what Gail did?"

She nodded. "Thanks to her, I got to have a normal life. It hasn't been perfect, but I've been free to make my own decisions which I would not have been able to do if I was a werewolf. For that, I have to be grateful."

Norah hesitated before broaching the next subject. "What about Parker?"

Madison stirred her tea. "I will always love Parker. He was my first love. But I've come to realise after all this that I can't let him be my only love. I want to be happy and to do that... I have to let go."

Norah took her hand. "I am so proud of you, Madison."

A car horn sounded outside and Madison stood up. "That's my ride."

They hugged. Norah picked up a scent she hadn't noticed before. "You've been close to Charlie! Wait - what -?"

Madison smiled nervously. "Baby steps."

Norah watched her go and couldn't stop grinning. She didn't know who she was more happy for - Charlie or Madison.

After that day, things continued to get brighter. Jenna and Meegan returned home the next day with a pleasant surprise. Meegan was a small girl with blonde hair and large brown eyes. In her arms, she carried Jared, who had arrived into the world only one week before. The premature labour had been the reason they had taken so long to arrive. They may have been late, but it was all worth it for the look of wonder on Luke's face at seeing his newborn son.

Norah was so focused on the baby, she didn't noticed the older woman sidle up to her. "You must be Norah."

Jenna was tall with black hair tied in a long braid. There was a tinge of sadness in her eyes blended with curiosity.

"I am," she held out her hand. "It's nice to meet you -"

Jenna crushed her in a hug and Norah glanced at Rylan in shock. Rylan grinned. "Where's my hug, Grammy?"

"Oh hush -" she released Norah and gave Rylan an equally forceful hug. "I hope he's good to you, Norah. If not, just say the word and I'll sort him out."

"Well..." she pretended to consider and Rylan yelped as Jenna put him in a head lock.

"Norah, why?" he wheezed.

"It's okay!" She quickly rectified. "He's very good to me. Too good even."

Jenna let him go, a twinkle in her eyes. "I think I like this one, Rylan. You better not stuff it up."

Norah remembered Holden saying something similar when they first met and smiled.

"I won't, Grammy."

The arrival of all three helped to lift the mood in the Montoya home. A baby always seemed to have that effect on people. New life was a thing to marvel and it was what the Montoya's desperately needed. Norah knew it would take time for the pain to fade, but watching Cassie coo over her grandson, she knew the healing process had begun.

Two days after they had returned, Norah and Rylan slipped away back to her home, eager to spend some alone time together. It was a rare warm Autumn day and they sat in the sand, contemplating something Norah had to do.

She needed to shift. Rylan said it was time and the longer she waited, the more painful it would be. She was nervous. "What if I can't do it properly and I only shift partially?"

"Never happens," Rylan lay back, arms crossed behind his head. "You should be more concerned about what colour your fur will be. I mean what if it's some crazy red or something? I don't know if I can love mmph -"

Norah shoved sand on his face and he rolled away, coughing. "You were saying?"

"I'll love you no matter what colour fur you have."

"Hmmph." She stood up, pulling something out of her pocket. The blue velvet pouch shone in the sun and she poured the contents into her palm.

Rylan stood behind her. "Decided what to do with them?"

She nodded. Clenching her fist, she threw them into the waves, finally saying goodbye to the last reminder of that awful chapter of her life.

"Perfect." Rylan nuzzled her ear. "I'm sure the flounder will appreciate the bling."

Elbowing him, she stepped away and started stripping. Rylan's eyes lit up. "Not what you think," she warned.

His face fell. She sighed, shifting self consciously. "Help me do this right and maybe later."

Rylan instantly perked up and she grinned. She loved an idiot. He gave her a quick kiss and stepped back. "You ready?"

"I'm ready."